AS HANDSOME DOES

AS HANDSOME DOES

Paul Williams

To Terry

With best wishes

from

Paul Williams

JANUS PUBLISHING COMPANY
London, England

First published in Great Britain 2001
by Janus Publishing Company Limited,
76 Great Titchfield Street,
London W1P 7AF

www.januspublishing.co.uk

**A CIP catalogue record for this book
is available from the British Library**

ISBN 1 85756 444 8

Typeset in 10pt Baskerville

Cover design Peter Clarke

Printed and bound in Great Britain

CHAPTER ONE

'Quick, Dolly,' Bill shouted, 'there's a kid on with no arms.'
Dolly put down the saucepan she was holding and ran to the front room as quickly as her arthritic legs would carry her. She loved children or, to put it more exactly, she loved disabled or sick children or, to put it more precisely still, she loved seeing them on television. (Seeing them in the flesh tended to prompt her to question why their parents or guardians had to bring them out, upsetting people.) Any disability would do. She never missed the type of programme in which they were paraded, and she could sit for hours in front of the screen going 'ooh' and 'ah' and 'love 'em', putting her head on one side and making funny faces at them. Bill indulged her habit, sensing that it was more harmless (and almost certainly cheaper) than a lot of habits she could have gone in for, and would scour the television magazine to see what programmes were coming on which were likely to have a suitable quota of such children for her to gawp at. They always put her in a good mood (or a less bad one) and when they were over she would sigh with that satisfied sorrow peculiar to English people who think they are being compassionate and say: 'It makes you realise how lucky we are,' and sometimes added: 'I've got too big a heart, me, that's my problem.'

She was almost too late. She did manage to get a glimpse of the little girl in question before the scene changed to something else entirely. It was a local news review and they did not spend long on each item. She sighed with disappointment.

'It was a bit about a new type of artificial limb they've invented,' Bill filled in for her. 'Never mind, that 'ospital documentary comes on at eight o'clock. There'll be plenty of sick kids in that.'

It probably goes without saying that Dolly had not had children of her own. True, her two nephews, Spike and Dean, had been living

1

with them since their parents' death in a road accident nearly four years earlier, but it was not the same. It wouldn't have been the same even if they hadn't been anything but trouble, in their different ways, since the moment they arrived. Besides, they weren't exactly kids any more - even if, as she often told them, they behaved as though they were.

She lit the gas under the potatoes and returned to the front room, seating herself beside her husband.

'So,' she said, pursuing something Bill had said earlier, 'you've got a buyer for the 'ouse.'

'Looks like it,' said Bill. 'Cash, too.'

It was not their own home to which they were referring, but the house next door. Old Stanley Peters had lived there for over fifty years until his death earlier that year. Bill, a builder and decorator, had been waiting for him to go for the last five. He knew that Stanley's daughter would be glad to be rid of the place, tip that it was, and he was able to get it from her for a snip. With Spike, his eldest nephew, working for him (and Dean, the younger one, during the school holidays) he was able to get most of the work done for under 7,000 quid. Knowing the right people to do the roof and the windows had also helped. Not the best, to be sure, but between them they'd managed to get the place looking right classy, even if Bill did say so himself. Bill kept his own counsel as to the exact figures, but with the recent recovery in the market he suspected that he could make a cool 40,000 on the place. His hopes now appeared to have been realised.

'That big Asian family, I suppose,' said Dolly resignedly.

'No,' said Bill, 'you couldn't be more wrong. That la-de-dah old bag.'

'Not the one Dean said looked like Barbara Cartland after an all-night rave party?'

'That's her. Seems she went down to The Kitchener's after she'd looked at the place and got in with old Sid and Albert. Turns out her dead 'usband was an officer in the same regiment as Sid in Italy. She can knock 'em back, too, according to Albert. I didn't think any more about it when they told me but then she rings up today to say she'll 'ave the place. Only a couple of thousand below the askin' price, and I thought I was being cheeky. Of course, she 'ad some snotty solicitor with 'er, kept grabbing the phone off 'er whenever she sounded too keen. Left to her, we'd probably 'ave got the full amount. Anyway, there was her saying she'd 'ave it, and 'im saying subject to contract and survey, but I reckon she knows 'er mind for all the wankers round 'er trying to sober 'er up.'

'Well, let's not count our chickens,' said Dolly.

'I know, I know, but I've got a feelin' about this one.' He tapped his nose. 'Keep it between us, though, I mean about getting a good price.'

'Huh, as if I'd tell them!' said Dolly, knowing that he was referring to the boys, who were just coming in.

'As if you'd tell them what?' asked Dean, whose hearing was better than most.

'Oh, there you are!' flustered Dolly.

'Yes, here I am,' said Dean. 'Tell us what?'

'You mind your own business!'

'You old rat bag!' said Dean, and went upstairs to join his brother, who was getting ready to take a shower.

Spike and Dean would never have been taken for brothers, not least because they weren't really, not by blood. Spike was blond, about average height, not, it was generally thought, academically inclined and painfully shy, a fault he tried to conceal by making himself look as macho as possible. Dean was dark (a West Indian parent or grandparent was assumed to be in the background, nobody knew for sure and probably never would), tall, clever and, if not exactly extrovert, certainly unafraid to speak his mind. Spike's parents had adopted him shortly before the tragedy that had forced him and Spike to come under Bill and Dolly's loving care. Yet their relationship was closer than that of most real brothers, circumstances having forced them to look out for each other. Dean, although the younger, did most of the looking out, aware that Spike was the most vulnerable.

'They're plotting something,' said Dean, entering the bedroom they had to share.

'I think he's sold number 12,' said Spike from the bathroom.

'And made a fortune out of your work, no doubt.'

'Well, don't make a scene about it,' pleaded Spike wearily, turning on the shower.

Dean had every intention of making a scene about it. He had not had a good argument with Dolly for weeks and this was as good a pretext as any. It was obvious from her attitude that Dolly, too, had been missing the exchange of pleasantries that had punctuated his long stay under her roof. He bided his time, though, and waited until they had all eaten their dinner. Spike liked his food and Dean did not want to spoil it for him.

'So,' he said, when he saw that Spike had finished the last of the apple crumble, 'how much are you getting for the house?'

'Well,' mumbled Bill, 'we er . . . haven't fixed on a price yet, not for sure, for certain, I mean. She'll probably try to knock somethin' off after the survey, they always do.'

'She?' said Dean. 'So it is the old bat who came yesterday. Rolling in it.'

'Excuse me,' said Dolly, straightening in her chair and using a posher voice to enhance her authority, 'if you don't mind, I'll thank you not to interfere in what doesn't concern you.'

'So you have got a good price!' said Dean, knowing that, had it been a bad one, they would have been told soon enough.

'And so what if we have?' asked Dolly with increased hauteur.

'So what! Spike's slogged his guts out doing that house for you' (Dean was speaking to Bill), 'and all you've ever done is look in on the way to the betting shop or the pub.'

'I did the skirtin' boards, didn't I?' Bill defended himself, 'and arranged the roof and window people. You don't see the paperwork.'

'No, that's true,' observed Dean, 'nor does anyone, especially not the Inland Revenue!'

'He gets paid, doesn't he?' said Dolly.

'Half what you'd have to pay anyone else. By rights he's entitled to a cut of whatever you make on that house, and you know it.'

'Calling us thieves now!' laughed Dolly. 'Him of all people!'

It was time for the fainter-hearted to depart. Spike crept quietly upstairs while Bill cleared away the dishes and went into the kitchen to wash them up (for Dolly ensured a roster was kept and it was his turn). Alone, Dean and Dolly could really let rip and they settled down to enjoy themselves. They were both of a theatrical bent and so understood the pleasures of a good argument even if Bill and Spike did not.

4

'If he had any more he'd only give most of it to you,' said Dolly. 'That's what you're really after.'

'No. I wish he'd get a job where he wasn't being fleeced so he could get out of here. You've treated him like shit ever since he came here and now you're robbing him, too.'

'Huh! Why doesn't he get a better paid job if he can? Who else would employ a freak like that?'

'Don't you insult him, you old cow! He's not as big a freak as you!' retorted Dean.

'Oh yeah? So how come you always have to stick up for him? Ooh, you're a funny pair. There's something odd about the way you two stick together. And it's not natural, him going on for twenty and you having to fight his battles for him, not to mention telling him what clothes he should wear, what type of haircut he should 'ave. "Ooh Spike" - she put on a mimicking voice - "that Ben Sherman shirt would really suit you. Ooh Spike, you'd look so good with a haircut like that!"'

'Nearly all the problems he's had you've caused or they've been made worse by you and your nasty tongue,' said Dean. 'You can insult me, but don't insult him. We've got one thing in common, you and I, you old bag. We both came off the streets, even if it was a hundred years ago in your case. But Spike came from a good home, the best in fact. He's got class, like his mum and dad had.'

'You speak for yourself. I didn't come off the streets. I've sung at the Hackney Empire. I could 'ave been someone if I 'adn't been daft enough to marry that old layabout.'

'It's a pity you never became a star. You'd look better from a few million miles away!'

'Oh, quite the little comedian, aren't you? You should 'ave been a professional, like your mother!'

Neither Dean nor Dolly was quite as quick-witted as this exchange might imply, for sometimes they both separately spent their quieter moments thinking up the lines they could use in anticipation of their next quarrel.

'Besides,' she went on, getting back to the subject of Spike, 'I showed him kindness, and patience, but he didn't even try to get any better. How long was I supposed to put up with all that nonsense, still 'ave to, sometimes? And as for his dad having class, well, he wasn't much of a businessman was he? Borrowing money on 'is 'ouse just before he got 'imself killed and not sorting out the insurance properly. If he was so wonderful how come there was nothin' much left for you two?'

'If he'd known what Spike was going to have to go through here he'd have been more careful, that's for sure.'

'Spike this, Spike that, you really are obsessed aren't you? Well, you'd better go to your precious Spike. Probably bawling his head off by now, or takin' another one of his showers. If you hurry up you might catch a glimpse of him in those designer underpants you persuaded him to buy. I've got your number, my lad, even if he hasn't yet!'

Dean was momentarily thrown. He knew that Dolly was as capable of being offensive as he was, but she had never ventured down that particular road before. A limp 'you dirty-minded old bag!' was all he could manage.

'Well, I can't think who else will benefit from them. No woman's likely to see him in 'em for a good while yet, the way he is ... Oh Christ!' she interrupted herself, 'that 'ospital programme's coming on now.'

Even Dean in full flow knew better than to interfere with Dolly and her hospital programme. Besides, his flow had been somewhat stemmed on this occasion, and he was not altogether sorry that the argument was coming to an end. With uncharacteristic tact he withdrew. 'I've got to get ready to go out anyway,' he said with pretended defiance, lest she was in danger of thinking that it was obedience that prompted his departure.

Spike, who was lying on his bed reading when Dean entered, gave his brother an admonitory look.

'Well, at least I don't smash the place up any more,' Dean reasoned. 'Why do you let them get away with it? You must know they're ripping you off.'

'Well, I'm not as badly paid as you make out. And they've had to put up with a lot from us too, you know.'

'From me, yes. Not from you.'

Dean leant over Spike to see what he was reading and was gratified to see that it was one of his own little collection. For some time he had made it his mission to help Spike rediscover the finer things of life.

6

Anyone who had heard the recent goings on between Dean and
Dolly would probably have been surprised at Dean's taste in literature, for blood and guts, murder mysteries and political intrigue
were not on the agenda where he was concerned; he preferred the
more elegantly written type of novel. He had introduced his
favourite novelist to Spike, who persevered with some of her works
but was not impressed. Dean had read nearly all of them, about
eighteen to date, but for Spike this would be the tenth.

'It looks like its going to be like all the others,' said Spike in exasperation. 'Another woman who lives off money she's been left, has a
flat somewhere within a two-mile radius of Sloane Square, doesn't
have many friends and feels life is passing her by!'

'They're not the same,' said Dean patiently. 'Be fair, in the last one
you read the woman was a college lecturer. It's the way the novel is
written that counts. Her genius lies in getting inside the heads of her
characters and describing their feelings. Besides, she does have a
man as her central character sometimes.'

'Yes, but they're just like her women only with trousers on. And
nothing much ever happens. Things are always moving
"ineluctably" in one direction, usually a pretty dull one, and most of
the times they spend with anyone else are "wordless". Their lives are
totally regulated and they always seem to shop in Harrods or
Fortnum and Mason. They read a lot of French novels and as often
as not they have a parent who was French, or at least from the
Continent, and she's always looking for any old excuse to get them
to say something in French. If they go away anywhere it always seems
to be Paris, except when it's Switzerland. And she's always talking
about them going to bed early and getting too much sleep. If they
have boyfriends or husbands it's always some boring older prat who
doesn't understand them.'

'Actually,' said Dean, 'if you read this one you'll find she does fancy
a young bloke,' and then added somewhat limply: 'though nothing
comes of it and she remains faithful to her husband, who is a good
deal older than her. He dies in the end, and she's left alone.'

'In Chelsea, I suppose, or Paris.'

'Well, no, it's when they're living in Switzerland, actually, though
she still keeps her house in Chelsea.'

Dean ducked gleefully as Spike threw the book at him.

'Now, now Spike! It's not like you to be so untidy!'

'But do you think people like that really exist?'

Dean felt like saying that yes, they did exist, and that for all his affected butch walk and pseudo-skinhead haircut, Spike was the nearest person he knew to being just like them. He could also have pointed out that Spike's paternal grandmother had been French and that Spike's parents had taken him to Paris quite frequently in his younger days, as a result of which Spike's own French was not at all bad. In the end he took the coward's way out.

'Good God, no!' he laughed. 'At least, you won't run into any in Walthamstow.'

This observation seemed perfectly reasonable at the time but, reflecting on the conversation a few days later, Dean was to be forced to admit to himself that he could hardly have been more mistaken.

Marianne Raseur walked from the museum to her home in Lucerne Court, Brookner Street, popping into Fortnum's to buy a cake on the way. She always enjoyed walking, not only for the exercise but because it took more time, and she knew her evenings at home would be long enough however early she went to bed.

There had been about six visitors that day. It was a private museum and library devoted to manuscripts and other artefacts relating to French writers, owned by Dr Sentier who was now in his seventies and only called in from time to time. The day-to-day running of the place was left to her and Judith Cohen. Marianne was not paid well, but that hardly mattered since she could have lived comfortably on her inheritance in any case. Judith was paid even less, but that mattered little either since she lived with her parents in Golders Green and did not go out much, though not, perhaps, as infrequently as Marianne.

In the lift at Lucerne Court, Marianne met Stella, who worked in a small bookshop near Charing Cross. Marianne saw that Stella also had a cake from Fortnum's.

'Had a busy day?' asked Marianne as the lift progressed ineluctably to the third floor.

'Hardly,' said Stella. 'We had about a dozen customers.'

'That's twice as many as came into the museum,' said Marianne.

'Though one of them was quite interesting. A postgraduate who's writing a thesis on the theme of death in Zola's novels.'

'How fascinating,' said Stella.

As Marianne opened her front door she could not help thinking of Roger Dusalon and the wry smile her exchange with Stella would have elicited from him. He had made no secret of his view that the women of Lucerne Court were a pretty dull bunch. Indeed, it had reached her ears that he had even described them as the most boring set of women in Christendom.

Entering her flat she called out *'Je suis là, maman, j'arrive.'* Her mother had been dead for five years, but out of habit she still replied to the now non-existent *'C'est toi, Marianne?'* for her mother's voice still seemed to emanate from the bedroom in which she had chosen to spend much of her time during the last years of her life. Marianne sometimes wondered why she maintained this ritual, for she had been no happier when her mother was alive than she was now. Her only really happy memories (not that they were many) had not had anything to do with either of her late parents. And yet she had stayed with Alexandrine, her mother, to the end, though their time together had become increasingly wordless. Such silence can often be the mark of a strong bond but, Marianne knew, in their case this could hardly be offered as the reason. For her mother had clearly found Marianne a disappointment, and the smile Alexandrine invariably gave her, when she returned home, was primarily in anticipation of the Belgian chocolates and the glossy magazines (the sort that featured the homes of the rich and famous), that Marianne had bought for her.

She had been in only a few minutes when the phone rang. It was Daphne, who lived on the floor below. Daphne had really been a friend of her mother's but Marianne had inherited her along with the flat, the furniture and the cleaning lady.

'Hello, is that you Marianne? Is it still all right for this evening?'

'Yes,' said Marianne. 'Just give me time to change.'

'I'll be up in half an hour, then. You needn't go to any trouble, I've bought a cake from Fortnum's.'

Marianne decided not to say 'so have I'. If she did not get through her own cake she could always give it to Mrs Turner, the cleaning lady, who lived way out in somewhere called Stockwell and so probably did not get to Fortnum's as often as she would like.

She changed from her expensive Harrods suit and put on her more modest attire, which she had bought on her last annual trip to Paris. These trips were the one extravagance she allowed herself. She always stayed at the same hotel on the rue du Roule, which was small but exclusive, and rarely crowded. She spent her time visiting museums and libraries and went to bed early. Only once, four years earlier, had she stayed up relatively late in Paris, but the memory - or rather the shame - of that evening was now painful to her and she tried not to think about it. It occurred to her now that she had not yet booked her annual week in Paris, and made a mental note to do so. In truth, after nine years on the trot, she was finding these visits a bit of a drag but she lived in hope that she might run into the Porters again. Perhaps they had forgiven her. Oh Gregory, you cruel boy, where are you now? And your kind, beautiful parents, where are they? Did I really disgrace myself so badly that I should be cut off so completely?

As she changed she caught sight of herself in the long mirror on the door of the large fake Louis Quinze wardrobe (her late mother's choice, of course). She knew she was, at the very least, relatively attractive - her body was more or less the right shape, given that she was now approaching 30, and no crows feet as yet had trotted over her naturally clear face - but, despite the copious amount of sleep she made sure she acquired, she could somehow not summon up the energy to work hard at 'making the best of herself' (as occasionally urged by Mrs Turner, who in fact meant that she should dress in a more contemporary style), though she was always smartly dressed. Once or twice a resemblance to the late Grace Kelly had been remarked upon, though Marianne herself had not been particularly flattered. Her mother had been the first to make this observation, and Marianne, only too well aware of Alexandrine's hopes and expectations for her, could not avoid understanding the deeper meaning. Play your cards right, she was saying, and you will end up marrying a rich man, and you (and I) will be able to live in the kind of house featured in these lovely magazines. That, indeed, was the message her mother had, sometimes implicitly, sometimes explicitly, drummed into her since she was a child. Marianne recalled now with a sigh that Miss Kelly, in her rôle as Princess Grace, had become somewhat matronly in build as middle age progressed, and she wondered if the same fate would befall her. No doubt there were others who would tell her that this was all the more reason why she should pull her finger out (though Marianne herself would hardly have used such an expression) while there was still time.

Daphne arrived exactly on time as always. Daphne was a large, articulate, confident (sometimes overpoweringly so) woman, qualities which alarmed Marianne a little, though she had to concede that they could be helpful on occasions, most recently in her dispute with the boiler-repair people. Daphne was good at putting people in their place.

'I saw an old friend of yours today,' Daphne observed as Marianne handed her a glass of wine.

From the nuance in Daphne's voice Marianne knew instinctively to whom she was referring. She said nothing but gave what sounded suspiciously like a snort.

'You know who I mean then?' said Daphne. It was not often that Marianne made such an unladylike sound, indeed by Marianne's standards it was the equivalent of blowing a raspberry. 'Roger, of course. He dropped in at Cynthia's while I was there. He was asking after you. I think you might still be in with a chance, you know.'

Marianne flushed. Clearly Daphne did not know all the details.

'Has he finished with his precious Dolores, then?' Marianne asked, doing her best to appear unruffled.

'Oh, Marianne,' Daphne admonished, 'you shouldn't take life so seriously. Men such as Roger have to be allowed their little flings. It means nothing to them. For a while we all thought you were practically engaged. He's a fair-minded man, you know. He'd be quite happy for you to be unfaithful, too. You could be content and very comfortable if only you learned the rules. And let's face it, he's the nearest you've come to the aristocrat your mother had in mind for you.'

'Why didn't my mother marry an aristocrat if she felt like that? In the event she simply married a Frenchman with a dress shop in Bond Street. She might just as well have stayed in France herself.'

'Well, when it came to it I don't think she had the courage of her ambitions. Still, she didn't do so badly. She thought that, given the right education and upbringing, you'd take the next step up.'

'I think my mother may have been just a little bit too French!' Marianne laughed.

'You do the French an injustice,' said Daphne. 'If you look around London these days you'll see not a few Czech, Polish or Hungarian girls with very similar attitudes to those your mother had when she arrived. If you don't get in quick Roger will probably end up with one of those.'

'I dare say. They'd most probably know rules about turning a blind eye when Roger requires them to do so and, if they don't like them, necessity will doubtless force them to put up with the situation. Perhaps I'm too comfortable to have to.'

'Being comfortable is hardly the same as being happy,' said Daphne, who then decided to change the subject as she realised that she was probably treading on dangerous ground. 'Anyway, I haven't come to try to marry you off to Roger or anyone else. The truth is I have a little favour to ask. It's your afternoon off tomorrow, isn't it?'

Marianne confirmed that it was, expecting the usual suggestion that they undertake a shopping expedition.

'Well,' said Daphne, with uncharacteristic caution as she took a slice of cake, 'you know that my sister Elizabeth has been thinking of moving from her flat in Knightsbridge?'

'Yes, of course. I understand you were trying to persuade her to move in here.'

'Well, yes. But she's turned very odd lately you know. Drinks too, of course. When I suggested she move to Brookner Street she said, "not on your life!" I can live with that, in fact there are advantages in her not being too close. She has found somewhere though, a little house apparently, and she's made an offer on it. I feel I really should take a look at it to see for myself that she isn't doing anything too rash. I was hoping you would accompany me.'

'Yes, of course, I'd love to. There aren't many little houses in this area, though, except a few mews cottages. But perhaps it's in one of those streets off the King's Road?'

'No', said Daphne, looking nervous again, embarrassed in fact.

'Oh dear! You don't mean it's south of the river?' Marianne was aware of the loss of status this would involve, in Daphne's eyes at any rate.

'If only! Quite the opposite direction. Walthamstow!'

Daphne could not have spat out the final word with more distaste if it had been a town in Serbia.

'Walthamstow?' Marianne mused, unable to place it at first. 'Oh yes, at the end of the Victoria Line. Oh!'

Daphne took the 'oh!' as agreement that it was a dreadful move. In fact Marianne was more alarmed at what she had let herself in for in agreeing to accompany Daphne. The suburbs were alien places at the best of times, but she had never been to the very end of a tube line (apart from Heathrow) in her life.

'But why on earth there?' Marianne asked.

'Well, it's partly financial. Properties are much cheaper out there, apparently. And she stayed in a theatrical boarding house in Leyton when she mixed with that crowd from the Theatre Royal, Stratford, forty-odd years ago. Anyway, the other day she fell asleep on the tube after she'd been for a lunchtime drink with that odd friend of hers, the one who used to know Nancy Spain, and woke up in Walthamstow. She took it into her head to get out there and go for a walk. She passed an estate agent near the station and saw that houses were fairly cheap. She found she can sell her place in Knightsbridge and the residue will add considerably to her savings, which, between you and me, are not substantial. It's that wretched husband of hers. Left half his money to that awful sister in Belgium.'

'Perhaps it's not so bad,' reasoned Marianne. 'It's still on the tube line after all, and you don't have to tell people where she lives. It might be a very pleasant house.'

'It's a little terraced house,' wailed Daphne. 'She showed me the estate agent's thingy. Oh, new roof and double glazing and all that. Just what people who can only afford that kind of thing are supposed to find lovely. She even said there was a handy pub on the corner. I can just see her there, plonking on the piano with a double gin on top of it, giving her version of "We'll Gather Lilacs."'

'Well,' said Marianne, seeing one relatively bright line of argument, 'Walthamstow doesn't appear on the news much, so it must be a fairly quiet sort of place.'

'You don't know about these things,' said Daphne, somewhat irritably. 'You've never been beyond Marylebone, none of the women in Lucerne Court have.'

By 'the women' Daphne did not mean literally all the women, but the six or seven single or widowed ones that made up their little set.

'That's not fair,' protested Marianne (choosing to misinterpret Daphne's exact meaning). 'Some of us have been to Paris and I've visited my relatives in Angers several times, and my friend in Switzerland. And don't forget I went to school in Kent.'

And, she chose not to add, she had visited Amsterdam with Roger only a few months earlier, accompanying him on a business trip. Not a good idea. Still, the fact that she was left alone during the days meant that she was able to visit several museums. Roger had escorted her only once on one of her educational trips, agreeing to meet up with her after lunch on the last day so that they could visit Anne Frank's house ('at least that won't be full of paintings of fat Dutchmen who all look the same'). Unfortunately, he had lunched a little too well, not that it showed overmuch at first. They did the crowded tour of the secret annexe in which the fugitives had hidden, the atmosphere inducing tears in some, and then proceeded through the house next door, which had been converted into a museum dedicated to the victims of anti-Semitism in particular and of racism in general. Here were photographs of the Frank family and their friends, taken in happier times. 'Typical Jews, weren't they?' Roger had said rather loudly, observing their facial features. Marianne, trying to rescue the situation, ventured: 'I think Anne had a very intelligent face,' but the damage had been done, and the looks being directed at them prompted her to usher him out as quickly as possible. 'I don't know why they had to look so pious,' Roger had protested, 'I bet they'd all thought it themselves.' Marianne did not venture an opinion as to whether he was right in this, but resolved then that she could never bring herself to spend the rest of her life with someone so irretrievably insensitive.

Her mission accomplished, Daphne did not stay much longer. She knew that Marianne liked to go to bed early after spending an hour or so reading some ancient French novel, and she did not want her to have any excuse for feeling unwell the next day.

Alone, Marianne felt rather ridiculous for looking forward to a trip to the suburbs with such trepidation. She had always tried to fight against the tendency to snobbery that her mother had attempted to cultivate within her but she was now forced to admit that she had never been put to any particularly difficult test in this regard.

Perhaps this little adventure was what she needed. All the same, she hoped that they would arrive home by the early evening.

As a reward for agreeing to go with her to Walthamstow, Daphne insisted on treating Marianne to a late lunch at the Ritz, which was conveniently near the Victoria Line.

It was a very hot day. There were many tourists about and the train was quite crowded for mid-afternoon, although they did manage to get two seats together. As they progressed beyond central London, Marianne noticed that the ethnic balance of the passengers altered perceptively on a couple of occasions. The tourists (mainly European and North American) had all but disappeared by the time they reached King's Cross, and from there as far as Seven Sisters there appeared to be a high proportion of Afro-Caribbeans. From then on it was a mix of Anglo-Saxon and Asian. Marianne found these demographic changes quite interesting, though she suspected that Daphne was making similar inward observations with a more critical eye. Not that Lucerne Court itself was without some ethnic diversity, but all of its occupants enjoyed a comparative wealth which put an entirely different light on things.

As they left the station Marianne was horrified to see 'Spencer is a cunt' scrawled on a wall. Daphne was every bit as outraged as expected. 'They can't even spell "count" properly,' she sniffed.

Daphne knew the name of the estate agency and that it was near the station, and after asking a policeman (whom they both agreed was most respectful) they found it remarkably quickly. The young man who greeted them was extremely smart, very, very polite and did his best to disguise a strong cockney accent, belatedly picking up his aitches when he dropped them.

'Hello, I'm Simon. How can I 'elp - help - you lydies?'

'We would like to take a look at number 12, Prentice Road, if we may,' said Daphne authoritatively.

'I'm sorry, madam, but that house is under offer. But we do 'ave - have - many similar properties in that price rynge.'

'I am not looking for myself,' said Daphne, not attempting to hide her irritation that anyone could think that she was. 'I believe the offer has been made by my sister, Elizabeth Palmer-Gosforth. She has asked me to take another look at the property on her behalf.'

Simon (whose real name was Wayne) correctly suspected that she was most probably lying, at least in implying that it was her sister who had asked her to come. But what could he do? If the Palmer-Gosforth trout had interfering relatives who might try to get her to change her mind, he had best butter up the said interfering relatives and try to rescue the sale as best he could.

'Ajit,' he called to the back of the office. 'Can you take over for a while? I have to show these lydies a property.'

An equally smart Asian youth emerged, eating a hamburger, which he hastily attempted to conceal when he saw just how expensively dressed the ladies were.

'If you'll wait here lydies,' said Simon, 'I'll bring the car to the front.'

They looked curiously at the scenes around them on the short drive to Prentice Road. They passed one end of Walthamstow Market, which Marianne cheerfully said was not dissimilar in appearance to some of the markets in Paris. Simon spotted through his mirror that Daphne did not look quite so benign.

'Prentice Road is very near Lloyd Park,' he said, 'an 'ighly sought-after area. William Morris's house is in Lloyd Park. Now a museum.'

'*The* William Morris?' asked Marianne, interested.

'The wallpaper man? Wasn't he a socialist?' asked Daphne, determined not to be impressed.

'Oh, but he was a very great artist,' said Marianne. 'You have to expect them to be peculiar in some ways.'

And indeed, as they passed Lloyd Park and the large mansion by its entrance, even Daphne admitted that the area did seem to be 'picking up.' She soured again as they turned into a road of terraced houses.

'Well', said Marianne as they got out of the car, 'they all seem to have very neat little gardens.'

All but one, that was. What had been number 12's front garden was covered in builders' debris.

'Of course, all this will be cleared up when the work's finished,' said Simon hastily. 'They're still working on it. In fact they're most prob'ly 'ere - here - now.'

Marianne could see that the house had the potential to be quite passable when it was finished and when there were curtains on the spanking new white double-glazed windows, the sort which followed as far as possible the style of the originals. Marianne was in no doubt that had the house, or for that matter the entire road, been located in Chelsea, Daphne's enthusiasm for it would have known no bounds.

The new mock-Tudor front door suggested good intentions, but even Marianne had to concede that it was not entirely in keeping with the period of the house. Simon opened the door and they entered a very narrow hallway, with an even narrower staircase ahead. A strong smell of fresh paint and emulsion met them. They could also hear a banging noise coming from the back of the house.

'Mr Clarke!' Simon called out.

'There are no carpets on the floors!' exclaimed Daphne.

'No, but there will be,' Simon soothed. 'The beauty of Mrs Palmer-Gosforth getting in early is that she'll be able to choose the colour.'

A man in his late fifties emerged from a room at the end of the passage.

'Ah, Mr Clarke,' said Simon. 'These lydies are relatives of Mrs Palmer-Gosforth. They've come to look at the house.'

Marianne caught the cautionary look he gave Mr Clarke.

'I'm not a relative,' she thought she had better clarify, 'I'm a neighbour of Mrs Gainsborough, here.'

'Well, we 'aven't finished yet, as you can see,' said Mr Clarke apologetically. 'Spike's just puttin' the kitchen units up now. I'll show you the lounge first.'

He led them through the first door into an unexpectedly large room, clearly made out of two.

'Not many 'ouses round 'ere 'ave the original fireplaces,' said Mr Clarke proudly, 'and Spike 'as done these up a treat. They'd both been 'idden under about sixty years' worth of paint.'

Marianne could see that his pride was not without foundation. Both of the marble and slate fireplaces had been restored most tastefully, and she said as much to a sniff from Daphne. At the far end there was a French window through which they could see a not unpleasant, if overgrown, garden.

They were led upstairs. On the way up, Daphne turned and whispered to Marianne.

'You really shouldn't show that you like anything.'

17

Marianne knew what she meant but she really wondered if Daphne had to look quite so disapprovingly at everything.

The bathroom was excellent, with surprisingly expensive-looking fittings and a separate shower cubicle. The tiling was faultless and positively pretty. Again Mr Clarke said something about Spike's workmanship and led them into the second bedroom, then the first. The latter was a good-sized, bright room with two large windows. Mr Clarke did most of the talking, accompanied by rather irritating asides from Simon about no expense having been spared.

They descended the stairs and made towards the back. A small breakfast room (with another charming fireplace) led into the kitchen, whence came the industrious sounds that had been in the background throughout their visit. The door was half closed and Mr Clarke gently pushed it open. Two youths were putting up the last of the kitchen units.

'Well, they've nearly finished by the looks of things,' said Mr Clarke. 'Plenty of work surfaces, you see?' ('And integral oven and hob,' Simon threw in.) 'And plumbing for a washing machine under there. A big pantry' (he opened a door to show them) 'and bags of room for a table. We extended this room ourselves.'

'I suppose it's fairly adequate for this type of house,' conceded Daphne, for all the world as though it were not twice the size of her own kitchen in Lucerne Court.

Marianne surveyed the two youths. The younger must have been about 18, fairly tall and of mixed race, wearing jeans and a tee shirt. She thought him moderately good looking, though she did not know what to make of the grin that crossed his face when he saw them. The other, not quite so tall, had his back to her as he tested one of the units to ensure that it was secure. She noticed with some alarm that he was a skinhead, or bordering on one, for his head was covered by a faint blond stubble (which made her shudder: she had witnessed an extremely unpleasant incident involving skinheads and a hapless old man a few weeks earlier). He had nothing on but a pair of denim shorts, obviously cut off from a pair of jeans. His fairly muscular arms, legs and torso, combined with his haircut, suggested to Marianne that he was not the sort of person anyone would wish to cross. When he had satisfied himself that the door was not likely to drop off for the foreseeable future (or at any rate not until after the sale was completed), he turned towards them.

Marianne gasped. She had expected to see a harsh, bulldog face, or at least a few scars. Instead she saw the gentlest, most beautiful eyes she had ever seen, set in a clear, open face. Well, almost the most beautiful, because she had seen a face very like that before, unless...But that was not possible. No, she had to be mistaken. For one thing these eyes, however attractive, did not appear to have quite the sparkle that had characterised Gregory's. On the other hand, it was nearly four years.

'These are my two nephews, Spike and Dean,' explained Mr Clarke, failing to be specific about which was which.

The darker of the two smiled again, and looked slightly bemused, obviously wondering who these daft-looking bags were. Perhaps it was just friendliness, but Marianne had a suspicion that he was having difficulty preventing himself from bursting out laughing. The fair one smiled too, but in a more shy way, although he was clearly the elder. He half looked away, as though a little frightened of them, but then quickly and all too briefly looked back at Marianne, perhaps realising that he recognised her. Was it really possible? Marianne urged herself to caution. She had made a fool of herself before. She had seen a boy at the far end of a crowded carriage on the tube, had been so sure it was he. 'Gregory,' she had shouted, and ran past the standing passengers, practically knocking one or two of them over. The boy had turned and she saw her mistake. Perhaps this was wishful thinking again.

Then she recalled that Gregory had told her his nickname, but she had remembered it as Smike. Had it simply been a case of her having read too much literature? Now she thought about it the Gregory she had known would hardly have been given a name like Dickens's Smike, unless as a sort of joke, as when a very short person is called lofty or someone with very straight hair Curly. Yes, it could have been Spike, and the more she thought about it the more she thought it quite likely. Funny how the memory plays tricks. And the name Dean rang a bell, too. Had that been the name of the newly adopted brother about whom she had been told?

'Well, I don't think we need take up much more of your time, Mr Clarke,' said Daphne breezily.

'But you haven't seen the garden...'

19

'I can see it from here, thank you. Besides, there isn't really much point. It will be my sister's decision, after all.'

'Well,' said Simon, trying to conceal his alarm at this decidedly dismissive note, 'I'll take you lydies back to the station if you like.'

'Perhaps,' Mr Clarke put in hastily, 'the ladies would like a cup of tea before they go. We only live next door,' he explained to them, 'and I'm sure my wife 'ud be only too pleased to do the honours.'

'Well, I don't know...' said Daphne.

'Oh, I really would like a cup of tea,' said Marianne, surprising herself.

'Well all right,' said Daphne reluctantly.

Spike (for Marianne now knew perfectly well which was Spike, or hoped she did) looked at her again, nervously and questioningly, but said nothing. So he should look nervous, Marianne thought severely, but then changed her mind. It was she who had the most to be ashamed of, wasn't it? But what on earth was he doing here?

They gave each other one more hasty glance, as though silently agreeing to keep their own counsel.

Simon pushed off shortly after that, only too pleased to leave Daphne and Marianne in the capable hands of the Clarkes. Dolly sat them in the front room and went off to make the tea.

'Most unsuitable!' said Daphne when they were alone.

'To be perfectly honest,' said Marianne, 'I don't think it's half as bad as it could have been. It really does have some quite attractive features.'

'If she came here, she'd be burgled within the month,' said Daphne. 'You can be sure those two young thugs will pass copies of the keys to their friends. I've read about those types.'

'We don't know that they're thugs,' said Marianne. 'They seemed inoffensive enough to me. They're not the sort of people we're used to, that's all.'

Daphne looked at Marianne curiously. Since when had she ever thought at all about the sort of people she was not used to?

Dolly brought in a tea tray and sat down to join them.

'This is a very nice room,' said Marianne, aware that Daphne would probably not be able to bring herself to say anything so polite. And it was pleasant, despite the rather too colourful carpet and the preponderance of statuettes on every available surface (doubtless described as 'collectors' pieces' in the advertisements aimed at those who had not the foggiest idea what a collector's piece was. Marianne had always wondered, while perusing the Sunday supplements, who could be stupid enough to fall for such blandishments. She suspected she now had her answer), not to mention the large commemorative plate on one wall depicting the late Diana, Princess of Wales and engraved with the words (lest there should be any doubt) 'Our Queen of Hearts.'

'Well, it's a bit small,' said Dolly. 'We 'aven't made it a through lounge like next door. We thought about it but decided against when the boys moved in. We thought it 'ud be better to have a separate room they could go to get out from under our feet.'

'Still, it's been very well done. I suppose having a builder husband is an advantage.'

Dolly laughed sardonically.

'Don't you believe it! Left to 'im the place would fall apart. It was Spike did this room, though I chose 'ow it would be done, of course. Spike said I should have plain carpet and curtains, would you believe! Said something about it being too busy what with the wall-paper and my nick-nacks. Men! They've no idea, 'ave they?'

'Have the boys lived here long?' asked Marianne cautiously.

'Nearly four years. Their mum and dad was killed in a car crash. Well, I say their mum and dad, but it's only Spike who's our proper nephew. The other one was adopted just before they passed on. Of course, we 'ad 'em both.'

'Oh, how awful!' said Marianne, suppressing with difficulty the full extent of the jolt this information had given her.

'How good of you to have them,' said Daphne, softening a little.

'Well, there was no one else. My 'usband and I didn't 'ave any of our own, and you've probably noticed we're gettin' on. I can't say it's been easy, takin' them in at that age.'

'But they seem very nice boys,' said Daphne, somewhat hypocriti-cally in Marianne's view.

'They could be worse, I dare say. But it was difficult at first. It was the shock of their mum and dad goin', I suppose. They were a right pair of terrors for a while. Well,' she modified, 'Dean was the terror. Spike was just...worrying. I didn't know 'ow to 'andle them, I don't mind admitting.'

'Is Dean the younger one?' asked Daphne.

'Yes, that's right. Half-caste father, not that he ever knew 'im. In and out of childrens' 'omes. Spike's mum and dad - she was my 'usband's sister - fostered him, then adopted 'im. If the adoption 'ad happened a couple of months later I don't suppose we'd have had to 'ave 'im. Still, he's the cleverer one, believe it or not. Just finished the sixth form. He's 'elping out in 'is holidays. Probably go to university, though he hasn't had 'is results yet.'

'But Spike is obviously very talented, too. We've seen the fireplaces next door,' said Marianne.

'Oh yes, he likes to keep 'imself busy. A hard worker, I'll say that for 'im. He tries to be a good boy. You have to laugh sometimes, despite everything.'

'He's quite a nice-looking boy,' Daphne put in. So she had noticed too.

'Well, 'e would be if it wasn't for that silly 'aircut. Sees 'imself as a proper little hard nut. Course, I know different,' she added, as though she could have said a lot more had she wanted to, and went on to confirm this impression by adding tantalisingly: 'Still, there are some things you don't talk about outside the family.'

She looked as though if pressed (and not pressed too hard at that) she would have been prepared to do that very thing, but at that moment they heard the front door opening.

'That'll be the boys,' Dolly said. 'If you'll excuse me I've got to give a message to Spike.'

She went into the passage from where they could hear her quite clearly.

'Fred phoned. He wants you in The Kitchener's as soon as possible. Annie's sick.'

For the first time that day Marianne heard his voice, that deep, virile boy's voice, richer now than ever.

'Oh, okay, I'll just change and shower first.'

Dolly returned. 'He's a funny boy. Has to 'ave his shower, even though 'e 'ad one at dinner time' (by dinner they rightly assumed she meant lunch). She smiled to herself again, then realised she hadn't done much nosing of her own.

'You're from up west, too?' (The 'too' was a reference to Daphne's sister, Elizabeth.)

'Yes, we live near Hyde Park Corner,' said Daphne. 'Marianne here is a neighbour of mine.'

'Oh, I thought you was mother and daughter.'

'No,' said Marianne, 'my parents are dead.'

'Oh, they must 'ave been quite young.'

'Not that young. I was born very late.'

Dolly thought it time to get down to the nitty-gritty. While making the tea she had been briefed by Bill about what to say. She turned to Daphne.

'Your sister 'ud be very comfy here, I think. And she'll be right next door to us, of course. On the other side of 'er is a very quiet young woman. Does something in the City. We 'ave quite a few people like that living round 'ere nowadays. And I could do her cleanin' for her and the boys would do any odd jobs that needed doing.'

'Well yes, but nothing's been settled yet,' said Daphne evasively, then rose to indicate that the visit was about to end. Marianne had little choice but to get up too.

'I can see that the work has been very well done,' Marianne said. Then she took a deep breath, for she was about to say something very daring. 'I wonder...I have a few jobs that need doing in my flat. Do you think Spike and Dean are likely to be free now that the house next door is nearly finished?'

'Well, to be honest, I think they will. There's not much work about at the moment. Can I just get a pen?'

She left them, leaving Marianne to face the expected outrage from Daphne.

'What are you thinking of? You surely don't want those boys coming to Lucerne Court?'

'Why not? They seem to do rather a good job.'

'But she's as good as said they're delinquents.'

'She said no such thing. She just said they've had problems. That's hardly surprising given what they've been through.'

'I had no idea you were such a liberal! Do you really think some of those so-called problems haven't involved the police?'

After an inordinately long time, Dolly returned with a pen and paper. Marianne wrote down her telephone number while Daphne looked on icily. As she wrote, they heard footsteps running down the stairs. The front door opened and banged closed. Through the bay window Marianne could see Spike rushing past, dressed this time in white jeans and a turquoise teeshirt.

'Can my husband give you a lift to the station?' asked Dolly anxiously.

'No,' said Daphne, 'that's quite all right, I think we can find our own way. It's such lovely weather, and it will give us the chance to see a little more of Walthamstow.'

And to find more excuses, Marianne surmised, to try to prevent Elizabeth from moving here.

They left the house and made for the main road, the same direction in which Spike had run. Sure enough, there was a pub on the corner and it was indeed called The Kitchener Arms.

'Didn't Elizabeth say she had been attracted to the local pub?' asked Marianne, trying to make the question sound as innocent as possible.

'Yes, come to think of it she did.'

Marianne slowed down. Her natural timidity when it came to new adventures was overtaken by curiosity and a feeling that there were some opportunities that could not be missed. The need for a quick decision made it imperative that she should be rather more bold than usual.

'Well, if you really want to get an idea of what she has in mind, don't you think we should take a look inside?'

'What? Go into an East End pub?'

'This isn't really the proper East End,' reasoned Marianne, 'and it's only half-past five so it won't be very crowded.'

'My dear girl, what has come over you? I thought it would be difficult enough getting you to come to Walthamstow. Now you actually want to go into a public house! Oh very well, to be perfectly honest a glass of sherry wouldn't go amiss, not that I suppose we'll get a decent one here.'

They entered and stood timidly in the doorway for a few seconds. The pub was unexpectedly well decorated and clean, had been newly renovated, in fact, in an Art Deco style which was marred only slightly by rather too much gleaming chrome. Marianne was surprised to hear a murmur of something approaching approval from Daphne. What she did not know was that Daphne had not been an

infrequent visitor to such establishments when her husband was alive
- one in particular decorated in a very similar style, albeit in a more
expensive part of London. Once inside, fond memories of those
evenings with Ronald and some of their friends came flooding back,
putting her into a mood bordering on the congenial. Furthermore,
she had the distinct impression that Marianne had an ulterior motive
for wanting to come in. She did not know that Marianne had actually
met Spike before, but they had both heard his exchange with Dolly
and Daphne suspected that Marianne's suggestion they try the pub
was not unrelated to the knowledge that he would be working there.
Daphne was intrigued.

There were not many customers yet. Two bus drivers were
chatting at the far end of the bar and a party of office workers surrounded one of the tables. There appeared to be no staff in attendance. Then Daphne, who reached the bar first, put her finger to
her lips and beckoned with her eyes towards a figure who was squatting down with his back towards them, putting bottles of Pils from a
crate into a refrigerated cabinet. The reason for her silent conspiratorial gesture became clear enough, for Spike's teeshirt was not long
enough to cope with his squatting position, and a two inch strip of
underpants showed above the top of his jeans. Emporio Armani, the
waistband proclaimed.

'Expensive underpants for a barman in Walthamstow!' said
Daphne loudly.

Marianne was not entirely pleased with Daphne for coming out
with this remark and hoped it would not reflect on her. She remembered Gregory once telling her that he found her elegant, and this
was not an elegant observation. Spike stood up and turned, flushing
as he hastily attempted to tuck his shirt into his jeans.

'They were a present,' he seemed to think he had to explain.

He reddened even more when he realised who they were.

'Hello. What brings you in here?'

'We were hoping to buy three yards of dress material!' said
Daphne. 'What on earth normally brings people into pubs?'

She ordered two dry sherries and to Marianne's even greater
surprise attempted to get on to a bar stool.

'You surely aren't going to sit here? There are plenty of tables free.'

'Of course I'm going to sit here. Now we're in a pub we might as well do it properly. I should imagine the after work crowd will be coming in soon and they're not going to talk to us over there, are they? I want to find out just what sort of people live in this area and come in here.'

Spike tried to avoid Marianne's eyes as he put their drinks on the counter.

'And I suppose you'd better have one yourself,' said Daphne.

'Er, thanks. I'll have half of lager.'

'You'll have a pint or nothing at all. A man with a half! I thought this was supposed to be Walthamstow.'

Spike smiled, and half looked away nervously just as he had done back at the house. Nevertheless, he did as he was told and poured himself a pint.

'That's quite right,' said Daphne, as she counted her change. 'You see, you're not as stupid you think you are.'

'Daphne!' said Marianne after Spike had gone to serve a group of people who had just entered. 'Why are you behaving like this?'

'Because I've decided that now I'm in here I might as well enjoy myself and it suddenly occurred to me that you should, too. You've hardly smiled since Roger started carrying on with that Spanish woman. Well, you wanted to come in here and now you're here I suggest you enter into the spirit of things.'

Marianne sat in silence for a while as she pondered the situation. She wanted Spike to be the Gregory she had known, but at the same time she did not want his parents to be dead. And yet she could not have the one reality without the other. Spike offered few clues. He looked embarrassed, but could it simply be the embarrassment of a shy young man who had observed an unknown woman looking at him strangely? It was not impossible that two unrelated people could look very much alike, and perhaps her memory was playing tricks, retrospectively smoothing over any differences between Gregory and Spike. Perhaps Gregory had never even said that his adopted brother's name was Dean, that only now, having heard the name, she was slotting it into the place she had convinced herself it ought to be. The pub was filling up quite quickly and a busy Spike glanced curiously at them from time to time, always turning his eyes away when he sensed that Marianne was looking at him.

'Do you want another one?' Marianne asked, seeing that Daphne had already finished her sherry.

'Well, I was going to suggest it but I assumed you'd say something about not wanting to be late.'

'Perhaps,' said Marianne, 'it might be as well to wait until the rush hour's over.'

It was not Spike who approached them this time but a scruffily dressed youth who had just arrived. His movements and his expression made it clear that he was bored with his job.

'I was right about one thing,' said Daphne, 'the sherry was crap. I'll have a glass of wine. Red. See if that's any better.'

Marianne thought this a good idea. Sherry always went to her head too quickly and she was fearful it might be making her sentimental. At Daphne's suggestion, Marianne ordered two rolls with the wine ('empty stomach and all that'), resolving that this would be the last alcoholic beverage she, at least, would consume. She looked around and saw that some chairs in one corner were being moved (Spike was helping), and a group of four young people, unmistakably students, were taking musical instruments out of their cases. Within a few minutes they had launched into a charming rendition of Mozart's Concerto for Flute and Harp, no mean feat since there was not a flute or a harp between them, but the clarinet and the violin did their best. It sounded unusual but it worked.

'My God, an orchestra!' laughed Daphne. 'We'll have to revise our opinion about Walthamstow.'

'They're allowed to rehearse here in the early evening,' explained a voice behind them.

It was Dean, now resplendent in street gear, a loosely worn check shirt which was not tucked into a pair of baggy trousers. He also had on a back-to-front baseball cap.

'Hello, my boy,' said Daphne. 'What are you having? I was just about to get 'em in.'

Dean seemed taken by surprise. Marianne sympathised. It must indeed have been difficult for him to reconcile this Daphne with the harridan he had met earlier.

'Don't be daft,' said Dean, who regained his balance very quickly. 'Remember I've got connections with the bar staff. What are you having?'

'Two red wines if you insist,' said Daphne, 'or even if you don't insist.'

Spike had seen Dean enter and ventured in their direction for the first time since he had last served them. He smiled broadly when he saw his brother and, for a moment at least, seemed to forget his earlier nervousness.

'The usual for me and two red wines for these ladies,' said Dean.

The drinks were served, and Dean handed over a solitary pound coin.

'That's the advantage of having your big brother working behind the bar,' Dean winked. Marianne noticed, however, that Spike furtively took some money from his own pocket and added it to Dean's contribution.

Marianne and Daphne watched bemused as Dean swigged his beer straight from the bottle, leaning with contrived nonchalance with his back to the bar as he looked around.

'Marianne's being admiring Spike's bottom,' said Daphne.

'I'm not interested in Spike's bottom!' said an exasperated Marianne, more loudly than she had intended. To her horror, a nearby conversation momentarily ceased.

'Why does he have such a silly haircut?' asked Daphne.

'Because he's got to be so, so macho, of course,' laughed Dean. 'Don't worry, he's not the sort of skinhead who goes about shouting "sieg heil". In fact I was the one who suggested he have it cut like that.'

'I like it,' said Marianne, before she could stop herself.

'I suppose you're another one who's going to try to sell the virtues of number twelve to me,' said Daphne.

'Well, as you said, it's your sister who has to make the decision.'

'But she values my advice.'

'Really?' said Dean. 'You surprise me.'

'You're a cheeky little bugger, aren't you?' Daphne laughed. 'Your brother doesn't appear to be quite as bold as you, though. I could swear he's been avoiding us.'

'Well, it's beginning to get a busy now,' said Dean. 'Spike would never be deliberately rude. Not like me. Or you,' he added, looking at Daphne.

'Oh, so I'm rude, am I?' said Daphne good humouredly. 'Young man, I'll have you know that nobody has dared reprimand me since

I was at school, and that was more than thirty years ago. Forty, if I didn't lie about my age.'

'Fifty, if you weren't still lying about it. But, you weren't exactly out to charm us today, were you? If I'd looked at you the way you looked at us in the house you'd have assumed I was about to mug you.'

Marianne could see that Spike was listening in on this conversation while he poured a sluggish draught Guinness for someone, obviously fearful that Dean might be overstepping the mark.

'I wasn't being rude,' Daphne explained, 'I was simply doing my job properly, as Spike obviously does. The job I'd set myself today was to come here to disapprove of everything I saw, and I believe in doing things properly. I do things properly when I'm being a snob, I do things properly when I'm trying to make estate agents feel small and I do things properly when I'm enjoying myself in a pub.'

'I hope he's not annoying you,' said Spike, who had to pass near them to take the Guinness to its purchaser.

'You'll have to excuse my brother,' said Dean. 'He takes life very seriously.'

'He has a lovely voice,' said Daphne, unwilling to use the word 'sexy', which is what she meant.

Dean smiled. He could hardly have looked more pleased if the compliment had been made to him.

'You seem to get on well with your brother,' Marianne fished.

'Who couldn't get on well with Spike?' said Dean, and she perceived that his guard dropped a little and he became momentarily softer as he looked in the busy Spike's direction. 'Though as you've probably guessed, we're not really brothers.'

'But I understand you were adopted,' said Marianne, 'so you are legally brothers. And in the eyes of each other you obviously are. Isn't that what matters?'

'Oh,' he said, 'I suppose Dolly's given you the low-down.'

'Well, she's told us something about what happened. I'm so sorry.'

'It was worse for Spike than for me. I'd only lived with them a couple of years, after all. He was the one who had face the biggest culture shock. He came from a nice area - not,' he added hastily, 'that that means anything to me. I'm a socialist. But his mum and dad were real cool dudes. When they died and we had to go to Bill and Dolly's it was just "here we go again" for me. It was different for Spike.'

'Still, I suppose you were lucky to have Mr and Mrs Clarke.'

'So she tells us,' said Dean, rather shortly. 'If you'll excuse me I'm supposed to be playing pool over there for a bit. And when you're ready, mine's a bottle of Becks. I thought I'd tell you now to save you having to come over to ask me.'

'I love a cheeky boy!' laughed Daphne when he had gone, 'especially when it's all so harmless. You know, I really think a couple of hours in here would do you some good.'

'My goodness, Daphne, and he a socialist, too!' laughed Marianne, for the self-importance with which Dean had come out with the remark had not been lost on them.

'Oh well, perhaps he has a right to be,' Daphne conceded tolerantly, 'just as long as he doesn't expect us to drink out of bottles and wear our hats back to front. You'd better keep on the right side of him, though. He might be useful in helping you get to know Spike.'

'Oh don't be ridiculous,' reddened Marianne. 'Spike's ten years younger than me. Nine, anyway.'

Fortunately, Daphne did not remark on the precision of Marianne's calculation.

'What's that these days? And nobody bats an eyelid if a man is ten years older than a woman. In fact your dear Roger is a lot more older than you than that, isn't he? The little clutch of single women in Lucerne Court don't often have flings, but when they do it's nearly always with old Casaubon types. It's time someone reversed the process.'

'I've never seen myself as much of a trend-setter,' laughed Marianne.

The pub was now quite full and they silently took in the atmosphere. After a while, they were alarmed to see that an altercation was taking place between Spike and a most unpleasant-looking man who had recently come in and had stood at the bar near them. Marianne remembered reading somewhere that some Victorians believed that there was such a thing as a criminal face, and she could not help thinking that this was just the sort of face they most probably had in mind. The man was not old but the eyes seemed decidedly malevolent and both his gaunt features and his bearing suggested that he was no stranger either to alcohol or to other drugs. He was arguing that he had given Spike a twenty pound note, Spike was insisting, with professional politeness, that it had been ten. The argument ended with Spike caving in and giving the customer another ten pounds. The look of roguish triumph on the man's face (which both Daphne and Marianne spotted) as he pocketed the extra cash clinched for them the question of who had been correct. Unintentionally, perhaps, they both gave him a look which made their feelings clear, aware that any shortfall might have to be made up from Spike's wages. He glared back at them and they attempted to carry on with their conversation, the subject-matter of which they altered, aware that a hostile ear nearby was hanging on to every word. Marianne explained to Daphne the difference between Art Deco and Art Nouveau, though she was put off somewhat when she noticed that the man was sarcastically mouthing every word she was saying. Eventually Daphne turned and gave him one of her most withering stares.

'Fucking bitches!' he expostulated.

'Excuse me, are you referring to us?' Daphne asked haughtily.

'Too fucking right!' he confirmed. 'You and your airs and graces. You're no better than me.'

'I hadn't said we were,' Daphne said, reddening at the possibility of an incident but determined not to let her own authority be undermined, 'though at this particular moment you're not doing much to prevent us thinking along those lines.'

'Oh, so I'm "not doing much to prevent you thinking along those lines," he said, mimicking her accent. 'And where are you from? Out slumming it tonight, I suppose.'

'Bugger off, Ian,' said the voice of a rescuer. It was Dean.

'Bugger off yourself,' said their tormenter.

'These ladies are friends of ours,' said Dean sternly. 'If you don't want to get yourself barred I suggest you finish that drink pronto and home to sober up. Or at least go somewhere else.'

Spike had also come in their direction, and stood behind the bar opposite him. To their great surprise the repellent interloper, after hesitating a moment, downed his whisky and, with a defiant 'I was going anyway,' made for the door. Before finally leaving, however, he threw back: 'And I could say one or two things about you, Dean Porter.'

'Sorry about that.' Dean apologised. 'He's not very well.'

'I think we gathered that,' Daphne agreed.

Marianne was thankful that the obnoxious Ian had gone, but relief at his departure was mixed with a profound gratitude to him. The name Porter had clinched it for her. So Spike was Gregory. Spike seemed to notice the effect this information had on her but, after a moment of mutual realisation, his response was to go and serve another customer. And it dawned on her that perhaps he, like her, had not been entirely sure if this had really been the person he thought it was.

That meant that Mr and Mrs Porter really were dead. She felt her sight blurring. She thought it best to excuse herself and made for the ladies. There, standing in a cubicle, she automatically repeated the little prayer for the dead she had learned as a child. The Porters had also been Catholics, she recalled, not overly zealous ones but probably less nominal than her own parents. 'And let perpetual light shine upon them,' she prayed, and then wondered if having perpetual light shining on one could really be all that comfortable. Probably quite annoying, really. To her own surprise she started laughing. It was like one of the jokes George Porter would have told, and she almost felt that it was he who was telling it now. And how, she wondered, would the Porters have taken to being described as 'cool dudes'? But Dean's description was apt for all that. After dabbing her eyes with toilet paper she emerged from the cubicle and rejoined Daphne and Dean. She looked around for Spike but he seemed to have disappeared.

'He's been summoned home for his dinner,' Dean explained, answering the question before it had been asked. 'He won't be long.'

So Dean, as well as Daphne, had most probably noticed the way she had looked at Spike and he at her. But how exactly had he looked at her? As someone who wished to resume contact or as someone who was wary of doing so? She tried to put this question out of her mind while she had a pleasant little conversation with Dean about the universities he had applied for. All, she noted, were in and around London. Clearly he did not wish to travel far, could not, most probably, bring himself to be separated from Spike. Dean could be a problem. He might even possess a veto.

And then, on this day of shocks, came the biggest jolt of all. For Spike had returned from his brief meal break and was serving a customer quite near them. He was no longer wearing the teeshirt but had donned a blue and white rugby shirt. His eyes met hers and this time he looked at her intently for a few seconds as if to gauge her reaction before looking away again. He had worn that shirt the last time they had met and ever since she had pictured him in no other attire.

'I spilt a bit of gravy on the other one,' he explained before moving off.

'I bet it was just a speck!' laughed Dean. 'He has a bit of a cleanliness obsession, I'm afraid. I haven't seen him in that rugby shirt for years, though. It's one of his old school ones.'

Marianne knew that she could now relax a little. 'Yes, I do want you to know it's me,' was the clear message, and her own reaction must have made her feelings plain. And yet this removal of any last doubts for either of them did not visibly alter his diffidence. It was still to be their secret, it seemed. But half an hour later he had to stand very near Marianne while he poured another Guinness, and he stood with one hand resting on the counter very near hers. Cautiously she edged her hand towards his until their fingers touched. And then he smiled. Oh, yes, yes, yes! thought Marianne.

'I've given my address to your aunt,' she said, trying to be casual but realising that her voice shook. 'I have a few jobs I would like you to do for me.'

Even Marianne had seen one or two of the *Carry On* films, and was horrified by the thought that some double meaning could be read into her words. Fortunately Spike did not seem to notice. He probably thought her incapable of being able to think in such a way.

'Yes, she told me,' he said, 'but we'll have to finish number twelve first.'

'You mean you spent the whole evening in a pub in Walthamstow?' said Judith incredulously, handing Marianne another black coffee. 'And with Daphne!'

'I had no idea she was such a raver,' said Marianne, using the word she could vaguely recall Dean using to describe Daphne round about ten o'clock, just after she had playfully started to undo his shirt.

To tell the truth, everything after about eight was a vague recollection for Marianne. She could remember little snippets but not the bits in between. She knew that there had been something of a lull in the place between eight and nine, and Spike had been allowed half an hour off, during which he played pool with his brother and some other youths. She and Daphne had gone to watch for a while and she became a little irritated with Daphne who insisted on digging her in the ribs every time Spike bent over near them. She also recalled that Spike, his turn on the pool table over, went round the place with a cloth polishing the chromework before returning to his duties behind the bar.

'Don't tell me he's the cleaner here, too,' Daphne had said.

Dean had raised his eyes to heaven in despair as he noticed for the first time what Spike was doing.

'He can't stand muckiness,' he had explained wearily. 'He's probably spotted a couple of finger marks and they've worried him. You should try sharing a room with him. It's like being in the army.'

Marianne could also remember the big farewell kiss Dean had given them both as their taxi finally arrived at twenty past eleven and, more to the point, the nervous way Spike stood in the background, only daring to give them a wave as they were safely passing out of the door.

'Well,' Daphne had said in the taxi, 'I suppose we'll have to face the possibility that he's the other way. He certainly didn't show much interest in your advances.'

'But I didn't make any advances,' Marianne had protested. Not on this occasion, anyway, she could have added.

She told Judith of the visit to Walthamstow only as faithfully as safety permitted (no mention of having met Spike before), though this was more than enough to impress her colleague.

'And are you going to make this a regular thing?' Judith laughed.

'I doubt it,' said Marianne, referring to the amount of wine she had consumed rather than to the visit to Walthamstow.

'Well, if her sister is going to move there you'll have the opportunity to go sometimes.'

This had, of course, crossed Marianne's mind.

At home that evening, her hangover long since conquered, Marianne was able to contemplate the events of the previous day with more clear-sightedness, though the clarity was not entirely welcome. For one thing she had to face up to the possibility that Gregory might have someone else in his life. Was this not the most likely explanation for his caution? Worse, however, was the discovery that Lottie and George Porter were dead, and it was in deference to their memory that she allowed herself to recall the first time she had met them at the hotel in the rue du Roule, rather than the second, when her attraction to the older Gregory had pushed his parents into the ranks of supporting cast.

On that first occasion Gregory had been 13, nearly 14. She had come down later than usual to breakfast (normally she would be one of the first, but as she was getting ready that morning a programme about Balzac started on the radio and she stayed to hear it out), and found herself having to share a table with the amiable couple. Mr Porter, she noted, was a good-looking man with a humorous face; Mrs Porter reminded her instantly of Greer Garson in her role as Mrs Miniver. Both, she estimated, were in their early forties and looked well for their age, or perhaps it was their air of contentment which gave this impression. Mrs Porter was perusing a guidebook.

'I suppose we'll have to take him to Versailles sooner or later,' she had observed.

'I don't think he's likely to learn much from that crap, at least no more than he'd get from a passable history book and a glossy brochure. If you've seen one palace from that period you've seen them all, though I'll admit Versailles is more gaudy than most. I thought we could go on one of those tours of the sewers of Paris. I'm sure that would be far more educational. Or perhaps you want to frit about pretending you're Marie Antoinette. Just bear in mind that she ended up being guillotined.'

'Not until after her husband was,' said Mrs Porter. 'Besides, sewers can't be that interesting either. After you've been along one section the rest must be pretty similar.'

'Oh, I don't know. You can only get out of them what you put in.'

Mr Porter then proceeded to laugh most heartily at what, it transpired, had been meant to be a witticism. He laughed alone, for Mrs Porter was embarrassed and Marianne had not realised in time that a joke had been intended.

'You'll have to excuse my husband,' Mrs Porter apologised. 'He...Oh, here's our little soldier at last.'

'Little soldier!' Mr Porter expostulated with good-humoured contempt. It was his turn to be embarrassed now by his wife's maternal expression, which did indeed seem a trifle excessive considering Gregory's age. Marianne had expected to see a boy of six or seven rather than the early teenager who had arrived on the scene. Mrs Porter proceeded to compound the offence by tucking Gregory's shirt into his trousers before he sat down. Marianne did notice, even then, that Gregory was an attractive boy, though not yet arousingly so. He looked at her curiously for a moment and then smiled, a smile she returned.

'Your father wants you to spend the day down a sewer,' said Mrs Porter after the maid had brought a pot of coffee ('Best place for him,' Mr Porter muttered).

Gregory thought about this for a moment.

'Have you been down a sewer?' he asked Marianne (these, she now recalled with a thrill, were the first words he ever said to her).

'Well, no,' conceded Marianne, 'but I'm sure it must be terribly interesting.'

'I thought you had. You look flushed.'

For the first time, Mr Porter looked with approval at his son and they both laughed. Mrs Porter sighed by way of further apology.

'I'm afraid he gets his sense of humour from his father,' she said.

Marianne was secretly envious. Her own father had rarely told jokes, in fact he had not often laughed much at all. He had smiled occasionally, usually when presented with a particularly fine cheese or a rare bottle of wine, and he had even smiled at her sometimes. She could only once remember anything approaching a guffaw, and that was when he had heard that a business rival had been declared bankrupt. Moreover, Gregory's instant, uninhibited little pleasantry at her expense suggested that she was welcome among them, an impression borne out by Mrs Porter's polite but sincere inquiries about how she was enjoying her stay in Paris. Marianne appreciated their friendliness but was a little frightened by it. Most of the other guests at that hotel were strictly introspective, confining any acknowledgement of each other to a sometimes grudging nod, and it was almost as though the Porters were not aware of the rules. Worse, she had a vague feeling that they might think she was somehow lonely as she recounted her solitary pursuits.

'So,' said Mr Porter to his son, who was enthusiastically buttering a croissant, 'may we ask why it took you so long to join us?'

'Oh, I was just finishing the last chapter of my book,' said Gregory, and added for Marianne's information: 'It's about the Elephant Man.'

'I've read it,' said Mr Porter. 'It doesn't tell the whole truth about him, though. It's not commonly known that he could be quite bad tempered.'

Mrs Porter and Gregory both groaned. They had already heard the snippet of information that was to follow.

'Oh, I didn't know that,' said Marianne.

'Oh yes. When anyone contradicted him he could turn quite ugly.'

Marianne wondered why they all looked at her so expectantly, suppressed smiles on their faces. A response of some sort appeared to be anticipated.

'Well,' she said thoughtfully, 'I suppose his condition must have been very frustrating for him.'

She planned to visit the Père-Lachaise cemetery that morning and was already behind her schedule, and used this as an excuse to finish her breakfast more quickly than usual before bidding them a polite farewell. Gregory grinned at her as she left and she found herself smiling involuntarily in return. As she waited at the lift by the breakfast room, she assumed that Gregory or Mr Porter must have told another of their jokes, for she heard uproarious laughter in which, on this occasion, Mrs Porter appeared to be joining.

It was as she was walking around the cemetery that the significance of Mr Porter's remark about the Elephant Man hit home. *When contradicted he could turn ugly.* It was perhaps unfortunate that she was passing the grave of poor Edith Piaf, at which a group of deferential matrons were paying their respects, when the joke hit her. She burst out laughing. Indeed, she chuckled to herself several times during the course of the day.

The following morning she went down to breakfast at the later time again, wondering if she would see them, but that morning it appeared they had set out for their day's adventures earlier than usual.

It was on the evening of following day that she next ran into them. She normally dined at a place she had come to know on the rue des Francs Bourgeois, and it was to there that she set off. As she walked along the rue des Archives, she caught sight of the Porters seated at a cosy table by a window. She walked on for a while and then, almost without knowing why, retraced her steps. She entered the restaurant and was shown to a table in a corner. From there she could see the Porters quite clearly, could see Gregory and his father laughing at something, and was soon feeling a little annoyed that they had not spotted her. Finally they did, though not until after she had ordered. Gregory was dispatched to ask her to join them.

'Well, yes, why not?' she said, after a suitable show of surprise at 'discovering' that they were there.

Mr Porter and Gregory were greatly amused at the waiter's vexation that Marianne had dared to move from her own table without asking permission.

'You'd think he'd be grateful that a table has been freed,' said Mrs Porter.

'Oh, I expect he is,' laughed Marianne, 'but he's a Parisian waiter, and has his authority to uphold.'

She found out a little more about the Porters during the meal. They told her that Spike was their only child, but they fostered children from time to time, sad cases most of them, it seemed. Difficult too, Marianne supposed.

'It does Gregory good,' said Mrs Porter. 'Stops him being spoilt.'

'He is spoilt, though,' said Mr Porter.

'Stops him being more spoilt, then,' said Mrs Porter.

Marianne thought that they were probably being a little hard on Gregory, who did not seem remotely spoilt to her. Precocious, yes, but that was altogether a different thing. If anything, it was his self-confidence that made him attractive. How different, she thought now, from the shy Gregory (or should she now say Spike?) she had just encountered.

'We've got this new kid coming next week,' Gregory said. 'He came last weekend to get to know us. Weird little bloke. Thumped Dad in the face.'

Gregory said this as though it was the one thing about the newcomer of which he approved.

'Not a very good start, surely?' said Marianne.

'Ah, that's the challenge,' said Mr Porter, who appeared to see assault as an occupational hazard. He turned to Gregory. 'He's had a hard life, not mollicoddled like some people.'

'Gregory's really quite good with them,' said Mrs Porter, but added somewhat apprehensively, 'though it looks as though Dean certainly will be a challenge.'

'If he thumps me, I'll thump him back,' said Gregory.

'You'll do no such thing,' said Mr Porter. 'He's younger than you, so it wouldn't be very gentlemanly, would it? In fact it would be downright cowardly. Don't forget you can feel secure, but he won't be able to until he knows us better.'

For a moment, Gregory looked genuinely chastened at this questioning of his manhood, but then observed: 'I feel insecure sometimes. Especially when Dad's driving.'

'Close your eyes, then,' suggested Mr Porter.

'I thought that's what you did,' said Gregory.

Marianne reciprocated their openness by breaking the habit of a lifetime and saying a little about herself: that she lived with her mother (for this was the year before Alexandrine died), who was French as her father had been, that she had been to school in Kent ('Oh, I could never send Gregory away to school!' Mrs Porter had said. 'I could!' grunted Mr Porter, though everyone knew he did not mean it. Marianne wished more than ever that she had had parents like these), that she had graduated the previous year and was now working in a little private museum and library devoted to French literature, frequented mainly by academics.

'It sounds really boring,' said Gregory.

'Don't be rude,' said his mother. 'To some people listening to you talking about Spurs all the time must be boring.'

'I bet more people go to see Spurs than go to her museum,' said Gregory, and Marianne laughingly agreed that this was certainly the case.

They walked back to the hotel together.

'Perhaps you'd like to come out for a little nightcap with us later,' said Mrs Porter to Marianne, 'after we've made sure Gregory's safely in bed.'

'Thank you,' said Marianne, 'but I feel I should have an early night. But thank you for a lovely evening.'

'Thank *you*, Marianne,' said Mrs Porter, in a way which made Marianne feel that she really had contributed something. It was preposterous, of course. Their evening would have been complete enough without her there. And yet, as she prepared herself for bed, she somehow felt a little more significant than she had before she met them. She certainly felt more cheerful.

Marianne ached with regret now as she recalled that time. Why, why, why had she declined the invitation from those kind, warm people? She had not even been tired, in fact she was nearer to being awake than she had been for a long time, or would be again until she ran into them at the same hotel a little over two years later.

CHAPTER TWO

Mr Clarke did not ring that week about the work Marianne had suggested might be suitable for Spike and Dean, in fact the phone did not ring at all until late Saturday afternoon. For a few seconds she allowed herself to hope, but it turned out to be Roger of all people.

'Marianne,' he said cheerfully, as if their last meeting four months previously had been amicable, 'how go things?'

'Roger! I didn't expect to hear from you.'

'Well, you know me: I like to surprise.'

His confidence annoyed her intensely, partly because it appeared so insulting, but mainly because she could not match it. She thought a silence would serve.

'Are you still there?'

'Yes,' she sighed wearily, knowing that her continued presence would doubtless only give him grounds for supposing that his cheek was paying off.

'Good. Look, I've got a couple of tickets for *Figaro* this evening. Thought you might like to come out. Let bygones be bygones and all that.'

'Has that Spanish woman stood you up, then?'

'What?...Oh, her. Haven't seen her for a couple of months. Look here, it was only a fling. And nothing was agreed between us, you and me, I mean.'

It was true so far as it went. They had never formally been a couple. Others had sometimes assumed it, Marianne had often taken it for granted, but no, nothing to that effect had ever been said.

She found herself agreeing to go out with him that evening, Heaven knew why. But as she prepared herself she realised that she did know why. She had to get out that evening, even at the expense of the loss of face involved in going out with Roger. Her trip to

41

Walthamstow had somehow revealed (or rather reopened) a hole in her life, a hole that had to be boarded up in some way, however temporarily. Well, Roger would be the tacky piece of cardboard she would use to cover it up that evening (and probably that night: she knew him well enough to know that a trip to the opera was most probably not all he had in mind). And, she thought, as she put on her lipstick, she would let him know that she was changing, that she could not be manipulated quite so easily as he thought. She would tell him of her recent adventure, make him aware that she was quite capable of going to places like Walthamstow if she wanted to.

He was surprised at her affability when he arrived to pick her up, and a little thrown by it, though delighted nevertheless. Perhaps the usual attempts at explanation would not be called for after all. The opera was excellent, they both agreed on that, and when, afterwards, he gave the taxi driver instructions to take them to Lucerne Court he had even more occasion to be surprised, for she said that she would quite like to go somewhere to eat.

'But it's gone eleven,' he said, recalling the hours she kept.

'It's Saturday,' she shrugged. 'If I can stay out late in the week, why not tonight?'

He told the driver to take them to a place he knew on Kings Road, and it was not until they had ordered that he recalled what she had recently said.

'So,' he said, intrigued, 'and where did you get up to in the week that's given you the taste for fast living?'

And so she told him, and he was immensely amused.

'Well, who'd have thought it of old Daphne! And was she right in thinking you had the hots for this young drip?'

'He was not a drip!' she said, surprising herself with her vehemence. 'You haven't been listening properly. He was just incredibly shy.'

'A shy boy of that age is what I call a drip. You make him sound like a little princess, fluttering his eyelashes and turning away. I'm surprised he hasn't been laughed off all the building sites in East London. The brother sounds more interesting. If you want a bit of rough trade, I'd try there.'

'How coarsely you put things,' she admonished. 'You haven't changed, have you?'

42

'So you have got the hots for him!' he laughed.

'Would be jealous if I had?'

He paused, knowing that an answer either way could be miscon-strued. He decided to be honest.

'No,' he said. 'Sorry if you weren't expecting that. I want us to be friends, even sometimes to...well, we are adults and unattached. But no, not disappointed. In fact, if you were to pursue it, I think I'd be impressed. Even if you didn't succeed, I'd be impressed. For one thing, you'd have to be just about the first woman in Lucerne Court who's gone after a younger man.'

'Funny,' she mused, 'Daphne said that too. Do we really come across as that staid? Anyway, what would be so impressive about my making a fool of myself?'

'Surely it's better to make a fool of yourself over someone young and fanciable than over an ugly old rake like me? Let's face it, there are fewer years between you and him than between me and you.'

'Ah, that's the point. I wouldn't want him to look on me the way I look on you.'

He smiled at her uncharacteristic impertinence. 'Don't you mean that you wouldn't want others to see it that way? But you denigrate yourself too much. Many boys would fancy a woman your age, and a lot older. You never fancied me exactly, what young woman could? They might fancy the security I could give - no financial worries - but not me.'

'You're wrong. I did fancy you, or at least you were in the category I'd assumed was the one destined for me. But...'

'But now you've been to a working-class suburb and all that's changed.'

'That's horrible. You make me sound like some rich bitch after a bit of flesh, preferably flesh that can be bought.'

'Not necessarily. You're saying the things, I suspect, that have probably been going through your own mind. You are fanciable enough not to have to buy anyone. The kudos in knowing someone such as you would be attractive enough to many working-class young men.'

'Someone such as me?'

'Well, affluent to be sure. Educated. Expensively dressed. What he or his mates would probably refer to as "a classy bird".'

'I think you may be showing your age if you think they still use expressions like that,' she said, with all the authority of someone who has recently spent an evening in a pub in Walthamstow. 'Anyway, he has a certain class of his own. He came from a good home. Not rich by your standards, but by no means *lumpenproletariat*. And he obviously believes in hard work.'

'Well, now you disappoint me. If he's upper working-class or lower middle class, or whatever they call it these days, I suspect he really is as boring as he sounds. That middle range are the most tiresome, and certainly the biggest prigs.'

'Why do rich people and poor people talk such nonsense about those in the middle?' she asked, genuinely interested. 'Is it jealousy, because everyone really knows that it's they who keep everything going? Is it because rich people see the more intelligent and hard-working "lower classes" as a threat to their assumptions in just the same way as the welfare state victims conditioned to live on handouts do?'

'All of those things,' he laughed, touched by her quaint defence of Thatcherite values. 'But, more to the point in your case, it's the middle range that are most likely to be hopeless in bed.'

'How would I know? I've only been to bed with the likes of you.'

And she could have added that she had never found it particularly wonderful, but she did not because she was not sure if the fault did not lie with her.

'How come you know so much about his background?'

'Because,' she admitted, allowing him (to his further surprise) to pour her some more wine, 'I've met him before. I wasn't sure at first, but I know it's him.'

He was suitably intrigued so she continued. 'It was in Paris. In the hotel in the rue du Roule. More than once. The first time was when he must have been about thirteen, nearly fourteen. A bright boy, I thought, with pleasant parents. I didn't see them the following year, but the year after that they were staying there again at the same time as me. I couldn't help noticing how he had developed in the two years since I'd last seen him. He had a really deep voice by then and I loved the sound of it. I remembered wondering what he would be like in another two or three years. I rather hoped I would see them again, but I never did.'

'Sounds like *Death in Venice*,' he laughed. He had never read the novel but had seen the film.

'Yes,' she said, not the least bit offended, 'though I will say in my own defence that I was attracted by the 16-year-old Spike more than the 13-year-old, and perhaps not so much attracted as curious to see what he would be like when he was older. Oh, and by the way, from the references you've made so far you seem to think he's some male version of a Barbie doll. Put that idea out of your head. While not short he's not that tall, he's muscular - he was even four years ago - and his face is too broad to fit into the classic Greek idea of puerile beauty, not to mention a slightly snub nose. I don't think Thomas Mann's Aschenbach would have fallen for him at all.'

'Are you quite sure your memory isn't playing tricks with you? You saw a boy then, and having seen someone similar you may be projecting this one on to that one.'

'No, I thought that was probable at first. In fact it seemed impossible that the general dogsbody I saw this week could be Gregory. But I deduced enough for me to know, and he recognised me.'

'But he didn't say anything?'

'No,' she admitted, 'not openly, but I know he knew who I was. Perhaps the memories of those days must be painful to him now. But the voice, the smile - when it came - the eyes, yes, that's Gregory all right.'

'Well,' he laughed, 'you've had your wish at last. You've seen what he'd be like a few years later. And up to expectations, if my instincts are correct.'

'Oh, yes, fully, except that...well, he seems so lacking in self-confidence now. Gregory was never like that. I remember going to sit by a playground near the hotel to read a book, but ended up watching him playing football with some local boys. That was when he was 16. His French was excellent and they'd obviously taken to him straight away. He could only have met up with them that day, perhaps the day before, but already he seemed to have become the leader of the pack. In fact it was that same evening that his parents asked me to take him out to dinner while they attended a business function.'

'Hmm. A dangerous age to be going to dinner with a woman in her twenties.'

'Yes, so I found. It nearly led somewhere, but both of us were too well brought up in the end. He did make me laugh, though. He really had quite a sophisticated sense of humour for someone his age. I was shocked when I realised how tempted I was.'

'Well,' he laughed, 'your self-control does you credit. I think *Death in Venice* would have been quite a different novel if Mrs Whatever-her-name-was had asked that old queen to look after young Tadzio for an evening. I shouldn't think it would have been published at all, at least not until the 1960s or 1970s, and then only after a court case or two.'

'But I think you've missed the point of the novel,' said Marianne, with the air of someone who is trying to reintroduce a sense of decorum into a conversation. 'It's supposed to be about love of classic beauty, not about sexual desire.'

'And do you believe that?'

'Good heavens no!' she laughed. 'I shouldn't think anyone does.'

She was grateful to Roger for listening and not being as scornful as he might have been, and in her indebtedness she found herself inviting him in when the taxi reached Lucerne Court. In theory it was for coffee, in reality it turned out as it usually did.

Her memory had not failed her. It was as though the procedure were a ritual they had to perform, just to prove that they were both adults and capable of doing it. He touched and caressed in his pokey way, but only enough to make respectable what was to follow, as though he wanted her to know (and he did not quite succeed in doing so) that they were sharing something. When the ritual was over so was the affection, assuming that is what it had ever been. She was not particularly disappointed, for it was no worse than she had expected in her limited experience with Roger or, indeed, with the two other lovers she had had in the last four years. They had always seemed as little fulfilled as she, but all sides seemed happy (or relieved) that they had not totally disgraced themselves. That appeared to be their definition of success. Had it not been for her imagination it would not have been bearable for her. For when with them it had not been their faces she saw when the light was switched off, but another face entirely, a face she was fearing might be fading until her memory had been given a top-up in Walthamstow a few days earlier.

Roger fell into a sound, slightly alcoholic sleep, but Marianne willed herself to stay awake to savour the memory of that second occasion on which she had found herself staying in the hotel on the rue du Roule at the same time as the Porters.

She had not known they would be there, for no addresses or phone numbers had been exchanged the first time. It was a hot day, she recalled, and after visiting the Delacroix Museum (which she had found disappointing) she had taken a book and seated herself on a bench by a somewhat dusty open space near the hotel. It was not a prepossessing spot, but her legs ached a little after traipsing around the museum and this was all that was on offer in the near vicinity of the hotel. Some boys were playing what was obviously an impromptu game of football, for they were not kitted-out properly and appeared to cover a wide age range, from about 12 to 17. She did not take much notice of them, although on one or two occasions she was obliged to do so when the ball came in her direction, to be retrieved apologetically by one of the players. It was the sound of an English voice shouting commands and advice that made her pay more attention. The French was good, but the accent was definitely English, spoken in a deep, pleasant voice. She looked up and deduced that the voice had to be that of the fair-haired boy, one of the older ones. Recognition came slowly, for although she caught sight of the face it was the rest of the healthy body, in white teeshirt and blue shorts, which held her attention. Gradually it did dawn on her that she had seen the face before, though she could not immediately link it with Gregory Porter. Only when he recognised her and waved did she realise who it was.

She waved back, unable to conceal her surprise. Could such a transformation have taken place in the space of two years?

Perhaps Gregory had become used to this reaction, for he smiled back as though anxious to reassure her that it was really he. He carried on playing, looking at her from time to time, as if to make sure that she was watching. When the game was over he announced to the others that he had to go. A couple of the younger boys ran to him, remonstrating in disappointment. With the confidence of a film star who knows he is idolised, he playfully held one of them in an arm lock before leaving them and approaching Marianne.

'Why, Gregory!' said Marianne, too overwhelmed to consider her phraseology carefully, 'you are a big boy now!'

He smiled and sat on the bench beside her.

'Are you staying at the same place?' she asked.

'Yes,' he said. 'Boring, isn't it?'

'Oh, I don't know, I find it suits me.'

'Yes,' he said thoughtfully, 'I suppose it would.'

She had hoped that he had told his team-mates he had to go because he wished to converse with her, but it transpired that he was supposed to be meeting his parents at Au Printemps, was already late, in fact. He said he would see her later and she watched him until he turned a corner.

She made her way back to the hotel, her fatigue forgotten.

She bathed and changed with uncharacteristic cheerfulness. She would almost certainly be invited to dinner with the Porters again, assuming she managed to run into them (something that was not necessarily inevitable even in a small hotel). She made herself up rather more carefully than usual and then stood by her open window, looking down at the street below as she consumed a bottle of mineral water she had taken from the minibar (a new feature that year: the twentieth century was catching up even with that establishment). Suddenly she saw the three hoped-for figures coming in the direction of the hotel, Gregory still in his shorts and teeshirt.

Well, if she really wanted to run into them now was her opportunity. She grabbed a couple of postcards she had written and made her way quickly down the stairs. She was only on the second floor and there was a strong possibility that she could miss them if she waited for the cranky lift. Her plan succeeded only too well, for Gregory was making his way up the stairs just as she reached the bottom flight. They both smiled as they passed each other, and she turned, still descending, to catch a back view of Gregory as he made his way around the bend in the stairs. She had not deliberately intended to take in his bottom and thighs, but there they were, level with her eyes. Her concentration lapsed momentarily and she missed her footing. She fell down the six or seven remaining steps and landed unceremoniously in the foyer in front of Mr and Mrs Porter, who were waiting for the lift.

The suddenness of it all dazed her a little. She could hear Gregory, alerted by the commotion, coming down the stairs behind her as she raised herself with the assistance of Mr Porter.

'Are you all right, Marianne?' asked a concerned Mrs Porter.

'Oh, yes. . . yes, I am. My mind must have been somewhere else,' said Marianne as she hastily readjusted her dress, aware that, for a moment at least, a large section of her knickers had been on show.

'Yes, I think it must have been,' agreed Mrs Porter, and Marianne wondered if she had noticed just what had caused the lapse.

'The carpet rod's come away,' said Gregory, and they all agreed that it had, though it was unclear if this was the result of Marianne's fall or a contributory factor to it. Monsieur des Salles, the proprietor, had emerged from his little office to see what was happening and was just in time to catch Gregory's observation. Only a few weeks before an American woman had threatened to sue the hotel for ten million dollars when she had slipped over on a splodge of marmalade outside the breakfast room, bruising her ample posterior. Although she had quickly forgotten her threat once she had calmed down, Monsieur des Salles saw it as a sad reflection on the times and a reminder of the perils facing contemporary hotel owners.

'I'm really all right,' said Marianne, in response to his rather histrionic gestures of concern.

Monsieur des Salles, relieved but not wishing to take any chances, decided to settle there and then. Ten million dollars might be the going rate for an American but for the English a pot of tea usually sufficed.

'Please,' he said, 'come into the lounge to recover. I will tell Anwar to bring you some refreshment.'

Sensing that the Porters knew Marianne, he made it clear that the invitation extended to them. Mrs Porter sat her on the sofa and Marianne noticed that, as she did so, she threw an admonitory glance at her husband and son. Mr Porter had seated himself in an armchair, Gregory on one of the harder ones. Both seemed to be biting their lips and their shoulders were shaking as they very obviously tried to avoid each other's eyes.

The little tea party went well enough, even if it did turn out to be rather brief. The Porters asked after her mother and expressed their condolences when Marianne told them of her death the previous year. They explained to her that they had just been out shopping buying a birthday present for Dean, their other son.

'I didn't know you had another son,' said Marianne.

'Well, we didn't the last time you met us,' Mrs Porter explained. 'It's the boy we'd been fostering. We've adopted him now. It was all finalised a couple of weeks ago. It's a pity he can't be with us, but he's gone on a school trip.'

'Oh, how lovely!' said Marianne, referring to the adoption. She wondered if it would be appropriate at this juncture to say something like 'you must all come and visit me some time,' but thought it better to wait at least until the first cup of tea was finished, lest she sound like the late Mae West. She was bitterly disappointed to discover, during the second cup, that the Porters were due to leave the day after tomorrow and would be out all of the following day visiting old friends in Orleans.

'Perhaps we could have dinner this evening,' Marianne ventured.

'Well, I'm afraid that won't be possible either. We have to attend a business function in Malmaison. It's not something I'm looking forward to, I can promise you.'

'I am,' put in Mr Porter, his usual good-humour deserting him for the moment. 'I intend to give that old crook a piece of my mind.'

Marianne deduced from the look Mrs Porter gave her husband that this was no time to be discussing his business affairs. Unfortunately this reminder of their evening's activities prompted a worried glance at her watch from Mrs Porter, and within a few minutes they were bidding her farewell.

Marianne made her way a little sadly to the postbox, but brightened on her way back as it occurred to her that, after this further meeting with them, it might not look too brazen of her if she were to leave a note for them at the reception desk, just a short note giving them her phone number and suggesting they pop in to see her if ever they were in the West End.

Arriving back at the hotel Marianne was surprised to see that Mr and Mrs Porter were standing in the reception area, as though awaiting her return.

'I'm sorry to bother you, Marianne,' said Mrs Porter, 'but I'm not sure if we should be taking Gregory with us this evening. It will be very much a business affair. I wonder, would you mind awfully taking him out to dinner for us?'

'Of course I wouldn't mind!' beamed Marianne.

'But you must let us pay,' said Mrs Porter.

'Oh no, I wouldn't dream of it,' said Marianne.

'We will pay,' said Mrs Porter, with rather alarming firmness.

'Or perhaps,' suggested the more practical Mr Porter, 'you could go Dutch.'

At that point, it has to be said, Marianne was more pleased at the opportunity to be helping out the Porters than she was thrilled at the prospect of spending an evening with Gregory. What on earth do I say to him? she thought. For she had hardly ever spoken to a boy 16 or thereabouts before, or at any rate had never had a proper conversation with one. Nor, even when she was a teenager herself, had she ever indulged in romantic fantasies about them. Having attended an all-girls school it was an age she had somehow bypassed: at 11 she had thought all boys beasts, at 15 she looked towards men in their twenties, at 18 (largely as a result of her mother's influence) to those older still. There were girls at her school who had posters of rather puny-looking young pop stars on their walls, but her best friend, Caroline Farnham-Trainor, was contemptuous of these. 'You must come and see the new blacksmith's apprentice who's putting new shoes on Heseltine,' they had excitedly been told one teatime (Heseltine was one of the school's own ponies), 'he's drop-dead gorgeous.' 'Why haven't you dropped dead, then?' Caroline had retorted, and she and Marianne stayed while the others stampeded towards the stables. 'Behaving like a lot of teenyboppers from a council estate!' Caroline had said scornfully, 'and over a mere boy!' (Marianne's mother had approved of Caroline. What she never knew was that, after a year at a finishing school, Caroline took a sudden lurch to the left and was last heard of living in a squat in Bermondsey.)

It was agreed that she should meet Gregory in the lounge at half past seven. 'Make sure he doesn't go to bed too late,' Mrs Porter urged.

As she entered the lounge at the appointed time she found Gregory wearing jeans and a blue and white rugby shirt. This necessitated a hasty reconsideration of her plans, for she had intended to disregard Mr Porter's suggestion that they go Dutch and treat Gregory to something a little grander than his father had almost certainly had in mind. This was not so much to impress Gregory (or so she told herself) as to fulfil an ambition of her own. She had always intended to visit one or two of the more renowned establishments (Lucas Carton had been recommended to her and, nearer, La Tour d'Argent) but as she was invariably alone when in Paris she had never before considered it a serious proposition. She was a little disappointed at first that she would have to make do with the less pretentious restaurant at which she usually dined, but as they made their way there she realised that this could be an even better option. She would not now be asking for her usual table for one, and the slight look of pity she sometimes suspected seeing on the face of Madame Volin, the proprietress, would no longer be called for. 'I'm looking after the son of some friends of mine,' she could say, and did just that when they arrived. Madame Volin's reaction (and that of the two flamboyant waiters when they saw Gregory) gave her even more pleasure than she had anticipated.

'Shall we get a bottle of wine?' Gregory asked, surveying the list.

'Well, I don't drink much,' she said, 'and I'm not sure your parents would be very pleased if I let you drink most of a bottle. Perhaps a half bottle.'

He could not dispute this point, but when the waiter came (they were more attentive than usual, Marianne noted) Gregory gave her his sweetest smile as she was just about to order. She closed her eyes and let her mouth carry on without her.

'...And a bottle of the St-Emilion,' she found it saying.

'You'll just have to make sure you drink most of it yourself,' he reasoned, to help resolve her crisis of conscience.

'Ah, so you're trying to get me drunk, are you?'

'Why should I do that? You fall down the stairs quite beautifully enough when you're sober.'

She laughed at his impertinence. 'And a great deal of amusement it gave you and your father.'

'Oh,' he assured her, 'I'd have laughed even more if it had been him, and he would, too, if it had been me.'

Marianne did not doubt the truth of this and began to feel at ease, even a little frivolous.

'But there are other reasons why gentlemen try to get ladies to drink more than they're used to,' she said mysteriously.

'Are there?' he said, with pretended incomprehension. 'Tell me about them.'

She blushed but could not help smiling nevertheless.

'You're very elegant you know. Mum and Dad said that after we first met you.'

And she realised that he was as flattered to be out with her as she was pleased to be with him (and she was pleased to be with him, if a little nervous of the situation. He had apologised to her for his attire on the way to the restaurant, explaining that he had wanted to wear his suit and tie but that his mother had said that casual dress would do. Why, she wondered, had Mrs Porter not wanted him to dress up too much to go out with her? The obvious answer made her wince). Much as she enjoyed the flattery, she knew that it would probably be safer for both of them to divert the conversation.

'So, you've just finished your GCSEs,' she observed, recalling some of the information he had given her on the way there.

'Yes,' he said. 'I don't think I've done that well, to be honest. Dean's the brainy one.'

'But your French is excellent,' she said, and she could have added that his humour was sharp.

'That's only because my dad's mum was French. I don't like any of the other subjects much, not the ones that involve essays and things, anyway. I prefer woodwork, stuff like that. I was hoping to persuade Mum and Dad to let me leave school soon and start working, but they won't have it.'

'I should think they won't.' said Marianne.

'If things go on as they are for Dad, he might have to change his mind,' he said, looking serious for the first time. 'He imports kitchen furniture, most of it from France. Apparently, he paid in advance for a load of it a year ago and the stuff still hasn't been delivered. The bloke who's to blame will most likely be at this do they're going to this evening. That's why they didn't want me there with them, in case there's a row. The housing recession hit Dad's business hard. Apparently, when people don't move a lot they don't want new kitchens so much. He paid for another lot in advance three years ago and the firm he ordered it from went bust before he got it. He's had a whole lot of people not paying up either, and he's caught in the middle. He had to borrow money on the house to keep going.'

'Oh dear!' said Marianne. 'But I don't think they'd like you telling me this.'

'No, perhaps not,' he said, and then brightened. 'Actually, Dad's got another contract in the pipeline which he thinks should help things along.'

'Well then, perhaps things will turn out all right,' she said.

At that moment, back in the horrible present, Roger started snoring loudly. She got up and went ruefully into the kitchen, suspecting that the interruption would make it impossible to return to her reverie. Then she spotted the wine rack, and recalled that there was a bottle of St Emilion there. Remembering her Proust, she wondered if the smells and tastes of times past could work their magic for her as they had for him. Perhaps a small glass could do no harm.

She sat in the drawing room, the lights dimmed almost to their lowest. The first few sips of the wine tasted harsh, and then she realised that it had not had time to breathe. But that in itself was an introduction to the past. 'This wine tastes foul,' Gregory had said. 'It's not had time to breathe,' she had explained to him.

It had taken a while for her to realise that she was becoming captivated. He spoke about Spurs and their chances of winning the cup in the forthcoming season, about his school rugby team, about his parents and Dean, now officially his brother. It did not matter what he said so much as the way he said it, for he spoke without malice to anyone, enthusiastically and unselfconsciously, his soothing baritone such a sharp contrast to the shrill bitchiness she recalled from the time she was that age. She had no illusions about the ability of boys to be nasty, but she could now see that there was a side of them of which she had not really been aware. True, Gregory could poke fun at people (had she not already been the victim of that?) but he did it without cruelty, and he took no offence when the fun was being poked at him. His features were at a crossroad. When he smiled it was like seeing a happy infant in a pushchair, when he frowned he seemed to be older than his years, and she saw how he might appear a few years hence. As she looked at him across the narrow table she wondered what it was that made him so attractive, that made her want to reach out and touch him. Perhaps it was his animation, or maybe his innocence. And he was innocent, although he did his best to pretend not to be.

The innocence would not last, she reflected sadly, could not. In a year or two he would be fully aware of his power to attract and, notwithstanding the Porters' excellent parenting, would be spoilt by others with whom he came into contact. He would find he could break hearts and probably learn to enjoy it.

'Didn't you ever resent your parents fostering those children?' she asked at one stage, 'and then adopting Dean?'

He seemed surprised by the question.

'Well, at first perhaps. But it was fun, in a way, and some of them were so pathetic you had to feel sorry for them. When he first came Dean was the most pathetic of all. He could be really violent, sometimes, and you never knew what was going to set him off. To be honest, I think there are things about his background I've never been told. Perhaps they will tell me now I'm older, or maybe he will, one day. I used to have to make sure he was all right at school, although I'm two forms ahead of him. Other kids used to make fun of him, but I used to make sure he was okay. The only trouble was he used to follow me around a lot, still does a bit. That's why Dad thought it would be good for him to go on this school trip, so that he'll learn not to rely on me so much.'

Marianne recalled seeing how the younger boys had adored Gregory that afternoon during the football match and had no doubt that Dean idolised him even more. As she thought about it now, and having witnessed the way Dean had looked at Gregory (or Spike, as she was apparently to have to get used to calling him) in the pub in Walthamstow, she sensed that the years had not diminished that adoration. The only difference appeared to be that Dean was now the leader, the protector perhaps. How had this curious reversal come about?

'Do you have any cigarettes?' Gregory had asked when their meal was over and the coffee ordered.

Marianne gave him a narrow look. Despite his benevolence to Dean it was obvious that Gregory was no saint.

'I'm as certain as can be that your parents wouldn't approve,' she said. 'Besides, I don't have any.'

He shrugged resignedly, but before Marianne knew what was happening, Serge, one of the waiters, came forward with a packet of cigarettes and a lighter. Trust him to be listening in, she thought. Almost absent mindedly, she took one herself, bemused by the lingering look

Serge gave Gregory. She did not smoke much, but for practical reasons sometimes had a cigarette when on a date with a man who did so, as it balanced up their breath in case of any mouth-to-mouth contact later. But why had she taken one now?

'Poof!' said Gregory, when Serge had reluctantly departed.

Marianne was a little disappointed in Gregory for using such an unpleasant word. Still, he was from the suburbs she reflected, and he had his own manly image to uphold. She thought she would experiment to see if he really was capable of taking as good as he gave.

'You seem quite good at spotting them,' she said playfully. 'On the lookout, are you?'

'Oh, I've had a few approaches,' he said, with a worldly air. 'They usually back off when they find they can't afford it.'

Marianne looked at him in astonishment for a few seconds before realising that it was a joke. When that realisation came, something happened that had not happened to her since the second form. She had a fit of the giggles. She started by laughing quite normally, but the more she looked at his butter-wouldn't-melt expression the more she lost control. She choked on her cigarette and had to put it out.

'Well, it wasn't that funny,' he said, although he had been a little infected by her mirth himself.

'Oh, it was,' she disagreed, recovering at last. 'You and your father would make an excellent double act, you know. I still laugh to myself when I think of one or two of the things he said when we met a couple of years ago.'

'Crikey, Marianne, you must have led an incredibly sheltered life! Mum and Dean pretend to block their ears when we get going. Silly puns are Dad's speciality. Mum says they constitute mental cruelty.'

They may pretend to block their ears, Marianne thought, but she was pretty sure they listened all the same, and laughed. The picture of life in the Porter household was becoming clearer and, as it did so, Marianne's envy of it grew. Perhaps it was laughter as much as anything that had tamed the once wild Dean.

It was as they were finishing their coffee that something happened which was to imprint itself in Marianne's mind almost as much as her first sight of Gregory earlier that day. The restaurant had become quite busy and a young Arab girl of about 17, usually confined to the kitchen, was helping to serve the food. She was not very bright, that was obvious, and her agility was impaired by a club foot. She had already been reprimanded by Madame Volin for delivering dishes to the wrong table and now, as she was passing by them laden with two plates of food, she tripped over the handle of a bag that had been placed on the floor by the next table. The plates she was carrying smashed noisily on to the stone floor. A roar of delight went around the restaurant. Marianne looked at Gregory, expecting him to be laughing louder than most, but far from laughing he was looking around at the other diners with something akin to anger. A moment later, he was crouched on the floor helping the distraught girl pick up the chards of crockery. Madame Volin emerged from somewhere and began berating the girl while at the same time insisting politely that Gregory resume his seat. Gregory ignored her, at least until Serge arrived with a mop and bucket. In tears, the girl was led back to the kitchen by the other waiter, followed by continued laughter from the customers and expletives from Madame Volin.

When the kerfuffle was over Marianne ventured to speak to Gregory, who seemed surprisingly shaken considering that the incident really had nothing to do with him.

'Where has your sense of humour gone?' she asked. 'I would have thought you'd find it more amusing than anybody.'

'Why?' he asked, as though she had said something astonishing.

'You laughed at me when I made a fool of myself this afternoon.' she pointed out.

'But you have everything. That girl has nothing, not very much anyway. And everyone could see she was upset. It isn't witty to laugh at people who are at a disadvantage.' Then he smiled, relaxing a little, 'not so they know, anyway.'

What did he mean, she wondered, when he said that she had everything? She somehow knew that he was not referring solely to her financial status. She could not but be flattered, especially as the remark came out almost by accident, as part of an explanation for something else. A direct compliment would have impressed her less, for she was used to receiving those, usually towards the end of an evening when sleeping arrangements had not yet been finalised. But the glow she felt was secondary to another feeling that struck deeper than flattery. She recalled something Roger had said (for she had known Roger and his little set for some years before she and Roger had become 'an item,' albeit a somewhat loose one). It appeared that when he had worked in the City in the late 1980s he and some colleagues had sometimes amused themselves on summer evenings by putting Superglue on to one side of fifty-pence pieces and sticking them on to the pavement in front of their favourite wine bar. They derived much pleasure from watching as tramps, druggies and other hopeless cases tried tried to pick up the coins. She had expressed doubts as to whether this was a particularly pleasant thing to do, and Roger had berated her for her lack of humour. 'You should lighten up,' were the words he had used. For a while, she had wondered if he might not be right. Now she was with someone who, even at 16, had a better sense of humour than Roger and all his pals put together and yet he would not have found such antics amusing either. Gregory could not know it, but he had touched her in a place nobody had touched her before, in a place she had not even known existed until now. She looked at him and smiled to herself as she recalled the words she had said when the gâteau trolley had come round half an hour before: 'I shouldn't really, but I don't think I could resist one of those!'

Neither of them wanted the evening to end but they had already lingered as long as possible in the restaurant. They walked slowly back to the hotel, looking into shop windows at merchandise which was mostly identical to that which could be bought in London.

'I've just remembered,' said Gregory. 'Mum's brought some photos with her to show these people we're going to see in Orleans, tomorrow. Shall I go up and get them? We can have a cognac in the lounge, perhaps.'

Marianne seized on this opportunity for an extension to the evening. 'Oh, that would be lovely!' she said. 'But I think we had better make it coffee rather than cognac.' When Anwar's attention was caught, she asked for cognacs, of course.

And so they sat in the lounge while he showed her some photographs of their house by Epping Forest, and the lake opposite with its swans, ducks and geese which he and Dean fed every night before going to bed, sometimes getting into trouble for using up all the bread. She also saw a picture of Dean at last, though she did not really take him in properly as he was seated next to Gregory. As they pored over the photographs, their heads side by side, she found herself putting her hand around his already quite broad shoulders and then to the back of his neck (as one does). She did not intend the movement to be seductive, but neither did she desist when it occurred to her that there was a chance it could be interpreted in that way. He put his arm around her and rested his head on her shoulder, and eventually kissed her neck.

She drew away (after allowing herself to touch his eyebrows, something she had wanted to do all evening), her inbred instincts of propriety more powerful even than the not inconsiderable natural instinct to let him continue.

'I'm old enough in France,' he reassured her.

'That's not the point,' she said, taking his hand. 'You know your mother most certainly wouldn't approve.'

'Can we be friends in England?' he asked, unable to contradict her on this point. 'I'll be 16 next week.'

'And I'm 25.'

'So? Anyway, I only asked if we could be friends. Perhaps before long I'll have caught up with you.'

'If I thought you meant it, I'd wait,' she laughed, only half joking.

It seemed a reasonable enough compromise. She went to the small writing table in the corner of the lounge and took a piece of the hotel notepaper. She wrote down her address and telephone number, which he folded and put in the back pocket of his jeans. Then he took some paper himself and gave her his details.

'But I think I should let your parents know that we've exchanged addresses and phone numbers,' she said.

'Well, I suppose so,' he laughed. 'Anyway, we have met before. And I do have other friends, you know. Some of them girls, believe it or not. I'll ring you, but if you do ring me say you want to speak to Spike. That's what my friends call me. I hate Gregory.'

They were still there when Mr and Mrs Porter returned at half-past twelve.

'What, still up?' Mr Porter admonished his son.

'It's my fault,' apologised Marianne on his behalf. 'I hope you don't mind. He's been showing me some photographs and telling me about his new brother.'

'Well, as long as he hasn't been boring you,' said Mrs Porter.

'Oh no,' Marianne assured her, 'he most certainly hasn't!'

The Porters joined them for a quick drink, over which Marianne asked them if they minded that she had given Gregory her telephone number. 'Why should we mind?' laughed Mr Porter. 'You're hardly likely to want to begin some torrid affair with a monster like that.'

The following day the Porters went, as planned, to Orleans. She saw them leaving the day after that, went down to see them off, and she and Gregory smiled sorrowfully at each other as he climbed resignedly into the car. He patted the back pocket of his jeans conspiratorially, reminding her that her address was in there. This now meant more to her than Mrs Porter's somewhat distracted observation (she was getting into the illegally parked car at the time, making haste necessary) that they must keep in touch.

That was the year Marianne altered her usual routine (an extension to her vacation was possible now that her mother was dead), for after Paris she went to visit her relatives in Angers and then on to see an old school chum in Switzerland (Celia, one of the girls Caroline had despised for liking pop stars. She and Marianne had not really become good friends until the final year, but had remained so since). This meant that it was three weeks before she arrived back in England, and she spent that time bitterly regretting that she had not told Gregory this. She suspected that time to a boy of his age probably went more slowly than for someone older, and that if he really intended to ring it would most probably be sooner rather than later. In three weeks he would have given up, assumed that she was not interested in seeing him again or, worst of all, forgotten her.

Nevertheless, she lived in hope. She was determined that nothing physical should pass between them (the very thought!), but looked forward to being able to invite him out, to take him to the theatre, maybe to a restaurant or two, to watch him grow into manhood (manhood as defined by statute, that is, for according to Nature's rules he had clearly already arrived at that point). She spent much of her time in Switzerland picturing the things they would do, the ways she would impress him. She even mentioned him to Celia, who professed incomprehension at her uneasy conscience. 'Lots of women on the Continent see it as their duty to initiate at least one boy,' she laughed. Marianne was less sure. She had always been a little surprised by the widespread belief in Britain that there was greater sexual freedom on the European mainland. Even allowing for the possibility that her own dour French relatives might not be typical, she still doubted very much whether your average Madame Dupont or Frau Schmidt would be more overjoyed at finding that her 16-year-old son had been seduced by a woman in her twenties than your average Mrs Brown or, more to the point, Mrs Porter. She was not without some hopes along those lines but was prepared to wait. Her 25 years to his 16 made immediate gratification impossible, but 28 to 19 would be less disreputable. Another year still and she might even be able to count on the blessing of respectable society. By then he would be in a position to make an informed choice, and if the choice did not go as she wished she could at least take comfort from the thought that, by then, she would be able to count him and his parents as close friends. That in itself would be no small prize.

When she returned to London, she waited for his call, and waited. Oh, why had she never treated herself to an answering machine? If he had telephoned while she was away, she would have had a reason to ring him back. But how could she make the first move without looking ridiculous? After a month she did ring but there was no reply. A few weeks after that she rang again. A man with an American accent answered. Puzzled, Marianne nevertheless asked for Spike (or perhaps Smike). She was told that nobody of that name lived there. Maybe it was a wrong number. She rang again, and the same man answered. With a heavy heart, she put the receiver down.

But still there was a glimmer of hope. Surely the Porters would send her a Christmas card? She sent one to them three weeks before the day itself in order to give them plenty of time to reply, carefully putting her own address on the back of the envelope in case they had lost it. But no card came. And it was only after another futile call on a bleak, lonely evening in the middle of January that she was finally forced to face reality.

'You stupid, pathetic woman!' she said aloud to herself. She had to assume what she had fearfully put off assuming for nearly six months, that Gregory had given her a false number, that to him the whole incident had been nothing but a cruel boy's game. He had probably laughed about it with his friends. (There was actually an even worse scenario, which she could still not contemplate at length: that the Porters suspected her motives and had vetoed any further contact.) And yet she was not as angry with him as she was with herself. For weeks afterwards, she found herself weeping with shame - and bereavement. Her period of mourning over, she returned to her old lifeless routine, determined that she would never put herself in such a position again.

And yet here she was, she thought, as she returned to bed and the snoring and unlovely Roger, waiting anew for a telephone call. No doubt Gregory - now officially Spike, it seemed - was laughing all over again.

Although Roger left before lunchtime, she put off her usual Sunday walk until later that day, as she wanted to watch the omnibus edition of *EastEnders* on the television. It had not been a programme which had interested her before, though she had caught a few minutes of a couple of the weekday evening editions while she prepared her dinner. She wondered now if it could give her any ideas about the way East Londoners thought and acted, but after sitting through the ninety minute version she concluded that Walthamstow must be very different from the fictional Walford. In Walthamstow people smiled occasionally and were nice to each other sometimes, whereas in Walford they all seemed to be shouting, plotting somebody's downfall or on the fiddle. The men were mostly louts but were positively benign compared to the women, who appeared to have the vilest personalities Marianne had ever seen on television, at least in such profusion. Marianne was furious at the misrepresentation. She even considered writing to the BBC to say that she had actually visited East London herself recently and it was not a bit like that.

While on her walk, Marianne's mind turned back to Gregory. She began piecing together the details she knew of the timing of the events in question. Mrs Clarke had said that Spike's parents had been killed nearly four years before. This meant that the tragedy must have happened not long after she had last seen them. She also remembered being told that Dean's adoption had taken place just before the accident. Yes, it must have been very soon after their return to England, in weeks or perhaps even in days. The highly mortgaged house was lost with the death of the Porters, and poor Gregory and Dean had had to go and live with the Clarkes. The new occupants of the house may well have known that the previous owners had been the Porters, may even have known that they had sons called Gregory and Dean, but how could they have known that Gregory's nickname was Spike?

She told herself not to get too excited. It was probable that Gregory would not have called her even if his parents' death had not intervened. But now she at least had a hope which, try as she would, she could not suppress.

Soon after her return from her walk, the telephone rang. It was Mr Clarke.

'Sorry I haven't given you a bell before,' he apologised. 'I wasn't sure when number twelve would be finished, but it looks as though Spike and Dean will be free from Wednesday on. Would that be okay for you!'

'Oh, yes,' she said, as casually as she could. 'That would be fine.'

'Is it a big job? If it is, I'll 'ave to bring the van. If it's just paintin' I can send them on the tube and they can go out with you to get the stuff. I suppose there's somewhere local you can get it?'

'It is only light work,' she agreed. 'And I know where we can buy the paint and emulsion, and the caretaker here can give them ladders. I'd love to...I mean I can go with them to choose what I want.'

'Okay then.' he said, obviously relieved that he would not have to be involved himself, 'they'll be there Wednesday. And don't let Dean give you any cheek.'

The imminent arrival of Spike and Dean meant that Marianne would have to find something in the flat for them to do. The kitchen, the drawing room, her own bedroom (with its en suite facilities) and the hall had been redecorated relatively recently. The dining room had been papered expensively by her mother shortly before her death, and as it had hardly been used it showed few convincing signs of needing refurbishment. The principal bathroom was mostly tiled, but she decided that the parts that were not might benefit from a lick of paint. The spare room, too, could be freshened up.

On the Tuesday evening she returned home via Fortnums and bought some supplies with which to feed her young workmen. She realised that she should not go over the top (or at any rate should not appear to be doing so) and reluctantly by-passed the caviar. In the end she settled for some smoked salmon, a turkey and a gâteau.

She rose early on the Wednesday morning and spent some time deciding what to wear. Given the heat, she opted for a light flowered dress and her mother's pearls with matching earrings. As she looked at herself in the mirror she wondered if the time might not be coming for her to heed Mrs Turner's advice and dress in a slightly younger fashion.

While she waited for them, she occupied herself preparing the salad she would serve with the salmon and turkey. They were only a little late, but to Marianne it seemed like an age.

'Sorry,' Dean said cheerfully, 'there was a body on the Victoria line.'

Spike stood behind his brother, looking nervous. She caught his eye and he looked away again. She wondered sadly if he would always do that. On the other hand, she did notice that he had obviously squirted on a good quality cologne and wondered with a thrill if this had been for her benefit.

She showed them what needed to be done and offered them a cup of coffee before they all set off for the DIY store. Spike looked up occasionally at her while Dean spoke to her about his A-levels, but said very little. She had a growing feeling that his reticence was due as much to reproach as to nervousness. One thing was certain: there was to be no acknowledgement of their past while Dean was there. Once this was established, Spike seemed to relax a little.

They enjoyed themselves looking round the store. Marianne chose some white paint for the woodwork and a pink shade of emulsion for the walls of the spare room, the existing blue for the bathroom.

As they worked, she pretended to read in the drawing room, but she had left the doors open so that she could quite easily hear their conversation coming from the bathroom. After they had decided where they should start from, they began speaking in a slightly daft way about their friends in Walthamstow.

'Pete Bettles has gone to Lloret de Mar for his holiday,' Spike observed.

'Best place for him. Though Tossa would probably have been more appropriate.'

'I shouldn't think he'll know where he is most of the time, at least not after his first eight San Miguels.'

'His sister fancies you, you know. I heard her the other night. Says you're like a teddy bear.'

'I'm not sure I'd be much use if I was one,' observed Spike. 'All the Teddy bears I ever met have had their dicks removed.'

'I wonder why they do that,' laughed Dean.

'So as not to frighten little girls.'

'I'd have thought removing them would be more frightening to little boys. And what do they do with them?'

'When I was a kid someone said that's where they got cocktail sausages from. Anyway, Tracy Bettles has a thing about teddy bears. Collects them.'

'Always steer clear of women like that,' Dean advised, and Marianne silently agreed with him.

'Oh, don't worry, I decided to steer clear of her ever since she sent me that thank-you letter for arranging her eighteenth birthday party at The Kitchener's. A little heart on the back of the envelope with SWALK on it, and she had that big clear writing with little circles instead of dots over the "I"s. She spelt "love" LUV, and she sent this luv not only from herself but also from her cat, her teddy bears and the goldfish.'

Marianne could sympathise. She knew several such women herself. She was surprised that they had them in Walthamstow, too. She had assumed most of them came from Surrey.

'She calls you Spikey-Wikey, too, and me Deany-Weeny.'

'Lucky neither of us is called Frank,' observed Spike.

Marianne smiled to herself as their conversation carried on in this vein for some time. They broke off to discuss the job in hand ('No, not that brush for that narrow bit, you plonker!' 'Ooh, you can be so masterful!') and then Spike started helping Dean with his oral French. She was impressed. Spike corrected Dean's *il faut que je suis* to *il faut que je sois*, resisting the temptation to go in and tell them that the subjunctive could have been avoided altogether if he had only used a more congenial construction in the first place. 'Why didn't you just use *devoir*?' asked Spike, and Marianne realised that her advice would have been superfluous. She felt a glow of pride on Spike's behalf.

She prepared the lunch and served it up in the dining room. They seemed a little overwhelmed when she called them in.

'You didn't have to go to all this trouble,' Dean said. 'We could have gone to a local sandwich bar or a pub.'

'They're all a bit expensive in this area,' Marianne explained, trying not to notice the funny look Spike had given her when he saw the spread.

They tucked in, appreciative of her efforts. They both had good appetites, even Spike (whatever his misgivings), and this pleased her immensely. It was so much more rewarding than when she entertained the somewhat picky women in Lucerne Court, and she told them as much. 'You should have seen us before we became anorexic!' Dean laughed. After they were more or less replete, and she had poured them a second cup of tea, Dean excused himself for a few moments and she found herself alone with Spike.

'I was so sorry to hear about your parents,' she said simply.

He looked down, then after a few seconds raised his head again.

'Why didn't you ring?' he asked.

'I did, but only after I had been to Switzerland to see my friend. I'm sorry, I should have told you I was going on there. Did you ring me, then?'

'Yes,' he said, 'a few days after we got back. But then...'

He lowered his head again.

'Well,' she said brightly, 'you're here now, aren't you?'

'I know I must seem a bit different to you compared to how I was then,' he said, in a tone which suggested that she must find him disappointing.

'You're even better looking now.'

'So are you.'

They both burst into a smile, and this time he did not look away. Progress at last!

'Does Dean know we've met before?' she asked, aware that it was important to know how to behave.

'No. At least, I told him a long time ago that I'd met you in Paris, but he doesn't know you're the same person as you.'

She smiled at his confused syntax.

In the afternoon Spike and Dean's conversation turned to football. It was obvious that Spike was still a Spurs supporter, while Dean favoured West Ham. They hurled pleasant insults at each other's team until teatime ('I don't think Spurs are really so bad,' Dean generously assured Spike. 'In fact I'd buy the whole team and the ground if I had two thousand quid.').

'That's the bathroom done,' Spike told her when they emerged. 'We can make a start on the bedroom tomorrow.'

She went to admire the work they had done so far, and her praise was perfectly genuine. Even her mother would have approved. While she made some tea, Spike asked if he could take a quick shower, having brought a towel with him for the purpose. When he returned she could not help noticing that he had applied some more of the pleasant cologne. As they left soon, she concluded that perhaps it had not been put on for her benefit after all, and wondered if Spike might not have someone else in his life. Perhaps the renewal of their friendship had come too late.

If Spike had looked sheepish on the first day, on the second he looked positively withdrawn. Marianne noticed that they appeared to work less cheerfully that morning, though clearly not from want of trying on the part of Dean, who said 'Cheer up, for God's sake, it's not the end of the world' on one occasion, and on another: 'You don't want to take any notice of that old bag.' For a horrible moment she wondered if she might be the old bag in question, but the context suggested it was more likely to be Dolly.

'Whatever's the matter with him today?' she ventured to ask Dean as he came into the kitchen ahead of Spike for their morning coffee.

'Oh, nothing,' said Dean evasively.

'Has he had a row with someone?'

'Well, yes,' admitted Dean, surprised by her prescience.

'His girlfriend?' she pursued. Well, she had to find out.

'Oh no!' smiled Dean. 'He hasn't got one, though there are plenty of hopefuls.'

'His boyfriend, then?'

Dean laughed out loud at this. 'What, Spike? Don't ask him that, for Christ's sake. He'd be most offended.'

'What are you two laughing at?' asked Spike touchily, coming into the room. He looked suspiciously at Dean.

'Nothing you need worry about,' Dean said reassuringly.

Spike did speak a little while they drank their coffee, but it was on the safely neutral subject of how they intended to proceed with the redecoration of the spare room. They were just about to get on with their work again when the door bell rang. It was Stella, and she had in tow a young man in his early twenties, looking, Marianne thought, slightly ridiculous in a goatee beard and absurdly baggy trousers.

'Hello, Marianne,' said Stella, walking straight into the kitchen as was her wont. 'This is Jerome, my cousin. I thought I'd better let you know he's staying with me for a few weeks until he finds a place of his own. Got a job in London...Oh, you've got visitors.'

Marianne made the introductions, mentioning in passing that Spike and Dean came from Walthamstow.

'Ah, East Seventeen, eh?' said Jerome, impressed. 'Cool!'

She noticed for the first time that his little beard, his hairstyle and his dress suggested imitation of one of the members of the pop group to which he was referring. His dress appeared even more absurd when he spoke for, as Marianne would have expected in a cousin of Stella's, his accent was pure Celia Johnson. The final 'Cool!' seemed so out of place from one with such stilted intonation that even Spike grinned.

'You're a fan, I take it?' said Dean, trying not to laugh.

'You bet! It's great they've got back together again. Do you know any of them?'

'One or two of them have been into our local,' Dean lied (to a look of astonishment from Spike) and added thoughtfully: 'Did I see you at Benjy's on Sunday night?'

'Yes, that's right, I was there,' said Jerome, looking as surprised as he was pleased. 'I didn't see you two there, though.'

'Oh, Spike wasn't there,' laughed Dean, as though the idea was somehow preposterous.

'I have been there, though,' Spike put in.

'But that was on a Saturday night,' Dean said, which seemed to mean something to Jerome, who involuntarily gave an 'ah' of both understanding and disappointment. It seemed that in this, at least, Marianne and Spike had something in common: they had not the foggiest idea of what this little conversation was about, whereas even Stella appeared to, for she raised her eyes to heaven momentarily in a sort of amused despair.

'The music's different on a Sunday night,' Dean explained.

'Well, these good people have their work to get on with,' said Stella, with uncharacteristic firmness, Marianne thought, as she dragged the reluctant Jerome away.

It was obvious that Spike and Dean would finish their work on the

Friday. Marianne's only consolation was that Spike was in a much better mood that day, and he and Dean spent the morning doing passable imitations of a range of celebrities and acting out a somewhat imaginative scene in which President Clinton tried to seduce Dolly. During their lunch break, Spike happily browsed through her bookcase looking at her French titles. She wondered how she could broach the subject of another possible meeting. Offering to lend him a few books would be a good start, but she wondered if that would not look a little obvious. As it turned out, succour came from an unexpected quarter: Jerome reappeared in the afternoon as Spike and Dean were clearing up.

'We've got three extra tickets for *Les Misérables* tomorrow night,' said Jerome, with the tone of someone who was asking a big favour. 'My parents and sister were due to come, but I got things mixed up and forgot they had to go to a wedding. I was wondering if er . . . you, Marianne, would like to come with us, and er . . . Dean and Spike could have the other two.'

'Why, that would be lovely,' said Marianne.

'Can't do it tomorrow,' Spike apologised infuriatingly when the idea was put to him. 'I'm working in the pub.'

'Oh, bollocks!' said Dean. 'You can have the night off. You know perfectly well they can find someone else if they have to. And you've always liked Victor Hugo.'

'Well, it would still be difficult. I've said I'd put together old Ma Carlaw's new garden shed tomorrow. I'd never have time to eat, wash and change.'

'Well,' said Marianne brightly, 'I could prepare something before we go or maybe put a slow casserole in the oven. We could come back here and eat afterwards.'

After a little more persuasion from Dean, Spike caved in.

'Cool!' said Jerome.

When they spotted Spike and Dean approaching (they had arranged to meet at Cambridge Circus, just outside the theatre), Marianne was gratified to hear a subdued 'wow!' from Stella. It was clearly not Dean to which she was referring. Oh, he looked sweet enough in his street gear, complete with back-to-front cap, matching exactly the style Jerome had adopted. But Marianne guessed that to one of

Stella's more conservative tastes it had to be Spike in his smart navy suit who had caught her eye. He had obviously been working in the sunshine all day and his healthy colour stood out above his light blue shirt and red silk tie. His very short hair (which had grown just a little since the week before) added to his immensely clean but interesting appearance. His best yet, Marianne thought.

Marianne herself had gone to some pains; in fact she had spent three hours in the hairdresser's. She had put on her white and blue Regency-style dress, the colours of which could have been designed to complement Spike's suit. Her efforts had not been in vain, for Spike remarked how nice she looked.

'Upper circle, I'm afraid,' Jerome apologised, but they all said that that didn't matter and cheerfully mounted the stairs.

'Take that silly cap off,' Spike remonstrated with Dean, who instantly took it off and put it on Spike's head, much to Jerome's amusement. Spike pulled it off, only to have it replaced with Jerome's.

'Stop it,' said Spike, laughing but embarrassed. Stella and Marianne smiled at each other as they witnessed this horseplay. This was not the sort of company in which either of them had ever been to the theatre before, and they found it a refreshing change. Jerome seemed to have decided in advance how they should be seated, for Marianne was placed next to Spike, Stella in the middle, then Dean, with Jerome at the end. Marianne was grateful for the arrangement and thought that Jerome must be more perceptive than she had given him credit for. The performance was almost over before she found herself surreptitiously taking Spike's hand in hers, and he willingly allowed it to be taken. It was a warm hand, and the contact sent a surge through her which she instinctively knew was mutual.

Marianne had been relieved to discover that the casserole was just right when they had arrived at her flat. Everyone complimented her, and Spike and Dean had not lost their healthy appetites. Marianne could tell that Stella was impressed by their good manners, and after a little wine they all seemed to feel remarkably relaxed. Dean enjoyed telling them all that the Thénardiers were just like Bill and Dolly, but conceded that this was probably a little unjust when Spike remonstrated with him. He agreed that it was certainly unlikely that Madame Thénardier had ever made an apple crumble quite like Dolly's.

'Dean sees himself as Gavroche,' Spike laughed.

'Well, I was a bit of a revolutionary,' Dean agreed. 'Before I went to the Porters I had my own ways of ensuring wealth got redistributed.'

'Were you a thief, then?' asked Jerome, obviously thrilled at the idea.

'Well, not a big-time one, but when you're in care you get to mix with all sorts, and I wasn't averse to being trained in that direction. My most lucrative scam wasn't from thieving, though. There was this old woman whose house we used to pass on the way to and from school. My mate Craig convinced her I was dying of leukaemia and she swallowed it for months. She always had a little present for me whenever I passed. I dropped hints as to what I wanted and you could bet it would be there next time I passed. I got trainers, computer games, even a snorkelling outfit and, of course, lots of money. I had to give Craig commission, of course.'

'And did she ever find out the truth?' asked Stella.

'No, it all fitted in quite nicely. When I went to the Porters in Snaresbrook I had to change schools, and Craig told her I'd died.'

'He must have been a bit cut-up about losing a nice little earner,' Jerome observed.

'Oh, no,' Dean reassured them. 'He found another kid who pretended to be deaf and dumb. Mind you, that one ran into trouble eventually. The kid fell over going up her steps and said "fucking hell" or something similar. They tried to pretend it was a miracle, said he'd drunk some Lourdes water that morning, but it didn't wash even with her.'

They were all greatly amused by this story, except for Spike who was visibly embarrassed.

'I don't think conning an old lady is anything to be proud of,' he said.

'She was loaded and we were company for her,' Dean reasoned. 'Anyway, it's all right for you to be so pious. You had a lovely house opposite a lake and your mummy to give you everything you wanted.'

Marianne had seen Spike blush often enough, but never Dean. This omission was now rectified, for Dean instantly realised that he had overstepped the mark. The wine, perhaps, Marianne thought.

'Sorry,' he said, 'I shouldn't have said that.'

'Have you got any music?' Jerome asked Marianne, patently altering the subject.

'Well, I'm not sure I have anything you'd say was cool.'

'I'll go and get some CDs, if you like,' he volunteered, and invited Dean to go with him to Stella's flat to help him choose something appropriate.

'We have our criminal element in Lucerne Court,' laughed Stella, by way of reassuring Spike that Dean's confessions were not so terribly shocking to them.

'What, here?' said Spike. 'I don't believe it! Was someone a week late paying their television licence?'

'Oh, even worse than that. Mrs Steeden, the kleptomaniac. It took everyone time to realise it was her, but loads of things went missing whenever she visited. My silver milk jug, for one.'

'And Daphne's carriage clock,' Marianne added. 'I was lucky, I only lost a couple of apostle spoons. Still, you have to feel sorry for her. They say it was the shock of her husband dying. In the end, she was caught shoplifting in the Burlington Arcade, the second time, apparently. She went to live with her sister in the middle of nowhere, where there was less temptation I suppose.'

'I can't say I feel all that sorry for her,' said Stella. 'She was affluent enough, after all. I can appreciate that she may have had some kind of problem which gave her the temptation, and I suppose some allowance has to be made for that. But at the end of the day adults know if what they're doing is wrong.'

The doorbell rang and they assumed it was Jerome and Dean returning. It turned out to be Roger. Marianne was slightly thrown by his unexpected arrival, especially so late at night. He had a bottle of wine in his hand, expecting, no doubt, that he would be sharing it alone with her. If he was annoyed that this was not to be, he hid his feelings well. As it happened, he was intrigued, after the introductions, to find that he was in the presence of the mysterious Gregory. He saw straight away that the boy, although not tall, did have a certain presence, and the handshake was certainly not limp. For his part Spike was naturally somewhat disappointed that Marianne could be in the habit of receiving such late-night callers. Both Marianne and Roger sensed this, and it was to Roger's credit that he made every effort not to queer Marianne's pitch.

'Marianne and I are old soul mates,' he explained (Marianne herself would not have put it quite like that). 'Totally platonic, I hasten to add.'

This lie suited a relieved Marianne. Not that it was a lie now, for she had resolved that that was just how their relationship would be from now on. Spike swallowed it, though for a reason which would not particularly have pleased Roger had he guessed it. For Spike, having taken a better look at Roger, concluded that there was no danger that he and Marianne could ever have had relations of an intimate nature. A woman such as Marianne could only be attracted to beautiful people (that was why, in his insecurity, he still found it difficult to comprehend that she could really be attracted to him).

'Someone stood you up tonight, then?' asked Stella, who had met Roger before and did not particularly like him.

'How perceptive you are!' said Roger, who did not think much of Stella, either. Another rich and boring little cow. At least Marianne had some personality, even if it was practically unused. 'So I toddled off to my club and then thought I'd better come to Lucerne Court to make sure there wasn't a homicidal maniac on the loose, out to deflower the good ladies here before cutting them up into little pieces.'

It was clear that Roger did not consider this an unpleasant thought. It was also apparent that he had had quite a lot to drink already, although Marianne dutifully offered him a glass of wine, which he declined in favour of a whisky.

'Well, you needn't have worried about us tonight, as it happens,' said Marianne, trying to inject a more gentle brand of humour into the proceedings. 'We have three strapping lads here to defend us.'

'Three?' said a puzzled Roger. 'Now I've often seen four people when there should be two, when I've had a few drinks, but this is the first time three have been condensed into one. Must have been the new malt whisky I tried at the club.'

'Stella's cousin, Jerome, and Spike's brother, Dean, have gone to get some CDs,' Marianne explained.

'Ah, music,' said Roger. 'Isn't that a bit daring for Lucerne Court? Though I must say, the one so-called strapping lad I can see seems a little quiet. Is he all there?'

'Yes,' said Stella. 'He just happens to have good manners.'

'Ah, then he is middle class. Just as I thought.'

'I shouldn't think someone who does labouring and part-time bar work could be called middle class,' observed Spike, who found Roger quite amusing. He was used to having fun poked at him by Dean and some of the regulars at The Kitchener's, and took it as a sign of acceptance from Roger.

'Ah, it speaks!' said Roger. 'But your accent gives you away my boy, and your manners. I'd heard you'd gone from riches to rags. Hoping for a reversal in those fortunes, no doubt.'

Spike did not understand that this could be construed as an insult, but Marianne and Stella most certainly did. They gave Roger a look which even he could not misinterpret.

'What I mean is,' he said, climbing down for once in his life, 'is that I hear you work very hard. That's commendable.'

'Well, I'm sure it's altered Spike's life for the better now that he knows he has your approval,' observed Stella, 'though I wasn't aware that you were that well acquainted with hard work.'

'Now there's a sexist remark!' said Roger, who had resolved that if he could not spend a night with Marianne he would at any rate have a good argument. 'Observe these ladies, Spike. Men are supposed to work hard, and they're condemned if they don't, but women of their sort have the choice as to whether they work hard or not, in fact they consider themselves heroically virtuous if they do any work at all. Though they'll be surprised to learn that it has been a hell of a week. Turns out the accountant in our East London office has had his hand in the till. Had to get in a whole team of consultants to sort it all out, and then there was the Fraud Squad.'

'Well, let's hope they don't dig too deep,' said Stella. 'We might see you behind bars before long.'

'Sorry to disappoint you, but I'm clean as a whistle, at least this time.'

'What do you do?' asked Spike politely.

'Furniture,' said Roger. 'Expensive stuff. A rip-off, really, but there are always mugs ready to buy the stuff, so who am I to complain? When you're the third son you have to try your hand at trade.'

'Roger's brother is Earl Norborough,' Marianne explained to Spike, wondering if he would be impressed but then instantly feeling ashamed at this hint of snobbery. It was just the sort of thing her mother would have said.

'We have a bloke called Earl who comes into the pub sometimes,' said Spike. 'It's an unusual name.'

Roger found this immensely amusing, but Marianne could not help noticing the private little smile Spike also allowed himself. Could it possibly be that Spike had been enjoying his own joke in response to her pretension? But no, surely not.

'Where are Dean and Jerome?' she asked, trying to veer the subject away from one which would allow Roger to talk about himself.

'Probably listening to the CDs before they decide which ones to bring in,' said Stella. 'But it is a bit rude of Jerome. I'll go and get them.'

'Spike won't mind going, I'm sure,' said Marianne.

'No,' said Stella, with surprising firmness, 'I'll go and see.'

'Well,' said Roger to Spike, when Stella had gone, 'so Marianne's got you here at last. She's been waiting a long time for this, you know.'

'Roger!' said Marianne in exasperation.

Stella returned fairly soon with an apologetic Dean and Jerome.

'My God, it's a pop group,' laughed Roger, for the two returnees were still wearing their back-to-front caps.

'It's really Dean's head that's on the wrong way,' said Spike, as Jerome put on some ghastly (in the view of everyone else) music.

Roger took out a packet of cigarettes and offered them round. The only takers were Dean and Jerome. Spike gave his brother an admonitory look.

'It's a dirty habit, isn't it Spike?' said Dean, as Roger gave him a light. 'Spike like's everything to be nice and clean, don't you Spike?'

'And quite right, too,' said Marianne, who did not think much of Dean's ragging. She suspected he was showing off to Jerome. All the same, she could not help inwardly remarking that Spike's attitude to smoking had altered radically in four years.

Marianne thought that the following hour went surprisingly well, despite the presence of Roger who seemed, to his probable disappointment, to have found nothing particularly objectionable in Spike. Spike and Dean told them more about the house they had just renovated, the one Elizabeth was buying, and Dean waxed lyrical on the subject of the lovely Dolly. He related her passion for television programmes about disabled children, and was particularly amusing when telling them about the time he and Spike had walked in unexpectedly one evening and found her attempting to put in a suppository for her piles, her drawers round her ankles with one leg on a chair, revealing, as Dean put it 'the bottom from hell.' Their merriment was only enhanced by Spike's vain attempts to dissuade him from telling the story.

'It had a dreadful effect on Spike,' Dean explained to them. 'He had nightmares for weeks afterwards.'

At last Marianne realised that it was time to offer coffee. She did so with regret, for it would signal that the evening was drawing to a close. She saw that Spike was beginning to look tired (a youthful drowsiness, which to her seemed to make him look more attractive rather than less) and she remembered that he had been working that day. She hinted that he might help her get the coffee, a hint he took. She ignored the smirk on Roger's face as they left the room.

She switched on the coffee maker while Spike took out the cups. Then she ventured to touch his cheek. 'Poor Spike. It's been a long day for you.'

He put his arms around her and she stroked his head. He responded with a blissful look, closing his eyes and raising his face upwards in ecstasy, like a dog with an itchy back being scratched.

'You can stay tonight, you know,' she whispered.

'Oh, no!' he said, drawing back with what momentarily seemed like offensive haste. He kissed her by way of apology, a kiss which made her shudder with delight. So her memory had not misled her. She allowed her own hands to wander and was pretty sure that it was neither impotence nor indifference to her that made him so coy about staying.

'I can put you both up,' she said, assuming that he might be thinking of his brother. 'Dean can have the spare room.'

He drew away again, and this time there was no mistaking a frightened look.

'What is it?' she asked.

'It just isn't possible just now,' he said nervously.

She could see through the open door that someone was going into the bathroom, and that they had most probably been seen. She saw with relief that it was only Dean. The thought of Roger seeing any intimacy between them made her cringe.

'You're a strange boy, aren't you?' she smiled.

'That's what Dolly's always saying,' he said, in mock admonition.

She knew that she could not press the point without making herself look a little pathetic, assuming she had not done so already.

'I'm presuming too much, aren't I?' she said. 'When we turned up in Walthamstow I thought for a while that you didn't want to know me.'

'Oh, it wasn't that. It's just that I didn't know...I mean, I thought I might have been imagining that it was you. I couldn't face finding out for sure that it wasn't. But I hope we can meet again. It's Dean's eighteenth birthday next week, and I know he intends to invite you to that.'

She was delighted. What she had taken for reluctance was probably, she surmised, no more than the mirror image of her own fears. They finished making the coffee, both smiling broadly. She noticed that, despite his fatigue, his enchanting glow of four years earlier seemed to be returning.

She reluctantly called a taxi for them after the coffee was finished. What she hated most was that Roger would still be there after Spike and Dean had gone.

The cab arrived all too promptly. Dean was with her in the hall as Spike said goodbye to the others.

'Don't worry,' Dean said to her reassuringly, as though aware of her thoughts. 'He's just a bit nervous of being away from home. You really mustn't rush him.'

She saw them down to the front entrance, any lingering worries dispelled by the warmth of their final farewell. On her return she found Roger getting ready to leave. He knew as well as she did that any thoughts he might have had of staying the night would be best forgotten.

'Sorry,' she said, as she saw him to the door. 'Things are different now.'

'Yes, I can see that,' he said, without rancour. 'As a matter of fact, I hope it goes well. I've a horrible suspicion I quite like them.'

Marianne brightened. He said it with such obvious regret that she knew he must be telling the truth.

Spike had been unintentionally inaccurate when he said that Marianne (along with Stella and Jerome) was to be invited to Dean's birthday celebration, to the official one, anyway. A do had been arranged at The Kitchener's on the Saturday night, a function which would include not only Bill and Dolly but also a collection of the more boisterous locals. Both Spike and Dean, for slightly different reasons, thought it best that their Lucerne Court friends should be spared the spectacle of an authentic Kitcheners' knees-up.

'They'd take the piss out of them,' Dean said, referring to the locals as the probable culprits. 'It could get a bit complicated.'

Spike agreed, assuming that Dean's concern was primarily for Marianne and Stella. In fact Dean was more worried about the reception which would be given to Jerome. The odd combination of street gear and Eton accent might be seen as an endearing eccentricity in W1, but in E17, at any rate in their circle, it would be open to all sorts of interpretations, especially as Jerome would most probably stick to Dean like toffees stuck to Dolly's false teeth.

'What I'd really like,' Dean said, 'is for us all to go for a picnic by Hollow Pond on Sunday afternoon. We could hire a boat.'

Spike approved of the idea. 'Then I could treat us all to a meal afterwards,' he said. 'We owe them for taking us to the theatre and feeding us.'

Stella and Jerome approved of the plan, too, when Dean telephoned, and it hardly needs to be said that Marianne did. She looked up Whipps Cross Road and Hollow Pond in her *A to Z* of London, and invited Jerome and Stella in for coffee so that they could work out the best way of getting there, for Jerome would be driving. Stella looked on, amused, as Marianne and Jerome enthusiastically debated the merits of going through the city or via Euston Road, and of approaching the pond itself from Lea Bridge Road or Leytonstone High Road. A safari in Africa could not have been anticipated with more excitement.

'And on Saturday,' said Marianne, 'we could go to Fortnum's to get some stuff for the picnic.'

'Don't you think Fortnum's would look a bit excessive for a picnic in East London?' suggested Stella. 'Besides, I'm busy on Saturday.'

'Stell's probably right,' Jerome conceded. 'Anyway, we have to buy him presents.'

So Jerome and Marianne went to Harrods. Their presents com-
plemented each other, for Jerome bought Dean a couple of CDs
while Marianne bought him a personal CD player. She knew that it
would look a bit odd if she were to spend too much on someone she
had only known for little more than a fortnight and reluctantly
decided that she should try to keep her gift relatively modest. She
was surprised that Jerome considered her choice somewhat over-
generous as it was.

'What would you have given him if he hadn't been Spike's
brother?' he asked.

'Oh, a box of handkerchiefs I suppose,' she admitted.

Despite getting lost three times on the way, they were not very late
arriving at the appointed place. As agreed on the telephone with
Jerome, Dean was waiting for them near the boat shed. Spike was
guarding the spot they had chosen a little further round the lake. As
they approached Spike, Marianne was perturbed to see that two
young women were sitting with him.

'Oh, Christ!' groaned Dean. 'It's Tracy Bettles and her chum.'

Introductions were made, pleasantries exchanged. It was clear that
Tracy and her friend Susan were not to be staying long, for they were
with another group sitting (unfortunately) not far away. Marianne
recognised one or two of these from her visit to The Kitchener Arms.
Marianne had to admit that Tracy had the makings of a pretty girl,
though the swimsuit she was wearing suggested rather vulgar tastes.
She had a voice that had an affected juvenile sound and what to
Marianne seemed like a rather false smile. And it was abundantly
clear that Tracy had her sights set on Spike.

'Is Marianne your auntie, Spikey?' Tracy asked before rejoining
her own friends, with a pointedness that belied the little girly image
she had cultivated.

It was a pleasant spot. The lake was irregular in shape, with lots of
little inlets and promontories. The hot day had brought out quite a
number of people, though the size of the area did not make it feel
overly crowded. There was a wealth of surrounding woodland which
Marianne intended to invite Spike to help her explore before the day
was over.

The agreement had been that Marianne and Stella would provide
the food for the picnic in return for Spike's playing host at the meal

later, though Spike and Dean had brought some delicious cakes and pastries provided by Dolly. Marianne's enjoyment of the food and the atmosphere was somewhat marred by the knowledge that they were being scrutinised from a distance by the persistent Tracy. Indeed, on one occasion she paid them another brief visit, bringing along one of several teddy bears which she had insisted on taking for a day out.

'Guess what he's called?' she simpered.

'Don't tell me. Spike.' said Dean.

'There, so he does look like him.'

'No he doesn't,' said Dean. 'For one thing Spike's got clothes on, and for another if he did really have such an enormous bottom and ears like that I doubt if you'd want to know him. Not to mention a big black spot for a nose.'

'And no hands,' said Jerome.

'Oh, you're all so cruel,' said Tracy, looking almost as though she were about to cry. 'You know just what I mean. He's so cuddly. I've got a monkey I was going to call Dean, but I won't now.'

'I'm heartbroken,' said Dean.

'I'm flattered that you're calling him Spike,' said Spike, ever the gentleman.

Tracy beamed. She smiled at them all before departing, though the look she gave Marianne was tinged with extra meaning. 'I saw him first' it seemed to imply. Marianne smiled back sweetly, knowing how wrong Tracy was on that score.

When they had eaten, lounged about for a bit and given Dean his presents (with which he was gratifyingly overwhelmed) they hired a boat for a couple of hours, taking turns to have a go on the water. Marianne only had about half an hour alone with Spike, and that was marred by constant cries of 'Coo-ee, Spikey!' from a now familiar voice in another boat. Marianne and Spike were the last in the boat, and when they returned to the others they were having a political argument.

'Socialism isn't dead,' Dean was telling them. 'In a few years time it'll be all the rage again.'

'Oh, for Christ's sake, Dean,' said Spike, who thought such subject-matter a little heavy for a lazy Sunday afternoon.

'Now there's a reactionary if ever there was one,' said Dean.

'As far as I can see,' observed Stella, 'Spike's just about the only one of us who's a real, live worker. I can understand your wanting to send Marianne, Jerome and me to the guillotine, we thoroughly deserve it, but Spike's the sort you ought to be fighting for.'

Dean gave a scornful laugh. 'Bourgeois to the bone. Hopes to own his own house.'

'How wicked!' laughed Jerome.

'Dean wants to kill off all the people who actually work for a living and leave only those who live on social security and student grants,' Spike explained. 'I wonder how long they'll last once we're gone.'

'We'll survive,' Dean reassured him.

'I suppose you'll live on creative thoughts and Marxist critiques,' suggested Jerome.

'Something like that,' laughed Dean. 'But I'd have thought the women would be on my side. Take Stella. She looks as if she needs liberating.'

'Dean!' admonished Spike.

'Actually,' said Stella, who was not a bit offended, 'I quite like a world in which women bring up the children. It's allowed us to indoctrinate little boys into believing that they're the ones who have to go out and be killed to protect us, and do all the dangerous jobs.'

'As I thought,' said Dean. 'A female Uncle Tom.'

'Anyone fancy a little walk?' asked Marianne, who had noticed that the ubiquitous Tracy was looking in their direction again.

'You lot can go,' said Stella. 'I'm feeling far too lazy. I'll stay here and look after the things.'

The woodland surrounding the lake delighted Jerome and Marianne. Once they had gone off the beaten track, the number of other ramblers diminished noticeably, and one could almost imagine one was in the country.

'Better not stray into that part,' said Dean at one point, as they approached some particularly dense woodland. 'That's where the naughty men hang out.'

'How do you know?' asked Jerome mischievously.

'Lottie told me never to go in there,' Dean explained.

'Is this near where you used to live, then?' asked Marianne, perceiving the reference to Spike's mother.

'Well, fairly near,' said Dean. And she noticed that he looked a little anxiously at Spike.

They veered to the right in order to avoid the naughty men in question and found themselves in an exceptionally pretty opening in the woods. There was a bench carved out of a tree trunk and, in the distance, they could see an imposing edifice.

'Looks just like Hampton Court,' said Jerome. 'Let's go and have a look.'

'Well, actually, you can't get close to it from here,' explained Dean. 'If you want to see it at its best you have to go to the other lake, and look across from there.'

'There's another lake?' asked Jerome, who seemed quite excited by the prospect.

'Oh yes,' said Dean. 'And a very beautiful one.'

'I think I'll go back,' Spike said suddenly. 'It's not fair leaving Stella on her own.'

'Oh, come on Spike!' Dean remonstrated. 'Sooner or later you've got to...'

'See you later,' said Spike, who was already disappearing. In a somewhat distressed state, Marianne could not help noticing.

'What's the matter with him?' asked Jerome.

Marianne did not have to ask. She suddenly remembered their meeting in Paris and the photographs Spike had showed her, photographs of the beautiful lake in front of their house and the stately building beyond it. So here they were, she thought with a thrill. Part of her wanted to run after Spike, but on balance she wanted to go on.

'Sorry,' said Dean. 'It's too much for him, coming here.'

'And doesn't it upset you too, coming back?' asked Marianne.

'Well, I was only here for a couple of years. Spike was brought up here.'

They walked on, and soon came to some water. This turned out to be the edge of the lake Dean had meant, though a full view was obliterated by a foliage-packed little island, pretty enough in itself, but Marianne was itching to get on to the main road she could now see to the left of them. From there, she knew, she would see the lake as the Porters would have seen it from their house.

And when she saw it she knew what Spike and Dean had lost. So many swans together she had never seen in her life before. They walked along a promenade by the road, from where the Tudor-style

palace they had glimpsed before could be seen across the lake in all
its glory. Dean explained that it was now the Crown Court, although
it had formerly been an orphanage.

'Not the one you were in?' asked Jerome.

'Oh no, it stopped being one long before my time. Besides, I wasn't
from round here. I started off in the darkest depths of Stepney. It
was like coming to Narnia for me, coming here.'

'Yes, I can imagine,' said Marianne. 'And did Spike live here all his
life?'

'Pretty well. His father's people had always lived round here.
That's why I came and put Spike's mum and dad's ashes into the
lake.'

So this was their grave as well as their home.

'It sounds rather morbid, I suppose,' said Dean.

'No, I think it's cool,' said Jerome.

'That's another reason why Spike won't come here,' Dean smiled.
'I think he thinks they'll give him a telling off.'

'Why should they tell him off?' asked Marianne.

'Oh, he seems to think he'd be a disappointment to them. That's
stupid, of course. I've heard it's usual to go through a period of
feeling guilty when people die, but Spike doesn't seem to have got
over that stage.'

Marianne again had the impression Dean was withholding something, but thought it would be churlish to ask too many questions
since he had already told them so much. Perhaps in time she would
find out the rest.

'I think he ought to come back and get it over,' Dean went on. 'If
he did that he might well...I don't know.'

'You mean he could start getting back his confidence?' suggested
Marianne.

'Yes, something like that.'

They were walking along the promenade by the lake, which was
quite crowded with people feeding the swans, ducks and geese.

Dean suddenly stopped, and instead of looking at the lake turned
and looked across the road at one of the houses.

'Is that the house?' asked Marianne.

He led them across the road by way of answer. It was unremarkable in many ways, though a little larger than usual for a semi-

detached 1930s-style house. Nevertheless, it was obviously a home that could be loved, especially given the magnificent view it enjoyed. It had once been a happy house, Marianne reflected, probably happier than any of the apartments in Lucerne Court.

'God, it's still got the same curtains,' said Dean, in some surprise. 'And the garden hasn't changed. The lawn needs mowing, though. The Porters would never have let it get like that.'

They reluctantly made their way back towards the woods. When they returned to Stella and Spike, by the other lake, Marianne noticed that Spike, aware of where they had been, gave Dean a reproachful look. Marianne felt her underlying exasperation with Spike rising to the surface again. Why did he have to be so absurdly private?

After their picnic, Spike invited them to go to Dolly and Bill's place to freshen up before their evening out. She and Dean knew that it was most probably because he wanted to take a shower himself, though for once he was not considered particularly perverse in this, for it had been a very hot day. The guests were politely allowed to use the facilities first, and while Spike and Dean got ready Dolly played host (Bill was in the pub). It was Stella who mentioned the Porters and the visit to their house, and Dolly took out a photograph album that had belonged to Mrs Porter. They were fascinated by the pictures of the young Spike and of his parents, and Marianne could tell (as, no doubt, could Dolly) that Jerome and Stella had noticed the contrast between the elegance of the Porters and their old home with the more proletarian aura surrounding the Clarkes and theirs.

'Lottie passed her eleven plus,' Dolly explained. 'She was much younger than my 'usband, and only 'is 'alf-sister, you see. Her mother was a bit more refined than Bill's 'ad been. Unfortunately she came along too late to teach 'im any manners! Anyway, Lottie went to grammar school and then university and mixed with a different crowd, became a bit odd if you ask me. Went all lefty, like most intellectuals did in them days. Don't get me wrong, I've always been Labour myself, so 'as Bill, but she went too far. Used to go on them Ban the Bomb marches, and started stickin' up for blacks. She settled down when she married George, though, and 'er views changed a bit. His people came from Woodford.'

They all agreed that this must have been a steadying influence.

'Not that she didn't still 'ave some funny ideas,' Dolly pursued. 'She still said you shouldn't 'ang people. And George was almost as bad. Bleeding 'earts, Bill used to call them. Lottie worked so hard, I'll say that, yet she always looked good. They fostered awkward kids, seemed to think it was some kind of duty to stop 'em being aborted. She lost a child the year after Spike was born, you see, and she was told she couldn't have any more. And George and his people were Catholics, although I don't think there was any Irish in them. His mother was French.'

'But France is mainly Catholic, too,' Marianne, who should know, explained.

'Really?' said Dolly, surprised. 'The Irish get everywhere, don't they?'

Having been thus entertained by Dolly they were taken by Spike and Dean to the most magnificently tacky Indian restaurant they had ever seen. That, at any rate, was their first impression, but the food was outstanding and it turned out to be a more pleasant evening, if possible, than the one Marianne had enjoyed the previous week, not least because there was no danger of Roger turning up out of the blue. The conversation was frivolous for the most part and often downright silly, especially when Dean and Jerome were arguing about politics. The drift into this territory had been Marianne's fault. Recollecting some of the things Dolly had said earlier, she ventured to ask Spike about his parents' politics. It had seemed a good opportunity to add a little more to the jigsaw.

'Oh, Dad was a One Nation Tory,' said Spike. 'Not that I ever found out what that means.'

'It comes from Disraeli,' Marianne was keen to explain. 'He argued that the rich and the poor were like two separate nations, and he wanted to recreate the Tory Party so that it could include the interests of both.'

'A bit like Mussolini and his Fascists,' said Dean acidly.

'Not quite,' said Jerome. 'Disraeli widened people's freedoms, whereas Mussolini limited them. The early Fascists were mainly ex-socialists, you see, so I suppose limiting people's freedom was in their nature.'

Marianne soon regretted bringing up the subject. For the next half-hour Jerome and Dean engaged in a most acrimonious argument. Dean, like many sixth-form socialists, had until then clearly had any easy ride, having had only ill-educated or easily tired family and friends to contend with. Jerome, although only about four or five years older, had the benefit of Oxford and much wider reading to help him. By upbringing, Marianne, Stella and Spike had been inclined to take Jerome's side but, as he referred to Sorel, Bukhanin, and a host of other names to back his arguments, the onlookers could not but conclude that he was being a bit of a clever-clogs. Before long, Dean was clearly out of his depth, and they began to feel sorry for him despite the fact that he was talking rubbish, or rather being manoeuvred into talking rubbish. Marianne should have rejoiced, for she could remember her own university days and the way socialists had used similar tactics, using a jargon that could not be vanquished because of its very inaccessibility and irrelevance. But Dean's heart was in the right place, and she did not wish to see him being humiliated. Neither, clearly, did Spike, for she had noticed that he had more than once given Jerome a look that suggested that he did not much like his self-assurance. Indeed it was Spike who put an end to it all, in a way which belied the shyness she had lately associated with him. When Dean needed saving, it appeared, even Spike could be stirred into action.

'Come on you two, we're all being bored shitless,' he said. 'Who votes we get another bottle of wine?'

Jerome took the hint and the vote was in the affirmative. The question about another bottle of wine came up again later, while they were discussing the imminent arrival in Walthamstow of Daphne's sister, Elizabeth. As a result, Jerome was obliged to concede that he would not, after all, be driving them home, and Marianne and Stella agreed they should take a taxi. That he would have to leave his car in Walthamstow did not appear to be a great inconvenience to Jerome, since it gave him the opportunity to arrange a lunchtime meeting with Dean the following day, presumably to argue some more.

CHAPTER THREE

Elizabeth insisted on having a moving-in party, in fact she was discussing it even before the completion date. Daphne tried to dissuade her but she was adamant.

'It will only be a few friends,' Elizabeth protested, 'maybe something quiet one Sunday afternoon.'

During her first week at number twelve, however, her circle of friends widened more dramatically than ever before in her long life. On her first evening, immediately after Daphne had taken a taxi home in despair ('I'll come in the morning to see if we can sort out some more of this mess. At least your bed is made'), Elizabeth had put on the gown she had worn for the Silver Jubilee and tottered down to The Kitchener Arms. She and Daphne had already had several sherries to fortify themselves during their labours and Elizabeth was reluctant to retire quietly. She was pleased that the move had finally taken place and the furniture was all now in place (thanks more to Spike and Dean's assistance than to the modest efforts of the gormless removal men she had hired. Perhaps that silly Marianne had been correct after all in suggesting she should have used Harrods) and she was on a high.

Spike and Dean had seen her entering and were able to turf out Bob Daniel and his mates from the table at which they were ensconced to make way for her. Sid, the nice old gentleman who had been in her husband's regiment, was also there and he and his chum joined her. The chum's grandson and his friends were there, too, and gathered round, intrigued by the cheerful old bag in the flamboyant dress and the feathers. They listened politely as she told them of her younger days, before she had lived in Knightsbridge, when she had stayed in East London and mixed with the people from the Theatre Royal, Stratford.

'It hasn't changed,' she said happily. 'Everyone is so kind' (she said this as the fifth gin and tonic was placed before her). 'I do believe this is the best move I've made.'

She went to The Kitchener's (as the locals called it) every evening during the following week and was not without company however quiet the place was, even when Spike and Dean were not there. It was on the Saturday evening that she mooted the idea of a party at her place.

'I thought a few friends next Sunday afternoon would be nice,' she said.

'Sunday afternoon would be awkward for a lot of people,' said Bob Daniel. 'That's when people have to visit their grannies in loony bins or fix the car. And the pub football team plays on a Sunday, too.'

The majority of the football team, standing nearby, agreed that it would certainly pose difficulties for them.

'Saturday night would be the best option,' Dean explained. 'People don't have to get up in the morning.'

'There hasn't been a decent party round here for ages on a Saturday night,' said Bob.

Actually, Elizabeth quite liked the idea of an evening party. It meant that the more stuffy relatives in Sittingbourne and Berkshire probably wouldn't come.

'I thought I could sing a few songs on the piano,' said Elizabeth. 'I once won a competition with "The White Cliffs of Dover".'

'Marty Johnson has a disco,' said Dean

'What's that?' asked Elizabeth.

'It's a sort of gramophone with lights,' said old Sid.

'Oh, that would be useful. I have some lovely records, and not all of them old-fashioned, whatever you might think. Cliff Richard. But I do hope I'll be able to sing a few songs myself.'

'Well,' suggested Dean, 'you could sing a few earlier on' (while most people are still in the pub, he meant), 'and we can bring the disco along later.'

'That's a good idea,' said Elizabeth. 'To tell the truth, I always find it more difficult to remember the words as the evening wears on.'

Daphne was horrified, of course, when Elizabeth phoned her.

'Next Saturday evening!' she gasped. 'And you seem to have invited everyone in the pub.'

'Well, you should feel at home,' said Elizabeth. 'I gather you are quite well known to some of them. They still talk about your visit a few weeks ago.'

'Oh that,' laughed Daphne mirthlessly. 'I was just trying to show that droopy Marianne a good time. And she fancies Spike.'

'Oh, she does, does she? Well she can jolly well get to the back of the queue. Anyway, it's arranged now. Invite some of those daft girls from the morgue you live in. Give the people in Walthamstow a good laugh.'

In the event, the contingent from Lucerne Court consisted of Daphne herself, Marianne, Stella and Jerome. Daphne did also ask Fiona on the first floor, but she had already arranged to attend a lecture on melancholia.

Daphne was relieved to find that the house was relatively empty when they arrived at 8.30. Dolly, who was in the breakfast room laying out the food, explained to them that Elizabeth was still upstairs putting on her face. Bill was in the lounge trying to make conversation with Hesketh, the only other relative present, and his wife, Helen. They clearly resented being in Walthamstow and one of the first things they told Daphne was that they would not be staying long. This did not appear to come as too much of a disappointment for Daphne. Indeed, it was their opposition to Elizabeth's move that eventually prompted Daphne to support it. They knew that they had a place in Elizabeth's will, and that her reason for selling the mansion flat in Knightsbridge was so that she could selfishly spend more of her own money as she chose before snuffing it. They sniffed with quiet dissent when Marianne said how nicely the house had been renovated.

Fortunately, Elizabeth chose that moment to make a somewhat dramatic entrance. 'I'm ready for my close-up now, Mr De Mille,' Jerome said under his breath and Stella started giggling. For Elizabeth had on a flowing pink and green gown and had overdone the lipstick and rouge (Daphne thought this was no bad thing as it would camouflage the colour her face was likely to turn as the evening wore on). She kissed them all effusively and Hesketh and Helen declared that they were just saying what a lovely house it was.

Elizabeth seated herself at the piano and without any introduction launched into 'A Nightingale Sang in Berkeley Square.' They all tried to look enchanted and applauded dutifully when it was over.

'I thought I'd try to liven things up a bit,' said Elizabeth. 'You all look a bit droopy. Never mind, the boys will be here with the booze in a minute.'

They did not have to wait a full minute, in fact, before a commotion outside announced the arrival of the boys in question. Bob Daniel and Peter Bettles struggled in with a large keg, accompanied by Tracy Bettles, several of the football team, and an embarrassed-looking Spike and Dean behind, laden with heavy carrier bags full of goodies from the local off-licence. Most of the new arrivals seemed happy to stay at the rear of the house, away from the more staid guests, but after depositing their loads Spike and Dean joined the party in the lounge.

'I'm sorry,' said Spike to a bemused Daphne. 'At least I've managed to stop them bringing the disco.'

This was true. When Spike had heard of the intentions of some of the regulars in The Kitchener's as to the type of party this would be (he had been busy behind the bar when the original plans were being made) he had put his foot down. He had put the word round that it was to end by midnight, thus ensuring that the more raucous regulars would be put off. He was helped in this by the general knowledge that there was another party planned for that night in Bedford Road (for which, fortuitously, Marty Johnson and his intemperate disco had already been booked), one which would be more to the liking of noisier set - not to mention those whose taste in smoking went beyond tobacco. Spike's barring powers in the pub gave him a modicum of respect, and he felt he could be modestly confident in ensuring that only the more respectable neighbours would attend Elizabeth's do. However, 'respectable' is a relative concept, and he could see from the looks of some of those in the lounge that his efforts would probably not be appreciated.

'I'll make sure everyone's out by twelve,' he added, aware that this would probably not help matters in the eyes of Elizabeth's relatives. Daphne smiled reassuringly, delighted at Hesketh and Helen's discomfort at the new arrivals.

'Now you're here, young man', she said, 'we can all breathe more easily.'

Spike and Dean politely asked everyone in the lounge what they would like to drink and then went to carry out the orders.

'Do you know those boys, then?' asked a surprised Helen.

'Indeed, yes,' said Daphne. 'They live next door. I don't know what we'd have done without them the day Elizabeth moved in.'

'Well, I hope they can be trusted,' said Hesketh.

Marianne was not, by nature, given to dagger-like looks, but she managed quite a good one for the benefit of Hesketh and Helen who, realising they were outnumbered, toned down their opinions. They were, in any case, genuinely mollified by the size of the drinks Spike handed them.

'Gregory restored those fireplaces,' said Marianne proudly to Helen and Hesketh. She thought it best to refer to Spike by his posher name.

'Lovely,' said Helen, though it was obviously a strain.

'I should be good at fireplaces', said Spike. 'My dad said I was named after one.'

'How can anyone be named after a fireplace?' laughed Jerome.

'Haven't you heard of Pope Gregory the Grate?' asked Spike.

Hesketh and Helen were less amused than the others.

'I'm afraid we're not really ones for religious jokes,' said Helen. 'We're Christians. Bible Christians,' she added pointedly, knowing there were Papists present.

'So no Pope here,' said Jerome, mischievously putting on an Ulster accent.

They heard the voice of Cliff Richard coming from the breakfast room (Spike had persuaded the others to allow one or two records from Elizabeth's collection to be played and they had clearly started early to get them over with. He hoped now that the laughter which exploded when 'Bachelor Boy' came on would be misinterpreted).

'Did you know Cliff Richard is a Christian?' Helen asked Dean.

'Is he really?' said Dean, with suspicious politeness. 'He's kept that to himself.'

Unable to keep straight faces any longer, Dean, Spike and Jerome went to join the other youngsters at the rear of the house. Marianne wondered how long it would be before she could decently consider joining them there, but before she could do so Dolly, her chores over, came in and sat next to her. Marianne complimented her on the food she had prepared.

'Oh, just a few bits and pieces,' Dolly said modestly. 'The boys 'elped, of course.'

'They do seem very helpful,' Marianne agreed.

'Oh, don't believe what you 'ear about youngsters today,' said Dolly, by way of agreement. 'They're good boys, really.'

There was a hint of the negative about the 'really.' Was it still possible that there some delinquency which merited this qualification of wholehearted praise? Fortunately, their conversation was for all practical purposes private, for Elizabeth was telling everyone else about the time she had been stuck in a lift with Lady Docker. Nevertheless, Dolly had lowered her voice, which pleased Marianne. There were advantages in Dolly seeing her as a confidante.

'I imagine Dean can be a handful,' she observed.

'Well, he's got a tongue on 'im, that's for sure,' laughed Dolly. 'It's Spike that's been the biggest worry though, I don't mind admittin'.'

'He does seem a little shy,' Marianne agreed, hoping that Dolly's misgivings had no cause deeper than this.

'I keep tellin' 'im he's got to start actin' 'is age,' she said, in obvious despair. 'But what can you do? He's nearly twenty, for 'eaven's sake. 'Ow is 'e ever goin' to settle down and find a nice girl if 'e doesn't start sortin' 'imself out?'

'He hasn't been in any trouble, has he?' asked Marianne, suppressing her anxiety.

'Only with me,' laughed Dolly, which Marianne found immensely reassuring. Then, to her great surprise, Dolly added: 'You like 'im, don't you?'

'Oh, I...' said Marianne, not knowing if it were a neutral observation or an accusation.

'Oh, don't worry, it wouldn't surprise me. It's just that he would take a lot of understanding.'

'Well, I know that,' said Marianne, not entirely truthfully, for she had no idea what Dolly had in mind.

'I know I've probably come down too 'ard on 'im sometimes,' pursued Dolly. 'I was too old. Dean's right in some ways, I can be an old bag. And I 'ave to admit, I was jealous. He's always turned to Dean. I felt I was some'ow outside them. I always loved Spike, though, even when 'is mum and dad was alive. I never had kids, you see, and I thought he'd see me as 'is mum. It wasn't fair of me, I know. We 'ad a big row once when they didn't buy me a Mother's Day card. I was hurt, I 'ave to say. It was the first one after 'is own mum 'ad died, or *their* mum, I suppose I should say. It's only now I realise how 'e must 'ave felt. But when you 'aven't had kids of your own, you do find yourself trying to pretend.'

Marianne could not help feeling for Dolly, even though she had to agree that she had not been fair. The scene was all too easy to picture. Dolly, childless but now with children, expecting the same consideration as a lifelong mother, and Spike, mourning (as he still mourned) his own parents and his former life. And the next in line for Marianne's sympathy on this occasion had to be Dean, for she could not help noticing that he appeared to be mentioned always as an afterthought. Understandable, too, since he had been a late arrival on the scene, but she suspected that Dolly had not been able to conceal the pecking order.

'You'll 'ave to excuse me,' Dolly said as she looked at her watch, just as a great many questions began forming in Marianne's mind. 'We 'ave to go off now. It's a friend of mine's twenty-fifth anniversary. In Leyton.'

And with that she left with Bill, leaving Marianne feeling a little frustrated.

Helen and Hesketh also left early, as expected, and some of the guests from the kitchen filtered in to listen to Elizabeth's efforts on the piano. Dean's music centre had been requisitioned for the evening but had been placed in the breakfast room for the benefit of those who preferred to stay nearer to the food and drink, at a volume that would not be too disturbing to the neighbours or even to those in the lounge. Spike obviously saw himself as something of an MC, or perhaps even as a bouncer, for he had dressed in his best suit and divided his time ensuring that everyone in the lounge had enough to eat and drink while keeping a wary eye on those who stuck stolidly to the rear of the house. The most worrying of these began trickling off at about half-past ten (taking care to kiss Elizabeth before leaving: even they knew the price that had to be paid), most probably to the party in Bedford Road. As they left, they were replaced by old Sid and a couple of his cronies who had been in the pub.

'Well,' said Spike, breathing a sigh of relief as he sat down in the front end of the lounge with Marianne, Daphne and Stella, 'that's the most likely source of trouble out of the way.'

'You've done marvellously,' said Daphne. 'I must say, I had my misgivings. I'd forgotten you would be here to take care of things.'

Spike looked embarrassed at the compliment, then he caught Marianne's eye and they instinctively smiled at each other.

'Where is Jerome, I wonder?' said Stella.

'I think I heard Dean saying something about showing him the pub,' said Daphne.

'No doubt,' said Stella, an apologetic note in her voice. 'Jerome's always been one for trying out new pubs.'

'Oh, come on,' said Daphne. 'Who can blame them for wanting to get away from Elizabeth's screeching for half an hour?' And to confirm her point Elizabeth was at that very moment commencing a duet with Sid: 'If You Were the Only Girl in the World.'

'If you were the oldest girl in the world, more like,' laughed Daphne.

'Well, it's nice to see her enjoying herself,' said Stella.

Daphne turned to Spike. 'You're looking very smart, young man.' Unlike Marianne and Stella, she had not had the benefit of seeing Spike in his suit before.

Spike, Marianne noticed, had been looking thoughtful, so much so that he had not caught Daphne's observation. She had to repeat it after he had looked up, slightly startled, on realising that he was being addressed.

'Oh, yes. To be honest, I may go and change into something more comfortable in a moment.'

'You do that,' laughed Daphne. 'You'll enjoy yourself more if you don't have to worry about spilling drink on yourself. We're all dying to see you get a bit tipsy. Marianne, especially.'

Stella found this amusing, while Marianne reddened along with Spike. He got up, asked them to excuse him for a moment, and went next door.

'I still prefer him in jeans,' Daphne confided. 'You can see so much more. That suit jacket almost obscures his bottom. Marianne's feeling quite short-changed.'

'You'll go to hell, Daphne!' warned Stella, laughing.

They cosily awaited the return of Spike, commenting at the same time on the now long absence of Jerome and Dean. But Spike did not return very soon, either. In fact the first of the missing trio to appear was Jerome, though not in the circumstances they had expected. For he entered alone and, saying nothing, seated himself in the armchair Spike had vacated. They knew that something was amiss but could not tell straight away what it was. Jerome appeared to be patting his nose with his handkerchief.

'What on earth...' said Stella as she realised there was blood on his handkerchief.

'It's okay,' said Jerome.

'Your nose is bleeding!'

'Don't fuss, Stell, it's nothing. I fell over on my way in, that's all.'

They made him put his head back, and he sat for a while as they looked on nervously.

'Where's Dean?' asked Marianne. A good question, both Stella and Daphne thought.

'Oh, next door,' said Jerome, the bleeding having stopped at last. They noticed that he still looked shaken, more so than a mere fall would have warranted.

'Did Dean punch you?' asked Marianne, echoing the same unspoken question from the others.

'No, not Dean,' he said, and realising that this probably gave away more than he had intended, added again: 'Don't fuss.'

His aversion to further questioning was manifest, and they felt it prudent to say no more for the moment. He was clearly not seriously injured, but it was obvious that he had been involved in a fracas of some sort.

'Was there a fight in the pub?' Stella ventured.

'What pub?' he asked, and then, realising where he was supposed to have been, added: 'No, I told you, I fell. Why do you keep going on?'

But their attention was soon diverted from Jerome, for Spike had reappeared. He had not changed out of his suit, though he seemed to have loosened his tie. On closer inspection it looked as though he (or someone) had pulled it loose with something of a jerk. He looked in their direction nervously, saw Jerome and, with a face of pure animosity, made for the breakfast room. Marianne gave him a few moments before following him out.

He had seated himself on a dining chair next to the table on which the remains of the food was laid out. He was shaking slightly, a look of bewildered fury on his face, although he appeared to have sustained no physical injury.

'What on earth has happened?' asked Marianne.

'Nothing,' he said, looking away.

'It doesn't look like it!'

'Nothing to concern you, anyway. Look, you don't want to spoil Elizabeth's party, do you?' He looked up again, but not at her so much as past her. She turned and saw that Dean was standing in the doorway. He glared at Spike, who glared back, his anger enhanced. Dean retreated.

'Have you had a row with Dean? And was it you who punched Jerome?'

'Oh, fuck off and mind your own business!'

Some might have argued that this was the most sensible thing he had ever said (or ever would say) to Marianne. In the event he put his head into his hands and said: 'I'm sorry. Just leave me alone for a minute. Leave me alone.'

Marianne thought it best to do as he asked. As she returned to the lounge she encountered Jerome and Dean engaged in a frantic whispered conversation in the passage, which they abruptly ceased as she passed them. All she heard from Jerome was 'That moron!' and, from Dean: 'He didn't mean it. It was a shock for him, that's all.'

Marianne, Daphne and Stella sat in embarrassed silence for a while until Jerome returned and suggested it was time they left.

'Are you okay to drive?' Stella asked anxiously.

'Oh yes, I'm fine,' Jerome said. 'Let's go.'

Only Dean followed them out. 'I'll say goodbye to Spike for you,' he reassured Marianne. 'He's a bit upset at the moment.'

Marianne forbore to mention that Dean looked pretty agitated himself.

'Well,', said Daphne, when the car was a safe distance from Prentice Road. 'Who'd have thought it? And I was beginning to think that boy was a wimp.'

'What happened?' asked Stella, as well she might. For she, no less than Marianne and Daphne, was absolutely satisfied that Jerome's bloody nose had most certainly not been caused by his falling over. It was as clear as anything possibly could be that it was the result of a punch, a punch undoubtedly landed by Spike. Stella, however, did have an advantage over Daphne and Marianne in that she knew her cousin slightly better than they did.

'Jerome! You surely didn't try to make a pass at Spike?'

'What, he of the padlocked underpants? You must be joking.'

'So what were you doing?' she pursued, with surprising severity.

'Well, what do you think we were sodding doing?' he snapped. Marianne and Daphne, in the back, sat up. There was something emerging from this exchange that suggested their attention would be well rewarded.

'And Spike caught you at it?'

'Yes, the stupid moron. Mind you, it was partly Dean's fault. He's the sort who sounds as though he's in agony when he's enjoying it most. Spike comes into the bedroom and assumes I'm raping his precious little brother.'

'Well,' said Daphne, after the news had sunk in, 'if he really thought that I think you're incredibly lucky to have got away with only a bloody nose.'

'Oh, don't you worry, he'd have done a lot more if Dean hadn't grabbed him. He managed to establish fairly quickly that I wasn't assaulting him, but Spike didn't seem to find that a particularly soothing thought. If Dean wasn't being raped it followed that he must be doing it voluntarily, even Spike's solitary little brain cell could work that one out. And, of course, that opened up a whole new can of worms.'

Not so much a can of worms, thought Marianne, as a pit full of vipers. There were so many different levels on which Spike would have been shocked by what he came across that evening that it was difficult to know where to begin. First and foremost (and probably most hurtful of all), he would have realised that Dean had held something back from him, something vitally important about himself, and Spike could not but assume from this that all along he had never really known Dean properly. That, by itself, would have been enough. But more: Dean had shown that he could share an intimacy with others of his own sex which he had never and could never share with Spike. That had to provoke a certain jealousy, whatever Spike's own sexual orientation. There was also, of course, the residue of prejudice about such activities that lingered from less enlightened times, which, although now virtually eliminated in more sophisticated circles, still lingered in corners and crevices in places such as Prentice Road (and Spike was hardly sophisticated; that, indeed, was his charm. Now Marianne had discovered a context in which it could be a drawback).

'Anyway,' pursued Jerome, correctly assuming that they would want to hear the account in full, 'I'm on top of Dean with my back to the door, and all of a sudden I'm grabbed from behind. I look round and instantly get bopped on the nose. Dean gets up, grabs Spike and pushes him away from me, telling him to calm down. I get up to hit Spike back, but forget my trousers and pants are round my ankles and fall over. Spike starts blubbing, Dean starts blubbing, so I make myself decent and piss off as quick as possible.'

'You mean,' said Stella, with some surprise, 'that Spike had no idea that Dean was almost as big a screaming queen as you are?'

'Not an inkling. Though it's difficult to believe someone could share a room with Dean all these years and not know. I suppose idiots like that only see what they want to see.'

Marianne thought it best not to handbag Jerome while he was driving.

'Well, he must be pretty thick,' Stella conceded. 'I knew the moment Dean came out with his first bitchy remark. And surely you must have known, Marianne?'

'How could I have known?' asked Marianne incredulously.

'You mean you fell for that Cock and Bull story of Jerome's about those spare tickets for the theatre a few weeks ago? Do you really think we'd have been in the upper circle if they were ones his parents had bought? Once you all agreed to come he had to rush straight round to the box office to get what he could. And what do you think they were doing when they were so long collecting those CDs when we were at your place?'

'Oh, shut up, Stell!' said Jerome irritably.

'Well I wish you'd told us earlier,' said Daphne, with only a little less irritation. 'It would have been so much more interesting if we'd known what was what from the start.'

'You mean the eventual outcome wasn't interesting enough?' laughed Stella.

Marianne, feeling that it would be politic to allow Spike and Dean a little time to sort out their differences, made no attempt to get in touch that week. She hoped, of course, that one or the other of them would contact her, but Friday came and she had heard nothing. She told herself that it would not be too forward of her to give them a ring the following day, and walked home that evening planning her usual early night.

She had only been in ten minutes when the telephone rang. It was Spike. It occurred to her when she heard his voice that this was the first time he had actually taken the initiative to phone her and that this, in a sense, was the very call she had been waiting for all these years. Her joy was short-lived, however, for he sounded agitated.

'Marianne,' he said anxiously, 'are you doing anything this evening?'

It was not the voice not of someone who was planning a social engagement but of one who needed some kind of assistance. To Marianne that hardly mattered, in fact to be able to assist Spike in some way could be even better.

'No, nothing much *this* evening,' she said, doing her best to make it sound as though this was quite unusual for her.

'Would you mind if we could meet? It's just that...well, Dean's disappeared. He went off a couple of days ago and I haven't seen him since.'

She knew that for Dean to go off leaving Spike in the dark as to his whereabouts was indeed a significant occurrence.

'He didn't say anything about where he was going?'

'No. He left a note saying not to worry, he'd be back in a few days. That's all.'

Marianne was slightly puzzled. 'But if he said he'd be back in a few days, and it's only two days ago that he left, what on earth is the problem?'

'But he's never gone away like that. And I said some nasty things to him...I just have to see him soon. I think I know where he might be. He used to go to the West End sometimes. I didn't know where, but I know now it must have been to the gay pubs. I wondered...do you know where they are? And would you come with me?'

'But Spike,' she reasoned, 'there are loads of them these days. It would be like looking for a needle in a haystack.'

But what was she saying? While their chances of finding Dean were slim - even assuming he had decided to go out at all that evening - the search would involve her having a night out with Spike, and for the first time neither of them would be chaperoned. Not an unattractive prospect.

'I've got to look, though,' he said frantically. 'I know it sounds like a silly request but I don't really want to go to them on my own. I know he mentioned Old Compton Street sometimes. Are there any there?'

Are there any! thought Marianne. As it happened, she could be more help to him than he realised. A few months before, a student, David, had come to help out temporarily at the museum. He was an amusing boy who wore his sexual preferences about as discreetly as Liberace had worn his jewellery. She and Judith had quite liked him, and on his last day he had invited them for a drink in Old Compton Street, in the very sort of establishment which would be as good a place as any to start looking for Dean. She had quite enjoyed that evening out, although the pub had become hideously crowded as the evening wore on. For women such as she and Judith the atmosphere had been, if anything, more congenial than the pubs into which they normally (if rarely) ventured. David and his friends had a wicked sense of humour (not so different from Dean's, it now occurred to her) and absence of any threat of untoward advances had made them both feel unusually relaxed.

'There are quite a few in that area,' she agreed, and she arranged to meet him at half past eight outside Leicester Square station.

Although she arrived a few minutes early he was waiting for her, impatient for the search to begin. He was casually dressed, which made her feel a little silly, for she had gone to some pains to look her best. Not that she objected, for he looked just about perfect as he was and, as always, he was squeaky clean. She could feel agitation in his kiss, not that it was any the less welcome for that.

'I'm sorry to drag you out,' he said.

'Oh, don't worry, I'll probably quite enjoy it. I know a place we can start. I went there a few months ago. A going-away drink for someone from work.'

'Didn't you mind going there?' he asked, surprised.

'Not in the least. It was fun.'

'It's a pity he had to go off like that just now. A letter came for him yesterday from the university people. He's been accepted at the place that was his first choice.'

'Oh, but that's excellent news!' said Marianne. 'Someone who comes into the library has just finished there. It really is an achievement to get on that course.'

'Anywhere with "Queen" and "Mary" in its name must be the right college for him,' Spike concurred morosely.

It would not have been a bad joke had it been said in the right spirit. On this occasion, however, it was prejudice rather than humour that appeared to have prompted it. This saddened Marianne.

'I think,' she said, 'you might try to reflect a little and try and see things from his point of view for a change.'

She regretted the 'for a change' part as soon as she had said it. It had been unnecessary and was probably unjust. He was silent until their first port of call.

'Well, here's the one I know,' she said.

'Well, you go in and see if he's there. I'll stay here.'

'What, you mean you just want me to go in and come out again?' Marianne had thought they would at least have a quick drink in each place. Who knew, by the end of the evening it might have put Spike in a more congenial mood.

'Well, there's no way I'm going in,' he bristled.

'In that case I think you'd better find someone else to do your errands for you,' she said. She would certainly not have risked such a precipitate end to their evening out if she had thought for one moment that her bluff would be called but she judged, correctly, that his desperation to find Dean made this extremely unlikely. He looked hesitantly at the doorway, almost quivering.

'Do you want me to pop back for a crucifix and some garlic?' she asked. Then she grabbed his hand. 'If we go in like this will it make you feel better?'

'Well, as long as they know I'm with you.'

They entered the very crowded and fairly traditional pub. She sensed that Spike was surprised that an orgy was not in full swing. As it turned out there was just a large crowd of ordinary-looking people inside: mainly male, to be sure, and mainly young, but to Marianne the only thing which really marked it as a gay pub was that the clientele were more stylishly dressed than was the norm. In fact she noticed just how many of the younger men had on a similar type of bomber jacket to Spike's. And the same very short hairstyle. She thought it best not to tell him, but to an observer he would have fitted in perfectly. She led him to the only vacant space, near the cigarette machine. He reluctantly agreed to a stay for half a pint and she insisted on buying the first round in order to show him that going up to the bar and ordering a drink was no great feat. It also allowed her to 'forget' what he had ordered and buy him a pint of strong lager.

'Well, it tastes okay,' he conceded when she returned. 'Are you sure it's Black Label, though?'

'They had to change the keg,' she lied, 'so I got you that to save waiting.'

'Well, he's not here,' he said despondently.

'Maybe if we stay a while he'll come in. Let's face it, if we just go from one to the other we're more likely to miss him.'

He saw some sense in this. 'There's an upstairs,' he noticed. 'Perhaps he's up there.'

'I'll look,' she said, putting her white wine on top of the cigarette machine, and added, with a touch of irony, 'are you sure you'll be all right on your own?'

'I'll manage it.'

When she returned she saw that Spike was looking at one of the free gay newspapers that someone had left on top of the machine. He did not look pleased. She recalled curiously flicking through one when she had come with David, and some of the articles and pictures hardly reflected traditional family values. He came to a full page advertisement for a rubber and leather shop, resplendent with a fanciful drawing of a well-endowed macho man in a pair of leather briefs and a harness. She noticed that the face of the man was similar to Spike's: cropped hair, soft eyes, cute nose and a firm jaw, with just the hint of a cleft chin. It occurred to her, as she looked at a picture on the wall, that this sort of face appeared quite regularly in gay illustrations. He put down the paper crossly but said nothing, aware that to do so would provoke amusement from her.

'You know,' she said, 'I think you have become something of a prig since that time in Paris.'

'That was different,' he said.

'I don't know that it was. You were barely sixteen and I was in my mid-twenties. Some people might have said that was a little sick, at least on my part.'

'Nothing happened in the end, anyway,' he pointed out. 'Besides, that was perfectly normal, natural anyway.'

'I didn't realise your views on what's natural were so papal,' she observed. 'People use contraceptives to thwart what nature intended, so I presume that also constitutes unnatural sex. Or do these rules only apply when it comes to people who want to do something you've never particularly wanted to? Or is it that rules for the majority can always be more flexible than those for the minority?'

'You're saying just what Dean said.' He made it sound as though this were proof that it was nothing more than a silly excuse.

She smiled. 'So what exactly do you intend to say to Dean if we do see him?'

'Only that I'm sorry for being nasty to him. After last Saturday we didn't talk much. Then on Tuesday evening he brought it up again, said that he was gay and that was that, and he didn't see why it should make a difference to us. I said it made a big difference, though I agreed to put up with it as long as no one else knew and I didn't ever have to meet any of his boyfriends. He said that was impossible. He said he'd always wanted me to know he was gay, and to meet his gay friends and be friends with them. He even said he wanted everyone in The Kitchener's to know, too, and he'd bring his friends there if he wanted to. I said I didn't want him showing me up like that. I mean, if I were seen with a load of queens people would start to think I was one, too. Surely that's reasonable?'

'No, Spike,' said Marianne, her principles overcoming her desire not to cross Spike of all people, 'it was not reasonable. What it all comes down to is that you were only thinking of what people would think of you. Has it ever occurred to you that a lot of your other friends might think you were a bigger person for being able to accept Dean for what he is?'

He looked chastened, and seemed to think hard for a while.

'I know you're right in a way,' he said at last. 'I was thinking mostly of myself. And Dean's been so good to me. I don't think I'd have got through the last four years without him. I...'

He stopped, clearly unable to go on. She sensed rather than saw a slight glistening in his eyes and thought it best not to pursue the matter further. She pressed his hand. For a moment Spike had dropped in her estimation, but she knew now that he was not really so selfish, just rather confused at the conflict between reality and the prejudices others had inflicted on him.

'Anyway,' she said, when she thought it safe to do so, 'do you really think it's a good idea to look for him like this? He might think you're spying on him.'

'Do you think so?' he said thoughtfully. 'On the other hand,' he brightened mischievously, 'it could be my way of showing I'm not frightened of walking boldly into a gay pub and meeting him and his friends.'

'You hypocrite!' laughed Marianne, really rather impressed. The last remark showed that Spike was, after all, capable of laughing at himself, a quality incompatible with dyed-in-the-wool bigotry. She also noticed with approval that he had already drunk most of the lager, unaware, no doubt, of its strength.

'I still don't understand how you can have enjoyed yourself in here,' he observed.

'Well, sometimes a woman likes to be in the company of men who want to explore her mind and not those who only want explore her body,' she laughed.

'And which are the more disappointed?' he chuckled.

She was delighted by the joke. This was the Gregory Porter she had known in Paris, his father's son when it came to the instant riposte. The lager appeared to be working even better than she had hoped, and so far he had only had the one.

They had to move slightly to allow someone to use the cigarette machine. A tall, athletic young man. He took his cigarettes, and nodded at them in thanks and apology for disturbing them. Then his eye caught Spike's face. Oh no, Marianne thought, if he starts showing too much interest in Spike the progress made so far could be undone. She had already noticed that quite a few hopefuls had been casting lingering glances in his direction.

'It's Gregory Porter!'

It was an exclamation of genuine recognition rather than a chat-up line.

'John Warner?' said Spike questioningly - and smiling too!

'How are you, old mate,' said the young man effusively. 'Good to see you.'

He shook Spike warmly by the hand, and Spike, to Marianne's surprise, was not averse to having his hand so shaken.

'This is Marianne,' said Spike, to what was obviously an old friend.

John shook hands with Marianne. He turned to Spike again. 'What happened to you. You never came back to see us.'

'Well, you know about...' began Spike.

'Oh, yes, of course. I'm so sorry. But I didn't think you'd disappear so completely. You only went to Walthamstow, I'd heard.'

'I don't know,' said Spike. 'I just never felt like going back to Wanstead.'

'Do you mind if I join you for a while? I'll just go and get my drink.'

'John was a school friend of mine,' Spike explained to Marianne, not without enthusiasm. 'In the year above me. And in the rugby team.'

'Oh well,' smiled Marianne, 'that make's it all right for you to talk to him, then.'

John returned. 'Well, I never expected to see you here,' he said. 'I had you down as a confirmed straight.'

'I am,' said Spike. 'I was just hoping to see Dean, my brother. Remember?'

John seemed to have to think about this, as though he could not recall Spike having a brother.

'Oh yes, Dean the Mouth! That kid your parents fostered?'

'Adopted,' Spike corrected him, and Marianne was touched by his determination that his relationship with Dean should not be considered less than it was.

'Well,' laughed John, 'don't be embarrassed about being straight. You've obviously dressed the part to come here tonight.'

Spike looked puzzled rather than offended. Then, as he took a look around him, he seemed to realise what John meant. 'I'll kill him!' he exclaimed.

'Who?'

'Dean, of course. He came out with me and made me buy this jacket. Said it was fashionable. And he said I should have my hair cut like this. Said it suited me.'

'And did he buy you that shirt?' asked John, lifting the flap of Spike's jacket so that they could see the motif on the front.

'Yes. Said he'd got it at a club that's all the rage.'

'And didn't tell you it was a gay one, I suppose?'

Marianne burst out laughing, as did John. After a few seconds of fuming even Spike started smiling.

'The little sod's been dressing me as a gay all this time.'

'Well, it's come in handy tonight,' laughed Marianne.

'Would you like a drink?' asked Spike, his own glass now empty. He went to the bar, apparently having forgotten his inhibitions.

'Poor Gregory!' said John. 'They were such a lovely family.'

'I know,' said Marianne. 'I don't think he's over it yet. He's had an argument with Dean and he wants to find him. They're very close, really.'

'Well, thank heaven for that. He'd have nobody, otherwise. Unless...I'm sorry, are you his girlfriend?'

'Well, sort of...'said Marianne, who wondered exactly how their renewed acquaintance could be described. 'I must say, he's brightened up a lot since you came in. Were you and Spike very close friends?'

'Spike? Is he still called that?' John looked amused.

'I think he thought it was more suited for Walthamstow,' Marianne explained.

'I used to love going to the Porters' house,' said John. 'His father used to make everyone laugh, and they always made you feel so welcome.'

'Yes, I can believe that,' said Marianne, feeling a pang of regret that events had made it impossible for her to have shared in that hospitality.

Spike returned with the drinks, and she noted that he had bought himself a pint. She guessed that, now that he was reconciled to staying for a while, one with his image to maintain could hardly stand around with a puny half-pint glass. She knew that he was not normally a big drinker and was pleased that he was letting his hair down.

He and John reminisced about old times and she enjoyed listening to them talking about the tricks they played, the people they had known. It was obvious that Spike had been extremely popular and, on the part of some at least, loved and perhaps lusted after. She did not mind this overmuch, since the lust had only ever remained a fantasy to those gripped by it. She could only applaud them for their good taste.

John agreed to help them in their search for Dean and suggested two or three other places they could try. Spike's worries about Dean dissipated a little as John explained to him that queens were fond of flouncing out, but always came back. He and Marianne listened to John telling them about some of the naughtier things he had got up to, and they found themselves reciprocating with the story of their evening out in Paris. When chucking-out time arrived in the last pub, in Rupert Street, John invited them to a club.

'Dean could be there,' he used as bait. 'When the pubs spill out a lot of people go there.'

Marianne was all for it, although she could see that Spike was beginning to show the effects of the five pints of lager he had consumed.

'Do I look drunk?' he asked anxiously.

'Good Lord, no!' they said, carefully walking each side of him to ensure that he did not fall over on the way to the club.

'I must be a bit tired,' Spike apologised as he stumbled at the entrance. 'I've been laying a patio in Chingford all day.'

'Lucky patio!' said John. 'Anyway, you'll come alive when you get inside. It has that effect on people.'

John was not wrong. They persuaded Spike to have just one more pint, and Marianne was able to have a brief dance with him. They found a settee by a vacant table in a quieter corner and carried on chatting, John and Marianne amused at Spike's increasingly slurred speech. To them he was equally charming drunk as he was sober, and Marianne was convinced that this departure from his usual staid habits could do him nothing but good (she of all people should know how soul-destroying an over-fastidious lifestyle could be). He insisted on orange juice for the last two rounds, unaware that a double vodka had been put in one of them. Finally he began dozing off, and Marianne was thrilled by the delicious weight of his head on her shoulder.

'I don't think he's going to get back to Walthamstow tonight,' said John.

'No,' agreed Marianne happily.

They had to rouse him so that they could leave. At the coat check Marianne agreed with John how they should proceed. John knew a cab office next to the club and suggested he drop them off at Lucerne Court before going on to Notting Hill, where he was looking after a friend's flat. Spike suddenly seemed to come awake as these plans were being made.

'No, I must go home,' he said firmly.

'That's far too far for you to go tonight,' said Marianne. 'The tube stopped running ages ago. Don't worry, I'm not trying to seduce you this time. You can sleep in the spare room.'

She meant it. There was always the morning, after all, when he need not be embarrassed by his present inebriation.

'I can get the night bus,' he said.

'You'll never make it on the night bus,' John observed.

'A taxi then.'

'Do you trust me so little?' she asked.

'No, it's not that,' and he kissed her, aware of the offence she had taken. 'I really would like to go back with you. It's just that...Tell you what, we'll go back to your place for a coffee to sober me up, and I'll get a taxi from there.'

The compromise was agreed. In the cab to Lucerne Court, Spike was affectionate enough, and Marianne was reassured that he was indeed fond of her.

Back in Lucerne Court she guided the heavily sleepy Spike to the Chesterfield in the drawing room and went to make the coffee. He was dozing again when she returned. She sat next to him, lifted him up a little, and put her arms round him.

'I wish I could stay,' he said wistfully.

'But you can,' and added, when there was no response: 'What is it Spike?'

'Oh, nothing. But I have to go back tonight. Please don't try to persuade me to stay. It really isn't because I don't want to. I'm too drunk and Dolly would freak out if she found I hadn't got home at all. I'll come tomorrow and we can have a proper night out. I'd really like that.'

'Well, okay,' she said. It was an appealing compromise. 'When you've finished your coffee I'll ring for a taxi.'

As he drank the coffee he seemed to rally and said what an enjoyable evening it had been. Then he tried to raise himself but fell back again. She was actually quite pleased that he was so unused to drinking. She helped him up and led him to the spare room.

'Why don't you lie down just for half an hour?' she suggested. 'I'll call a cab for you then.'

He lay on the bed wearily.

'Stay here with me then. Lying down does make me feel a bit better. But don't let me fall asleep. I've got to get back. It would be nice if we could just talk for a bit.'

She stroked his head. 'Is there someone else?'

'Oh no. You've always been the only one, really. I mean, I've been with one or two other girls, but only when I thought I wouldn't see you again. I dreamed of seeing you again, over and over. That's why I...why it's got to be right. Nothing must go wrong.'

He smiled in mockery at his own soppiness.

He fell sound asleep within minutes, shortly after informing her that the room was going round and round. She really had intended to do as he asked and call a taxi but sensed she would have difficulty waking him and, even if she could, doubted whether any cab driver would accept him in his present condition. Gently she pulled off his jeans, resisting the temptation to divest him of any more. She sat looking at him in wonder for a full half-hour, occasionally gently stroking his chest and his face. 'You have ruined me,' she said softly, 'I can never again be content with anything less.' Then she tugged down the bedclothes and put them over him. After one last kiss she put out the light and left him.

Marianne could not remember rising so late. She had forgotten to set her alarm and when she looked at her bedside clock she was shocked to see 10.44. At first she wondered how she could possibly have let this happen, then she remembered.

She crept into the spare room and there was Spike, much as she had left him seven hours earlier. So it had not been a dream.

She saw with a thrill that his face was covered with a faint stubble. It had never occurred to her that he had to shave. The stubble was a shade darker than his hair, and she found herself gently touching it. There was a vague smell of lager in the room, the result, no doubt, of Spike's inebriated respiration. She was used to this: Roger had often had quite a bit to drink when they had been together. On those occasions it had not been something she found particularly pleasant. Now it delighted her, as though, along with the stubble, it symbolised Spike's coming of age.

She left the room, deciding that if she were to wake him it would be with a cup of tea: that somehow seemed more respectable. She went into the kitchen and found that she had no milk left, and remembered that she had used the last of it in the coffee the night before. She dressed hastily and went to ask Stella if she could borrow some.

In the corridor she passed Jerome, who had clearly just left his cousin's flat.

'Is Stella in?' she asked.

'Yes,' he said, and she noticed that he looked a little sheepish.

'Is anything the matter?' she asked.

'No,' he said quickly, and added, as he was halfway down the stairs, 'Sorry, I'm just in a hurry.'

She rang Stella's bell and her instincts told her that Stella, too, seemed a little odd, although polite as always.

'I've managed to run out of milk again,' Marianne apologised.

Stella stood there for a moment, as though unsure whether to ask her in. They had both borrowed things from each other before and each had always invited the other in on such occasions. Conscious, no doubt, that it would appear offensive not to follow the same procedure now, Stella stood aside and led Marianne into her kitchen where she proceeded to pour a cup of milk from a large carton.

Marianne could hear that there was someone in the bathroom and was surprised that Stella should be so coy at having a guest. While they both had lived pretty dull lives, neither were nuns and each had never expected the other to behave as such.

'Will this do?' Stella asked.

'Perfectly,' said Marianne, taking the cup. She was in the hallway on her way out when Dean emerged from the bathroom.

'Dean!' exclaimed Marianne, suddenly realising why she had been given such an odd reception. She had knocked at Stella's door the previous evening, before setting off to meet Spike, to ask if she or Jerome knew of Dean's whereabouts. Stella had responded in the negative.

'Hello, Marianne,' said Dean nervously.

'Dean is staying for a few days,' Stella explained, somewhat super-fluously.

'You...you won't tell Spike I'm here, will you?' Dean asked.

'Why ever not?' asked Marianne.

'Well, I don't want him causing a scene here, that's all,' and he added petulantly, 'It's none of his business, anyway.'

'He's been looking for you, you know that?'

'Oh, I dare say he has. And has he roped you in for the search?'

'It might interest you to know he's been very worried.'

Dean snorted and made for the drawing room. Marianne followed. Stella wisely made herself scarce.

'It wasn't very good of you to leave like that,' Marianne said. 'You must have known how it would upset him.'

'It's only for a few days, for Christ's sake! I said I'd be back. I just needed a bit of time on my own.'

'From what I can see you haven't been on your own exactly.'

'Away from him then, from all of them. Though I admit Dolly and Bill aren't as likely to be as worried about me as he is. A bit of time to think might do him some good, though.'

'I think you've already made the point you set out to make. He had me traipsing round the gay bars with him looking for you last night.'

Dean laughed despite himself. 'Spike, in a gay bar?'

'Take it as a measure of just how worried he was,' she smiled. 'And how sorry. As it happened he ended up quite enjoying it. He got quite drunk, in fact.'

'Dolly must have loved that when he got home!'

'Well, in the end he didn't go home. He stayed at my place,' and she added hastily, 'in the spare room.'

He looked at her in astonishment. 'He stayed at your place? He's getting adventurous!' Then he looked apprehensive. 'Was he all right this morning?'

'Well, I looked in on him and he seemed all right. He's still sound asleep. To be honest, he didn't really intend to stay, but he flaked out and I had no choice but to put him to bed.'

'Oh my God!' said Dean, horrified. 'How much did he drink then?'

'About six pints of lager and a couple of vodkas. He met an old schoolfriend of his.'

'Oh my God!' repeated Dean, putting his hand to his head.

'What's the matter?' asked Marianne, surprised at Dean's over-reaction. 'Isn't he entitled to get drunk occasionally?'

'Well yes, but...Oh Christ!...I must go and see if he's okay,' he said, making for the door.

'I haven't raped him if that's what you're worried about!' said Marianne somewhat crossly as she followed Dean into her own flat, the door of which she had left ajar.

Dean did not answer as he rushed into the spare room. He leant over Spike and gently shook him awake.

'Spike, Spike, wake up! I'm here now.'

Spike drowsily looked at his brother, who instantly put his arm round him.

'It's me, don't worry.'

Marianne, standing in the doorway, was greatly surprised at the affection and concern with which Dean said these words, so different from his attitude just a few moments before.

'Dean!' Spike said, still drowsily, perhaps still not quite sure where he was.

Dean leaned further over Spike, almost as if he were shielding him from Marianne. 'Are you okay?' he said softly.

She retreated, sensing that it was impolite to eavesdrop on this tender reconciliation. She went into the kitchen to put down the cup of milk she was still holding and put the kettle on. Dean entered not long after.

'I'm sorry,' he said, looking a little nervous. 'Spike and I have one or two things to sort out. I know it sounds rude, but do you think we could have a little while alone together?'

'Well, yes of course,' she said. It was only natural after all. 'Do you think you can be friends now?'

'Oh, yes,' he said, as though having difficulty recollecting that they had so recently fallen out. 'I er . . . just want to get one or two things out of the way. No time like the present and all that.'

'Well,' she said, 'why don't I pop out and get us something for breakfast? I'll go out for an hour, give you time for a heart-to-heart.'

'Thanks, Marianne,' Dean smiled. 'I know we must seem like an odd pair to you.'

'Not at all. You will stay for breakfast, won't you?'

'Of course,' he said quickly, and returned to Spike.

CHAPTER FOUR

Marianne luxuriated in the warm glow one feels when a job has been done well. Spike and Dean had been reconciled and she, albeit unwittingly, had played no small part in that reconciliation. She was of use, after all.

She went into a supermarket on Edgware Road to buy some bread, milk and bacon. One important item she already possessed, for some weeks earlier Dean had happened to mention that Shreddies were Spike's favourite breakfast cereal, and she had kept a packet in her pantry ever since. Her shopping done, she walked along Oxford Street and browsed around the ground floor of Selfridges. At least she pretended to browse, for her elation made it difficult to take in very much. She was restless to be back home, to witness just a little of the happiness that she had helped bring about. But she had promised them an hour and an hour she would give. In his own way, she mused, Dean was as shy as Spike. She smiled to herself when she thought of the nervous way he had asked her to leave them alone for a while, no doubt due to a misplaced concern that their emotional reunion might be taken for weakness.

She made her way back along Oxford Street, realising that she was going to be ahead of the time she had promised, but she felt sure they would forgive her if she broke her word by five minutes or so. She would cook them all a good breakfast, the sort she had not taken during the years she had been alone. She knew that they were hearty eaters, and she wanted to cement this new landmark in their friendship in a way they would appreciate. She told herself that she should not jump the gun, but her fortuitous discovery of Dean would surely earn her some credit in Spike's eyes.

She looked at the pavement some of the time as she walked, finding the sight of faces a distraction to her daydream. Passing the entrance to Marble Arch tube station she was forced to pay more

As Handsome Does

attention as a throng of recently disgorged passengers made their way into the street. As she looked up, however, her eye was caught not by somebody coming out of the station but by someone going in.

For Spike was before her. Strangely, he was carrying a large holdall, her holdall, she at once recognised. He did not see her straight away as he fought his way through the oncoming crowd.

'Spike?' she said, questioningly, not because she was unsure that it was he - there was only one Spike, after all - but because he should not have been there. Nor could she see any reason why he should be carrying her holdall.

He gave her a look of what could only be interpreted as terror and ran into the station. She followed him, aware that she could not fail to catch him at the barrier. When he realised that she had followed and that there was no escape that way (he had not yet purchased a ticket and could not get past the barrier without one) he made his way out of the station again, obstinately staring straight in front of him as he brushed past her. She retraced her steps and watched him run in the direction of Oxford Circus, run faster, despite his luggage, than she had ever seen anyone run in a crowded street, except once when she had watched as a shoplifter was pursued by security guards.

Except when she had seen a thief being pursued...She froze. Her holdall! He had had nothing with him when they had met the previous evening, so what could he be carrying now? Whatever it was could only have come from her flat, and the holdall was positively bulging, bulging at least as much as when she had used it to take some old clothes to Daphne at her charity shop the day before. She recalled that on her return she had left it in a corner of the drawing room, had just been about to put it away when he phoned her. She remembered Mrs Steeden who had taken to shoplifting after her husband died, and she recalled the way Dolly had implied that Spike was always getting into trouble for something, the details of which she had infuriatingly seen fit to keep to herself. Kleptomania, perhaps?

Pursuit was now pointless. Her own unsensible shoes were no match for a lithe youth in trainers, especially not for one so determined to escape from her. Her instincts told her that she would, in any case, be better occupied returning to her flat as soon as possible

114

to see exactly what was missing.

Not that the missing items, whatever they were, whatever their value, were her main concern. As she made her way back to Lucerne Court the horror of it all grew. Kleptomania made it sound like an innocent medical condition, but it was still theft. Besides, how many kleptomaniacs had accomplices? She had left Spike with Dean, so the theft could hardly have taken place without the latter's knowledge. And it had been Dean who had been so determined to get rid of her.

She remembered all the programmes on television she had seen, some fiction, some fact, about women who had been fooled by good-looking young men, and not all of those women had been particularly ridiculous, either. Less ridiculous and gullible than she, most of them. And now she had been cheated as they had been.

In retrospect she saw that it had all been too good to be true. She would not be eating a late, leisurely breakfast with two of the most genuine people she had ever met, she would be contemplating her broken illusions. She had no doubt that Dean would also be gone, by a different route no doubt, and probably carrying more booty. The only question in her mind was whether they had planned this all along or whether temptation had got the better of them when they had found themselves alone in her flat. Perhaps they had calculated that her fondness for Spike, for both of them really, would prevent her going to the police. That prospect did indeed present new horrors. 'Well, officer,' she could only say, 'I went to Walthamstow a few weeks ago and became friendly with a young decorator. I put him up last night and popped out this morning. When I returned I found he had stolen all my valuables...' It did not require much imagination to picture the barely concealed smirks. Her one hope now was that they might have been moderate in their theft, taking enough to satisfy themselves but not enough to force her to seek justice, with all the humiliation that would involve.

Poor Lottie and George Porter, she thought. To think that the son they had so carefully raised had turned out like this! Clearly, he had learned more than they had intended from the delinquents they had fostered, the last being the biggest delinquent of all. But then, what had she really known about the Porters? Perhaps they had been latter-day Fagins who had run a training school for young villains. Perhaps that business function they had attended while in Paris had been a gathering of international crooks. And the following day they had gone to Orleans, supposedly to visit friends. Marianne recalled that there had been a big bank robbery that day in Tours, a mere 100km from Orleans. Was she really expected to think that it had been a coincidence? Something told her that she could be letting her imagination run away with her, but allowing it to do so was her only comfort, or at any rate her only self-defence. The panic she had seen in Spike's face left little room for doubt. It was the panic of one who had been caught in wrongdoing of a fairly heinous nature.

She trembled as she put her key in the door, not so much with fear as with anger. She saw at once that the door of the linen cupboard in the hall was ajar and she looked inside. She could tell that it had been disturbed, and remembered reading an article about burglars and how they searched in linen cupboards and even laundry baskets because that was where some people tried to conceal their valuables. So much for letting her imagination run away with her! Hard luck, Spike, she thought grimly, you got it wrong there. She entered her bedroom, which was nearest, and saw that several of her drawers had also been opened and not completely pushed back. Nothing much appeared to have been taken from them, nor had they been violently rifled, but then the thieves would not have been particularly interested in scarves and handkerchiefs. And on this occasion the thieves had plenty of time, time she had given them. She made for the drawing room, wondering what sort of state that would be in.

The room was perfect, if anything tidier than when she had left it. The only things missing, in fact, were the two coffee mugs that had been left on the occasional table the night before. The table itself was clean, as though recently wiped. She was nonplussed for a moment. It was not Mrs Turner's day to come in. Then she realised there was someone in the kitchen, for she heard the sound of crockery being moved. Thither she went, her rage giving her courage.

Dean stood by the sink. 'Hello, Marianne,' he said.

'What...what on earth is going on?'

'I just thought I'd wash up for you while I waited for you to come back,' said Dean, with an apparent innocence that infuriated her further.

'Why have I just seen Spike running off with my holdall? What was in there? And why was he so terrified when he saw me?'

Dean said nothing for a moment, then came out with a rather limp 'oh!' It was the 'oh' of someone who had been rumbled, there was no mistaking that.

'I've put some coffee on,' he said nervously. 'Would you like a cup? There's something I have to explain to you.'

'I'll bet there is!'

'No, please Marianne. Don't make it more difficult for me, or for Spike.'

While he certainly sounded like someone who had something difficult to say, he was good at making it sound as though there was some sort of rational explanation. Professionals, no doubt, prided themselves in the ease with which they could explain their way out of holes. She sat down at the kitchen table while he poured out the coffee. Handing her a cup he sat opposite her.

'Does he make a habit of this?' she asked, determined not to allow herself to be put off by soft words.

'Oh, so you've guessed,' fumbled Dean, obviously surprised by her attitude (or pretending to be). 'Well, I have to admit it does happen occasionally. He's much better than he used to be. Just after his parents were killed he did it all the time.'

'It's such a relief to know he only does it occasionally!' she said sarcastically. 'And is this what poor Dolly is supposed to be so nasty to him about?'

'Well, yes...'

'And who can blame her!'

'Is it really so unforgivable?'

'There are some things,' said Marianne, with a still shaking gravity, 'that are beyond the pale. Beyond excuse.'

'Oh, no,' said Dean, angrily, 'not you, too! The poor sod can't help it, and this time you have to take some of the blame for persuading him to drink so much last night.'

Marianne was in no mood for zany theories about the criminal really being the victim, or that alcohol could be used as an excuse for crime. On this occasion they hardly served, except to make her more furious.

'I'm surprised he isn't behind bars by now. Has no one ever called the police?'

Dean looked at her as though she were mad.

'Oh, so you think it's normal to take other people's things, do you?' she fumed.

'He hasn't taken anything. I mean, not really. He'll bring them back, or more likely I will. He'll be too embarrassed.'

'Oh, and I'm supposed to believe he's just borrowed them! And I should think he will be embarrassed. Is that supposed to make me feel sorry for him? Well there are some things I won't make excuses for, not even for Spike. He's not the Spike I thought he was, anyway. That's over and done with. And to think I thought so highly of his mother and father! Some parents they turned out to be, bringing up a...a...'(she searched for an appropriate word) '...an animal like that!'

Dean's anger now matched hers. He got up.

'You're a hard bitch, aren't you?' he said. 'I suppose nothing like this has ever happened to anyone in pure, pristine, everything-as-it-should-be Lucerne Court. And don't you insult Lottie and George. They were worth a hundred of any of the stuck-up shits who live in this dump!'

'Oh, I expect you'll be telling me next it's social conditioning. And what exactly did he take?'

'Well, the sheets, of course, and the towel he used to dry himself after he had a shower. And I did have to go into your room to look for a teeshirt for him. He'll wash them all and I'll bring them back, as I said. And frankly, Marianne, I hope that's the last he or I ever see of you again. You must be one of the cruellest people I've ever met, and you even beat Dolly for over-reaction. The police indeed!'

He made for the door leaving Marianne wondering if she had not missed something somewhere. Was she really supposed to believe that Spike had taken the sheets to wash them? What the...?

And then there was light.

'Dean!' she shouted, running after him and catching him as he was about to close (or, more likely, slam) the front door. 'I think...I think we may have been talking at cross-purposes. Come in and sit down, please, and let's start again.'

Somewhat reluctantly Dean allowed himself to be led back into the kitchen and plonked back into the chair he had just vacated.

'What exactly are you talking about?' she asked.

'What were you talking about?' he rejoined.

'Well, when I saw him running along with my holdall, I naturally thought he'd taken things, especially as he wouldn't stop. Ran away from me, in fact.'

'Spike, take things? You mean steal them?' he said, a smile beginning to cross his face.

'Yes,' she said, smiling too as she realised the nature of the misunderstanding. 'I thought he must be a kleptomaniac or something.'

'Spike's the last person who would ever steal anything.'

'Yes, I know that,' she said, relief overwhelming her as she realised that it was true after all.

'It's just that he had a bit of an accident. He had to get away before you got back, he was too embarrassed...'

Dean dutifully looked embarrassed on Spike's behalf. She burst out laughing.

'Oh you stupid, stupid boys. What sort of a dragon do you think I am, for heaven's sake? He did have rather a lot to drink last night. And yes, that was my fault.'

She laughed again. She knew Dean's humour well enough, and expected that by now he would be laughing with her. But he was not laughing. He did smile faintly, but it was more in sadness than mirth.

'Please, don't misunderstand me,' she said hastily. 'I wasn't laughing at Spike, just at the situation. At my stupidity, really.'

'I know that, and if it was a one-off mishap due to too much to drink we could probably all have a good laugh and then forget about it. But Spike's had more problems than I think you realise. I know you think he's shy, and that it's terribly endearing, but you don't know the torture behind what you take to be shyness.'

And as he said this his voice quivered. He made an effort to control himself but it was useless. He put his head in his hands.

'Oh, poor Spike,' he sobbed. 'It's all my fault. I shouldn't have gone away like that.'

She got up and put her hands round his shaking shoulders.

'Well, he did say some nasty things to you. He knows that.'

'He didn't mean it. It was a shock for him, that's all, finding Jerome and me like that. He's never deliberately hurt anyone in his life. I just had to get away for a few days. What with all this I'd forgotten that yesterday was his birthday. He must have thought I was really serious when I didn't come back for that.'

'But he never said it was his birthday!' said Marianne, horrified at

119

herself for not knowing, though in truth there was no way she could have.

'No, he wouldn't have told you. It's not a day we celebrate exactly. You see it's also the day his mum and dad...'

He could not go on, but Marianne understood his meaning all the same. She tore off a piece of kitchen roll and handed it to him.

'Thanks,' he said, blowing his nose.

'Well,' she said, speaking with mock solemnity, 'now I've found out about this hideous secret is there a chance you'll stop shutting me out?'

He looked at her thoughtfully. He seemed about to say something, paused, and then went ahead anyway.

'He thinks it's his fault they were killed.'

'But why? Surely he wasn't there.'

'We'd gone to Southend that day, him and me. It started to rain so we looked around the shops. He saw a pair of rugby boots he'd wanted for a long time, and they didn't have those ones in the sports shop near us. So he used nearly all the money we had to buy them. When we got to the station he'd lost the return tickets. They must have dropped out of his pocket when he'd taken out the money for the boots. The shop was shut by the time we got back so we had no choice but to ring his dad. His dad was annoyed, but his mum said they might as well come and pick us up and we could go out for a meal there. We'd planned to go to a restaurant that evening anyway, to celebrate his birthday. George told us to wait outside a hotel in Westcliff he knew. We waited and waited, two, three hours. We rang home a couple of times but there was no answer, so we knew they had to be on their way. A doorman from the hotel kept coming out and asking us why we were hanging around, and eventually he called the police. They didn't seem to know whether to believe us, that we were waiting for our mum and dad. Telling them we were brothers only increased their suspicions. The police took us to the cop shop and the doorman said he'd keep a look out for George and Lottie, said he'd tell them where we were if they came. The police didn't seem to know what to make of us, just gave us each a cup of tea and made us wait by the inquiry desk. We heard them talking about a pile-up on the M25 but still didn't think that had anything to do with us. I began to cotton-on when they started being nicer to us. Spike had probably never been in a police station before so he didn't know that something must be really wrong when the police start being nice to you, especially when you're a teenager. They were even nice to me. They asked us again what sort of car it was, and the number, and a bloke took us to the canteen for something to eat. Spike was really enjoying his meal when another policeman came in and beckoned to the one who was with us. I saw from his face what it was about and it was I who gave the game away. The policemen looked at us, as though deciding to let us finish our meal before coming over. I somehow saw it as inevitable, but Spike had been born to sweet delight, as the poem says, and now it was all over. I suddenly knew that and, when he saw my face, he knew too. I've often wished I could have pretended a little bit longer, just so that he could have finished those egg and chips!'

Dean blew his nose once more before continuing. 'He took all the blame on himself. Kept going on about them not being there if he hadn't been so selfish, buying those rugby boots so that they had to come and pick us up. He was concerned about me, too. He thought that it was his fault I'd lost them, and my home. And the last words his father said to him were "You're a bloody nuisance!" He couldn't get that out of his mind. He fell to pieces totally for a while. Always worried, thinking everything was his doing. Sometimes he couldn't accept they were really dead, either. He said they were punishing him for something, that it was all a joke. You've no idea how different he was from the Spike I'd known before.

'You see, I was 12 when the Porters first took me in. I was what the social workers called difficult, and they weren't exaggerating. In fact, just before I'd gone to them I'd run away from the home I was in and spent a month on the game round Victoria Station and Soho before they caught me. I thought the Porters would be another pair of wankers, but no matter what I did they never gave up on me. But it was Spike who really took me in hand. He was two years older than me, the same as he is now, and I have to admit I fancied him gutless. He helped me with my homework, took me round with him, treated me as an equal. Everyone at school seemed to love him. He was good at sports, and God! so beautiful. At least he was to me. I felt so proud I could call him my brother. I started working hard at school to please him and found I was quite brainy. I'd never have known otherwise. If it hadn't been for him and his mum and dad I'd probably have been dead by now. At the very least I'd be inside.

'After the accident the Clarkes didn't really want to have me, that was obvious. Not that I particularly wanted them, either. But there was no way I'd let them take me from Spike, nor would he let them separate us. The social workers said that as my adoption had just been formalised I was legally as much the Clarkes' nephew as he was. Mind you, they got paid well for having me.

'At first they weren't too bad to Spike, thinking he'd get over it fairly quickly. But when it looked as if it might take longer than that it was a different matter. Dolly liked the praise she got from other people for taking us in but the novelty soon wore off. I suppose you have to look at it from their point of view. They'd been alone so long and they weren't used to having any kids, let alone a difficult pair like us. Not that Spike was really that difficult, it was just that Dolly saw fit to make a meal out of the one little problem he had. I was the one who really gave them trouble. I didn't see why they should tell me what to do - when I should come in, what I should wear and all that. They weren't the Porters and never could be. And the way they treated Spike infuriated me, and I let them know it. I was angry with Spike, too, for not standing up to them, but he didn't seem to have any spirit left. Poor sod still didn't know what was happening to him. He'd lost everything, not just his parents but his home, his self-esteem, just everything. He seemed to agree with Dolly that he wasn't fit for civilised people to mix with. Eventually I calmed down only for his sake. I realised I was probably only making matters worse for him. So I knuckled under, or at least pretended to. He'd helped me and it was my turn to help him. I got him to come out more, to start doing things and at least try to enjoy himself. He still had all sorts of hang-ups, always thinking he wasn't clean enough, thought that everyone he met knew all about him and were probably laughing at him. To counter it, he developed his totally over-the-top macho image, but still looked as though he'd burst into tears if anyone tried to get too close to him. Anyone but me,' he added, not without some pride.

'Anyway, he started working for Bill and that helped. If his parents had still been around he'd have gone on to college, but he didn't seem able to apply himself to academic work any more. Physical labour was different. He threw himself into the job and eventually Bill came to realise what a little goldmine he was. Everyone said what a fantastic job he did. Later on he also started helping in the pub sometimes. Keeping busy was what he needed. What worried him more than anything was that soon I'd probably leave. Recently he started saying that we should get a flat together, which I'd like too, but I knew I'd have to sort out something else with him first. There are other things I intend to start doing now I'm eighteen. Besides, I couldn't stand being in the closet for any longer where he was concerned. I wanted him to know, because it wasn't right that I should hold it back any more. I couldn't lie to him of all people. As it was, when he did find out it must have seemed as though I'd been lying to him all the time.'

Marianne took his hand. 'Poor Dean. Why do you talk as though it's only Spike who's suffered? Wasn't the loss of your adopted parents and your home as bad for you?'

'No,' said Dean, with less visible emotion than he had shown hitherto, 'nowhere near, although I do miss them. You see, he lost the people he loved the most. I still had the one I loved the most.'

'Tell him not to be worried about what happened here,' said Marianne after a long pause. 'No harm's been done. You must have noticed the mattress cover on that bed. I look after a neighbour's three-year-old daughter sometimes.'

'Sure!' laughed Dean. 'That's bound to go down well with our little macho man, telling him he's in the same category as a three-year-old! That's just what Dolly has always told him, more or less.'

'Well, you don't have to put it quite like that, then,' smiled Marianne.

'I don't think he'll ever see you again,' said Dean sadly.

A little of the fear Marianne had felt earlier returned. 'You can't be serious. That's too unjust to both of us.'

'You just don't understand how hard he is on himself. I expect at this moment he's at home piling those sheets into the washing machine accompanied by the usual jeers from Dolly. He'll give them to me to give to you, washed and more neatly ironed than you've ever seen them. But he won't ever be able to see you again. Not now you know.'

She realised that she had been a little hypocritical in asking Dean

123

not to shut her out. He had been honest with her, but was she not still being a little dishonest with him? Perhaps it was time for her own confession.

'Has Spike told you that we go back further than the last few weeks?' she asked.

He looked at her curiously. 'I did think you seemed to recognise each other the day you came to look round number twelve.'

And so she told him the whole story, and not just the bare narrative, for she also mentioned the impression Spike's parents had made on her, to Dean's obvious approval.

'So it was you!' said Dean, in astonishment and delight.

'He has told you, then?'

'No, not that it was you. His parents were killed about a week after that last trip to Paris. He was put on sedatives for a few weeks and he didn't always make much sense. He kept going on about the lady they'd met in Paris, and seemed to think that Lottie and George must be staying with her, that it was some kind of prank to teach him a lesson. When we finally managed to persuade him that they were definitely dead, that they'd been cremated, he then changed the story a bit. Apparently the woman now wanted to marry him!'

Marianne murmured in sympathy at this further evidence of Spike's temporary derangement.

'Anyway,' Dean continued, 'he said her address was in our old house somewhere but I couldn't find it. He never went back, you see. I went with Bill and Dolly to get some of our stuff but much of it was left in the house when it was sold. All the furniture stayed, and a lot of other things, to try to get as much for it as possible. If the bank repossessed it we'd have been left with nothing. Dolly told him that if his precious lady had really wanted to know him she'd have been in touch by then, anyway. Everyone thought he'd gone a little bit mad, not mad like a real nutter, but with grief. It was his way of facing the truth gradually. Even I didn't really believe him.'

'I had to go on to Switzerland,' she explained. 'I didn't get the chance to tell him that. In any case, when I got back I was frightened to ring, frightened of what his parents would think. I didn't know they were dead by then. I waited for him to ring me. When I did ring at last it was too late. The people there hadn't heard of him. I thought he must have given me a wrong number on purpose, that it was a game for him.'

'Oh, it certainly wasn't that. He spoke of you as though you were the most beautiful, the most elegant and sophisticated woman he'd ever met. I must say,' Dean added, 'you're not quite as I imagined you.'

'Thank you very much!' said Marianne.

'I must go to him now, though,' said Dean, rising.

'Yes,' she said gently, much as she wanted him to stay, 'I think you should.'

She followed him dolefully to the door.

'In a way it's worse, now I think about it,' said Dean. 'He's thought about you and hoped to see you again for so long. For this to happen here of all places, and for you to know about it...Christ, it doesn't bear thinking about.'

'I understand that,' said Marianne. 'But let's face it, he still sets a lot of store by your opinion. If anyone could persuade him...'

'Well,' Dean admitted, flattered by her faith in his powers, 'perhaps I could talk him into not giving up hope. But give him a little time. In any event I'll most probably be coming to Lucerne Court quite a lot now, to Stella's I mean, so I can keep you informed.'

She hugged him.

'So you did exist after all!' he said again, as though only now absorbing the full implications of it, and chuckled to himself as he made his way down the stairs.

Marianne had suspected that sooner or later Roger would hear about the events at the previous week's party at Elizabeth's. He was acquainted with Daphne, who was a prodigious telephone user. When he finally visited Marianne on the Sunday afternoon (the day after Spike's chagrined exit and her heart-to-heart with Dean), she was only surprised that it had taken him a week to come and gloat.

'Well,' he said, waiting only until she had provided him with a glass of whisky before launching into his piece. 'A dicky bird tells me that young Spike packs quite a punch. Not to mention what I've heard about Dean and Lady Face-Ache's young cousin.'

'You shouldn't believe everything dicky birds tell you,' said Marianne.

'This was a very reliable one,' he assured her. 'And not unsympathetic, no more than I am.'

'You sound sympathetic,' said Marianne with irony.

Roger smiled. 'You have to forgive us our little gossip, we're only human after all. I must say, I'm impressed. He's turning out to be infinitely more colourful than I thought. And have you seen the young pugilist since?'

'Yes, as a matter of fact,' said Marianne brightly, hoping that this would put Roger's nose out of joint. 'We went out on Friday evening. Had a most enjoyable time.'

'Ah,' he said, looking amused. 'And did you finally get your wicked way with him?'

'I think that's between him and me, don't you?' she said.

She certainly had no intention of telling Roger of all people about the more recent catastrophe: the entertainment he would derive from it would be beyond endurance. They had too many mutual acquaintances, and not only would Roger dine out on the story, those to whom he told it would be able to dine out on it too. 'You know that young lad from East London Marianne has the hots for? Well, she finally managed to get him to stay the night, and you'll never guess what happened...' She had no doubt that however carefully she explained the situation Spike, in the telling, would soon be transferred to her room and her own near drowning would become an essential ingredient of the story, made all the more amusing by her prim and proper reputation. And knowing Roger and his set she would probably receive not a few swimming costumes for Christmas. If she really thought she might never see Spike again she would probably have risked letting Roger into her confidence, but she had every intention of seeing Spike again. Indeed, she still had hopes of presenting him to her (and, in the main, Roger's) friends, and liked to picture their faces when they saw him. She did not want her moment of glory marred by any suppressed sniggers at Spike's expense, though they could laugh at her as much as they liked.

Fortunately Roger did not pursue the point. There were other things on his mind.

'I've got to be in East London tomorrow,' he said wearily. 'Probably have to go every day this week. That crooked accountant of ours is on trial. I suppose I've got to put in an appearance to see justice is done.'

126

'Is he likely to be put away for long?' she asked.

'Could get at least five years apparently. Done it before, it turned out. Gave us false references when he came to us.'

Marianne was not overly interested in the delinquent accountant, but Roger gave her a few more details nevertheless. It was only when he mentioned that the case was to be heard at Snaresbrook Crown Court that she found herself sitting up.

'Probably some inner-city dump,' he moaned.

'It's certainly not that,' she was able to inform him. 'I've seen it. It's in a beautiful old building set in lovely grounds surrounded by woods. That's where we went for our picnic a few weeks ago.' She forbore to mention that it was near Spike's old home.

'I shouldn't think that will make the proceedings any less tedious.'

'As it happens,' she said cautiously, 'I have lots of leave owing me at the moment. I could go with you tomorrow if you want some company.'

She had intended to go back and visit the area on her own at some stage and this opportunity seemed too good to miss. After a quick telephone call to Judith to ensure that she did not also propose to have the following day off, the outing was arranged.

'You're not wrong, for once,' Roger observed as they drove into the grounds of the Crown Court the next day. No doubt for those who faced the possibility of being sent down for a long stretch the architecture and location of the place in which they were to be so condemned was immaterial, but spectators could allow themselves the luxury of such aesthetic considerations.

It was indeed a tedious morning in Court Number Eight, every bit as bad as Roger had anticipated. The jury was sworn in, the opening statements made. Then there was a brief adjournment while the defence team argued some point of law. Embezzlement did not lend itself to very much romance, even though the alleged embezzler did look a bit like Crippen. The rest of the morning was taken up by a couple of accountants who explained how the book-keeping system at the firm operated. A nice murder or sex scandal would have been worth sitting in on, but this was excruciating. It was not even as though they could enjoy a relaxed lunch. After a quick sandwich with her in his car Roger had to go off to phone his partners to inform them of what had happened so far.

'Why don't you go off for a walk?' he suggested, realising that it could not be much fun for her. 'It doesn't seem a bad area.'

She had intended to do just that.

'Would you be terribly offended if I don't come back till quite a bit later?' she asked. 'It's a lovely day, and I would like to do a bit of exploring.'

'No, I won't mind,' said Roger, surprised at how daring she seemed to be becoming. 'Try and be back by about four, though, in case they adjourn early.'

She started off by looking round the grounds of the court, which were open to the public. Some people were eating their lunch on a large lawn and she sat down on a perimeter bench to soak up the sun for ten minutes. She wondered who of those around her were the families and friends of those on trial, who were jury members and who, like herself, mere onlookers. She noticed a row of handsome trees in front of her, beyond which was the lake. She decided to take a look.

She peered across and with a stab of joy caught sight of the Porters' old house, the sun glinting on its windows in a way that almost made her think it was making eyes at her - or beckoning her. Yes, that was definitely it, one of the half-dozen or so between the large Georgian one and the modern but comfortable-looking home for the elderly.

She had to get across. She had to take another look at that house, and not only at the house. She wanted to stand and look at the view Spike had looked at so many times, to try and imagine what it had been like for him in those happier days. She began walking to her left, but saw that a substantial fence separated the court's grounds from the forest. She retraced her steps and walked towards what looked like a gatehouse. She was right in assuming that where there is a gatehouse there would most probably be a gate. She found herself on a pretty but relatively busy road which she followed for five or six minutes, then took the first left. Yes, this was it! The lake was now to her left, and she walked along what was effectively a promenade. Women with children fed the swans, ducks and Canadian wild geese which flocked to the edge in chaotic greed. And yes, after a couple of minutes, there on her right, was that house, to her the loveliest house of all, though in truth identical to its attached twin.

She crossed the road and stood in front of it. The same curtains, Dean had said, but was that so surprising? It had been only four years, after all, though no doubt such a period has a different dimension to one of Dean's age. And as she looked at the house she knew that she had to get closer still. In the ten minutes of her walk an idea had developed in her mind, though she had not seriously thought she would carry it through. It had been more of a daydream than anything else: she could knock on the door, she could say she was a friend of the Porters, that she had been abroad for some years and had now come to look them up. She would be shocked, horrified, to hear that they were now dead. Perhaps she would be invited in to be consoled. At the very least she would catch a glimpse of the hallway, and whatever else happened she would have stood on the doorstep.

It was not until she was halfway up the garden path that she realised that she was actually putting her plan into operation. She marvelled at her impulsiveness, but was also strengthened by it. If she faltered now, her courage would quickly dissipate.

She rang the bell, one of those old-fashioned, integral bells set in the wall by the door, the bell which would have been familiar to Spike. There was no answer. How could she have expected there would be? It was a weekday, after all, and its occupants would no doubt be at work or school or shopping. And yet this absence also presented opportunities, for as the house was semi-detached she could walk around the side. If seen and questioned, her original story could still explain her presence. She had rung and no one had answered, and she wondered if they might be in the back. She did so want to catch the Porters while she was in England.

She made her way around the house and noticed that the back garden was a little overgrown. She did not have much time to survey it as a furious barking began - from the garden next door, fortunately.

'Now what's got you going, Senator?' she heard an elderly lady's voice say, and a few seconds later the source of these words was in the adjoining garden, surveying Marianne suspiciously over the fence.

'Can I help you?'

The question was put rather nervously. Marianne could only just see the very short lady's head.

'Oh, I'm so sorry if I frightened you,' said Marianne, summoning up all her acting abilities. 'I...I've been a Porter, and I'm looking for the broads. I mean I've been abroad and I'm looking for the Porters.'

The old lady squinted at her. Obviously short-sighted. Still, she did not look unkind.

'Oh, I thought you must be from Mr Newton's company. I have the keys, you see.'

Marianne did not see. Then the old lady looked even more worried as she recalled Marianne's reason for being there. 'Did you know the Porters well?'

'Not that well. I met them on holiday a couple of times.' Marianne realised that this was probably a rather vague claim to friendship and added with uncharacteristic disregard for the truth: 'but we became quite friendly, and I visited Lottie and George here once or twice.'

'Well, I'm afraid...oh dear, I'm afraid they've been dead for four years.'

'Dead?'

'In a car crash. I'm so sorry.'

'Oh, and not poor Gregory and Dean, too?'

'Oh no.' The old lady looked relieved, for she had had some doubts about Marianne's story but her knowledge of all the Porters' Christian names put her mind at rest on that score, at any rate. At least she could give the young lady some good news. 'They went to live with relatives.'

'Oh dear!' said Marianne, and wondered how good she would be at pretending to faint. She decided against. Although in many of the novels she had read women seemed to faint (or 'swoon,' for they were usually pretty ancient novels) on the slightest pretext, she suspected that it was not entirely fashionable these days and, with the arrival of feminism, not even particularly respectable. Besides, she was standing on crazy paving, not on a deep-piled carpet with a conveniently placed sofa nearby. She contented herself with putting her hand to her forehead.

'I'm so sorry dear. It must be a shock for you.'

'Well yes...It is. Oh dear, I suppose I must be trespassing then. How embarrassing. Oh...poor Lottie and George!'

'Have you come far?'

'From ... from Australia.'

'I meant today.'

'Oh, I see. Well, from Marble Arch. I'm staying with friends while I'm over here.'

Old Mrs Douglas was impressed. The mention of Marble Arch, combined with Marianne's accent, told her that this was no ordinary trespasser.

'Would you like a cup of tea?'

And so Marianne found herself sitting in Mrs Douglas's lounge sharing a pot of Earl Grey and some Battenberg cake. Her conscience was salved a little as she told herself that even the redoubtable Miss Marple had resorted to similar stratagems in her pursuit of information, and both Mrs Douglas and her respectable home would not have been out of place in an Agatha Christie novel. She was given details of the accident about which she was not supposed to have heard (absent-mindedly saying 'Southend' when Mrs Douglas said that the Porters had been on their way to Clacton) and of the additional tragedy of their having remortgaged the place shortly before their death to help finance the renovation of the house and, Mrs Douglas suspected, Mr Porter's failing business.

'I was hoping the boys would come back and see me but they never did. Gregory couldn't bear to come here. Such a nice boy. I did go and see him the once, a couple of weeks after the accident. Oh, it broke my heart. He'd always been so cheerful and full of life. But he just sat there, saying practically nothing, staring into nowhere, looking terrified. I told him and Dean to keep in touch, to come and see me as soon as they felt like it, but I somehow knew they never would. Senator missed them too, didn't you my love?' - she stroked the now docile Labrador's head - 'You miss those lovely runs in the wood with Gregory and Dean, don't you, yes.'

Senator cheerfully allowed his head to be stroked by his owner, though Marianne felt he was still looking at her rather suspiciously.

'And so much stuff was left behind!' went on Mrs Douglas. 'That brother and sister-in-law came and took a few things, but most of the furniture stayed to try to get as much as possible for the property.'

'Who took the house in the end?' asked Marianne.

'Oh, business people. Americans. In oil. Hardly ever lived in it after the first three months. His company transferred him to Bah-something or other. They only kept it because they were waiting for the market to pick up before selling it. Such a shame that a nice house like that should be standing empty, what with people sleeping in shop doorways.'

Marianne suspected that if the people currently sleeping in doorways were given occupancy of the house Mrs Douglas would be the first to object.

'And did they do much to the house?' she asked.

'Nothing. They had the outside painted last year, but that's all. They came a few months ago and stayed for a week, then off again. They thought of letting it but they don't want tenants in case they decide to sell, though Mr Newton occasionally lets colleagues from his company use it in emergencies. I thought you might be one of them. It frightens me, it being empty. You don't know who'll get in round the back. I've got the key so I can go in and put the lights on sometimes, just to make it look as if it's lived in. And I look out for leaks, of course. And I get the man who does my garden to keep the front tidy.'

So the Newtons would like to sell! Marianne told herself to stay calm but the temptation to race ahead was overpowering.

'I'll be coming back to England for good soon,' she said, 'and I'll be looking for somewhere. I've always liked that house.'

'Really? Well, as I said, they've not done much to it since the Porters were killed, God rest their souls. Not that it needed much doing. The Porters had just spent quite a lot on it. I don't know...perhaps they wouldn't mind if I showed you round - the Newtons, that is.'

'Well,' said Marianne, 'I wouldn't want to put you on the spot. I suppose you should really check with them.'

'Yes, I suppose so. Maybe I shouldn't show you now, then,' said Mrs Douglas.

'On the other hand,' Marianne added hastily, 'I haven't a lot of time, what with having to be back in Canada the day after tomorrow. Maybe it would make sense to take a look while I'm here.'

Fortunately Mrs Douglas did not notice that Australia had turned into Canada.

'You'll see,' said Mrs Douglas, as she opened the front door, 'it's just as it was when the Porters were here.'

Marianne was feeling much as she did when she had visited Victor

132

Hugo's house in the Place des Vosges. To think that this was the very place! But in this case even better, for most of the original furniture and fittings were here. This was the house they came from (and returned to) when she had met them in Paris. It was almost like touching them.

What struck Marianne at once was the unforeseen cheerfulness of the place. She had expected gloom, as befits a house with such a mournful past. But then, had its past been mournful? No tragedy had actually taken place in it, after all. They had simply left one day, never to return. The spacious hallway was carpeted in good-quality beige, and the walls were a pinky white. The white paint of the woodwork was yellowing very slightly, but not enough to give it an air of decay. They went first into the sitting room.

To anyone else the room would have seemed unexceptional enough: a pleasant three-piece suite covered in a bright flowered material; a tall mahogany cabinet; a fitted log-effect gas fire in a marble surround; a bookcase in the same style as the cabinet and a television. Yet to Marianne it was like entering paradise itself.

'Only the television's different. Their relatives took the old one.'

Marianne's elation grew as they went into the tastefully fitted kitchen, then a study (was it at that desk that Spike had helped Dean do his homework?), then the large dining room in the style of the George III period. Marianne, after thinking for a moment and taking in the furniture, agreed with Mrs Douglas's supposition that it was all just reproduction stuff. Most of the things, Mrs Douglas repeated, were just the same as when the Porters had the house, right down to bulk of the kitchen utensils and crockery.

'Yes,' said Marianne, in the dining room, 'I remember that grand-father clock. I always liked it.'

'I think that's one of the things the Newtons brought with them,' said Mrs Douglas.

'Oh, oh yes, of course. I'm thinking of one another friend of mine has.'

Marianne was relieved as she followed a slightly breathless Mrs Douglas up the stairs, for she had no need to pretend to know anything about the upper rooms.

The front bedroom was magnificent. Marianne had rightly expected that it would have a good view of the lake and the court beyond, but the reality far exceeded anything she had imagined.

'I suppose this was the Porters' bedroom,' she said.

'No, I don't think it was. She didn't like the traffic noise. Eventually they probably would have moved back in here after they had the double glazing put in, but they didn't have time. The accident happened not long after that. They used this room...'

Mrs Douglas led her into the second bedroom, still large but otherwise commonplace.

'And this must have been the boys' room?' said Marianne, pushing open the remaining door on that floor.

'No, that's the bathroom. The boys had a room each upstairs.'

Marianne had not initially taken in the narrower staircase leading upwards.

'The Newtons haven't touched that part of the house at all,' said Mrs Douglas. 'They just use it for storing junk. Would you believe some of the Porters' things are still up there, not just furniture, I mean boxes of stuff? Their relatives took some of it, and said they'd come back for the rest, but they never did. It's all old rubbish nobody would be likely to want, but as they never went up there the Newtons said it could stay there for a bit in case someone did come for it. They've never used those rooms so they're not bothered. They're so lazy! Do you know, they haven't even taken the posters and things off the walls.'

She looked apprehensively at the narrow staircase.

'Do you mind going up alone, dear? I'm not much good at stairs at the best of times these days, and those ones are a bit on the steep side.'

Marianne far from minded. She mounted the stairs, noticing that the carpet was of the same high quality as in the rest of the house, unusual for the approach to attic rooms. The Porters obviously believed that their boys should have the best. Quite right, too.

There were two rooms above, with another small bathroom in between. She entered the front one.

There was no possible doubt that this had once been a boy's room: the posters covering the walls said it all. Football ones, mainly, but a few pop stars too. And a couple of photographs. One, over the bed, was of a school rugby team. She peered at the sturdy 15 and 16-year-olds and yes, there in the front row was Spike, looking just as he had done in the rue du Roule. He was the best-looking then, too (though the one on the far left wasn't bad either, nor the one holding the ball), and the white shorts showed his thighs to good advantage. Marianne had to sit on the bed for a moment.

She looked at the large poster in front of her, the Tottenham Hotspur team of a few seasons earlier. So this was Spike's room then! She laid herself down on the bed for a few seconds to catch the scene that he would have experienced when he woke up in the morning. She ran her hand along the soft mattress.

'Are you all right?' Mrs Douglas called up.

'Just checking for damp,' Marianne called back.

She knew that she could not linger, much as she would have liked to. She went into the bathroom and, after trying to picture Spike in the bath, entered Dean's room.

It was much as Spike's but without the view. The posters here proclaimed the glory of West Ham United, and the pop stars were all pretty, young men. From the gaps it was clear that some were missing - ones, no doubt, that Dean had seen fit to take during the hasty and sorrowful removal. Latterly it had obviously been used as a storeroom, for on the floor were three or four tea chests full of bric-a-brac. Marianne rooted into one and pulled out a handful of old birthday cards. They were all ones that Mr and Mrs Porter had sent to Spike in his early years, lovingly kept, no doubt, by a doting mother. 'To our darling Gregory on his twelfth birthday,' was the greeting on the one she opened at random. Mrs Porter's words, no doubt, for beneath them were others in a different handwriting: 'You're a bloody nuisance but you're my favourite bloody nuisance.' Marianne smiled through her sorrow as she recalled George Porter's gruff but kind sense of humour. She remembered, too, Dean telling her of George's last words to Spike about his being a bloody nuisance. Perhaps one day Spike could be reminded of the punchline.

'Are you sure you're all right?' Mrs Douglas called again.

'Oh, yes, I'm coming,' said Marianne, not without some effort. She blew her nose and rejoined the old lady.

'It still has that effect on me when I go up there,' said Mrs Douglas sympathetically, for despite her short-sightedness she could sense Marianne's emotion.

'It's so sad,' agreed Marianne.

Before Marianne left, Mrs Douglas gave her the Newtons' address and telephone number. Marianne said that she merely wanted to find out how much they were asking, though in truth the sum was immaterial. She had made up her mind.

The purchase of the house went quickly and smoothly. Mr Newton had appeared hesitant at first but became more than co-operative once Marianne had made it clear that she was in a position to pay cash. She was sufficiently sensible to seek independent advice about the value of her purchase and to take Mr Newton down a little from the price he was asking, though not enough to risk his putting down the receiver in contempt. She suspected that he was quite a shrewd businessman, and would not be above putting up the price at the last minute if he was given the impression that she wanted the house at all costs. In the event, over several phone calls, they became quite amicable. A colleague in London was commissioned to act on his behalf, and Mrs Newton was to come to London in between exchange of contracts and completion (a matter of just a few days) to organise the removal of their personal effects (Marianne invited her to stay in Lucerne Court to facilitate the process). The furniture and most household items, it was agreed, were to remain with the exception of the grandfather clock which, the Newtons claimed proudly, was a family heirloom of their own and worth more than £2,000. Marianne laughingly agreed to this, knowing that it was the one item in the dining room which had not been acquired by the Porters.

Buying the house was relatively easy; telling Spike of the deal less so. Dean's services would be required, of course, and it was on the day contracts were exchanged that she finally plucked up courage to tell him what she was doing. She had heard from Stella that he would be coming to Lucerne Court that evening and asked him to pop in.

'I'm buying a house not too far from Walthamstow,' she said cautiously, 'and intend to let it out. Do you think Spike would be interested? I thought of you two the moment I saw it.'

Dean was more than interested.

'Where is it?' he asked.

'Snaresbrook,' she said.

He looked at her in the way she had anticipated, but the look quickly turned to disappointment. 'Sorry, Marianne, but I don't

136

think that's on. Spike can never bring himself to live there. Too near our old house.'

'Why exactly should that be a problem?'

'Can you imagine it? He'd have to see it sometimes, it's in a pretty prominent position, after all. It would just bring back everything he's lost. To be so near and yet so far.'

'And how would he feel about actually living in that house? How would you feel?'

Dean looked at her, not immediately grasping her meaning. The smile she could not suppress helped him along.

'You don't mean..?

'Yes, that's the house. The people who bought it have hardly lived there and want to sell. Everything's just as it was according to the old lady next door.'

'Mrs Douglas?' asked Dean, smiling as he recalled her. But his smile faded as he considered realities.

'I know you mean well, Marianne,' he said, after thinking some more, 'and in a way it could be the making of Spike to be back there, but I don't know if we could ever actually get him there.'

'Surely between us we could find a way?'

Dean mused for a moment, then looked less benign.

'What exactly is your game, Marianne?' he asked.

She realised it was a question he had a right to ask, one she should have foreseen.

'I don't know,' she said candidly, feeling a little deflated. 'I just found out it was for sale and saw it as too good an opportunity to miss. I'm not offering charity, if that's what you think. It's an investment for me, after all.'

'You must know we could never afford the going rent for a place like that?'

'Yes, I know that. But having the right tenants is worth a reduced rent. I know Spike would look after it.'

'Oh, he'd look after it, all right!' Dean agreed.

It was clear that despite any misgivings he was coming round. She knew perfectly well that it was not only Spike who had loved the house.

'I'd have to discuss it with Bill and Dolly,' Dean reasoned.

'You're both old enough to decide for yourselves, surely? In any case, I thought it was your intention to get a place of your own sooner or later.'

In the event Dolly and Bill turned out to be more sympathetic to the idea than Marianne had dared hope. Spike was working in The Kitchener's the following evening, and Dean arranged for Marianne to visit them while he was safely out of the way. At first Dolly was as suspicious of Marianne's motives as Dean had been, but grudgingly agreed that that house was where Spike belonged, perhaps what he needed, and that this opportunity was too good to pass up. Neither Dean nor Marianne fully knew what this admission was costing her, nor did they witness the agonies she was to suffer in private as the day of Spike and Dean's removal came closer.

'Let's make it a surprise, though,' said Dean, who was really getting quite excited now that he knew that their return to their old home was not a pipedream.

Mrs Newton turned out to be a somewhat scatty woman, nothing like the brash American Marianne had anticipated. She was apologetic about not having done very much to the house, but tried to make amends by helping Marianne and Dean get the place ready after her own belongings were packed and shipped off. Completion (and Mrs Newton's departure) was to take place on the Friday, and it was their aim to lure Spike there on the Saturday.

Dean marvelled at how little the house had changed, though it was not until Senator rushed towards him when he was in the front garden that Marianne noticed how affected he was. The dog recognised him immediately and almost knocked him over with enthusiasm. Old Mrs Douglas clapped her hands and wept with delight when she realised who it was (which took some time, for Dean was now about a foot taller than when she had last seen him) and they told her of their plans. Marianne was forced to apologise for her earlier subterfuge, but under the circumstances Mrs Douglas was more than willing to forgive her.

Dean punctuated their work with some enchanting little reminiscences about the Porters, each one triggered by a reminder of their occupancy. The best was probably the one he shared with Marianne just after Mrs Newton had left. It followed the discovery of a Pears *Cyclopaedia* in the bookcase in the dining room, left behind by Bill and Dolly at the time of the original hasty sort-out, most probably because the edition was out of date even then.

'This was what made me start thinking I might be quite brainy,' he smiled, tenderly opening it.

It had been a about a month after he had come to live with the Porters. He had steadfastly refused to look at a book or do any school work since his arrival, turning every effort to persuade him to do so into a scene, although he had curiously gone to watch Spike doing his homework from time to time. One evening, over dinner, Mr Porter had entered into an argument with Spike over which king had been beheaded.

'It was William the Conqueror!' Mr Porter had said firmly.

'No, I'm sure it was George II,' Gregory had insisted.

(A year or so later it had dawned on Dean that the whole thing had been a set-up, that Mr and Mrs Porter and Gregory had known who it was all along. By then it did not matter, as he was then on the road to academic success.)

'You're stupid, you two!' Dean had said, happy to be able to say it for once with undoubted truth on his side. He knew because he had seen the film. 'It was Charles I. Everyone knows that.'

'No,' George Porter said firmly. 'I'm quite sure it was William the Conqueror.'

'It was because he burnt those cakes,' Lottie Porter had thrown in.

'No,' Gregory said, with equal firmness, 'it was George II. It was because he lost the American colonies.'

Dean listened to their errors with increasing irritation and scorn.

'That was George III,' he said. 'And Alfred burnt the cakes.'

'Well, for someone who doesn't do any homework you seem to know an awful lot,' George had retorted scornfully.

The 12-year-old Dean got up from the table, unable to remain seated in his anger. It was not often that he had been in a position where he had known so absolutely that he was right and those arguing with him wrong. And he suspected that, even so, he would be belittled as he always had been before, be it in foster homes or institutions.

'Wankers!' he had shouted, resorting to the only weapons he knew. 'Silly shits!'

'Well,' Lottie said, as always infuriatingly oblivious to his dirty words. 'There's only one way to resolve this. Get the Pears out and let's see who's right.'

George took the *Cyclopaedia* from the bookcase. 'Somebody,' he said solemnly, 'is going to look pretty silly.'

George and Gregory peered into the book, arguing over how to use the index. Eventually they put it down, deflated looks on their faces.

'Well,' George admitted, 'it does look as though it was Charles I.'

Never before in his life had Dean known a victory quite like this. Nevertheless, he stood near the door, his short lifetime's experience suggesting that to be proved right could result in even greater retribution than being shown to be wrong.

'Well,' Lottie said, 'I think we all owe Dean an apology.'

'Sorry, Dean', George said humbly, a sentiment echoed by Gregory.

Dean cautiously made his way back to his place at the table. He remembered feeling quite sorry for them for having to admit they were wrong. Nobody had ever done that before.

'Will you look up whether it was George II or George III who lost the American colonies?' Lottie asked, handing the book to Dean.

The way the sections of the book were divided up made it difficult to find the right place, but Dean did so eventually, and all by himself. Triumphantly he showed them what the oracle had to say on the matter.

'Gosh, Dean,' Gregory had said respectfully. 'I had no idea you were so clever. Will you help me with my homework? I'll try and help you with yours, even though I'm not as brainy as you.'

'Oh, I'm not really that brainy,' Dean had said modestly, such unaccustomed praise bringing him closer to tears than years of brutality ever had. Was it possible that such people really existed, people who could be nice to him without wishing to put him down-or screw him?

And from then on, as Dean now explained to Marianne, he and Spike had sat together doing their homework, the understanding being that Dean, although the younger, was undoubtedly the cleverest. And Dean worked as he had never worked before, and the myth became reality.

'And was that when you first fell in love with him?' asked Marianne playfully.

'God, no! I fell in love with him the moment I moved in here. If I hadn't been in love with him already their little game would never have worked.'

Another little insight into Dean's relationship with Spike came as he was sorting out his old room. The first thing he did was to tear down the football poster. 'I never could stand football,' he explained. 'It was only to impress Spike and give me something in common with him, something for us to have conversations about. I don't have to pretend any more.'

On the Saturday morning Dean secretly brought some of Spike's things to the house. There he met Marianne as arranged. After a visit to Sainsbury's to buy provisions they set off in a taxi for Prentice Road.

This, they both knew, was the tricky bit. Spike had not seen Marianne since that embarrassing encounter in Oxford Street, and ever since he had remained in self-imposed disgrace. They had no idea how he would react to seeing her now.

'He's in the kitchen,' Dolly whispered.

They left Marianne to it. Spike sat at the kitchen table (on which he had neatly spread some pages of a newspaper) polishing a pair of shoes. He was so intent on his task that he did not register who it was, though probably aware that someone had come in. She watched him for a few moments, fascinated at his perfectionism, for although he had to be holding the shiniest pair of Doc Martens in London he still looked disapprovingly at them, cloth in hand, searching for a missed blemish which he could not bring himself to believe was not there somewhere. Then, sensing that the figure he could see in the corner of his eye was not one of those he would normally have expected (wrong shape for Dolly, and even Dean had not yet taken to wearing a dress) he looked up.

'Oh, Marianne!' he said, and blushed deeply.

She sat opposite him and smiled, reassuringly she hoped, but he looked down in embarrassment.

'You found out more about me than you bargained for,' he said.

'It was my fault,' she said. 'I put you in an awful position. It's just that I have this dreadful compulsion to try and seduce you all the time.'

'What, still?' he asked in wonder.

'Yes, I'm afraid so. But I promise to try and take things a little easier from now on. I can wait till you're ready.'

'That might be a long wait,' he said, still looking down.

'Some things are worth waiting for.'

She took his hand and he looked her in the face at last. She smiled, and then he burst into a smile too.

'If it's any consolation, my bowel control is excellent!'

So he could still joke, even at his own expense.

'Well, that is a relief!' she laughed. 'I shall certainly remember to mention it if ever I'm asked to write you a reference'. Then she added, as she remembered the ticking taxi outside: 'but I hope your claim won't turn out to be a case of pride coming before a fall. You haven't seen the surprise we've lined up for you!'

'Are you and Dean up to something?' he asked. 'He's been acting strange lately. I mean stranger than usual.'

'Ah, I should have guessed he'd give it away. Come on, there's a cab waiting for us.'

CHAPTER FIVE

Spike was shaken, but not in quite the way they thought. He let them show him round, saying nothing, showing no emotion. This frightened them a little, as they assumed that he was saving it up, that it would show itself in some other way, a way which would not necessarily be to their advantage. Perhaps he was angry; maybe the memories would have been best unrevived after all. He did not frown, he did not smile, most surprisingly of all he did not cry. He nearly did, as he entered the front door for the first time in over four years. But the very house that created the emotion gave him the strength to overcome it, or at any rate to postpone it. And the strength grew as every second passed, as the knowledge struck home that he would never have to leave again, not before he chose to, anyway.

For he was grateful, more grateful than he could express in words there and then. He sensed their excitement, but more than this he sensed their fear that he might be angry with them, and it was this, almost as much as the return to the house, that shook him. Why should he be angry with those who had shown so much concern for him? And why should they want to show him such concern? Why did they consider him so fragile? Yet these and other thoughts were still vague, and he felt that he needed to clarify them in his own mind. He needed that clarification as soon as possible, for only then would he know the proper way to react.

He knew that there would be time to show his gratitude later. There would be time to take a closer look around the house later too. What he wanted most urgently was the lake, which he was able to see from the lounge, from the big front bedroom and again from his own room. He looked longingly at the swans, the geese and the ducks. His very earliest memory was of feeding them. 'That's right,' his mother had said to the 3-year-old Gregory as she guided his hand, 'try and throw the bread into the water. If you get crumbs on the pavement they might come out and wander into the road.' It was these living creatures he craved now, maybe some of them the very ones he had fed before, or their offspring.

He had kept it his secret, but Spike had visited the lake and the woods on several occasions since his parents' death. He had once felt that he might be closer to them there, that he might gain some inkling of whether they had forgiven him. At the very least he had hoped he might be able to recall their voices and what they looked like. He could remember them, of course, but in a very superficial way. He was somehow unable to recapture their essence, the exact tone of voice, the facial expressions of affection. Those visits had always ended in bitter disappointment. Their old home had stood there, dark and barred to him, and all the joys he had known were likewise unobtainable. Father Stanwood had told him, on the day of the funeral, that he should try to talk to his parents, that if he did he was sure they would answer. But try as he would he was unable to do so, and they had not appeared to wish to talk to him, either. He had had a recurring dream in the first two years of his orphanhood: he was standing by the lake, feeding the assorted fowl, and had then gone for a walk in the woods alongside. There he had met his parents, who were both dressed up as though ready for a dinner party (he was aware that this aspect of the dream most probably had its origin in the way they were dressed for their evening out in Paris, a few days before their death, when they had attended the business function without him), but they had looked at him distantly. 'Mum, Dad,' he called out to them, but they always walked past him, saying nothing.

Now, he sensed, they might not pass him in silence.

'Is there any bread?' he asked when they were in the kitchen and Dean had begun making a cup of tea.

'Of course there is,' said Dean. 'We've stocked up on everything. Do you want some toast, then?'

Spike smiled for the first time since their arrival, and Marianne and Dean breathed a sigh of relief.

'No. I just want to go and feed the ducks. I won't be long,' he added, a hint that he wished to be alone, a hint they took.

He crossed the road to the lake (aware that he was being watched anxiously from the lounge window) and began throwing portions of the bread into the water. Within seconds, a flotilla of swans and geese were making their way towards him, with the poor little ducks in hot pursuit. As so often in the past he tried to aim the bread at the ducks, who always seemed to miss out. Some seagulls, inland now that the colder weather had arrived, also cottoned on to the fact that food was being dished out, and they swooped down in an attempt to beat the lake-bound recipients to the morsels he was dispensing. The seagulls were far more bad-mannered than the swans and the geese who, although greedy, were not violent. His father had once told him that it was because the seagulls were not from Snaresbrook and so had not learned good manners. They might even have been brought up in Canvey Island, so one had to make allowances.

'Tch, Gregory! You've dropped some of the bits on to the pavement,' said his mother. And this time the tone was absolutely right.

Spike looked at his feet.

'Sorry, Mum,' he said, picking them up and throwing them into the water.

And it was not until his supply of bread was exhausted that he realised that she had spoken to him, or at least that he had managed to recall what she would have said had she been there, for Spike was too sapient to believe in ghosts. What he did know, what he had longed for and, what he had known Father Stanwood had meant, was that his knowledge of them, the spirit and consciousness they had bred into him, would enable him to reclaim their presence in a way which, if anything, could be closer and more real than the company any mere ghost could give. He had seen programmes on television about people who had claimed to have seen ghosts, sad cases most of them, or born non-entities out for a bit of publicity, sometimes exactly the same people to be seen on other programmes talking about their previous lives. The shallowness of it all had angered him. People with real lives and real sorrows did not play such games.

He felt his vision blurring. A car had pulled up nearby, out of which an extraordinarily large family were emerging with bags of bread in their hands, and he thought it prudent to make for the side of the lake and the woods, away from the road. A merciful November dusk was falling and he realised that he would be able to make a fool of himself in privacy.

'Well, here you are then!' said his father cheerfully, diplomatically waiting until Spike was in the seclusion of the woods, but his tone immediately changed to irritation. 'Oh Christ! He's started blubbing. So much for this macho image he's been cultivating.'

'Sorry,' said Spike, after wiping his eyes with the bottom of his shirt. 'It's just that I'm only remembering you properly now.'

'I know,' said his mother. 'But remembering us properly wasn't important.'

'How can you say that? I was so lonely. And I wanted to know if you'd forgiven me.'

'You had Dean to think of,' said his mother, 'that was far more important.'

'And forgive you for what?' asked his father.

'He means about us being killed,' said his mother, replying for him. 'He reasons that if he had never called us out to pick them up we wouldn't have been in that accident.'

'Well, he's right about that,' said his father. 'He should feel guilty.'

Spike was dumbfounded. That was not what his father was supposed to say! This was all happening in his mind, after all. He was discovering that when one really lets one's imagination take over it does not always go in the intended direction, especially when talking to those who were a part of you.

'Well,' pursued his father mercilessly, 'you're quite right. If you hadn't called us we wouldn't have been on the road that night.'

'And I suppose your rotten driving had nothing to do with it?' said Spike, intensely annoyed at his father's attempt to spoil the touching little scene he had created. 'Or the bloke behind you who was three times over the alcohol limit?'

'Ah, but isn't all that irrelevant? You wanted to feel guilty so I'm obliging you, you spoilt little plonker. Feeling guilty was what you needed to keep yourself the centre of attention, wasn't it?'

'George!' admonished Spike's mother. 'That's a little bit harsh.'

'Well, I'm sick of him and his guilt. If he wants it, then let him have it. What about Dean? He lost as much as Gregory, but because he had nothing to feel guilty about nobody ever thought of his needs.'

'Actually, now I think about it, it's you who should feel guilty', said

Spike angrily to his father. 'it was your fault you got yourself and Mum killed, leaving us like that. Because of you we...'

Spike drew himself up sharply, shocked by his own anger and bitterness. No, he must not go down that road. That way lay lifelong misery. He rewound the conversation in his head. One can do that.

'Dad's right,' he said, starting again. 'I was useless. Looking at the last four years I see just how hopeless I was. Dean was the one who took charge. I never thought enough of him.'

'But you gave him the strength,' said Lottie, 'even if you didn't always have it yourself. And I think you knew exactly what you were doing. Dean was thrilled to be able to think he was looking after you. And you were more understanding than you pretended to be. You suspected all along that Dean was gay, just as we did. You knew why he took an extra delight in being with you, but you never let on.'

'I'm not sure if that was so kind,' said Spike. 'I should have said something long before the matter came out into the open in such a horrible way. I knew that things couldn't be the same once he knew I knew.'

'And,' his father pointed out, 'it was you who brought things to a head. You deliberately caught him with Jerome. You knew where they were that night and what they were most likely doing.'

'Well, Jerome got on my nerves,' said Spike. 'I wanted an excuse to bop him.'

'What you mean,' said George Porter sternly, 'was that you were frightened someone was at last taking Dean away from you and, if it had to come out into the open, you wanted it to be in such a way that you could appear to be the one who had reason to be most hurt.'

Spike knew that there was no reply to this other than to start crying again. It might cut some ice with his mother at least.

'Oh God!' said his father wearily. 'If it's not coming out one end it's coming out the other!'

'I was wondering when you'd bring that up,' said Spike crossly.

'We're not here just to go on at you,' his mother said, softening as he had expected. 'But you've got to start acting like a grown-up, you know that, don't you? The time's come for you to start being the strong one again.'

'Nothing's going to happen to Dean, is it?' asked Spike anxiously, hoping that his mother did not mean what he thought she meant.

For other another fear had gripped him over the past few years. It was this fear, more than simple prejudice, that had made it difficult to come to terms with his brother's sexuality.

'Not necessarily,' she replied evasively. 'But do you think this move back to the old house is entirely welcome to him? He knows perfectly well that it will be the making of you, and he went along with it all the same, although he doesn't know where it will leave him. Don't forget that, Spike.'

'There's no danger of that,' Spike reassured her.

'And don't forget Dolly and Bill, too. Poor Dolly didn't mean to be so harsh with you. She was just jealous that you always turned to Dean and not to her.'

'I know that, too,' said Spike.

'Well, good. Anyway, I think it's time you got back to the house. They'll start worrying.'

'Don't go yet, Mum,' pleaded Spike.

'I told you, you must be the strong one. And we're not going to be far from you now, you know that.'

'Did you organise all this?' asked Spike, hoping that more questions would keep them longer.

'About the house, you mean? No, we could only hope, though it was you who were hoping really. Start appreciating how lucky you have been.'

'What was so lucky about losing you?' asked Spike, with some reason. 'But yes, I have been lucky in other ways. I've always had so many people around me who care about me. But why should I be so lucky? Wars go on, even here in Europe, people buried in mass graves. And even those who are left have lost far more than I ever did. They must hope, too, but they'll never get back what they've lost, not even their homes.'

'That's true,' said his mother. 'But what did we always teach you, Gregory? It's down to those who are lucky to look out for the ones who aren't so fortunate. Remember that and we'll always be here.'

'You make it sound like an ultimatum,' said Spike.

'It is,' said his mother.

'Come on Lottie,' said his father. 'Let's go before he starts blubbing again.'

'Bye Mum, bye Dad,' said Spike, not too sadly now because he knew that they would always be there for him - just as long as he kept his side of the bargain.

His father's reason for wishing to leave him was not without foundation. Spike knew that he was in no fit state to go back to the house just yet, not if Dean and Marianne were to see the new Spike he wanted them to see. He walked further into the woods and sat in the semi-darkness on the bench carved from a log. There he bawled out a last farewell to his sorrow, a sorrow that for so long had been his constant companion, even closer sometimes than Dean. For happiness was being thrust upon him, or at least the beginnings of the prospect of happiness, should he choose to embrace it. So much was now down to him, and it was a daunting prospect.

Marianne was a little disturbed at the length of time Spike was away, but Dean was reassuring.

'He's gone in the woods to think,' he explained. 'That's what he used to do.'

She noticed, however, that after an hour even Dean began looking apprehensively at his watch every two minutes as they prepared the salad for their evening meal.

At last Spike returned. 'Sorry to have been so long,' he said. 'I went for a little walk.'

They ate cheerfully in the kitchen, both Spike and Dean remarking delightedly at the number of items that had belonged to their parents. Marianne had already gone through the litany with Dean, and knew that the teapot, the mugs and the crockery were all the Porters'. She did not object to hearing it all again, and agreed with Spike, as she had already done with Dean, that the salad bowl, obviously a product of the Newtons' term, was ghastly.

'Mum would never have had that in the house,' Spike observed.

'We'll get rid of it first thing,' Dean agreed.

'No,' said Spike thoughtfully. 'It's a perfectly good salad bowl. It can't help being ugly any more than some people can. You have to have some tatty things in a house, otherwise it isn't a home. This isn't a museum, after all.'

Both Dean and Marianne were a little relieved at this. The fact that it had been something of a museum had delighted them at first, but the practical difficulties of keeping it so had occurred to them both separately. Museums cannot be comfortable places to live in.

'I'm afraid I have to go soon,' said Marianne as they were finishing their cheese and biscuits.

'Why?' asked Spike. The time of Marianne's going had not occurred to him.

'I should have said before. I'm leaving for Switzerland tomorrow. I've arranged to go and see my friend there. I have to pack.'

'How long are you going for?' asked Spike.

'Three weeks.'

Spike looked at her. It was clear that he knew why she was going, and he silently thanked her.

'It'll be December by the time you get back,' he observed. 'What are you doing for Christmas, by the way?'

'Oh,' said Marianne, hoping her heart was not beating too loudly, 'I never do much for Christmas.'

'It's just that I was thinking of asking you to spend it with us here. But I suppose you prefer a quiet time. I'd hate to think you were altering your routine for us.'

He smiled, and she smiled back, her eyes admonishing him for his sarcasm. And yet it was a pleasant sarcasm. He had changed, that she could see. It was almost as though he were in control of the situation.

'And as for this evening,' he went on, 'I want to do what I was looking forward to doing the last time we lived here. I was just coming up to the age when I could, and then it was all snatched away. I want to go on a crawl of the pubs in Wanstead, with you two. And don't say you have to get back to pack, Marianne. I'm sure you can just as easily do that in the morning. You won't be stranded: the last tube's after closing time.'

He spoke with such authority that Marianne would probably not have refused if she had wanted to. The fact that she did not want to made acquiescence all the easier.

And it was indeed an extremely pleasant evening. For the first time there were no secrets between any of them, no repressed feelings that had to be guarded. They started off at the nearest, The Eagle, which was stately and ornate but not exactly humming with atmosphere. It had a restaurant attached, and had more the appearance of a hotel than of a pub. The main bar was not very crowded, but then it was early by Saturday-night standards. They found a table in one of the square bay windows overlooking the main road, and when they were settled Spike began by getting down to business.

'So how much rent did you have in mind?' he asked.

She knew that this would be a tricky subject. She was keenly aware of Spike's pride and a derisory sum would not have gone down well. She had originally planned to say £50 a week, but upped it to £70 on the spur of the moment.

'You'd could get a minimum of 200 a week, fully furnished, and you know it,' he said. 'We can't afford that, but I'm not that hard up and Dean gets his student grant now. Let's say 120.'

Marianne could not help noticing that Dean's smile faded a little at this, although he concurred with Spike's suggestion.

'No,' she said firmly, 'I won't take any more than 80. You have to leave yourselves enough to live on. I don't think you've allowed enough for that. As I've said, for me it's an investment. For the price I paid I can't lose. Trustworthy tenants are worth half the rent, and I'll expect you to do any repairs and redecorating.'

Spike eventually agreed to this, but did make a proviso.

'Okay, but only on condition you come and stay at weekends, and that you consider the main bedroom yours.'

'I won't be able to come every weekend,' she said, trying again to dampen the elation she felt at the suggestion. 'I have my own life to live, you know.'

'Really?' said Spike, 'and what exactly have you done with this life so far?'

She was both delighted and embarrassed by his impertinence. 'I have had my admirers,' she said, trying to inject a hint of jocular mystery.

'I've no doubt you have, but I bet you've succeeded in frightening most of them off. Besides, you can invite your admirers to Snaresbrook sometimes.'

She endeavoured not to let it show but the idea appalled her. The thought of being with the likes of Roger in that beautiful room, with Spike just a staircase away, was too hideous to contemplate. There was only one lover she ever wanted during her sojourns in that house, a fact which, by now, had to be as clear to Spike and Dean as it was to her. And yet she had made up her mind not to pursue such hopes, at least for the time being. Staying with them from time to time would be pleasure enough.

'No,' she said firmly. 'This will be where I come for good company, clean fun and pure air. That's all I want.'

'I shouldn't think the fun will always be that clean once Dean has settled in!' laughed Spike.

'You bet it won't!' Dean concurred.

The business over, they moved on to The Cuckfield. On entering Spike showed the first signs of disappointment.

'It's completely different,' he said. 'It used to have a carpet and lovely armchairs and things. Now it's all plain.'

'But it's been very expensively renovated,' Marianne observed as she surveyed the now polished flooring and the heavy light fittings, 'and it's obviously fairly popular.'

This was an understatement, for the place was positively heaving. Spike apologised that they could not find a table and suggested they move straight on to The George, but Marianne assured him that she quite liked standing. They were surrounded by mainly young people enjoying themselves, and while one or two looked as though they could be a little dangerous if crossed they were, in the main, not so very different from Spike and Dean: stylish, comely and with basic good manners (which were tested as they tried to push their way towards the bar) which she was reassured to find still existed. Many there, she realised, were entering their twenties just as she was leaving hers, and she felt a pang of regret for her wasted years, when she had allowed herself to succumb to the received opinion that it was predominantly a wicked, dangerous world. Did the purveyors of this false message really know the damage they were doing, the happiness they were stifling? Her mother, she knew, would have been appalled at her spending a Saturday night in a suburban pub, perhaps genuinely frightened for her. True, if Marianne had spent the last ten years in such places she might well have come a cropper from time to time, if not there then on the way home. But what could have been worse, more harmful, than spending a lifetime behind a bolted door? The risk would have been worth it. Still, she reflected, she was here now, and in the best company she could ever have imagined.

In a group near them she noticed John Warner, who caught her eye and Spike's at the same time. He joined them.

'Well, what brings you to this neck of the woods?' he asked.

Spike told him, told him that they were back for good, in their old house, that Marianne had bought it and was letting them rent it for next to nothing. Marianne noticed that at last Spike was letting himself get excited, and in his animation she noticed a return of the vitality which had so charmed her when she had known him before. John was thrilled at Spike's news, and within minutes was reintroducing Spike and Dean to several old schoolfriends whose delight at seeing them again was all too tangible. 'Why didn't you keep in touch?' was the universal question to Spike, and Marianne and Dean smiled knowingly at each other as he floundered for an answer.

Any thoughts of a pub crawl ended here, for it was obvious that they would not be allowed to get away. Marianne could have felt a little left out, but was so pleased to see Spike enjoying himself that she did not mind at all that nearly all the conversation was directed at him. Besides, she spent much of the earlier part of the evening talking to John Warner's younger brother, Ralph, a fresh-faced 18-year-old who seemed to have fallen in a little in love with her. Dean, she saw, was amused too as he looked across at them. Marianne and Dean were particularly diverted at the way Ralph spoke in perfect English to Marianne, while reverting to a kind of pseudo-cockney when addressing his friends. Spike had a similar habit. Marianne also had occasion to be amused at Dean's expense, for he was being blatantly chatted up by one of the young ladies present. Hopeful girl! she smiled. At last Spike noticed that Marianne was being left out of the conversation (or rather conversations) in which he was engaged, and made a conscious effort to bring her in. The others followed his cue and began being more attentive to her, though some of them must have been confused as to where exactly she fitted into the story. It seemed to be enough that she was with Spike and she marvelled at the speed with which he seemed to be re-emerging almost as the leader, courted like a monarch returned from exile. Marianne had difficulty following the different interlocutions, but they all delighted her. When she perceived it to be her round she made sure she got a drink for everyone, and everyone responded by making it clear that she had a place among them. At closing time they found themselves being invited to a party that evening.

'Sorry,' said Spike, looking carefully at Marianne and Dean. 'Not tonight.'

'I have to get back,' Marianne agreed, 'but there's no reason why you two shouldn't go.'

'No,' said Spike, and turned to the others. 'We can't make it tonight, but you know where we live. We'll see you all before long.'

Spike and Dean insisted on walking with Marianne to the station.

'Why aren't you going to the party?' she asked. 'Once you've seen me off you can go back and join the others.'

'No,' said Spike. 'This is our first night back in our old house. Now the shock's worn off I want to be able to savour it.'

And she realised that Spike was actually talking to Dean, who looked gratefully back.

'I've had a lovely evening,' Marianne said, as they stood on the platform.

Spike positioned himself in front of her and put his arms round her.

'I haven't thanked you properly,' he said, and she could see his eyes moistening.

'I've told you,' she said, 'it's just an investment for me.'

He smiled at this patent falsehood, then held her to him, unable to speak for two or three minutes. Holding her was easier than having her see his face. At last they could hear the train coming and he pulled away, embarrassed.

'I always seem to disgrace myself in one way or another when I'm with you,' he observed, trying to smile.

'You've never disgraced yourself, Spike,' she said.

'Can we come to the airport with you tomorrow?' he said, remembering his manners.

'That would be a lovely idea,' she said, 'but you have things to do yourself tomorrow. You have to go and pick up the rest of your things, and I think you should spend a little time with Dolly and Bill. I think they're going to miss you.'

The train was now at the station.

'Don't forget you're spending Christmas with us,' he called, as she jumped into the nearest open door.

'I'll have to think about that,' she laughed.

'But you belong with us,' he shouted, as the automatic doors closed.

It was only when she was seated and the train had left the station that his last words sank in. In the novels she had read, or the films she had seen, 'Will you marry me?' or 'I love you' were supposed to be the phrases most sought after by romantically minded women, but the divorce rate had much devalued the first, while the second often owed more to lust and its immediate satisfaction than to commitment. Marianne had never felt any particular longing for either. She saw now that what she had longed for, perhaps all her life, was to hear something like those words 'you belong with us,' all the more valuable, on this occasion, for being so spontaneous. Of course she was aware that they stemmed partly from gratitude, but they were none the less sincerely meant for that: Spike was not glib by nature. She did not know if they would ever become lovers, but at that moment that did not matter to her. He had said enough to make her more than content. And even if her friendship with Spike were eventually to fade (though the thought terrified her) she knew that her old soulless life really was coming to a close. He might think that he had much to thank her for, but it was nothing in comparison with what she owed him.

'Do you really not want to go to the party?' asked Dean as they left the station.

'In a way, I would like to,' said Spike, 'but there's other things I'd rather do tonight. Like look round our house properly, and then sit in the lounge and have a quiet nightcap, just the two of us. Unless you want to go, of course.'

'No, I like your idea better,' Dean smiled.

He tried not to give away just how much more he liked it. Dean had nothing against Marianne, was as grateful to her, indeed, as propriety demanded, but this had been the moment to which he had really been looking forward, when he and Spike could savour together the home which was theirs again. And savour it they did, both aware that it was still really too much to take in fully. And yet, for Dean, it did not bring unqualified pleasure. As they looked again at their two separate bedrooms he felt an unexpected pang of sorrow. He had often looked forward to having a room of his own again, and the obvious possibilities that presented, but now the time had come he realised the full implications of what that meant. There were occasions when a single room could be a lonely room. And

Spike was already different; he could see that just as Marianne had. He could never need Dean as much as he had done during the last four years. It had not occurred to him at the time, but Dean suddenly realised that the years of Spike's dependence on him may well have been his own halcyon years, a time that was now over. That very night they would go to their single bedrooms and two doors would separate them. As they descended the stairs to the lounge and the promised nightcap Dean was unusually quiet, but made a sterling effort to remain cheerful all the same. He did not want to spoil it for Spike.

'Well, you and Marianne certainly thought of everything,' said Spike cheerfully as he took two cans of lager from the refrigerator, and Dean felt relieved that he had not noticed. And yet, as they sat side by side on the settee in the lounge, Spike looked at him thoughtfully.

'This won't make any difference to us, you know,' he said.

Dean knew that this could not be true, even if Spike had meant it to be. Apart from the arrival of Marianne on the scene Spike had already made, or rather rediscovered, several friends in the few hours they had been there. True, they could now be said to be Dean's friends too, but he suspected that the welcome he had received had more to do with his connection to Spike than any merit of his own. It was hardly the sort of neighbourhood that would welcome the arrival of a youth of mixed race with open arms, and they had yet to discover that he was gay. He consciously made an effort to stop himself thinking along those lines. This was hardly the time to play the touchy black on the look-out for signs of disapprobation. It was bloody true, all the same. He could not help remembering his schooldays and the reason why Spike had had to be his protector. He had only been accepted eventually then because of Spike (and could that really be called acceptance?).

'Do you really think I'll forget?' Spike pursued, putting his arm around him. 'Nothing will come between us, nothing.'

'Be careful,' said Dean, trying to joke. 'I might not be able to control myself if you start getting romantic!'

'Oh well, you've controlled yourself all these years, so I don't think I've anything to worry about now. But we both have to grow up eventually. We're luckier than most. We can grow up and be separate people, but not have to be apart. And we can do it gradually, in our own time. Marianne's gone away on purpose to give us some time, so let's make the most of it. We've so much to look forward to.'

'I know,' said Dean, who was aware that the prospect before them was not unexciting, and was cheered immensely by the knowledge that Spike knew something of what he felt. 'I'm going to miss arguing with Dolly, though.'

'Perhaps we should argue more,' laughed Spike. 'We've made a good start, after all. Though I promise not to punch any more of your boyfriends.'

'Some of them would probably enjoy it,' Dean reassured him.

'Tomorrow, though, we must take Dolly and Bill out for a meal, after we've shown them round the house, of course. Dolly's certainly going to miss you.'

'Do you think so?' said Dean, realising for the first time that this was probably true.

'And there is one other thing,' said Spike apologetically. 'I know you'll think I'm a prat, and it won't do my image any good at all, but do you mind if we keep our bedroom doors open for the time being? Remember how we used to be able to see each other from our beds when the doors were wide open? It's just that I haven't been used to sleeping in my own room for so long and I think I'll have to be weaned into it gradually.'

'Oh, Spike!' said Dean, bursting into laughter (because it was the only alternative to bursting into tears) as he realised the extent of Spike's prescience, 'you're magic, absolutely magic!'

'Have I turned into a frog, then?' asked Spike.

'No,' laughed Dean, 'but I know one Frog who fancies you.'

'Hmm,' said Spike, understanding the reference to Marianne. 'Doesn't that bother you just a bit? I have wondered if you approve of her.'

'Of course I don't! I'm a bitchy, jealous queen after all. I'd hate any woman who fancied you. But I suppose I have to be tolerant given that you can't help being straight. Your mum and dad were good judges of character, though, and I know they met her a couple of times. Did you ever find out what they thought about her?'

'Oh yes,' laughed Spike, 'I know that. They thought she was nuts.'

'I think,' said Dean cautiously, 'they might think that all the more if they'd been around over the last few months.'

'I know what you mean,' said Spike thoughtfully, 'but it may be a little too easy to laugh at someone just because they're so obviously doing the chasing. If someone loves you so much it might be worth the effort to try loving them back just a bit.'

Dean found this remark extremely odd, and pondered it many times in the coming weeks. At first it had seemed to be a daft way of thinking, until he started to realise where he might be now if Spike had thought in any other way.

They did keep their bedroom doors open for the first few nights, but then the inevitable happened and Dean brought home a little friend after a night out in the West End. He (and the little friend) came in after Spike had gone to bed, though Spike heard them (hardly surprising since they mounted the stairs singing 'Give Me a Man after Midnight'). He heard Dean's bedroom door being closed and got up to close his own. Broadminded though he might try to be, Spike did not particularly want to hear the details any more than Dean wanted him to hear them. The doors remained closed from then on.

'Oh, Christ!' groaned Dean, putting down his pen crossly. 'Not again!'

If it was not the phone it was the doorbell. Dean was sociable by nature but even he was finding the celebrity status he and Spike had been given in the fortnight or so since their return to their old home a little wearing. Apart from their former schoolfriends, they had Mr and Mrs Porter's old chums to contend with, not to mention the neighbours. The day after their return Spike took it into his head to suggest that they both go to Mass to show their gratitude for the blessings that had been bestowed on them. Personally, Dean was of the opinion that two more hours in bed would be more beneficial of a Sunday morning, but had gone along with the idea since it made Spike happy.

To say they had been mobbed would not have been much of an exaggeration. People turned and looked, took double-takes and began whispering. Dean had a suspicion of what was coming before the consecration, but by communion it was clear that they were the centre of attention for an uncomfortably large proportion of the congregation. Dean knew that, had he been there alone (which was not very likely), he might not have been noticed, but Spike's face had not changed that much in the intervening years. The fatted calf (or at any rate coffee and biscuits) awaited in the parish hall, and thither they were dragged when Mass was over. 'I feel like a bloody pop star,' whispered Dean, trying not to show that he was enjoying it really, even though the fans on this occasion were not 15, 16 and 17 so much as 50, 60 and 70.

Ever since, there had been a stream of visitors, usually bearing gifts, cakes mostly, though Mrs O'Donnell brought along an ashtray the shape of a shamrock and Mr and Mrs Leszczynski turned up with a bottle of Polish vodka for Spike and a picture of Our Lady of Czestochowa for Dean. Spike had been immensely amused. 'I'll keep the vodka in my room,' he said, after they had gone, 'and you can keep the holy picture in yours.'

In addition their friends from Walthamstow came to have a nose round, and a delegation from Lucerne Court in the shape of Daphne, Stella and Jerome also turned up one evening. Now, having realised that fame was not what it was cracked up to be, Dean wished only to be allowed to catch up with his coursework. Clearly this was not to be.

Instead of the pious old lady bearing pastries that Dean had expected to find on the doorstep, he was confronted by Roger Dusalon. It took him a few seconds to realise that this was the chum of Marianne's he had once met at her flat. His surprise must have shown.

'A bit out of context, I know,' said Roger. 'I'm not usually a suburbs person. Nice duck pond, though. I'd assumed Marianne must have been seeing the area through rose-tinted glasses because it's where Spike comes from, but it really isn't bad, though the court looks a bit Hammer Horror from here.'

'Spike's out,' said Dean, a little abruptly. He suspected that Roger had come to check up on them in some way and, despite his pretended scorn for bourgeois values, was almost as offended as Spike and some of their neighbours would have been at hearing their beloved lake described as a duck pond, not to mention the description of the court. Nevertheless, he was in the Porters' old house now, and he felt honour-bound to show something of the hospitality they would have shown to a guest. Roger was invited in and offered a glass of the vodka they had been given (which Spike had not, of course, kept to himself).

'Not bad at all,' repeated Roger, though it was not clear if he was referring to the house or the vodka. He took out a packet of cigarettes and offered Dean one, which made Dean warm to him slightly.

'I suppose your brother wouldn't approve of us smoking in here,' he said.

'Well, he wouldn't say anything,' laughed Dean, 'just give us a pained look.'

'That's remarkably liberal by the standards of most non-smokers these days. I happened to be in the area, so I thought I'd pop in. We're taking over a shop in Woodford. I thought we'd do a few antiques and restoration work as well as our usual range. I've got to recruit some staff. I hope the two I saw today aren't typical of the material in this area.'

'Oh,' said Dean, without much interest. Snooty furniture did not mean a lot to him.

'And, by the way, don't let on to Marianne I came. She might think I'm prying.'

Dean smiled in a way that made his thoughts clear.

'Ah, that's just what you think I'm doing. Well, maybe you're right. But Marianne's invested quite a lot of money in this house, when you think about it. I'd like to see for myself she's done the right thing.'

'And do you think she has?' asked Dean, not sure if Roger had the power to turf them out if he disapproved.

'Well, I suppose that depends on what her motives were,' smiled Roger. 'But I suppose you've wondered about that, too.'

'You obviously have,' said Dean.

'You're more direct than your brother, aren't you?' laughed Roger. 'I think I quite like you. I'm not so sure about Spike, though. He's honest, I can believe that right enough. But I can't say honesty in itself has ever appealed to me much; I only count it a virtue in employees. I certainly wouldn't want many honest friends. You can't trust them.'

Dean laughed at Roger's somewhat Wildean humour.

'This isn't my first domestic visit of the day,' Roger went on. 'I told

Daphne I'd call in on her sister on the way here. I understand Spike restored those fireplaces. I must say I was impressed.'

'Spike has an artistic streak,' Dean confirmed. 'He doesn't like being called artistic, though. Thinks it's the same as poofy.'

'What a right little bore you make him sound,' said Roger. 'But then, Marianne can be pretty boring too.'

'Oh, Spike's not boring!' said Dean. 'I don't think Marianne is, either. Doesn't have to be, anyway. I suppose it's just the company she's been keeping up to now that's made her seem like that.'

'Touché!' laughed Roger.

'And what do you think are Marianne's motives,' asked Dean, picking up on an earlier point.

'Well, I'd have thought that's pretty obvious. She wants to impress Spike. The point is, is she wasting her time?'

Dean reflected. It was obvious that it was not only the house that Roger was checking out.

'I honestly don't know. Spike always sort of idolised her, but even people you've idolised can be somehow different once you get to know them.'

'That's true enough,' Roger agreed. 'And what about you? What sort of couple do you think they'd make?'

Dean thought again, not because he did not know how to answer - he had pondered on the matter himself recently - but he did not know whether it was in order to tell Roger what had been going through his mind. He could not help grinning mischievously, a grin Roger returned, clearly able to read his thoughts. After a few seconds they both burst out laughing simultaneously.

'They'd be ghastly!' Dean chuckled. 'Blissfully happy, I think, but ghastly, at least to people who had to watch them in action. If you think they're quaint now, try imagining them married! They'd live here, of course, and they'd keep it beautifully. Spike would be ever so attentive to her, and she'd worship him. They'd be flawlessly turned out, as they are now, and they'd have friends like themselves. Spike's already met up with quite a few of his old mates, and they all live in nice houses round here and have nice girlfriends, and they'll all live in similarly nice houses when they get married. The blokes will play rugby or football on Sundays, and they'll be allowed the occasional nights out when they'll do all the things predictable straight blokes round here do. If they feel really daring they might do something like stand in a circle and take their trousers down while they sing what for them is a naughty song. One or two will look rather attentively at Spike in his underpants but they'll hope no one is noticing. Other times the women will be with them, of course, and they'll have big group nights out in restaurants in Woodford or Chigwell, or maybe in the Conservative Club, and the women will go to the toilet in packs so they can talk about the men and help each other with their make-up. There may be one or two extra-marital affairs, but you can be sure that won't involve Spike or Marianne. No secret visits to the pox clinic for them.'

'And they'll have children,' said Roger, goading him on.

'Oh, they'll have children. Beautiful children, as you'd expect, and always beautifully dressed. Most of their friends will have children, too, and they'll have birthday parties in each others' houses, and hire blow-up bouncy castles to put in the gardens for the children to play in while the parents look on from the patio, drinking their wine and nibbling the canapés while they discuss house prices...More vodka?'

'Oh, well, maybe I can allow myself one more,' agreed Roger, who was enjoying himself more than he had anticipated.

'Not,' pursued Dean when he had refilled their glasses and accepted another cigarette, 'that you or I will be totally excluded. I might even be allowed to bring along a boyfriend as long as we're discreet and he's respectable looking and is something in the BBC. It'll make their friends feel they're quite liberal really. And they'll take comfort from the fact that I'm only partly black and can't stand rap music in any case. And your brother being an earl will allow you to bring along a tarty blonde half your age and get away with it. Though they'll all pull her to pieces something rotten when you've gone.'

'Ah,' said Roger, 'so Marianne's obviously been telling you about me. But I take it Spike's old chums are not exactly your kind of people?'

'In some ways Walthamstow's more me than this area, though I'm glad we were able to come back to this house. His friends aren't really that bad, I suppose, but I somehow wonder if Spike's really like them. Perhaps what I'm really saying is that I'm frightened he might become more like them. They reckon themselves a bit.'

(Dean was hardly likely to say so, but his ambivalent feelings

162

towards Spike's friends had a more specific origin. For the previous Saturday night some of them had been in The George when the subject of John Warner's sexuality had cropped up. 'You'd never have guessed that guy was gay in a million years,' Phil Corrie had said. 'That's what I thought,' Jerry Piper had concurred, almost with admiration, 'I couldn't believe it for months until he turned up last New Year's Eve with that boyfriend of his. He doesn't act like a poof at all.' 'His boyfriend looked like a proper bloke too,' conceded someone else. Dean thought that this would be an excellent opportunity to step out from the closet himself. Expecting gasps of astonishment he announced: 'Actually, I'm gay, too!' They all looked at him with the most unsurprised countenances he had ever seen. 'Oh, yeah, we thought so,' Jerry Piper had said, and the subject changed to football. The worst of it was that Spike had chuckled to himself for a good quarter of an hour after this exchange had taken place.)

'Marianne thought very highly of Spike's parents,' said Roger. 'But then, she didn't know them that well, did she? Surely they must have had some faults?'

Dean looked at Roger in some surprise. Nobody had ever asked him that question before. Surely Roger did not really expect him to slag off Lottie and George to a comparative stranger. What was he to say? That they were perfect in every way? Nobody had ever known it, but Dean did not think that at all. They had been guilty of one fault, or rather one glaring omission, which some might have found trivial but which to Dean was enormous, even though it did not affect him directly. For a terrible moment he almost thought he would blurt it out to Roger, almost started to, in fact.

'Well,' he conceded, 'even the best people can forget to do something they should have done...'

'Oh yes,' said Roger. 'Yes, of course. His father didn't sort out his financial affairs very well, did he? You'd think he'd have got insurance or something to make sure Spike and you were not left with nothing.'

Dean breathed a sigh of relief. That was not, in fact, the omission he had in mind, but it was another one, one which he did not mind touching upon.

'Well, he didn't expect to go like that when he did. He just got himself killed at the wrong time. It's a pity Spike's not more

Marianne's equal financially, though. I suspect he won't ever consider popping the question until he is.'

'I can see that,' Roger agreed. 'He'd have to tile a lot of bathrooms and restore a lot of fireplaces to catch up. Do you think he could go on to further education?'

'Oh, yes. I've always been thankful his parents were killed just after he took his GCSEs and not before. He did quite well. Now he's getting his confidence back he could carry on from there.'

'But,' Roger pointed out, 'Marianne is a bit older than him. If they were to want to have children and all the rest of it wouldn't be advisable to hang around too long. Perhaps it might be best for him to go for a job where his existing skills would be useful.'

'Well, it's a competitive world nowadays,' said Dean. 'A bit of further education would be an advantage. Unless...'

Dean stopped to consider. The germ of an idea was forming in his mind. Just how far was Roger prepared to go in helping things along?

'Unless what?' asked Roger, showing interest.

'Well, what I mean is...Well, Spike has had some experience in the retail trade. I mean, he works in a pub some evenings. He's very highly thought of. And as you've said, he's good at restoring things. Maybe with just a little training he could extend those talents a bit...'

'I must say,' said Roger, knowing perfectly well what Dean was driving at (he should have done since he had deliberately put out the bait), 'I've never thought of a pub as the retail trade, though I suppose at a stretch it could be considered so. I imagine he must certainly have had experience with awkward customers. And as I've said I had considered that the shop I have in mind for Woodford would involve some restoration work if we do decide to go in for the antique side. He'd have to do some training for that, maybe go on a course of some sort. Mind you, I've promised the manager's post to someone else. Old bloke. From our Kensington High Street branch.'

'How old?' asked Dean bluntly.

'Well, retires in six months, actually. He lives out here somewhere. I thought he could set the place up before I give him his fake gold watch. Wean someone else in, as it were.'

Dean took a deep breath. 'Do you think Spike could be the one he weans in?'

'Good heavens!' said Roger, looking amused at Dean's naiveté. 'It

164

takes years to work your way through the ranks in our organisation. For a very young man to be considered he would have to be exceptionally talented, exceptionally honest, exceptionally presentable-and exceptionally cheap.'

'How cheap?'

'Well, during the training period not more than 12,000 a year. As manager maybe 18,000, perhaps rising to 20 after a year or so of proving himself.'

'How about 15,000 to begin with?' suggested Dean hopefully.

Roger laughed. 'You really don't know much about this trade, do you? Or about me. An aspiring young revolutionary like you must have noticed that my main aim in life is to grind the faces of the labouring masses. If I weren't underpaying them it would have to mean I was overpaying them, and that would make me lose sleep at night. Mind you, now I think about it Spike speaks French, doesn't he? That could be handy for negotiating deals on the Continent. Maybe that could be worth an extra thousand or so.'

'Oh yes,' said Dean. 'He's practically bilingual. Though in some careers you probably reach the top quicker if you're bisexual. Anyway, I don't think you're as bad as you pretend to be. You don't want Marianne to think of you as a mean old fart, do you?'

'Oh, good Lord, she knows that already. If I pretended to change now, she'd wonder what I was up to. Anyway, enough of that. I want to have a look around this little investment of hers.'

Dutifully, Dean showed him round the house. He knew that someone of Roger's background could not possibly be as impressed as some of their other recent guests, but he was gratified by the (almost) polite admiration the tour evinced. He saved the dining room until last, as this was generally considered (by everyone except Marianne, who liked the main bedroom overlooking the lake) to be the best room in the house. Shortly before his death George Porter had had it extended into what had been a separate conservatory. This had been to accommodate the fairly long dining table as well as the large sideboard and bookcase. The only two original oil paintings were also in this room, two depressing views (in Dean's opinion) of a late Victorian shopping street on a winter evening.

'Reproduction stuff, of course,' he said apologetically, in an attempt to neutralise any possible look of contempt from Roger.

'Well, no doubt,' said Roger, 'but that doesn't automatically mean it's rubbish. Sometimes...'

Roger stopped suddenly. Reproduction? Unless years of experience counted for nothing, this was no reproduction furniture. On the contrary, it was one of the finest examples of a George III mahogany pedestal dining table he had ever seen. Instinctively he took one of the chairs and turned it over, gasping with delight at the joinery and the hand-cut screws. He went to look at the paintings.

'Pretty grim, aren't they,' said Dean.

'Not grim,' laughed Roger. 'Grimshaw. Atkinson Grimshaw.'

'Oh!' said Dean, rather surprised that they should be by a recognisable artist, not that he had ever heard of him.

'Tell me,' said Roger curiously, 'how much was the house sold for when the Porters were killed?'

'Well, for just a tad less than Marianne paid to get it back, I think.'

'And all this furniture was included?'

'Yes, and it was included when Marianne bought it. I suppose the Newton's didn't think it was worth the hassle of shipping it to America, though apparently they said a dealer had offered them a thousand quid for it. There was a nice grandfather clock here but they took that. Said it was worth a couple of thousand so they couldn't let it stay.'

Roger sat down on one of the chairs and, leaning on the table, put his head in his hands in comic despair. The shock over, he started laughing. Clearly, nobody involved in either transaction had any knowledge of antique furniture (though the 'dealer' who had offered a thousand pounds no doubt had). They say that two wrongs don't make a right, he thought, but two prats obviously can. It looked as though George Porter had left insurance after all. Perhaps only his wife had known about it. That certainly had been bad planning, getting themselves killed together like that. Roger got up and scrutinised the bookcase.

'This is George II. Look at the dentil moulded cornice with the broken swan-neck pediment. Kentian.'

'I always thought it smelled funny,' said Dean.

'You'd smell funny if you were 250 years old,' said Roger.

And then Roger noticed the flying ducks. 'What on earth are they?' he asked in disbelief.

'Oh, them,' said Dean. 'Spike found them in the garage and put them back up. His father had put them there originally. He thought it was a funny touch. I think it his was his way of saying he didn't take all this crap seriously.'

Nobody else had understood the humour behind it but Roger did. It was not difficult to imagine the Porters' snootier guests laughing with each other at this gauche intrusion, unaware that the joke was really on them for thinking it mattered. But was it entirely a joke? Who could possibly imagine that such valuable pieces could be in a room with flying ducks on the wall? Not that he thought it wise to let on to Dean about their probable value. He could be mistaken, but doubted it very much.

'I have to go soon,' said Roger. 'But I'll let you give me a cup of coffee before I do, if that's okay with you.'

At Roger's suggestion, the coffee was taken in the kitchen which, he had deduced from the open newspaper on the table, was the room they probably relaxed in most. Cosy kitchens had held a fascination for Roger since his childhood, probably because of the contrast they presented to the austerity of public school and comparative coldness of the more formal rooms in his own ancestral home. He had always considered it a treat to be allowed to visit the kitchen and enjoy coffee drunk from a mug, accompanied by a large slice of fruit cake or apple pie. He was aware that the hospitality he had encountered there was based to a large extent on deference, but he had thought he detected an element of genuine warmth, too.

Dean apologetically moved the paper away, with a hint of embarrassment as he realised that Roger could not have helped noticing that it was the *Daily Mail*.

'Spike's not one of the greatest intellectuals around,' he said, as though anxious to let Roger know that it had not been his choice.

'Thank goodness for that,' said Roger. 'I wouldn't want to employ him if he was some kind of *Guardian*-wielding wanker.'

'Oh,' said Dean. 'So you would consider employing him?'

'That's really why I came,' laughed Roger. 'I was going to offer 20,000 straight away and 30 after training, but I like the deal you've negotiated for him better.'

At first alarmed at his big mouth, Dean relaxed a little when it occurred to him that Roger would not have mentioned his original intention if he had no plans to go through with it.

'But can you just make up your mind to give him the job without interviewing other candidates?' asked Dean. 'I mean, what's your equal opportunities policy?'

'My what?'

'Oh, never mind,' said Dean. He was not too fussed about favouritism if Spike was to be the one favoured, though such generosity from one such as Roger gave rise to other suspicions.

'It's for Marianne rather than Spike that you're doing this, isn't it?' said Dean, seating himself after he had made the coffee and offered Roger a piece of the fruit cake Mrs Douglas had brought in that morning.

'Well, of course. I hardly know Spike. Though I hasten to add that I wouldn't be offering him a job unless I was sure, from what I do know, that he'd give value for money.'

'Oh, he'd do that all right. But supposing he and Marianne don't hit it off after all. Would he be out on his ear?'

'Of course not, not if he was good. What sort of man do you take me for? I'd simply cut his wages.'

Dean smiled, assuming that Roger was joking. But there was another question he had to ask, one which it would be best to get out of the way as soon as possible.

'And Marianne,' he said with some caution. 'Do you still want to...'

Dean paused. The question was more difficult to put than he had realised. Roger helped him out.

'If you're trying to ask what I think you are, the answer's no. I won't be claiming any *droit de seigneur*. But I can understand your suspicions. You want to know what's in this for me. Well, I suppose it's partly because I owe Marianne. I'd like her as a friend, but she's somehow incomplete. We both know what will make her more complete. Yes, I think I'd like to have friends like her and Spike. I want to be able to visit here sometimes and sit in this kitchen eating cake, or be invited to dinner and listen to you taking the piss out of them.'

'As if!' laughed Dean. 'Anyway, it'll most probably all turn out to be a waste of time. They'll never really get together when it comes to it. They're so fucking polite they'll blow it.'

'Left to themselves I've no doubt they would,' agreed Roger. 'It looks like it's down to us to make sure they don't!'

CHAPTER SIX

Marianne had been deliberately vague to Spike and Dean about the date of her return to England lest it appear that she was angling to be met at the airport. She had never had a welcoming committee before and could manage quite well without one now. What she was really looking forward to was seeing them settled in their new home (or rather their old one).

It was the cosiness of it all that struck her when she finally arrived. She had loved the house before, even when it was not lived in, but nothing prepared her for what she encountered. The gorgeous smell of the roast beef in the oven, the aroma of the coffee prepared for her, the comfortable cleanness, reminded her of the dreams she had harboured while at her somewhat stark boarding school. She had seen similar interiors through lighted windows on the way back from the playing fields to the school, had even caught the aromas as she passed. They were simple enough homes in comparison with the ambitions her mother harboured on her behalf, but she came to associate comparative smallness with warmth. She had fantasised about being invited in to share that warmth, to be served a meal at a table with a pretty tablecloth instead of the cold refectory tables for which she was bound. (True, she enjoyed home comforts during the holidays, but these were always marred by the knowledge that they would be all too brief.)

She had been a little afraid that Spike (and, to a lesser extent, Dean) might try to go too far in restoring the atmosphere which had prevailed when Lottie and George had lived there but, too far or not, this was one restoration which met her full approval. She knew instinctively that something like this ambience was what would have met Spike on his arrival home from school or on a Sunday when he had been playing rugby.

'It's all so lovely!' she could not help saying.

'It should be,' whispered Dean. 'He's been working non-stop for the last month.'

The faint smell of pine cleaner emanating from the woodwork bore testimony to Dean's statement.

Spike, who had been upstairs when she arrived, emerged and she saw at once that he was different. His shyness had disappeared almost completely and he even seemed physically bigger. Marianne was momentarily a little frightened by the change: in some ways the new Spike might be more forbidding than the old one - certainly more difficult to handle. But the warmth of his greeting reassured her. This Spike would take some getting used to, that's all. She suspected it was going to be worth the effort.

She hadn't realised that Spike was such a good cook, and complimented both in word and deed, for she found their appetites infectious.

'Oh, it's only simple stuff. Anyone can do mad cow,' he reasoned modestly.

'Well,' she said, 'I've had disasters with it. And the vegetables need a certain knack, at least to come out like this. Cauliflower cheese isn't easy, not to mention the Yorkshire pudding.'

'It's easy enough when the cheese sauce comes out of a packet,' he laughed. 'My mum taught me how to do the Yorkshire pudding.'

'Well, you remembered it pretty well, obviously,' she said. 'I'm beginning to get quite an inferiority complex.'

Spike did not tell her that he had gone into the woods that afternoon and asked Lottie to run through it again with him.

'If the trifle looks suspiciously like Sainsbury's,' Spike said, as he laid the dessert before them, 'it's because they're always copying my ideas.'

'Looks delicious to me,' said Marianne, and laughed as a witticism occurred to her. 'I suppose your father would say it was a mere trifle.'

'No,' said Spike thoughtfully. 'I don't think even my father would have told a joke that was quite as bad as that.'

Marianne looked at him, nonplussed for a moment, then spotted the slight flicker on the deadpan expression. So she was to be made fun of, too. Her joy knew no bounds. This was acceptance, Porter style.

'Was your mother a good cook?' she asked, testing the water to see if it would be possible at last to speak normally about Lottie and George.

'Oh yes,' said Spike, as she had expected, but he then added: 'except for her curry.'

'Oh God, yes,' Dean laughed. 'George used to say that her curry reminded him of that song from the musical *Oliver!*.'

'Oh, "Food, Glorious Food"?' Marianne supposed.

'Oh no,' said Spike, 'the one with the line: "Never before has a boy wanted more".' She always said she'd carry on trying until she got it right, and she did, although we tried to persuade her that she really needn't go to the trouble. She began doing it whenever she was cross about something, like the time we pretended to forget her birthday. That time something went wrong though, and she realised the curry was really going to be quite good, so she boiled the rice for an extra twenty minutes so that it became all sludgy.'

'How about your mother, though?' asked Spike when they had finished laughing. 'Was she a good cook?'

Marianne was a little thrown by the question. In truth her mother had not cooked a great deal, though she could rustle up the occasional French rustic dish she remembered from her earlier years. These efforts had been passable, though Alexandrine had also had the occasional disaster. Marianne wished that she knew how to turn some of these into an amusing story as Spike and Dean would doubtless have been able to do (her father's face had indeed been a picture sometimes as he suffered in silence). Had she that kind of humour, she sensed, she might be able to remember her parents in a slightly different light. It was too late now though, wasn't it?

'Oh,' she said, wishing to pass over the question as quickly as possible, 'she was okay.'

They told her of their plans for that evening. Apparently they had spent quite a few evenings over the past four weeks meeting up with Spike's old friends, and now Dean had finally prevailed upon Spike to agree to go out with him to one of his haunts.

'He put off agreeing to come until you were here protect him,' Dean explained.

After dinner, Spike showed her to her room, which had obviously been prepared with great care. It was not unlike a five-star hotel bedroom (well, four-star anyway), right down to the fresh flowers, the telephone next to the bed and the small, beautifully wrapped box of chocolates on the pillow (a touch Spike probably remembered from the hotel in the rue du Roule). Some deep-piled rugs had also been added, and there were three pleasant prints, ones she had admired in the art shop in the High Street when she and Dean had taken time out while preparing the house for Spike's return.

'It's beautiful!' she said. 'But why have you given me this room? By rights surely you should be in the master bedroom now.'

'Oh, I like my little room upstairs,' he said.

She looked out of the window at the lake. If anything, it looked more beguiling at night than during the day.

'Did any queen ever have a lovelier view?' she asked.

'Probably not,' he laughed. 'There's one queen whose room faces the back.'

'But all this must have cost quite a bit,' she said, turning from the window to survey the room again.

'Well,' he said, looking a little embarrassed, 'I think we can just about afford it. I've got a new job.'

He had been waiting for the right moment to tell her, but now realised that there was no right moment as such. A little hesitantly he explained that he had started working in the new shop that Roger had opened that week. He also felt obliged to tell her of the rather bizarre interview the week before, which had consisted solely of a pub lunch with Roger at which he was not asked a thing about his qualifications and experience, but much about his parents, what he thought of Marianne, and his attitude to weedy, teetotal vegetarian types. Fortunately, the way the questions were framed always gave a strong clue as to what the answers should be. He ordered rump steak, agreed with Roger's suggestion that they have a second bottle of claret (though while Roger was in the gents he managed to pour away one glass into a half-finished pint of bitter left on a nearby table), and slipped in that he had started playing rugby again. He passed with flying colours.

Marianne's reaction was much as he had anticipated.

'Hmm, I wonder what he's up to?' she mused, and immediately felt a little guilty at putting a damper on what to Spike must have been an excellent break. 'Of course, it could just be that he likes you and trusts you,' she smiled. 'Even Roger has a soul somewhere, although he sometimes pretends to have mislaid it. Congratulations, Spike. It gives us a pleasant extra reason for going out and having a good time this evening.'

(A few days later Marianne was to receive a visit from Roger and was able to tackle him about his interview with Spike. In response to her enquiry he replied, not without some mischievous intent, that he could not decide if Spike was another Brad Pitt or another Berty Wooster. Instead of the outrage he had expected she simply nodded in thoughtful agreement.)

Dean's plan was that they should go to a large and popular cabaret pub on Commercial Road, another area new to Marianne. 'We can get the tube to Mile End and take a taxi from there,' he had suggested. She could not help noticing how excited he was becoming at the prospect of the evening out. It would be his first trip to a gay venue with Spike, and he was clearly looking forward to showing him off. His enthusiasm was infectious, for Spike was also in a frivolous mood by the time they departed.

They decided to have a first drink in The Eagle before catching the tube. The place to which they were going had a late licence, which gave them time enough. Marianne and Dean seated themselves while Spike went to get a round in. They were bemused to see him approached, while at the bar, by a well (if plainly) dressed woman in her late twenties. She said something to him and he shook his head, and the lady looked decidedly disappointed as she returned to a table near them.

'What was that about?' asked Dean when Spike rejoined them.

'She asked me if my name was Keith,' whispered Spike. 'I think she's meeting someone from a dating agency.'

Both Spike and Dean seemed to find this amusing enough, but Dean suddenly began shaking uncontrollably, for he was the first to notice that a man who had been seated near them (next to them, in fact, though behind a low partition) was approaching the lady. The man was in his thirties, wearing a cheap suit and a gaudy tie. His hair was thinning dramatically, a fact he had inadvertently accentuated by trying to cover the area with a few long hairs combed over from the side.

'I'm Keith,' he introduced himself. 'Penny, is it?'

'Oh er...yes,' she admitted, and allowed herself to be escorted to his table.

'What a plonker!' whispered Dean uncharitably.

'Don't be so quick to judge people,' said Spike virtuously, as though he had not thought exactly the same himself. To Spike and Dean's obvious annoyance, the couple's conversation was drowned out by a rowdy group of youths who entered at that moment. Having purchased some drinks, however, they moved round to the other side of the bar.

'And what do you do in your spare time,' the bloke was asking.

'Well, I have so little spare time, what with my mother and the cats,' the woman replied. 'A group of us from the office sometimes go bowling. How about you?'

'Train-spotting, I expect,' whispered Dean.

'People say I look like a train-spotter,' said the bloke (making Dean look like a bit of a twit, which Spike enjoyed), 'but I don't know one end of a train from another. No, I help out a lot in the church, in fact people see me as the vicar's right-hand man. If I have a hobby at all it's collecting old cigarette cards. I've got over two-thousand.'

('Well, that's really put those of us who thought he was a train-spotter in our place,' smirked Dean.)

'Have you met many people?' asked the woman, 'I mean through the agency?'

'Well, only one. A disaster, I'm afraid. Brazilian. After the passport, I suppose. I thought Jenny was supposed to weed out people like that. And I'd specifically said a non-smoker but she lit up almost as soon as she saw me. Said she just wanted the one to calm her down, but she had four or five during the evening.'

(Dean mouthed an 'ooh' of mock horror at this outrage.)

'And has there ever been anyone before that?'

'Well, I did have a young lady I was seeing years ago, but she became a missionary. In Angola now.'

'And so what do you look for in a woman?'

'Oh, somebody not too flighty. Somebody who'll help me piece together the complicated jigsaw of life.'

Dean happened to be taking a swig of beer as the bloke said this, with the result that he choked badly, spilling some of it onto his shirt. Even Marianne, who could not at first understand what was so amusing, felt herself succumbing and assumed that the couple must realise by now that they were being overheard. Fortunately, some taped music began playing, making it practically impossible for them to hear any more. Spike and Dean were still laughing as they made their way to the Tube station.

Marianne had come to like travelling on the Tube, having discovered that there was usually someone interesting to study. Spike and Dean obviously felt the same, and they looked around for someone to laugh at the moment they boarded. As it happened the selection was pretty unremarkable on this occasion.

'They're all boring from Snaresbrook out,' Dean said. 'Middle-class reactionaries like you two, mainly. Let's see who gets on at Leytonstone.'

Leytonstone did not appear to yield much of interest either, nor Leyton. But at Stratford two very flustered elderly ladies entered through the door near them. They did not sit down immediately, reluctant it seemed, to believe they were on the right train.

'Does this go to Marble Arch?' asked one of them.

'Yes, all the way,' said Dean.

They sat down, relieved.

'We got on the wrong train coming.'

'The wrong train,' echoed her companion. 'She's quite right.'

'We went the wrong way.'

'The wrong way, that's right.'

'We got on at Tottenham Court Road and I began to think it was a long way.'

From the North, by the sound of it.

'Are you visiting London?' asked Spike politely.

'We won a prize in a raffle. A weekend in London.'

'Enjoying it?' asked Dean.

'Everything's so dear,' wailed the first.

'It's a nice hotel, but so dear. A cup of coffee, ninety pee.'

'Ninety pee. And set dinner's fifteen pounds.'

'So we don't have our dinner there.'

'And they don't take our Leeds passes on the buses here.'

'No!' said Dean.

'And you can't make head nor tail of the tubes. We were hoping to go to the Tower of London tomorrow. God knows how we'll find it.'

'The Tower of London's dear,' said Dean.

'Is it? How much do you think it would cost, then?'

'Oh, about five or six quid, I think,' said Spike.

Their faces simultaneously contorted into horror.

'You get a nice view from the outside,' said Spike helpfully.

'We'll do that then.'

'Trafalgar Square and lots of other sights are worth seeing,' said Spike, 'and they won't cost you anything. And the art galleries and museums are mostly free.'

'Oh, we can't be doing with museums, not with our legs. We did think of going down to Hampton Court, though. It might be worth seeing in spite of our legs.'

'If it's not too dear.'

'You may get in cheaper if you're pensioners,' said Spike, and added gallantly: 'but I suppose that wouldn't apply to you.'

'Oh, you!' they laughed, and seemed to cheer up.

'You're not out with your girlfriend tonight, then?' said the elder to Dean, who was seated on the other side of Spike from Marianne.

'I haven't got time to find a girlfriend,' said Dean, 'what with my mother and the cats. And it's so dear.'

'He does go train-spotting, though,' Spike chipped in.

'Well, it's nice to have a hobby. And are you two married?'

'No,' said Spike sadly, 'this lady is a nun. She's come from Angola to collect for her mission there. She's been in a missionary position for most of the last ten years. I'm still waiting for someone to help me piece together the complicated jigsaw of life.'

'That's quite right,' they said.

'He's the vicar's right-hand man,' said Dean.

They reached Mile End.

'Another eight stops for you,' said Spike as they got off.

'Ooh, thank you,' said the two old ladies gratefully, and it was clear that they were much happier than when they had boarded the train.

As planned, they took a taxi the rest of the way, informing the driver that they were from Leeds, having won their trip to London in a raffle. Dean got the next round in ('It's so dear.' 'You're quite right') and then suggested they make their way to the quieter end, away from the more crowded disco part of the very large pub ('What! With my legs?' said Marianne, finding herself entering into the spirit of things).

Dean actually had an ulterior motive for wanting to go to that end of the pub, for a little group of his friends were there. Spike clearly had the impact on them that Dean had anticipated, and Marianne noted how he glowed with pride as he introduced his brother. Poor Dean, she reflected, how long had he waited for this moment?

The group were all standing, except for one of their number who was seated at a table next to them. That he was with them was obvious from the way they looked down and spoke to him from time to time, and at first both Marianne and Spike wondered why he kept himself apart. Marianne thought she recognised the lived-in face, and had a feeling that the circumstances in which she had last seen it had not been pleasant. Then she remembered the repulsive creature who had insulted her and Daphne in The Kitchener Arms when they had first visited Walthamstow. And yet she could not but forgive, as she soon realised that he sat because he had difficulty standing, a difficulty that had nothing to do with inebriation. He was very thin, too, and (she felt guilty for thinking it) even uglier than before. The diagnosis was obvious enough; the prognosis, unfortunately, equally so.

'I suppose we'd better sit down for a minute with Ian,' said Dean, with a certain reluctance. 'Do you remember Ian? He used to go to into the Kitchener's sometimes. Lives on Forest Road.'

Marianne noticed the recognition in Spike's face, and the split second of horror which passed across it. But his smile was genuine enough as they all sat down.

'We haven't seen you for a while,' said Spike, shaking Ian's hand.

'I haven't been able to get out much,' replied Ian. 'I didn't think I'd see you in a place like this. So Dean finally persuaded you to come along. And is this your girlfriend?'

'Yes,' said Spike, making up for his earlier denial to the two old ladies on the tube. Although made as part of a jest, it had hurt Marianne just a little.

'Remember that argument we had over my change?' Ian mused. 'It was only a tenner I'd given you after all. I found the twenty-pound note in my pocket when I got home.'

'You didn't come back to tell me,' said Spike, smiling despite the censure.

'No, I know. I meant to,' (they all knew he was lying, of course), 'but I came down with pneumonia. You can probably guess what it is.'

They were interrupted by someone saying: 'The cabaret's starting!' and most of the little group near them began making their way to the other part of the pub.

'You've been saved by the bell,' said Ian, who had obviously noticed Spike's unease.

'We'll come back and see you afterwards,' promised Dean.

Any distress Spike felt at seeing Ian's plight was, temporarily at least, dissipated by the crush around the cabaret area. For on this occasion the star attraction was the well-known drag queen Chastity Crotchsniff ('The Mother of all Cackles', according to the billboard), renowned for her appalling singing voice and her vicious tongue, so vicious, in fact, that people of a nervous disposition tended to want to be as far away from her as possible lest they become her victims. Thus, although plenty of people wished to see her, few actually wanted to be near her. Naively, Spike and Marianne thought they were lucky to be pushed to the front. Dean had an idea what could happen but found it more amusing to keep his own counsel.

She started with a rendition of 'Waiting at the Church', which was apparently her signature tune. Some of the audience joined in, as they were supposed to, while others made a point of making it clear they were above all that. Dean participated, as Marianne would expect, but she was pleasantly surprised to see that Spike was doing so, too.

The sing-song over, Miss Crotchsniff started up on those members of the audience she had clocked as suitable targets. The first was a sitting duck, a gawky-looking queen in a suit.

'Your suit looks nice, Chuck. Just like the one we buried our dad in. I think he looked better in it though, he had more colour than you've got. Mind you, I like a man in a suit. I don't go in for casual sex meself.'

This was tame (not to say dated) stuff, and Dean guessed she was just warming up. She spied a group of lesbians.

'I see the dykes are in tonight! Hello my love, I've seen you around before, haven't I?' - she was talking to a plump girl in the middle of the group. 'Have you lost some weight?' The girl confirmed that she had, obviously pleased that her efforts had been noticed. 'Yes,' Miss Crotchsniff concurred, 'I thought you were looking shorter.'

That was nasty, Marianne thought. The drag queen's eye caught her, Spike and Dean. Marianne could feel Spike freezing.

'Now there's a man who's never been known to say no,' she said, looking towards Dean, 'though rumour has it he once said "enough".'

'I'd say no to you, don't worry,' said Dean. The audience seemed to love it, and Dean was obviously marked down in her book for further treatment after the next song, 'Walking Back to Happiness.'

'Don't get her going on us,' hissed Spike frantically, though all too late.

'Now that man's a priest,' announced Miss Crotchsniff as she pointed to a well-known clergyman who was often to be seen on the more right-on religious programmes on television. 'He's been unfrocked but he still holds a collection every time his friends come round.'

She approached a boy near them and asked if she could kiss him.

'Better not, I've had a curry and I've got bad breath.'

'Bad breath's the least of your problems, my love.'

'It's not the least of yours,' shouted Dean.

'Ooh, I see we've got a right little comedian in tonight. Mind you, with a face like that what else could he be?' Suddenly she noticed Marianne. 'Ooh, my dear, you do look nice. But if you don't mind my saying so you've made the same mistake a lot of cross-dressers make. You haven't dressed like a woman, you've dressed like a drag queen. It's a good forty years since a real woman dressed like that.'

The audience roared with delight, except for Spike who looked for a moment as though he was about to punch Miss Crotchsniff who, to give her credit, was not remotely intimidated.

'Don't worry, my love, it's all in good fun. I wouldn't really insult your friend's outfit. I know her mother must have saved a lot of coupons for that dress. Ooh, but you're a bit of a looker yourself, aren't you? But don't get excited boys, he's too butch and thick-looking to be gay. Any woman who doesn't fancy him can't be a lesbian.'

Having said this Miss Crotshsniff wisely retreated a few steps (though she had more time on her side than she realised, for it took Spike a little while to work out her exact meaning) and burst into 'Bird in a Gilded Cage.' Dean and Marianne judged it best to give the rest of the cabaret a miss and dragged a fuming Spike back to the quieter part of the pub. 'Evil old bitch!' was one of the nicest things he had to say about the artiste. 'If it was a bloke, I'd have punched his head in.'

They noticed that Ian was sitting alone at his table, abandoned for the moment. They asked him if he would like a drink and Spike sat with him while Dean went with Marianne to the bar.

'It's a bit unkind of the others to go off and leave Ian,' Marianne observed as they waited to be served.

'Oh, none of us here are really his friends,' said Dean. 'I don't think he has many. He always had a reputation for being a nasty piece of work. You can bet he knew what he was doing that time he diddled Spike in The Kitchener's. That was typical of him.'

'Well, really,' Marianne admonished, 'I think that now of all times you should all forgive and forget.'

'Well, we do try. But he's not beyond a bit of shit-stirring even now. People don't always become saints just because they've got Aids.'

On their return Marianne was pleased to see that Spike, at least, was deep in conversation with Ian.

'I think you should get in touch with them,' Spike was saying as she and Dean sat down.

'Oh, they chucked me out and said they didn't want to know me seven years ago,' said Ian. 'I can't see why I should make contact now. They'll only want to find out what they can filch from the flat when I'm gone. My dad's probably dead, anyway. Had asbestosis then.'

'And haven't you wanted to find out about them? You must have been curious,' said Spike, clearly shocked at the existence of such unfeeling families.

'No, why should I? She's not my real mother anyway, the fat old tart.'

'But things would be different now, surely?'

'Drop it, Spike,' said Dean softly.

'I always hoped you were gay,' Ian mused, looking at Spike. 'You used to dress a bit like a gay.'

'Well, yes,' laughed Spike. 'A certain person had something to do with that.'

The cabaret over, the others were returning. They ragged

Marianne and Spike over the insults they had endured at the hands
(or rather the mouth) of Miss Crotchsniff and then one of the boys
(the campest, in fact, with a refined Edinburgh accent which made it
inevitable that he was called Miss Brodie by the others) prevailed on
Marianne to go to the dance floor with him and a couple of the
others. She suspected, from the more pointed questions that were
interspersed with the jokes, that they wanted to find out from her if
Spike really was straight.

'I hope you're not too disappointed,' she said when the position
was made clear to them.

'Well, as long as you bring him along sometimes for us to look at.'

'Well, you can look,' she laughed, flattered on Spike's behalf
(anyone who agreed with her that Spike was worthy of attention had
to be counted a friend), 'but you mustn't touch.'

As the evening came to a close they noticed that Ian was carefully
counting his money on the table. Sensing that he was likely to have
difficulty with his cab fare Spike offered to drop him off in theirs
(although it was not really on their way).

'He's always doing that,' Dean said to Marianne as they collected
their coats.

'Who always does what?' she asked.

'Ian. That counting his money for the cab fare trick. He knows
someone will offer to drop him off. Trust Spike to be the mug this
time.'

When the taxi pulled up outside his flat on Forest Road Ian invited
them in for a drink. Dean seemed reluctant, but Spike and Marianne
somehow felt that it would be unkind to refuse. They had deduced
enough to suspect that Ian did not have much company and that he
secretly craved it.

It had to be the most revolting flat Marianne and Spike had ever
entered (Dean seemed less surprised, and this, together with the way
he had led the way in, suggested that he had been there before). It
was roomy enough, but grime covered the cheap and battered furniture and there were half a dozen ashtrays filled to the brim. An odd
smell, a mixture of cannabis, tobacco and mildew, met them the
moment they entered.

'I've got a bottle of plonk somewhere,' said Ian, struggling with difficulty to the kitchen. He could walk, but only just. A reluctant Dean

went to help him, leaving Marianne and Spike in embarrassed silence.

They smiled as though grateful when the grubby glasses of wine were handed to them, and sat bemused as Ian rolled up a joint. They suspected that Dean might have joined Ian if they had not been there, but he confined himself to an ordinary cigarette.

They did not have to do much talking as Ian did most of it for them. He started by telling them of his hated family in Laindon, of the father who used to beat him and the stepmother who had always wanted him out; of his brother who, last heard of, had been in prison for grievous bodily harm. All his friends, it appeared, had turned out to be bastards and toe-rags, who had robbed him or accused him of robbing them (unjustly, of course). He became angrier as he spoke, at times frighteningly so. But this was innocuous stuff compared to what was to follow. For he then treated them to a frank and detailed account of his sexual encounters, which became more lurid as he downed several glasses of wine. Clearly, he liked to shock (it was, after all, the only weapon left in his now meagre armoury), and he sensed that it would probably be a long time before he would have quite such a shockable audience (in Marianne and Spike, at any rate) again.

Dean cringed at first, wondering just how much Spike and Marianne would be able to take, but he became mildly amused as he realised that, whatever they might be thinking, their expressions of polite interest would barely change. This, he smiled to himself, was the middle class at it's finest. He realised, however, that there would be a point at which he would have to call a halt. This point arrived when Ian came to an uncomfortably graphic episode with a Dutchman who was into a particularly messy kink. Dean suggested, as gently as possible, that Spike and Marianne might not find such conversation particularly interesting.

'Oh,' said Ian, who did not like having his flow interrupted, 'so they may not find it particularly interesting!' he put on a sarcastic-sounding upper-crust accent. 'Who's a posh bitch from Snaresbrook now, then?'

'Perhaps we'd better go,' said Dean, suppressing his anger.

'"Perhaps we'd better go,"' mimicked Ian. 'Don't want your brother and his slag to find out what you've been up to, I suppose? You're funny brothers, though, what with you being half-coon.

Mother work round King's Cross, did she?'

Having said which he instantly vomited, partly on the settee and partly on the floor. He sat back, momentarily defeated, a look of unmistakable fear on his face.

'Are you okay?' said Spike, getting up.

'Yeah,' said Ian after a moment. 'I want a wank. If you don't want to watch I suppose you'd better go.'

They went. Dean first, but Marianne and Spike lingered for a few seconds, Spike to ask again if he was okay and Marianne, without a trace of irony, to thank him for a lovely evening. As they reached the bottom of the stairs they heard a voice behind them. 'Go on, you cunts. You're just shit like the rest of them, fucking shit!'

'Sorry,' said Dean, as they made their way to the nearest cab office. 'I did try to warn you.'

'I think,' said Spike,' 'he must be very lonely.'

'Are you surprised?' laughed Dean.

And some, Marianne thought sombrely, are born to endless night. And there was nothing anyone could do about it.

Spike had everything planned for Christmas and nobody was inclined to tell him that he was presuming too much in expecting them all to fit in with his arrangements. For he seemed determined that, in one way or another, everyone, far and near, was to be included. Christmas Eve was to be spent at The Kitchener's in Walthamstow, Christmas Day was to be close family plus Marianne (who, he took for granted, would be there throughout the whole season in any case) and on Boxing Day there would be a party for his rediscovered local friends, to which the Lucerne Court crowd plus Roger were to be added. Marianne was commissioned to relay the invitation to Roger who, surprisingly, accepted instantly. He was usually very much tied up with family, business colleagues and friends over the festive season.

'You will be coming then?' she said, unable to conceal her astonishment.

'You bet. It'll be the one event I'll look forward to. Besides, Spike is my employee now, so I have an interest in seeing what he gets up to. I've seen him sober, but the only way to judge someone is to see him drunk.'

As ordered (was there ever an order more happily obeyed?), Marianne arrived in the afternoon of Christmas Eve. She was laden with cases and bags, for as well as her own requirements for the next few days she had the presents to carry, and various other items which she thought might be a welcome additions to their Christmas fare. She had spent the previous hectic day with Daphne, who had shopping of her own to do. 'The poor don't realise how lucky they are.' Daphne had said. 'They don't have to queue up at Fortnum's at Christmas!' Marianne delightedly saved this gem for Dean who, as expected, was rewardingly outraged.

Marianne was a little surprised to see that they had put up an artificial Christmas tree, albeit a well-decorated one. There was a charming crib beneath.

'We found the tree and the crib figures in the shed,' Dean explained to her while Spike made some tea.

'You mean they were the ones that were here before?' she asked with a stab of joy as she realised the significance.

'Yes. Spike bawled his eyes out when we found them, though don't let on I told you.'

'And you didn't, I suppose?' she smiled, and his look gave her the answer.

That evening in The Kitchener's was pleasant enough, though Marianne was a little put out when Spike disappeared for a good hour round about ten o'clock. She ventured to ask Dean where he had got to, but Dean seemed as surprised at his absence as she was. Spike returned, explaining that he had popped in on old Ma Carlaw, a lonely old former neighbour, it appeared, who could not get out much. Marianne realised that the episode said more about herself than it did about Spike. 'I'm already turning into a ridiculous, possessive harridan,' she said to herself, and resolved not to let it happen.

It was Christmas Day itself to which Marianne had most looked forward. A day of dread in recent years, she was determined that this time she would enter into its spirit with more gusto than the reformed Scrooge. It was easier than she expected, for her hosts clearly had the same end in view.

Not that it started off entirely smoothly. Devoted brothers though they were, Spike and Dean were not ideally suited to share a kitchen.

Dean had been put in charge of the vegetables, leaving Spike to concentrate on the turkey and pudding.

'So what do I do?' asked Marianne, feeling rather hurt that she had not been given a definable role.

'Well, you can get the dining room ready,' Spike had generously offered.

It was a task that Marianne quite enjoyed, although she became increasingly perturbed at the sounds of discord which came from the kitchen.

'Not on there! I'm trying to stuff the turkey,' she heard Spike saying irritably.

'It's the only thing you ever will stuff, even with the help of a spoon. You should have thought of it earlier instead of waiting till it's nearly cooked.'

'Rubbish. This stuffing is the real McCoy. You can't do it too early or it gets overdone. Anyway, those potatoes are far too big. You'll have to make 'em smaller. And the sprouts should be cut at the bottom to make sure they're done inside.'

She ignored them for a while, but when she heard a crashing sound followed by a string of expletives and counter-expletives she felt intervention was necessary.

'Girls, girls!' she admonished, trying to sound like Alistair Sim in his headmistress of St Trinian's rôle.

'Why don't you take him out to feed the ducks?' suggested Spike. 'Though I know they'd probably prefer bread.'

Both Marianne and Dean thought this a good idea, and not for totally unselfish reasons. The kitchen was, unusually, a mess, and they did not particularly want to help clear it up. They suspected that, given a little time on his own, Spike would have everything back in order on their return. He would enjoy it, they reasoned.

'Do you believe in reincarnation?' asked Dean thoughtfully as they stood by the lake.

'I don't know,' said Marianne, surprised by the question. 'Why do you ask?'

'Well, if Lottie and George were reincarnated, I think it's likely to be as a couple of these ducks or swans, or maybe the geese. The thing is' - Dean looked a little guilty - 'when I came to tip their ashes in the lake this lot thought it must be food, and gobbled most of it up. I mean, look at them, they just grab first and ask questions later. See those two big white ducks over there?'

'Are they ducks?' Marianne asked. 'They look almost like little geese.'

'I don't know what they are. But they're always together, and they seem to be the only two quite like it. I know swans are supposed to be monogamous, but they don't ever seem to swim about in pairs like that. They go about as if they're not talking to each other.'

'Which only goes to show they must all be married,' laughed Marianne. 'I imagine if my mother was reincarnated it would have to be as a swan. I think she'd be most annoyed to be one of the ducks or geese.'

'But those dark little ducks with the funny beaks are quite cute. They always make a laughing sound which makes me laugh, too.'

'Cuteness and laughter are concepts I don't think my mother would have understood. Elegance was what counted with her.'

'Well, these swans don't look very elegant now, the way they scramble for everything.'

'Oh, elegant people sometimes know how to go for what they want,' laughed Marianne. 'Talking of elegant people' (it was meant with irony) 'have you seen your friend Ian since that time a couple of weeks ago? I felt quite guilty, our leaving him like that.'

'I think it was just as well we left when we did,' said Dean. 'And he's certainly not my friend. I know we're supposed to feel sorry for him, and that he must be very lonely and all that, but it really is his own fault. People have tried to be nice to him but he always ends up insulting them or trying to stir things up. Steve was chatting someone up a few weeks ago, and Ian had to get in there and tell the bloke a pack of lies about Steve, not because he had any hopes of getting him himself - he must have known that was ridiculous - but just because he was jealous. And that was while Steve was buying him a drink! Even at his best, Ian's conversation is boring or filthy. And he doesn't have to live in that sort of squalor. He gets quite good benefits, although he's always on the scrounge. Spends it all on booze and drugs. I'm afraid some people are just unhelpable.'

Marianne laughed. 'Now who's talking like a reactionary old Tory? I shall throw that back at you next time you have a go at Spike or me.'

'Well, in Ian's case I'm prepared to risk being branded that way. He carried on having unsafe sex with people even after he knew he was HIV positive. Not that anyone could mistake his status now.'

'Still,' said Marianne, 'you sometimes have to feel sorry for people when they've been brought low, whatever they did before.'

'This house must be having an effect on you. That's just the sort of thing Lottie Porter used to say,' said Dean, not realising just how much of a compliment Marianne took this.

As they expected, everything was under control when they returned, leaving them all time to change into their best before the arrival of Bill and Dolly.

Marianne had bought a new dress for the occasion, something not as expensive but a little more up to the minute than she was used to. She was pleased with the result. She was just leaving her room when Spike came down the stairs from the upper floor. He had bought a new suit, too. Light grey, purchased mainly with his new job in mind but more than adequate for this occasion. With the pale blue shirt and darker blue tie he looked stunning, and as they paused, taking each other in, it was clear that his opinion of her was equal to hers of him. They smiled in mutual admiration and vanity, and then Spike kissed her. At first it was a polite Christmas day kiss, but then he lingered and she drew him to her again. Only the doorbell made them disengage.

'Can I come and see you tonight?' he asked, then flushed and looked down.

'You'll see me all day,' she laughed, hardly daring to believe what she was hearing.

'You know what I mean,' he said.

'Well, if my door's unlocked you'll know you can come in.'

They both knew there was no lock on that door.

Dolly spent most of the dinner apologising for Bill's bad manners, though Marianne could not help inwardly remarking that Dolly's own manners were not up to much. For when not chiding Bill she made observations about what Spike and Dean should have done with regard to the cooking. And, of course, the Christmas pudding Marianne had purchased at Fortnum's was nowhere near as good as the one Dolly had obtained the previous year from Kwiksave. 'Still,' Dolly reluctantly admitted when the meal was finished, 'it was very nice.'

Spike and Dean smiled, realising what even this vague praise must be costing her, and Marianne finally understood, too. It was probably the first Christmas dinner for a generation that Dolly had not cooked herself, and the feeling of redundancy must have hurt a little. Dolly was redundant now in other ways, too, Marianne reflected, and probably saw her as the one behind that loss. Under the circumstances perhaps she was being incredibly polite.

They adjourned to the lounge just in time for the Queen's broadcast and then the presents were opened. It was a deliciously drawn-out process. Dean acted as Santa Claus, taking each gift from beneath the tree in turn and not passing on to the next until the current one had been opened and admired. They were all generous in proportion to their means and, in Spike's case, thoughtful. For Marianne he had bought theatre vouchers and she for him a camera, complete with film and other accessories. It was used straight away, of course.

Marianne noticed that Dolly appeared to become more and more apprehensive as the present-giving drew to a close. 'Bill,' she said, nudging her husband.

A rather embarrassed Bill took from his inside jacket pocket two envelopes and handed one to Spike and one to Dean. They both contained cheques. Spike's was for £10,000, Dean's for £5,000. They looked baffled, too much so to give proper thanks straight away.

'I know you think as we've been ripping Spike off all this time, what with 'im working for Bill,' Dolly explained, speaking primarily to Dean. 'In fact we was puttin' the money aside for when 'e needed it. And it's true we got the money from the Council for 'avin' you, even though you was family. We've been puttin' some of that aside, too. Reckon you're old enough to 'ave it now.'

'But,' said Spike, when it was possible to for him to speak, 'can you afford it?'

'Course we can,' said Dolly. 'As I've said, we've been puttin it aside. Special account, with interest. It's your money. It always 'as been.'

And she glanced again at Dean, with a look that he understood all too well. Whether they could afford it or not was immaterial: seeing him look such a Charlie made it all worthwhile. Her eye caught Marianne, too, and she smiled. Marianne also understood. 'Top that, madam!' Dolly was saying.

Spike and Dean remained somewhat shell-shocked for the rest of the day, though they tried to make it up to Bill and Dolly by letting them win the game of Monopoly they played after tea. The generous couple made their triumphant exit at about nine to go and see their friends Flo and Bert (though Bill had more the look of one who was wondering if the cheques really needed to have been for quite so much. Being the owner of Piccadilly, Mayfair and the Waterworks for an hour, even coming second in a beauty contest, did not fully compensate).

When they had gone Dean's humility immediately evaporated. Having had to kiss Dolly on her way out made him feel he had earned the money in any case.

'Yes!' he shouted gleefully, waving his fist in the air as soon as the front door was closed. 'Yes, yes, yes!'

His face made clear what was in his mind. They could see the pictures of leather jackets, designer shirts and expensive nights out in best colour photography.

'That money's not for wasting,' said Spike virtuously, knowing that the advice would be falling on deaf ears and anticipating the look of scorn it would earn him. Nevertheless, he carried on giving Dean wise investment tips for some time, and only stopped when Dean threatened to start calling him Prudence. In fact Dean was not the only one who found Spike's rectitude unwelcome, for Marianne had her own reasons for hoping that he was not going to be in too much of a respectable mood that night.

They watched a film on television. It was somewhat far-fetched in Marianne's view, about a penniless young couple in Las Vegas who meet up with a very rich man who offers them a million dollars if he can sleep with the woman for one night. Although ludicrous, sentimental and entirely predictable, it did have one or two romantic scenes from which, Marianne hoped, Spike might pick up a few tips himself. Unfortunately, he laughed all the way through them. The only good sign was that he did not drink too much during its screening, confining himself to one small Tia Maria while she and Dean finished off a bottle of Chardonnay between them. Spike obviously wanted to be in top form that night.

She bade them goodnight when the film was over.

'Not having a cup of something?' asked Dean. 'That wine can really dry you out.'

'No thanks. I'll have a glass of water after I've had a shower.'

She threw a conspiratorial look at Spike, who looked back as though uncomprehending. She could only wonder if he had forgotten. Perhaps he was going to spend the night admiring the cheque he had been given.

After her shower she settled in bed to read. Dean's present had been a novel by a writer who was new to her (very handsome, she noted, looking at the photograph on the inside cover. Probably why Dean had chosen it) about an affluent if rather boring young woman who is persuaded by a friend to visit an outer suburb where she meets a young man whom she had met a few years before in a foreign capital.

As she read she heard someone coming up the stairs, passing her room to the floor above. Spike's step, undoubtedly. She could hear the upstairs shower turned on and, five minutes later turned off. She felt herself tingling with anticipation, though she carried on reading, realising that the time would pass quicker that way. She was not entirely happy with the story, finding the principal female character rather irritating. She felt like shaking her and telling her to wake up instead of moping about hoping that the love of her life would come to her. She found it absurd that a woman with so many advantages could be so lacking in self-respect. She had little time for women like that, and would not have blamed the object of her desire if he had told her to go and find something more useful to do. Perhaps he would before the end.

At last she heard steps descending the stairs and there was a knock on her door. The knock disappointed her a little: she was rather hoping he would be bolder than that.

But she was not disappointed when she saw him. Modest still, he had on a pair of underpants, not just clean but spanking new by the looks of things. He had a packet of condoms in his hand, which he put on the bedside table with an apologetic expression. They looked at each other nervously as Spike sat on the bed. And then he smiled. Tenderly she drew him to her with one arm while trying to lift the bedclothes with the other.

Close up he was more substantial than he had sometimes seemed when he wandered around looking lost. He touched her breast nervously and instantly withdrew his hand, as though he had done something wrong. She took his hand and put it back. He smiled again at his own bashfulness and she burst out laughing.

'Do I really look that stupid?' he asked.

'Stupid was the last word I had on my mind,' she said, and put both her arms round his head.

After this somewhat hesitant start they settled down to enjoy themselves. His touch was like nothing she had ever felt before, all the more sensuous for his initial nervousness. For at first he seemed to look at her as though asking her permission for everything he did, bursting into that heart-stopping smile every time she herself smiled by way of consent. His potency and the firmness of his body made his gentleness all the more exciting, and she responded with an equal sensibility. Lust was there, it had to be conceded, but there was something else, something that had always been missing before. She searched in her mind for what it must be, even looked for the word to describe it, but could come up with nothing more poetic than 'kindness.' And then she realised that kindness was exactly what it was. Odd that she had taken such a crucial word for granted.

'I suppose I'd better take my pants off if I'm to be any use,' he observed.

'Let me,' she smiled. 'I've been waiting to get them off you for four and a half years. Don't deny me the pleasure now.'

The wait, she soon discovered, had not been in vain. He relaxed when it finally dawned on him that he was not doing too badly and they even found things to laugh at from time to time. She hadn't known that you were allowed to do that. She was aware of all the nonsense spoken about the earth moving in such situations, and was determined not to become the victim of any such silly clichés. Nevertheless, after the third time she did find herself blinking in wonder on seeing that the pictures on the walls were still hanging straight.

'It's at times like this,' she said, realising that even Spike must be in need of some sort of rest by that time, 'that I wished we both smoked.'

'That's out I'm afraid,' he said firmly, grimacing slightly at such a filthy suggestion. 'Even if I wanted to I wouldn't. We have to set some sort of example for Dean.'

'Oh yes, of course we must,' she laughed, amused at the total lack of irony with which Spike had made the observation.

'Let's have a cup of tea, though,' he suggested, and she readily acquiesced to this even better idea.

He searched for his pants, left, and returned a few minutes later with two steaming mugs.

'Do you know, he's still down there watching a dirty video? I wondered what that mysterious present from Jerome was.'

'How disgusting!' she laughed. 'And we've been up here for the last two hours saying our prayers! What was it about?'

'Well, two guys of course. One of them was eating trifle off the other's stomach.'

'Well, even gays have to eat,' she pointed out.

Spike laughed. 'You're developing quite a sense of humour, you know that?'

She was more flattered by this than he realised. And she felt more relaxed with him than ever, and he, it seemed, with her. In the past it had always been at this stage in the proceedings that she had felt most ill at ease with a man.

'Spike,' she said thoughtfully, sipping her tea. 'Do you think we could ever be...I mean, what do you want? Do you want this to lead anywhere?'

She did not know how to put it exactly, but he seemed to understand her meaning.

'I don't know what I want yet. Not completely. I only know what I don't want. And what I don't want is almost everything I'd have to put up with without you there.'

Well, that wasn't too bad, was it?

'I'd like us to be...well you know,' he pursued. 'But...'

'But'?...' she echoed, questioningly and a little fearfully.

'Why do you and Dean think so much of me?' he asked. 'I've never understood why. There's not a lot to me really. I'm just a mummy's boy who found himself without a mummy. I've always let people love me without giving a lot of love back.'

'There's more to you than that, Spike. If there wasn't, you wouldn't have said that. I've known mummy's boys. Come to think of it, I've met a few daddy's little princesses. For sheer ghastliness I don't think either of us would get past the starting line in competition with them.'

He sighed and put his unfinished tea on to the bedside cabinet.

'I suppose I'd better go back to my own bed now.'

'No!' she said firmly, putting her own cup down. She held him and manoeuvred him down beside her. 'You're not going to deny me the pleasure of waking up beside you. There are some risks you have to start taking.'

He was non-committal in his reply, but fell asleep before long in any case. We have been here before, Marianne thought, although something told her that this time there would be a happier outcome. She did not feel inclined to sleep herself for a while. Every minute holding Spike gave her more pleasure than any of the nights she had spent with anyone before. She sensed he was slightly larger than he had been earlier in the year, and found the prospect of his being a little chunkier rather exciting. If his new contentment was making him prone to put on weight, however, she would have to ensure that the extra weight was channelled in the right direction. Dean would agree with her on that. She would enrol them all in the local gym - it could be a little extra Christmas present for Spike and Dean. She would also have to ensure that Spike ate the right things. She recalled the last wedding she had attended. An old school chum, Isobel, had married someone big in the City and she grimaced as she remembered his enormous beer gut. Spike, she thought smugly, would wear his morning suit with infinitely more panache. But then, she reflected, some people might say she was jumping the gun.

CHAPTER SEVEN

The party on Boxing Day confirmed Spike's position as a key player in the social scene of the area, a position once clearly occupied by his parents, judging from the numerous anecdotes with which Marianne was regaled during the course of the evening. What intrigued her most, however, was the way in which Roger and Dean spent a good two hours chatting by the staircase, smoking profusely and breaking off their conversation only to replenish their glasses. She wondered what on earth they could have in common, rightly discounting the obvious theory, for she had no doubt that Roger was in no way attracted to young men in any sexual way. Roger had, indeed, brought along the (for him) obligatory escort, a not unattractive Polish girl called Kasia, of about Spike's age, whom Marianne could not decide was more stupid or more intelligent than she was pretending to be. Marianne suspected that it was on her insistence that Roger had announced, on arrival, that they could not stay for more than an hour or so, but the intention clearly went by the board as both Kasia and Roger found the event more stimulating than expected, for while Roger chatted and joked with Dean, Kasia was more than happy to be entertained by some of Spike's old schoolfriends in the dining room.

Spike, Marianne and Dean were invited to a fancy-dress party on New Year's Eve, and they thought it would be a diverting idea if Spike and Marianne were to choose Dean's costume and he theirs. Spike and Marianne dropped strong hints that they rather saw themselves as Antony and Cleopatra, but in vain, for they found themselves cast as Popeye and Olive Oyl. 'But Spike isn't a bit like Popeye!' Marianne protested, and was rather disappointed that nobody rushed to say that she was likewise miscast. 'Oh, so I'm like Olive, am I?' she asked peevishly. 'Not physically,' Dean reassured her. Not that Dean had the last laugh, for he had wanted to go as Shirley

Bassey, but Spike put his foot down and he had to be content with being Noddy. 'If you try doing anything naughty in one of the bedrooms this time,' Spike told him severely, 'the little bell on your cap will give you away.'

Over the next few weeks it became established that Marianne should spend her weekends at Snaresbrook, and very full weekends they were, for there always seemed to be something going on and she began to wonder if she would be able to keep up the pace. She enjoyed trying, nevertheless. Besides, even if she did find the going out a little hectic, the coming home made it all worthwhile, for Spike effectively moved into the big front bedroom when she was there.

Marianne was particularly impressed at the way Spike was able to juggle the variety of new roles that had been thrust upon him. During the week (and on most Saturdays, unfortunately) he was the little businessman, setting off importantly for work in his crisp suit (she stood by her bedroom window and watched him set out, realising that Roger had not been stupid in wanting him as an employee. How could any customer resist spending a fortune when attended to by Spike?), while in the evenings, at least at weekends, he was obliged to live up to his social position. He also still worked in The Kitchener's a couple of evenings during the week. Far from tiring as a result of all this activity, he seemed to thrive on it. Working hard and playing hard appeared to come naturally to him, and she could see his confidence growing as a result of it.

Her only criticism of him at this time was his annoying habit of being a little too cheerful on those mornings when he had to get up before her and Dean. As he washed and flitted up and down the stairs to his own room he sang joyfully about his luvverly bunch of coconuts ('Oh, for God's sake Spike!' an irate Dean would invariably shout from his room). Marianne sympathised with Dean, for she was not particularly interested in coconuts at that time in the morning either, even if some were as big as your 'ead. She came to see it in a different light, however, when Dean explained to her that George Porter used to rouse the house with the same song.

At first Dean seemed to appreciate the new Spike as much as she did, but by the end of January she noticed he had come to look increasingly down in the mouth, and on one or two occasions he said things which suggested a certain disenchantment with his brother.

Could it be jealousy? she wondered. Dean had, after all, for long been the undisputed life and soul of the party, a role which had now partially been usurped. On the Friday of the first weekend in February she had arrived to find an uncharacteristically strained atmosphere. Nothing was said to her, and they seemed to put the bone of contention between them on ice for the duration of her stay. Nevertheless, she could not help overhearing Dean mutter 'arrogant shit' as he looked at Spike laughing and joking with a couple of his friends in The Cuckfield that evening. As Spike was working on the Saturday she was able to raise the subject with Dean.

'Is something the matter?' she asked, after their now routine trip to Sainsbury's, during which he had been unusually subdued.

'No,' said Dean defensively. 'Why should there be?'

'I just had the impression you were rather annoyed with Spike last night, that's all. And you seem a bit quiet today.'

'Oh,' said Dean, in obvious discomfort, 'brothers have arguments all the time. You must know that.'

'You don't,' said Marianne.

'Well perhaps we're making up for lost time. Spike certainly seems to be.'

'Well, yes, maybe he is,' said Marianne, not quite understanding his meaning. 'But you have to allow that he's only just started to enjoy life again. You have to forgive him if it's gone to his head a bit.'

'Would you say that even if...' and Dean suddenly stopped.

'If what?' she asked. Such self-censorship was uncharacteristic of Dean.

'Nothing. It's me I suppose. I've had one or two problems lately, I mean at college.'

'Are you sure that's all?' she asked, becoming a little alarmed. Compared to the problems he had coped with quite adequately until then, such trivial matters ought to have been a piece of cake for him.

That evening Dean seemed to make a special effort for her sake but the following morning Spike announced that he had to work at The Kitchener's that lunchtime. The look Dean gave him was unmistakable in its hostility.

'Don't you like him going to The Kitchener's?' she asked, when Spike had left.

'Oh, I've no objection to that,' Dean said, and despite her questioning as to what the matter was he remained obstinately unforth-coming.

'Well,' she said, 'why don't we go to The Kitchener's ourselves for an hour?'

'Oh, don't do that, Marianne. I mean, he might think you're checking up on him.'

'Why should he think that?' asked Marianne, alarm bells beginning to ring.

The alarm bells were silenced, however, when Spike returned, for he was attentiveness itself. And yet, was there something guilty in that attention?

Marianne was soon to have a particular reason, and a very strong one, for hoping that there would be no falling out between herself and Spike. For she had discovered something else early in February, something she told herself was totally unexpected but, deep down, she knew was probably not. Just before the second weekend of that month she was finally forced to face up to the truth of it.

Spike would have to be told he was going to be a father, she was crystal clear about that, but how to proceed beyond that revelation was something about which she was not inclined to be too definite. She certainly had no wish to force him into anything against his will. She was solvent enough, after all, and was better placed to cope with such an eventuality than many women in her position. She wanted his child, of that she was certain, and would have it whatever his reaction, but she was aware that they were reaching a point from which they would have to go forward or backwards. That was the horrible truth, and she quaked at the prospect of having to find out which direction he might choose.

With superhuman effort she tried to appear as normal as possible when she arrived in Snaresbrook that weekend. Picking the right moment to tell Spike would be important and she was determined that, should his response be in any way negative, she would pass it off as no big deal (or try to, at any rate). Much as she wanted the child, the growing certainty that things between them could never be exactly the same again made her wish that it had not come quite so soon. A few months, at least, of that idyllic existence would have been nice.

She arrived as usual at about seven thirty on the Friday evening.

Unusually, Dean was alone in the house.

'Spike's working late,' he said, somewhat abruptly.

'When will he be back, then?' she asked, as it became increasingly apparent that she and Dean were to be eating alone.

'God knows!' said Dean, and added: 'Perhaps about ten. Paperwork to be sorted out, he said. And maybe he'll go for a drink afterwards.'

'But surely he'd let us know if he was doing that?' said Marianne.

'He might. Then again he might not.'

'Shall I ring the shop and ask him?'

Dean looked at her, a look which said everything.

'Better not do that, Marianne,' he said softly.

She pretended not to understand. They sat in the kitchen and ate in virtual silence, apart from a few mechanical words of praise from her about his cooking.

'It's sausages and chips,' he said, surprised that such a dish could be worthy of commendation.

They made some tea and went into the lounge. When she could stand the silence no longer Marianne broached the subject Dean was clearly dreading - though not, surely, as much as she.

'He's not at work, is he?'

'I don't think so,' Dean admitted.

'And you didn't think he was working at The Kitcheners last Sunday, either?'

'No. I met Pete Bettles last week and he said Spike hadn't been working there for some time.'

'Oh,' said Marianne, feeling immensely cold. 'It's that serious then. Do you know her?'

'No. He's tried to keep me as much in the dark as you. I know her name's Carol, though. She rang today. When I said he was at work she said she'd ring him there. Ten minutes later he rings to say he'll be home late. I wasn't going to tell you about it. I thought it might be something brief, something we could ignore.'

'And why does it bother you so much?' Marianne asked, for she had not realised until then that Dean was so much on her side.

'Because I know it has to be you - for him I mean. He knows that, too, that's the stupid thing. Why is he doing this? It doesn't make sense. Now of all times.'

The last sentence was curious. Did Dean suspect her own news?

'Why is it worse now?' she asked.

'I wanted us to be a family. Him, me - and you. For a while, at least. Just like when Lottie and George were alive.'

She said nothing and then, after taking a deep breath, he added: 'And I've found out I'm HIV positive.'

Her own inner turmoil, at least the turmoil she had brought with her, suddenly seemed unimportant.

'How long have you known?' she asked, after giving herself time to digest the information.

'Oh, about three weeks.'

She sat next to him on the settee and put her arm round him. They sat in silence for a quarter of an hour. Various questions presented themselves to her, but she thought it best that they should be left unasked.

'And you haven't told Spike?' she asked at last.

'What do you think?' he laughed, with some bitterness. 'To be honest, I was hoping you'd do it for me. But I don't suppose you'll want to speak to him now.'

'I don't know. Maybe this little fling he's having isn't too serious. He is just finding his feet, after all.'

'That's obviously not the only part of himself he's found!'

'He's still the same Spike,' she said.

'I wonder. I don't like some of those friends of his. They talk about women as though they're trophies. And they're so full of themselves.'

'And you think some of that may have rubbed off onto Spike?'

'Well, I suppose he'll never be quite like the others. But on the other hand...I always thought I knew how he'd react to things. I'm not so sure now.'

They sat quietly for a little while longer until Dean suddenly got up.

'Oh, for Christ's sake, Marianne! Look at the two of us! I don't know about you, but I fancy a drink. We've still got an hour until chucking out time.'

Marianne smiled. A change of scene would, she thought, be welcome. Dean's ability to bounce back impressed her, and she felt it was a quality she ought to try and emulate. Heaven knew, she would probably need to.

They made their way to The Cuckfield. As they turned into the High Street they saw the eastbound tube train trundling over the bridge, and then, in the distance, having obviously just alighted from the train, they saw Spike. He did not see them but walked towards the same destination as theirs, about a hundred yards ahead of them.

The same thought passed through both their minds. Why had he been on the eastbound train if he had been coming from the shop in Woodford?

'Shall we go to The Eagle or The George instead?' suggested Dean.

'Why?' asked Marianne. She was certainly not in the business of deliberately avoiding Spike; it went too much against the grain, even now. There was probably a rational explanation for it all. That was what she had to believe.

As always on a Friday The Cuckfield was very crowded and they were obliged to stand. Dean insisted on buying Marianne a drink, as though determined not to become involved with Spike and his cronies, whom they could see not far away from them. Jerry Piper and Derek Hammond were there, and Phil Corrie who fancied himself as the town stud (a particularly bad influence on Spike, in Dean's view) and a couple of other of the lager-swilling morons (Dean's description) Dean had latterly come to dislike, blaming them to some extent for taking Spike away from Marianne - and from him. Spike saw them and beckoned them over.

'I'm not going!' said Dean.

'Well,' Marianne hesitated, 'she doesn't seem to be with them, whoever she is.'

'Well, of course not,' said Dean, and added with a tone of deep contempt: 'this is the butch lads' Friday night out.'

The group somehow edged towards them, so that they found themselves part of it whether they wished it or not. Dean did not stand on ceremony.

'Nice of you to let us know you'd be here,' he said.

'Sorry,' said Spike, 'I've only just arrived. I got off the train and thought I'd pop in. I tried to ring you on my mobile to say I'd be here. You must have been on your way.'

He looked a little nervously at Marianne, as though aware that Dean may have been telling tales about him. While he was perfectly correct in this assumption, Marianne was not, in fact, as angry with him as he might have expected. For she was still clinging to the hope that Dean might be under a misapprehension. Perhaps his own unwelcome news had put him into a mood that had made him suspect the worst unjustifiably. Besides, just seeing Spike made it difficult for her to be angry with him. He certainly looked innocent enough, and something told her that sustained subterfuge was not in his nature. There was no evidence, indeed, that he had spent so much as one night with the mystery woman. And even if he had had a flirtation, who was she to judge him for that? He had made no pledges to her. She smiled at him and he seemed to relax a little.

Dean was not so easily mollified. He scowled at Spike in no uncertain terms, and made a point of not laughing at Phil Corrie's joke about the nun and the camel. When Spike was getting a round in he pointedly refused a drink from him.

'Ooh, she's in a right mood tonight!' said Spike, in an affected camp voice.

Dean snapped. If Spike had spoken to him in this way when they were alone or just with Marianne it would not have mattered in the slightest, but his doing so in order to amuse a bunch of posing Essex boys was something else. In his fury he found himself committing the ultimate treachery.

'You pompous prat!' he said, not bothering to lower his voice. 'Just because you've managed to go for a whole month without wetting the bed you think you're God's gift!'

Marianne blanched, and it was immediately obvious from Dean's face that he wished he could put the clock back just ten seconds. And yet was the situation irretrievable? Surely Dean's outburst could be put down to ratty younger brother's futile attempt to embarrass? A shrug and a laugh and it would have been forgotten. As it was there was a pregnant pause, as though Spike's companions could not really believe that such a juicy piece of information was being presented to them so cheaply. She had not taken into account Spike's extraordinary stupidity on occasions. For, assuming that all was now in the open, his only concern was to ensure that his achievement was not understated.

'It's more than two months,' he pointed out, from behind a traffic-light red face.

It was this, and the mixture of indignation and pride with which he said it, that made the others dissolve. Oh Spike, thought Marianne, what can anyone do to help you? She looked down, loyally attempting to hide the smile she could not repress herself and noticed that Dean was having similar difficulties. At least on this occasion Spike did not try to run away, but attempted to regain his shattered dignity while his friends composed themselves, which took some time. Fortunately he was able to look at the bar and not at them while he waited to be served.

'I will have a pint then,' said Dean weakly, now wishing only to make amends.

Spike had realised that his absence on the Friday evening had not gone down well, and to make up for it he left work early on the Saturday. He told Marianne of his plan to do so before leaving that morning, explaining that they now had an additional member of staff and that it would probably be okay. He was as good as his word, for they heard the key in the lock just after four o'clock.

Dean and Marianne looked at each other apprehensively, for they had agreed that this would be the time she would tell Spike Dean's news. After tea (during which Spike and Dean were stiffly formal to each other) Dean disappeared upstairs, in theory to get on with an essay. Marianne braced herself.

She was grateful now that she had not had a showdown with Spike herself, despite having had some grounds for doing so. Before going to The Cuckfield the previous evening it had been her intention to tell Spike that she did not wish him to share her room that night, if only to show that she was not that dependent on him, but events made her change her mind. His humiliation in front of his friends made her heart go out to him, and she had no wish to add to his discomfort just then. Besides, she could see no reason why she should punish herself to spite him.

He took the tea things into the kitchen and began washing up. He was a stickler for not leaving the dishes, though on this occasion she was determined to put first things first.

'Leave those for a while, Spike,' she said. 'There's something we have to talk about.'

'Okay,' he said, seeing the earnestness with which she made the request, and he followed her back into the lounge somewhat fearfully. He assumed that she was going to speak about their relationship, for he knew for certain now that Dean had told her about his inexplicable absences. She most certainly did intend to speak to him about that, but not just yet.

'It's about Dean,' she said, when he was seated next to her on the settee.

'Dean?' he said, with some relief.

'Yes. I...I don't really know how to put this. But you're going to have to be very strong.'

'Oh Christ!' he said. 'What has he been up to this time? I know something seems to have been on his mind recently. Caught doing naughty things in a toilet, I suppose. I knew it would happen sooner or later.'

'No, no,' she said. 'Nothing like that. But I'm sure you know he's always been in what they call a high-risk category.'

It took him a few meanings to follow her gist, and finally came out with 'oh, that' when he had done so.

'Well, Dean's had an HIV test recently, and it turned out to be positive.'

He looked at her for a few moments, and to her surprise he seemed to smile slightly.

'Do you understand what I'm talking about?' she asked.

'Oh yes. You're saying Dean's HIV positive.'

'Well, yes.'

'He told you that, did he?'

He pondered for a moment and then got up and called Dean, who joined them hesitantly a few moments later.

'Marianne tells me you're HIV positive,' said Spike cheerfully.

'Er...yes,' said Dean, sitting down.

'Well, who would have thought it? It must be particularly hard for you, what with the leukaemia you suffered from as a child and the terminal cancer you had a couple of years ago when you wanted me to pay for that holiday to Germany you had planned. My goodness, fate has dealt you some terrible blows!'

And Marianne at last understood Spike's levity. He did not believe it.

'Spike,' she said, urging caution, 'I know Dean hasn't always been truthful, but I'm sure on this occasion...'

'Hasn't always been truthful?' said Spike, with considerable scorn. 'Marianne, we are talking here about a world champion. He produces more pork pies than Melton Mowbray!'

'Well, I think that's a bit of an exaggeration,' said Marianne. 'But what reason would he have for lying about this?'

'I'm not saying I'm going to die tomorrow,' said Dean defensively. 'I'm not after sympathy or anything like that. I'm just saying the test was positive. I'll probably live for years yet.'

'I wouldn't be too sure about that!' said Spike, and his sarcasm suddenly turned to serious anger. 'I was happy, at last, getting on at last, in love with someone at last. You couldn't let that happen, could you? You had to try and ruin it. You had to remain the centre of things. What a coincidence that you should find this out now.'

Dean stood up, his indignation making it impossible for him to remain seated.

'You accuse me of being a liar?' he said, or rather shouted. 'You say I'm out to ruin everything for you? Who is it who's been lying about what he's been doing over the last couple of months? Who's Carol? You sanctimonious, hypocritical fart. I don't have to ruin anything for you. You're making a good enough job of that yourself.'

'You shut up!' said Spike, rising from his seat.

'Shut up yourself. You're so pious aren't you? "In love" my arse! You're nothing but a glorified rent boy, and a fucking expensive one. Marianne's bought you, and you know it. You're both as tacky as each other!'

Marianne could see that Spike's fists were clenched and for a moment she feared the worst was about to happen. But Spike seemed to realise the danger himself and sat down again.

'Why are you doing this, Dean?' he asked, only just managing to regain his composure. 'Last night you tried to embarrass me in front of my friends, now you're trying to break up Marianne and me. And, of course, you're dying of Aids!'

'So where have you been getting to then?' asked Dean contemptuously, and then, looking at Marianne, he suddenly stopped. He had not really intended to hurt her, but it had been the natural corollary of the insults he was hurling at Spike. He sat down, as though deflated.

'Well,' he admitted, echoing Spike's softer tone, 'perhaps I could have got the wrong end of the stick about one or two things. And I didn't really intend to humiliate you last night. You know my mouth doesn't always do the things I mean it to. But I'm not lying about the HIV test.'

Spike gave a disdainful snort.

'If you really want proof,' said Dean, 'I've got the test result on paper upstairs. And a letter from the hospital about counselling and what not.'

Marianne felt the jerk Spike gave at this. He paled.

'Are you serious?' he asked, fear now entering his voice.

Dean looked at him briefly and left the room. Spike put his head in his hands. Marianne noticed Dean pausing to look at him through the open door before he ascended the stairs.

Dean was gone a long time. After a while Spike got up and looked vacantly out of the window. She went to him and stroked his neck.

'Oh, Christ!' he said. 'What if I am wrong? Oh crikey! Oh shit!'

Quietly Dean returned. He had no papers with him.

'I...I can't find them' he said weakly, with the lameness of a school-boy claiming to have lost his homework.

Spike turned and looked at him, his eyes moist. 'Do they exist?' he asked.

Dean looked at him fearfully for a few moments, then said: 'No.'

'Get out of my sight!' said Spike.

Dean turned and reascended the stairs. Spike took a deep breath, wiped his eyes and gave a sardonic laugh.

Like Spike, Marianne's feelings were a mixture of relief and anger. Why had Dean told such a silly lie, one which was bound to be found out before long? And was everything else he had said about Spike's alleged infidelity now credible? But there was an explanation of sorts.

'I suppose,' she said, allowing a few minutes for Spike to calm down, 'he must have been feeling a bit left out lately. It's only because he loves you so much, Spike. I can't blame him for that.'

'Maybe,' said Spike. 'But this isn't funny. When I think of...of all the people who can't just say it was all a joke, who can't suddenly change their mind and decide that they haven't got Aids after all. This is just out of order. And then there's the things he said about us. I can't let it pass as though nothing's happened.'

'I'll let him have the keys to my place,' she suggested. 'He can stay there for a while.'

'Would you?' asked Spike, relieved at this way out.

'Only for a while, though. You mustn't fall out with him for too long.'

'Of course I won't,' he said, and then added sternly, 'but he needn't think I'm going to ring him tomorrow and ask him to come back. I'm not going to be so soft from now on.'

'Well, that's right,' agreed Marianne, but added, intrigued as to just how hard this new, strict Spike could be: 'How long did you have in mind?'

'I'll probably ring him on Monday,' he said.

Marianne burst out laughing. 'Oh, Spike,' she said, 'you are funny!'

'I don't see why we should let this spoil our evening,' said Spike, more in hope than anything else.

They had been invited to a little soirée next door to celebrate Mrs Douglas's seventy-fifth birthday.

'What, no Dean?' the old lady asked, disappointed.

'He had something else on, I'm afraid,' said Spike, doing his best to smile, though it was fairly obvious to Marianne that he would have difficulty putting the scene with Dean earlier that day out of his mind.

Most of the other guests were elderly women, though a few younger relatives were in attendance. Marianne tried as much as possible to be jovial, conscious of Spike's difficulty in entering into the spirit of things.

'I'll have to go,' he whispered to her at last. He made his apologies, citing paperwork he had to catch up on. Marianne dutifully stayed on for another hour in the hope that this would reassure everyone that nothing was really amiss, for Mrs Douglas had noted Spike's premature departure with some alarm.

When Marianne returned to their house Spike was sitting looking at an old photo album. He pretended to be blowing his nose when she entered but he was too late to prevent her noticing that he was wiping his eyes, too.

She sat next to him and put her arm round him.

'We ought to be so happy,' he said. 'Why did he have to say those things?'

'He's frightened he'll be losing you, that's all,' she said. 'I can't blame him. If I thought I might be losing you I'd lie and cheat far more than that if I thought it would work.'

'You don't believe I'm seeing someone else, do you?'

'Of course not,' she said, kissing him and trying to suppress the fear she felt.

The phone rang and she got up to answer, thinking it best that she do so in case it was Dean. In the event it was a young woman. She announced herself as Carol and asked if she could talk to Spike. There was nothing untoward in this, but it was Spike's reaction that set the alarm bells ringing again. And then Marianne remembered Dean's reference to a Carol. Spike reddened on being told who it was, and with barely concealed agitation went into the hall, almost closing the door behind him. Marianne listened from the lounge, catching Spike's words despite his speaking deliberately softly.

'What...oh....yes...You think so...oh. When was that?...Oh...yes. I'll come straight away, then.'

He replaced the receiver. 'I have to go out,' he said, with understandable trepidation.

'I rather gathered that,' said Marianne, anger rising despite herself, especially given her protestations of faith in him only a few moments earlier.

'It's not what you think,' he said.

'I don't know what to think. All I know is that Dean wasn't wrong when he said you'd been acting strangely lately, and now this. It's nearly eleven on a Saturday night, for heaven's sake. You're hardly going to tell me you have to open up the shop!'

He said nothing and rang for a taxi. To Shoreditch.

'Well,' she said, 'at least I know where to start looking for her. Pretty, is she?'

'It's not like that,' he said, almost shouting in desperation. It was not often he raised his voice. Now he had done so twice in one day.

'Spike,' she said, trying to keep her poise, 'I've believed you up until now. But if you go out tonight without something of a convincing explanation I don't see how there can ever be any trust between us again. If you want to see someone else then that's your right. But why be sneaky about it?'

And it was his right, that was the stark truth of it. She had said it in an attempt to make herself appear reasonable, but the words brought home to her just how little she could do if her hopes were disappearing as quickly as they now appeared to be.

'There isn't anyone else,' he said. 'Not in the way you think. And it looks as though it's going to be all over tonight, anyway.' He looked thoughtful for a moment. 'If you feel up to it, perhaps you'd like to come with me.'

'What!' she expostulated. 'So you want to end it, and you want me to hold your hand while you do it?'

'It's not how you think,' he repeated. 'I should have brought you before. I was going to anyway, but that's all been overtaken by events. Come on, get your coat.'

She looked at him, still doubting but recalling a time before when she had thought the worst about him only to be shown to be spectacularly wrong. He went upstairs and she could hardly believe her nose when, on his return, she realised that he had put on some of his most expensive aftershave lotion. Did he think this was funny?

He smiled slightly at the look she gave him, but she went to get her coat all the same, her curiosity to see her rival momentarily overcoming all other instincts. And who knew? If there was to be a showdown she might yet emerge the winner. But could anyone be the winner? Whatever happened she would have lost the Spike she thought she knew. Perhaps what he was offering her now was not so very different from the kind of relationship Roger had once offered her. So had she simply come full circle? Well, not quite. Spike was a sight sexier than Roger, after all. Perhaps, in the real world, one really has to accept such things. It was something she would have to think hard about before making any rash decisions. But she could not do other than mourn the time when she thought she would not have to do such weighing-up.

In the taxi Spike became increasingly unhappy-looking as they approached their destination. He seemed to be dreading something, and her doubts persisted.

He told the driver to stop at a most unprepossessing spot in Hackney Road and then led her towards a large building behind a small car park. At first she assumed it was a block of flats, but as they approached the entrance she realised that it was a hospital or clinic of some sort. They entered and Spike signed them both in. It was probably quite pleasant as such places went, but the quietness and the subdued lighting at that time of night added to her sense of foreboding. And yet it was not quite the same sort of foreboding she had felt earlier. This was not the place to which one came for a showdown with another woman. There was usually only one reason why people were called to hospitals at this time of night, and some of the posters on the walls of the corridor along which they walked to the lift made it abundantly clear exactly what sort of hospital this was.

As they took the lift to the third floor Spike looked at her apologetically and questioningly, wondering, no doubt, if she understood yet. A sort of understanding was dawning, but it was as yet unfocused.

They walked along another short corridor and stopped at a glass-panelled door. It was the only room with a light on. As he pushed the door open a nurse met him.

'He had another convulsion a couple of hours ago,' she whispered. 'Brain haemorrhage. He won't come out of this one.'

Marianne did not immediately recognise the emaciated and obviously dying man on the bed. She was reminded of the figures she had seen on archive film taken by the liberators of Belsen, the images of the skeletal unfortunates who had been beyond saving. Only when Spike leant over, took his hand and said gently: 'I'm here, Ian,' did she understand. A surge of emotion took hold of her and she left the room quickly. Her overwhelming feeling was one of relief, followed instantly by guilt that she could feel relief in the face of such suffering. Standing in the corridor she rooted in her coat pocket for a handkerchief.

A few moments later the nurse emerged.

'Why don't you come with me,' she said, and led Marianne to a pleasant room where two nurses, one male and one female, sat at a table drinking coffee. The nurse who had been with Ian sat her at the table and asked her if she would like a cup of something, and a dazed Marianne asked for some tea.

'Hello, Marianne,' said the male nurse, and she recognised him as Steve, one of Dean's friends whom they had met at the cabaret pub in the East End the night that dreadful Miss Crotchsniff was performing.

'Oh, Steve,' she said, composing herself gradually.

Steve introduced her to the other two nurses, Mandy and the one who was making the tea, Carol.

'Thank God for Spike,' said Mandy. 'It's so awful when there's nobody. Family doesn't want to know. It was good of you to come.'

'Well . . . I . . .', said Marianne guiltily. They were clearly unaware that she had not come voluntarily, did not, in fact, know what she was coming to.

Steve lit a cigarette and offered her one. She took it, sensing that this was one occasion when Spike would not be too cross with her. Odd, she could not help thinking, that so many nurses smoked.

'Not a pretty sight, is it?' said Carol sympathetically as she handed Marianne her tea.

'He never was a pretty sight at the best of times!' laughed Steve, with a humour that shocked Marianne under the circumstances. But she recalled that Steve had known Ian and could perhaps be forgiven.

'Does he know?' Marianne asked, the familiarity of a cup of tea and the friendly atmosphere restoring her sense of reality a little.

'You mean is he conscious?' said Mandy. 'To be honest it's sometimes difficult to tell how much they know. I somehow think he'll know Spike's there.'

'Spike's put on that aftershave Ian likes him wearing,' said Carol. 'He might recognise that.'

'Spike was the only one who came to see him,' said Steve. 'Not that you can blame the others. Ian could be a nasty piece of work. He insulted Spike too, a lot of the time, but you could tell he lived for his visits. In fact the last few weeks have probably been the high point of his life. Who could ever have thought it would turn out like this? Quite a famous actor died here a few weeks ago, someone who had once had everything. But his only visitors were hangers on, and even they trailed off except for one opportunist little prick who's now writing a book about it all. Yet Ian, who probably never had a real friend in his life, knew as the end approached that the sort of man he'd only ever dreamed about was there for him and would be there till the finish. Some of the richest people on earth have never had as much. I hope you know how lucky you are, Marianne.'

'I know,' said Marianne, making a sterling effort to keep her composure. The urge to be with Spike at that moment was too strong to resist. She got up.

'I'll go and see how he is,' she said, not knowing if she was referring to Spike or to Ian.

She made her way back to the room and opened the door gently.
Spike was still holding Ian's hand and was telling him about some of
the things he used to get up to at school. It would have been pretty
clear to anyone but Spike that Ian was beyond understanding
anything of what he was saying, but then, as Mandy had said, one
never knew. Spike did right to talk to him.

She stood behind the seated Spike and put her arms around him,
resting her chin on his head, and then pulled up a chair and sat
beside him. After about an hour Steve and Carol entered and said
that they would have to turn Ian over and see that he was comfortable. As the room was quite small they had no option but to leave.

They made their way back to the lounge area. Once seated, Spike
looked down guiltily, as though he believed she might still be cross
with him.

'Why didn't you tell us, Spike?' she asked.

'I was going to,' he said. 'It's just that I thought he'd have a bit
longer than this. It started when we were all at The Kitchener's on
Christmas Eve. I realised we were only up the road from his flat, and
I guessed he'd probably not be getting many Christmas presents so I
took him a bottle of whisky. He was far worse than when we'd been
to his place a couple of weeks earlier, his health, I mean, though his
manners weren't much better either. He said he had somewhere to
go on Christmas Day and that he had loads of friends, but when I
went to see him a few days later it turned out that it had been a load
of rubbish. He could have gone to this thing they'd laid on at some
centre in Stepney for people with Aids but, of course, he'd made
enemies of everyone there. Anyway, he got worse still in early
January and was in the Middlesex Hospital for a couple weeks. I
went to see him there quite a lot, and then he seemed to get a bit
better so they arranged for him to come here. Respite they call it,
only it turned out there wasn't to be much respite for him. Last week
he started having convulsions and they suspected a clot. I didn't
know whether it was the right time to bring you along. He said he'd
like to meet you again when he looked a bit better, but asked me to
keep it secret until then. I was going to tell Dean, too, but I knew he

didn't think much of Ian and would probably think it was funny, me doing this, especially as Ian liked everyone to think I was his boyfriend. Besides, I've always been a bit frightened for Dean, too...I mean...well, I think you know what I mean. That's partly why I was so angry with him, pretending to be HIV positive just to get a bit of sympathy. Seeing Ian, and the others here...I just didn't find Dean's little games very amusing.'

Marianne was unable to speak. Oh Spike, she thought, you'll have to stop stunning me like this.

'I only got sucked in by accident, really,' he said. 'Besides, I think my motives were a bit selfish. Ian told me they must be, said I was turning into a middle-class do-gooder. That's what Dolly used to call Mum and Dad. Ian being so rude and difficult reminded me of the kids they used to take in, and how Dad used to say that they were only like that because they'd been hurt. I think Ian was hurt a lot in his life. His people chucked him out years ago for being gay, yet they forgave his brother who tortured and nearly murdered an old lady whose house he broke into. I tried to get in touch with them a couple of weeks ago, but they put the phone down on me when I said it was about Ian. His sister turned up a few days ago but didn't stay long. I'm told she started asking the nurses whether his family shouldn't take charge of his benefits book now that he was so ill. There are some pretty awful families around. I've felt so much closer to my own mum and dad since we moved back to the old house, and I have you to thank for that. I can even pretend I'm talking to them sometimes, although I know I'll probably be carted off to the loony bin for saying it. I just had to do what I knew they'd expect me to do, so I could look them in the face again - not that they really have faces to look into, but you know what I mean. I was able to bring him over to our place in a taxi a couple of weeks ago when Dean was out. He was so pleased, you wouldn't believe. You'd have thought our little house was Buckingham Palace. I sat him in the lounge and we had a bottle of wine together, and I showed him our old photos. When I realised just how much I'd always had I wondered if it wasn't a bit cruel of me, bringing him there, but he said it was the best evening he'd ever had. If it was anyone else I'd have thought they were just being polite, but then I remembered that he didn't know how to be polite. He'd never learned because nobody had ever been kind to him.

Perhaps that was the saddest part.'

The nurses returned, their task completed for the moment.

'I'll go in,' said Marianne. 'You look as though you could do with a cup of tea.'

'Are you sure you want to?' Spike asked.

'Yes,' she said. 'I have some things I can say to him too, you know.'

Spike went in with her and showed her some little sponges on sticks next on the bedside cabinet.

'Moisten his lips with these every so often,' he said, and gave her a demonstration, though she had already seen him doing it earlier.

'Okay,' she whispered, stroking Spike's face as he left. She suspected he would not be gone for long.

She took Ian's hand.

'Remember me?' she said. 'Spike's girlfriend, not that Spike ever had much say in the matter. I'm expecting a baby, you know. Spike's, of course. He doesn't know yet. I suppose you think he's wasted on me, and you're probably right. He's had an awful row with Dean. Has he told you about that? I know they'll get over it - they can never fall out for long. Though Dean can be a right little sod' - she unconsciously drifted into the style of speaking that would most probably be most familiar to Ian - 'but then, they say you're far worse. I expect you are. Do you remember how you insulted us when we dropped you home that time? Your conversation was the filthiest I've ever heard, and you threw up. Still, I'm glad you became friends with Spike. We have something in common, you and I, and Dean. We're the only three people in the world who know what Spike is really worth, the only ones who appreciate him, I mean properly. I'll always love anyone who loves Spike. He's got loads of friends, of course, but a lot of them are only impressed because he's good-looking and screwing a rich bitch like me. I never really loved anyone before, perhaps not even my own parents. You and I have that in common too, an unhappy family. I hated them for sending me away to school, for trying to groom me into something they wanted me to be. And then I came across a family who were every-thing mine hadn't been, a beautiful, kind, happy family. Well, who am I trying to kid? I fancied the son in that family, that was the truth of it. And I may have him, but I can't be certain, and you can't have any idea how frightened that makes me. There, I'm going on, aren't

I? As though my fears can be anything compared to yours. But you have nothing to fear. And Ian, darling Ian, if you love Spike, as I know you must, please put a word in for me when your journey's over. I know I've no right to ask it. But I will love him as no one else could, I can promise you that.'

Spike rejoined her and there they stayed until release came for Ian at about a quarter past five. When it was over Spike and Marianne allowed Steve to treat them to more refreshment.

'It must be especially hard for you,' said Steve to Spike. 'What with Dean being so recently diagnosed.'

Marianne and Spike both shifted uneasily in their chairs. It had not occurred to them that Dean had been telling others the same fib he had told them. They said nothing.

'Oh Lord, me and my big mouth,' said Steve, misunderstanding the nature of their silence. 'Hasn't he told you yet? To be honest I didn't believe it at first, but Jason works at the place where he went for his test, and he confirmed it. God, I'm sorry for coming out with it like this. I really did think he must have told you both by now.'

Marianne's head started swimming. Why would Dean have told them and then denied it? But as soon as she posed the question she knew why. Spike had shown that he could not take the news, not yet anyway, and Dean had backtracked when he saw the effect that it was having on him. It was not the first time Spike had acted with anger when confronted with a new reality which he found difficult to take. And the reason why Spike had found it so difficult to take was clear enough now, too. Dean could be healthy for a long time, but to Spike HIV meant what he had, unbeknown to them, been seeing nearly every day for the past two months.

She dared not look at Spike.

Before leaving the hospital, Marianne secretly asked Steve if he could give her something to make Spike sleep that night. With a cunning that would have done credit to Lucretia Borgia she popped the potion into the cocoa she made for him on their return. She knew that the following day promised to be as traumatic as this one (though it was the following day now, she reflected, as they finally turned in at seven o'clock) and that Spike would need as much restoration as possible.

She herself rose at midday and left it an hour before taking Spike some coffee.

'I suppose I'd better ring Dean and apologise,' he said, after he had taken the first few sips.

'Perhaps it would be better if you went to see him,' she suggested, and after hesitating he concurred. The journey would give him time to decide what exactly he should say.

'Anyway,' she said, 'the apology shouldn't only come from one direction.'

'Maybe,' he said, and added: 'It's my fault, though.'

'What is?'

'His being HIV positive.'

'Oh, for heaven's sake, Spike, if there's one thing for which you can't be blamed, it's that!'

'Not directly. But for the last four and a half years I've been utterly pathetic! Perhaps if I'd been less self-absorbed I could have kept more of an eye on him.'

'Short of tying him up the whole time, I don't know how you could have prevented him doing what he was going to do. Anyway, you don't know when he contracted it. I'm pretty sure he's had the sense to play safe since he started going out over the last year or so. It's quite probable it goes back to the time before he came to live with you and your parents.'

'He was 12 when he first came to us,' Spike said, dismissing this theory.

'And just before he came to live with you he ran away from the home he was in and was on the game for a few weeks.'

'He never told me that. That's ridiculous! He was 12,' he repeated.

And more streetwise then than you are now, she thought.

'Just supposing it does go back to before he came to us,' said Spike. 'That would mean he's had it for six and a half years. That could mean he's already had most of the years the lucky ones are supposed to have.'

The logic was chillingly apposite.

'Well,' she said, rather lamely, 'some may be given a few years on top of a few years. The situation isn't quite as hopeless as it appeared to be a few years ago, or so I've read.'

'Will you come with me?' he asked.

'No, Spike. I think this is one thing you have to do yourself. I'll stay here and cook some dinner for us. Make sure you bring him straight back.'

He dressed, shaved, had some toast and put his jacket on. 'You can do it,' she said supportively, putting his cap on him and straightening his collar. He did not look so sure.

She stood at the window and watched him cross the road. He always crossed in front of the house so that he could walk by the lake. He was so young, she reflected, and the fear still in his face made him look younger even than his years. Too young for the new burden that had been placed on him. Too young, perhaps, to be a father?

He paused and looked at the lake - or perhaps beyond it. He stayed there for several minutes as though gathering his strength. This time, however, the lake did not appear able to work its magic. When he moved off again in the direction of the station it was with such manifest dread that it was all she could do not to run out and throw her arms round him, to tell him she would go with him.

When he was out of sight she sat silently in the lounge for about a quarter of an hour, for she had her own strength to gather.

The events of the last two days had put her own mad pursuit of Spike into perspective. She had discovered that there was more to him than the malleable, insecure creature she thought had fallen into her lap. She loved him more now than she even she had thought possible, and yet she was forced to recognise (at last, some might say) that he was a person in his own right, capable of making decisions on his own and, that deep down, he wanted that to be recognised. For she had no doubt that his secret visits to the dying Ian had not just been for the reasons he had stated. It was probably the first time he had taken a major decision on his own, off his own bat, since he had been orphaned. He seemed to be ashamed of his new-found ability to act for himself, which was probably the real reason why he had not told her or Dean. For he had become accustomed to having them shape events for him, and he knew that they expected to be able to do so in perpetuity. They had pretended to put his interests first, when all the time it was their own needs that were paramount. Spike himself did not appear to have reached this last conclusion, but how long would it be before he did? It was unlikely now that Dean would have to worry about the consequences of that realisation, for the turn of events had given him a new hold on Spike (which may have been why he had not greeted the discovery of his condition with as much trepidation as might have been expected). But before long she might experience a justified reaction to her manipulation.

For years the 16-year-old Spike had been put on ice. Then, at last, with his return to his old home and his rediscovery of old friends, he had been able to carry on from where he had left off. At the very least Dean would live for a few more years, she sensed that, and could help Spike grow in the independence which was his right. But what could she now do other than nip that independence in the bud? She could be proud of her part in helping Spike come out of his emotional coma, but did that give her the right to claim him as her own? She could still hope that he might one day be hers, but it was not right to expect it yet, not until he had lived a little, not until he could experience others with whom he could compare her.

The more she pondered the matter, the more coldly certain she became as to what she should do. She got up, knowing that she had to act quickly and decisively. She knew she was right and that hesitation might weaken her resolve.

She packed her things, neatness thrown to the winds in her frantic efforts to get it over. And yet, that task finished, she realised that she would have to give them sufficient time to have left Lucerne Court before she returned there. She allowed herself one last cup of tea in the kitchen and began writing a note. It would have to be carefully framed, for she could not afford to have Spike coming to her immediately and beating on her door. Were that to happen, she had no doubt that she could not but open it, they would be in each others' arms again and the problem would be shelved. And when his justifiable (and inevitable?) resentment finally emerged it would be all the more ferocious.

If there were those who thought Dean was spending his brief exile in Lucerne Court brooding about his lot and thinking bitter thoughts about Spike - or anyone else - they would have been mistaken.

For one thing, he had known about his status for several weeks, and had considered the possibility for several years prior to that, so the shock with which Spike and Marianne greeted his announcement was not, by then, shared by him. He was, in retrospect, amused by

Spike's refusal to believe it, and touched in an odd sort of way. He wondered why he had not expected it: knowing Spike he certainly should have done. His row with Spike was not pleasant to him, but he knew that Spike would find out the truth sooner or later and, when that happened, that Spike would be mortified. So mortified, in fact, that there would be little he would not do for Dean to try to make amends. In fact, Dean had already worked out what form the amends could take. A trip to New York would be nice.

Having let himself into the flat in Lucerne Court, thoughts of the advantages of being in the heart of London on a Saturday night took over in his mind. If this was meant to be punishment, he was all for it. He made himself a cup of tea, following Marianne's precedent and going to Stella's to borrow some bread and milk. Stella did not seem particularly surprised that Marianne should have loaned him the flat: he was Spike's brother after all. He was a bit disappointed to learn that Jerome was away for the weekend, but after thinking about it came to the conclusion that he might be able to enjoy a more interesting evening on his own. For that reason he politely declined Stella's invitation to attend a performance of Handel's 'Messiah' with her.

He found a tin of salmon in Marianne's cupboard and, having eaten a sandwich and drunk his tea, revelled in the luxury of being able to leave his cup and plate in the sink without having Spike moan at him, and then being allowed to spend as much time in the bath as he liked with his new Oasis CD on at full blast. Not that he spent too much time so luxuriating: Old Compton Street beckoned.

He had a good evening out. So much more convenient not having to think about the night bus times back to Wanstead. He did a few of the bars, met some old friends, and ended up in a club. Here he met a three young visitors to the metropolis from Newcastle and invited them back to 'his pad' for a drink. They were most impressed at the flat in Lucerne Court, and at his explanation that it was only one of several homes possessed by his wealthy family, this one being reserved for him and his brother when they were in town. After they had got through a sizeable portion of Marianne's drinks cabinet (his guests had gone easy in the club after discovering the prices) he generously offered to put them up for the night, the single one of the three having made it clear by then whose bed he would like to share.

All very safe, of course, but enjoyable nevertheless. The two who had slept in Marianne's room made some funny comments about the women's clothes about the place, and Dean had been forced to 'admit' that his brother was a drag queen (an assertion that gave him no little inner amusement when he thought of Spike). Later he had given himself a metaphorical slap on the wrist for these porkies, not so much because of any principled objection to lying but because it had been so unnecessary. Simply saying that the flat belonged to his brother's girlfriend would have been almost as impressive, after all. He wondered why he had done it, and put it down to force of habit. He decided that he would try to be more virtuous, what with being a sort of invalid now (or at any rate a potential one), and made a pious mental note only to lie when absolutely necessary.

Having got rid of his guests round about lunchtime he decided to make a few phone calls. He did not think Marianne would object to his making a local call or two and so confined himself to Europe. As it happened the tourist from Berlin he had met a few weeks earlier was out and, getting rather bored, Dean decided to ring Steve, whom he had not seen for some time and to whom he would like to show off his new, if temporary, accommodation.

The call to Steve, who told him everything that had happened during the night (and what Spike had been doing for the last two months), promptly brought Dean back to reality. It took a while for him to take it all in.

'Are you sure it's the same Spike we're talking about?' he asked incredulously. When assured that it was he felt a lump in his throat, one which for once had not been caused by his excesses of the night before, and the urge to see Spike became overwhelming. Of course it was the same Spike, how could he even have asked such a question? Of course Spike would have had to have gone back to that filthy little flat to see how Ian was. Only Spike, the reactionary, homophobic, oh-so-straight, rugby-playing moron would have ventured back there, when most of the gays of his acquaintance, who saw themselves as beautiful people (and whose compassion rarely extended beyond other beautiful people) had long since deserted Ian and his ilk.

And then he recalled the things he had recently said. Had he really embarrassed Spike in front of his friends like that? Even Dolly, for all her faults, had never publicly humiliated him in that way. And then there were the things he had said about Spike's relationship with Marianne. Oh Christ! Oh Jesus! He was fully prepared to grovel if he had to. After some hasty attempts to put things in Marianne's flat near enough (though not very near) the way he had found them he made his way to Marble Arch station.

It was a bugger of a journey on the Central Line that day. As so often on a Sunday the plonkers had decided to do some engineering work in the Stratford area. Everyone was chucked out at Mile End and had to take special buses to Leytonstone, from where they all had to get back on to the tube again. He finally got out at Snaresbrook nearly two hours after his journey had begun. He opened the front door somewhat nervously, and was surprised to see two cases, Marianne's, packed and waiting in the hall. The kitchen door was open and he could see her seated at the table writing something. She looked up when she saw him.

'Oh, hello Dean,' she said nervously.

The kitchen table was covered with her half-started efforts. Nosily he picked one up before she could stop him.

'My darling Spike,' it said, 'I know this will probably hurt you, but I think it's for the best. One day you will come to see that, I am sure...'

'Marianne!' he said in alarm, recalling the packed cases in the hall. 'What's all this about?'

'Oh, don't ask, Dean,' she pleaded, putting down her pen and attempting to gather up the half-dozen other sheets.

'Where's Spike?' he asked.

'Gone to fetch you,' said Marianne, realising for the first time that Spike was obviously on a fool's errand. 'But what are you doing here?'

'I phoned Steve,' said Dean. 'He told me about Ian and what Spike had been doing all this time. When I heard, I simply had to come back. But what about all this, though? Have you had a quarrel?'

'Oh no, far from it.'

'Then why...'

'I have to go back,' said Marianne. 'It was wrong of me, all this I mean. You were right when you implied I'd been trying to buy him. He's too young to be forced into anything. He deserves the chance to find his own way.'

'But you can't go, not like this. He'll blame me!'

'I have to,' she said, getting up. 'At least now you're here I won't have to think of what to write. You can give him the message for me.'

'I'm certainly not giving him a message like that! What on earth has brought this on? He's perfectly happy with you, you must know that now.'

'I have to go,' she said, determined not to be drawn into a discussion. 'He'll be back soon.'

'When did he go?' asked Dean.

'About an hour ago.'

'In that case you've got bags of time. The tubes are up the spout again. Let's talk about it over a cup of tea.'

'Well...' Marianne hesitated. She might not be able to speak to Spike, but perhaps she could try to explain to Dean. Some of it, anyway.

'Now, what's all this about?' he asked again when the tea was made.

Marianne found that the mass of thoughts which had passed through her mind earlier were difficult to collect together.

'Well, I suppose if I put it simply, I just don't think I'm good enough for him.'

Dean looked at her in some surprise. She was fairly rich, tolerably beautiful and didn't whinge and moan all the time. Nor did she possess a large collection of teddy bears and call Spike 'Spikey-Wikey.' All that made her good enough in his book. He decided that levity might help matters along.

'Oh, we all know that! Neither am I, and he's been stuck with me for long enough. The trick is, Marianne, never to let people for whom you're not good enough know it until they've found out for themselves. Why throw a good thing away before you have to?'

'I'm serious, Dean,' she admonished, and added thoughtfully, 'that's just the sort of thing Roger would say. The point is, he's not really the Spike you and I thought he was. He has a mind of his own.'

Dean said nothing. He was going to make a joke about doubting the possibility of Spike having a mind at all, his own or rented, but thought better of it.

'I mean,' Marianne went on, 'his secretly going off and visiting Ian. I think it was a sort of bid for independence. That's why he didn't tell us. Everyone else said Ian was a shit, but Spike still did what he thought was right. He had the strength to resist what other people said, even to go against what, not so long ago, were his own prejudices. Sooner or later anyone with that kind of strength is going to wake up to what I've been doing. I'd rather give him a bit of space now, and live with the hope of his one day choosing me of his own accord, than live with the terror of his turning on me and accusing me of manipulating him into everything. Because that's what I've done. And I am terrified, all the time. I was before, but now it's worse. I can't stand it any more.'

Dean was surprised that someone in with Marianne's advantages should know about that kind of terror. He had felt it all his life, in fact it was what had helped him survive. It had not always been to do with Spike. He had had the terror before he went to live with the Porters, though if anything it became worse then, for he had more to lose. Only in the years when Spike had needed him did it seem to abate for a while, but it had always been there really, because he knew that one day Spike might wake up and find that he was superfluous. Dean had braced himself for the day when Spike would meet a woman who might take him away and, after initial doubts, was grateful when Marianne came along because he sensed that she would not do that, not completely. And yet was Marianne right about Spike's motives?

'It could just be,' he pointed out, feeling his own eyes glistening as he said it, 'that he's his parents' son. They taught him to be kind to waifs and strays. That's why I ended up here. Any idiot can be nice to nice people. It takes an exceptional idiot to be nice to nasty people.'

Suddenly Marianne remembered that the events of the last two days involved more than her relationship with Spike. At least it gave her the opportunity to change the subject.

'But why, Dean, did you let us think you were lying yesterday? You told the truth then backtracked, made yourself look ridiculous.'

Dean smiled. 'I know. I just couldn't go through with it when I saw Spike's face. He's lost so much already, and it was obvious he couldn't take it. And he was right when he said I was angling for attention. I did enjoy telling you, in an odd sort of way. Whether it was true or not made no difference. I could have waited, I'm healthy enough after all. That's why I think you're wrong about Spike. He hasn't changed, it's just that you've seen a new side of him, a side I knew was there before and should have realised would come out again.'

'That doesn't alter the fact that I've been making everything go the way I wanted. There are lots of women out there, and he has a right to go out and play around with them before he's forced to settle down. I'm stopping him doing that.'

'What good would it do him, playing the field? I can't see that the other relationships we've seen round here have been any happier than yours. And I've seen some of the women who've been looking in his direction since we came back here. All bleach-blonde hair and white stilettos, not to mention their god-awful voices. They'd take advantage of his good nature and eventually make his life a misery. He's seen as a catch, and if he thinks you've really gone, they're the ones who'd catch him, because in some ways he'll always be a bit of a prat. There's hardly a couple in the world who aren't more suitably matched than you two.'

'Well, you've changed your tune. That's not what you said yesterday.'

'No, no, I was wrong. I don't want him to be with anyone other than you. All the alternatives can only be worse...I mean, nowhere near as good.'

She smiled at his near slip.

'Better or worse, he must find out for himself. It's as though he's been frozen these last five years. He's mature in some ways, but not in others. Even his generous impulses are those of a boy. I feel like I've been trying to catch him before he could know any better. Especially now that...'

She stopped. There were some things she had to hold back, even from Dean.

'Now that what?' he asked curiously. 'I sensed you had something to say this weekend, something momentous. Perhaps that's why I tried to get in first to top it, whatever it was. I thought for a moment you were going to ask him to marry you.'

Marianne frowned. She should have known Dean would have noticed, even if he had misunderstood her exact intentions.

'There are other ways a woman can have of capturing a man,' she found herself saying. 'More devious than a simple proposal of marriage.'

Dean looked at her, comprehension coming slowly but surely.

'You mean you're ...?'

'Yes,' she said, realising she had come too far now to retreat.

He looked at his cup for a while in silence. She tried to gauge from his features what he was thinking, but it was difficult. Then he looked at her suddenly and smiled.

'That's great!' he said.

'Do you think so?' she asked. 'I'd have thought it must make me all the more contemptible in your eyes. It wasn't deliberate, not exactly. Let's just say I wasn't too careful.'

Just how deliberate it was on her part was a question that had already started to cross Dean's mind. But then, if there had been any fault in this area it could not have been hers alone. Quite apart from the matter of contraception, he had always taken it as read that she and Spike would be careful for a more contemporary reason. Nevertheless, he felt it would be indelicate to pursue any questioning along those lines just at present.

'But why leave now, then?' he asked. 'Spike would make a smashing father. And he's got an old-fashioned streak to him. He'll want to marry you, now. I think he always had that in mind anyway.'

'I wish I could be so sure. I'm the one who's always planned the next move.'

'Of course,' he laughed, 'that's why Spike never had to. He's lazy in some ways. Not when it comes to plastering a ceiling or keeping the house clean, but when it comes to emotional things he's always been happy to let other people do all the work. That doesn't mean he doesn't approve, he's just frightened of making a fool of himself. For one thing he thinks you're too far above him for him to be able to seem too keen.'

'I'm too far above him!' said Marianne incredulously.

'That just goes to show how much you have in common. He feels he's not worthy of you and you think the same about him. A psychologist would have a field day with you two, you know that?'

Marianne sighed.

'You know,' said Dean, after thinking a little more, 'I think we've both underestimated Spike. I think you should just be totally honest with him just so that he can make a decision for once. I'd even say you owe him that.'

'True. But however generous his reaction to my news now, I still can't help thinking I'd be cheating him of something. I've liked seeing the way he's been developing since he came back here. He could be quite a Jack-the-lad. I think he should have the space to be just that for a while.'

'But you'd break his heart if you were to go now, you must know that. Don't give him another loss on top of the others. I'm not saying that just for him or for you. I want to see his children, see them at least begin to grow up. I didn't think I would, but now there's a chance of that.'

'You'll see this child, don't worry about that. So will Spike. As often as you both want to.'

'That won't do for Spike. He's very much a family-values type, as I thought you were. Now, all of a sudden, I am too. Depriving a child of a father is one thing, perhaps in some cases it's unavoidable, but to deprive a child of a father like Spike would be unforgivable. Well, he might forgive you one day - he forgives everyone except himself - but I never would.

Until that moment he had been sympathetic, albeit a little flippant at times. But she was shocked by the harsher tone his voice had taken on as he said the last few words.

'Well,' she conceded, 'maybe doing it this way isn't showing him much respect. But will you help me, I mean when I speak to him?'

'Go and unpack for now, at least,' said Dean. 'If you do decide to stay, he mustn't ever know how close you came to leaving.'

He scooped up her literary attempts and put them into the bin, which he then made sure he emptied into the bigger one outside. As he did so he could not help smiling to himself. It had not required much persuasion to make her change her mind, had it?

She had been upstairs only a few minutes when the phone rang. They both knew who it was likely to be, and that Dean must answer.

'Yes, Spike, I'm here,' she heard Dean saying. 'I came back, I wanted to see you...Yes, I know...Don't worry about that...Spike... Spike, look calm down, everything's okay. All the nasty bits are out of the way. There are some much nicer things to talk about now. Take a taxi, and we'll get the dinner on. Hurry up, I'm starving.'

'After dinner,' Dean told her meaningfully, 'we'll have a little con-ference.'

It came as a relief to both of them that Spike seemed much more composed when he returned. The roast safely in the oven, Marianne went to have a bath leaving Spike and Dean alone together, only rejoining them when called to dinner. Whatever they had said to each other appeared to have had a therapeutic affect on both of them, for Spike was utterly calm (or perhaps simply relieved that it was out of the way) and Dean looked positively cheerful. While he may have made his peace with Dean, however, Marianne was pretty certain that Spike had no inkling of the other bombshell that was about to hit him. Only when dessert was finished did Dean lean forward meaningfully and Marianne held her breath. She was more than happy that Dean was taking charge, though a little alarmed at the blunt way in which he came out with it.

'Spike,' he said, with impressive facility, 'Marianne's going to have a baby.'

Spike looked at him and smiled, assuming that this was a prelude to some silly joke.

'Marianne's frightened to tell you, so I hope she won't mind me doing it for her, although I know this is a bit unusual.'

Spike looked at Marianne and, seeing the look of embarrassed anticipation on her face, realised that this might not be a joke after all. He looked back at Dean, whose expression mirrored Marianne's. To Marianne and Dean's horror a look of profound disappointment crossed Spike's own face, with a hint of something that looked suspiciously like anger.

'Oh,' he said and, after hesitating a moment more, asked: 'Who's the father?'

Marianne was later to tell Dean that if there been anything to hand she would have thrown it at Spike. Dean was to be a little puzzled by this, for there were a number of things she could have thrown had she wanted to. The salt and pepper mills for one (or rather two), and the table mats. And if they had not been there she could have taken one of the flying ducks off the wall and bunged that at him. As it was she met the question with a stony silence.

'Who do you think is the father?' asked Dean, unable to conceal his own irritation at Spike's denseness.

'It's not you, is it?' asked Spike.

And now it was Dean's turn to be annoyed for, her own mortification notwithstanding, Marianne's response to this query was to burst out laughing.

'Well, it's not impossible, you know,' Dean admonished her. 'There's a couple of lesbians at college who've actually asked me to father a child for them.'

'Sorry, Dean,' Marianne apologised, realising that this was no time to start making enemies unnecessarily. She turned to Spike. 'I haven't been with anyone but you, not since we met again last year, anyway.'

'But...' began Spike and then added 'oh!' as he recalled the one occasion on which conception would have been possible. 'At Christmas...?'

'Yes,' she smiled, relieved that his memory had not failed him.

Dean did not understand this. He distinctly remembered Christmas himself, and Spike borrowing a packet of condoms from him. Still, the most important thing at that particular moment was that Spike was not questioning his paternity. This hurdle out of the way, Dean launched into business with precipitate speed in Marianne's view.

'And personally I hope you're going to do the decent thing and marry her, and so does Marianne, of course, although she's frightened you might regret it later.'

'Dean!' interrupted Marianne, horrified. 'I didn't ask you to propose for me!'

Dean carried on as though she had not spoken, justifiably confident that he was not saying anything she would not be saying herself if she had the courage.

'She thinks you're too young and ought to be given time to be a Jack-the-lad before settling down. I've told her not to be daft. Nearly everyone who gets married regrets it later. It's God's punishment to them for being heterosexual. Personally, I think you've a better chance of making it work than most.'

Spike was silent, understandably dazed at this volley of information. They sat in silence for a full five minutes. Spike nearly began 'I...' but then stopped.

'Of course,' said Dean, after getting tired of listening to the clock ticking, 'we know that this must be a bit much for you to take in. Perhaps you'd better go and speak to your mum and dad about it before you make up your mind.'

Spike got up.

'Yes,' he said thoughtfully. 'That's a good idea.'

'Be careful of the road,' Dean called after him anxiously, noting his somewhat distracted demeanour.

And so they waited. Marianne felt like someone on trial awaiting the jury's verdict and Dean, her defence counsel, also had no little interest in the outcome. They occupied themselves by doing the washing up and making the coffee, looking anxiously out of the front window a couple of times. On the first occasion Spike was standing by the lake, on the second he had disappeared.

'Don't worry,' Dean laughed when he saw the expression on Marianne's face, 'he hasn't run away. He's gone into the woods.'

'I know his parents won't approve,' she said. 'They've got too much sense.'

'His parents are dead,' Dean pointed out. 'Whatever they say to him will be what he thinks they would say. Everybody cheats a bit when they play those sort of games.'

They looked out of the lounge window a third time and saw Spike approaching the front door. They rushed back to their seats in the dining room like children whose teacher is returning to the class-room. He had only been gone about forty minutes, though to Marianne it seemed much longer. He sat down and poured himself a cup of coffee with deliberate slowness.

'Well?' said Dean. 'What did they say?'

'Well, first of all they told me off,' said Spike, 'and they also said Marianne should have known better.'

'And I'm not surprised,' said Dean. 'I think it's quite shocking myself. Such goings on!'

Marianne and Spike looked with justifiable surprise at the source of this moral outrage, although aware that Dean was being flippant.

'Still, they said what's done is done and we all have to consider how to proceed from here. They were quite set against the idea of my marrying Marianne just yet.'

Marianne's heart sank.

'However,' Spike brightened, 'I was able to persuade them that it might not be such a bad idea. They admitted I could do worse. What they did say, though, was that if we do get married we should make sure we get some things straight first. They agreed with the point about me being very young to make such a commitment, although I'm very mature for someone my age.'

Dean could not help letting out a 'hmph!' of disbelief.

'And they said that under the circumstances it was only right that I should be given a bit of freedom to be a Jack-the-lad, as you said. My dad said there's no reason why I can't still be that after I'm married.'

'Oh, he did, did he?' said Marianne, realising the extent to which Spike had, as Dean had anticipated, projected his own thoughts on to his parents. She was also aware by now that he was not being entirely serious and that the answer in any case was 'yes.' But she knew that she would have to suppress her elation long enough for this rather silly conversation to run its course.

'It was you they were thinking of,' explained Spike. 'They know how guilty you must feel, angling me into marriage like this, and that by giving me a bit more freedom than usual it would make you feel better about it.'

Dean and Marianne both laughed at this sophistry. Spike himself could not help smiling a little through his contrived air of solemnity.

'Frankly,' said Marianne, 'I take their point. But I've got a horrible suspicion that you'd be a very good husband and father, and you'd quickly forget the wilder role you've claimed for yourself, so I'd still feel guilty.'

'No I won't,' said Spike defensively, 'I'll be a rotten husband, I promise. I'll always leave you at home with the kids while I go out enjoying myself, and I'd come in at all hours hurling abuse at you and Dean. He'll still be here, of course, because we'll need a babysitter.'

'Well, it goes without saying he'll still be here,' said Marianne, glad that Spike had remembered to make that clear. 'But you've just said I'd have to stay at home with the children.'

'Oh, I'd let you come out with me occasionally,' Spike assured her, 'especially as I'd want to get drunk every night and you'd be useful to do the driving if we go beyond Wanstead. Mind you, I'd expect you to sit quietly in the corner with a half of shandy while I get on enjoying myself with the other lager louts.'

'Of course,' said Marianne. 'You'll make a lovely male chauvinist. I'll be the envy of all the women for miles around. You promise you'll develop a good beer gut?'

'Oh, definitely. Though you'll have to carry on looking your best, of course. I don't want you showing me up.'

And suddenly Spike realised that he had reached the limit of his ability to make light of the matter. He looked at Marianne, the enormity of the decision he had made striking home at last. And the relief of it, for this had been the moment for which he had not dared hope for so long. Dean also noticed the similar expression on Marianne's face, and the way their hands began edging towards each other. That must be how people look, he mused, when they discover they've won the lottery jackpot. He decided that it was now his turn to make himself scarce for a while.

'Yuk!' he said, 'this is the bit I was dreading. I'm going to get ready to go to Benjy's before I'm sick!'

Dean went upstairs, had a bath and changed. He rather expected not to see much of Marianne and Spike that evening but as he came down the stairs Spike emerged from the lounge.

'Do you mind changing your plans about going to Benjy's?' he asked. 'Only I thought...let's have our own little party tonight. The three of us.'

Dean beamed. He had thought that the two lovebirds would want to be left alone, and that had indeed been their original intention. But Marianne and Spike had not been so preoccupied with themselves that they had forgotten what a traumatic weekend it had been for Dean, too.

Spike went to fetch a bottle of vintage port, a Christmas present from Roger as yet untouched. Marianne allowed herself a small glass, and seated in the lounge they began discussing practicalities. The more they discussed them the more they realised how many things had to be sorted out.

'We'd better start going to Mass for a few weeks if we want to get married in church,' said Spike. 'They don't let you have a requiem Mass if they think you're not practising, and I want things done properly.'

'You mean a nuptial Mass!' Marianne laughed.

'You call it what you want to and I'll call it what I want to!'

'Any more jokes like that,' said Marianne, 'and you'll get a ball and chain put on your leg! Though I'll admit,' she added thoughtfully, 'it will mollify my relatives in France if we have the works. Perhaps I'd better go and see them.'

'My goodness me, yes,' said Dean. 'You've got some explaining to do, my girl.'

'Why should they need mollifying?' asked Spike, with some alarm.

Marianne could have bitten her tongue out. The truth was that she knew that the financial gulf between her and Spike could lead to suspicions in certain quarters. She attempted to turn the problem on its head.

'Well, you know, I am nine years older than you. Some people might call me a cradle snatcher.'

'Is that so great a difference?' asked Spike.

'I hope you realise that when you're 40 I'll be nearly 50, and when you're 50 I'll be nearly 60.'

'Never mind,' Dean reassured her. 'At least you'll always know as you approach old age that Spike was incontinent long before you were.'

'Thank you for that thought, Dean,' said Spike, markedly less amused than Marianne at the observation.

'I do my best to help,' smiled Dean sweetly.

'They'll think I'm a fortune hunter, won't they?' said Spike, returning to the subject of Marianne's relatives.

'It doesn't matter what they think. Nobody who's ever known you could think that.'

'I'll carry on paying rent for the house after we're married,' said Spike, his old worries resurfacing. 'And I don't want you to put more into the other expenses than I do. If you like I'll sign one of those thingies they have now, saying I've no claim on any of your money.'

'You'll do no such thing!' said Marianne. 'That's horrible. This isn't Hollywood. And I've always seen this house as more yours than mine. It's the one you were brought up in, for heaven's sake. You'll be putting in quite enough, I've no doubt. Nobody could accuse you of being a layabout. Roger seems to think you'll go far, and he usually knows. Frankly Spike, I'm just not prepared to talk about such things. In fact, if you mention it again, I'll give all my money away so that you'll have more than me. Will that satisfy you?'

'I'll have it, if it will help,' volunteered Dean.

'You'd take it too, wouldn't you?' admonished Spike good-humouredly.

'Of course I would,' chuckled Dean. 'And, if I did get it all, you two needn't think you can sponge off me!'

'I think that's what Jewish people call *chutzpah!*' laughed Spike.

'Actually, I want to give you both one little treat,' said Marianne. '... No, Spike, you needn't look at me like that. Let me explain. While I pop over to France to see my relatives, why don't you and Dean have a little holiday? I'm taking you from him, in a way. Let me do that at least that much for the two of you.'

'Well,' said Spike, 'I'm not sure if that's a good way for us to start.'

'Oh, stop being such a clot for once, Spike,' said Dean, who thought it rude not to let Marianne spoil them if she wanted to.

'Well, we'll see...'said Spike. He then got up as he remembered something.

'I won't be a moment,' he said as he left the room.

He returned with a little box. Dean murmured with approval, for he knew what was in it. Spike took out three rings.

'My mother's engagement and wedding rings,' he explained, 'and one my father wore.'

'They're all beautiful,' said Marianne. She was not talking about their value or their appearance, for they were really rather unremarkable as rings go, though the engagement ring was pretty. To her it was a beauty that went deeper than physical appearance or resale price.

'I should really buy you an engagement ring,' he apologised, 'and I will, of course. But if this one fits I'd like you to have it, too.'

'It does fit,' said Marianne, trying it on (it didn't, not perfectly). 'I really want no engagement ring other than this one. And, when the time comes, no wedding ring other than that one.'

'And isn't it time you wore your father's ring?' asked Dean. From the way he said it Marianne deduced that Spike had been reluctant to wear it until then - or perhaps afraid to.

Spike took the remaining ring and put it on his own finger. After looking at it thoughtfully for a few moments he removed it and, taking Dean's hand, placed it on his.

'You were his son, too.'

'Not really,' said Dean, looking down.

'Oh no? They chose you, whereas they were lumbered with me. They chose you just as I'm choosing Marianne. And if you have to go before me then I can wear it, and I'll wear it with twice as much reason and twice as much pride. And by the way, I am choosing Marianne. I haven't been manipulated into this, although you two seem to kid yourselves into thinking you can manipulate me. Although I suppose I should try to be a bit more romantic sometimes.'

Marianne and Dean looked at each other, the same thought crossing their minds simultaneously. From where they were sitting Spike seemed to be doing okay without trying, and it was all the more beguiling for his not knowing it.

'But that still leaves you without a ring,' Marianne pointed out.

'Yes, it does, doesn't it?' said Spike. 'Well, you'd better do something about that as soon as possible.'

Marianne thought for a moment. 'Oh, I'm far too mean to pay for a ring all on my own. If Dean doesn't mind, I'd like him to go halves with me on it. It will be from both of us.'

Dean looked at her in surprise and gratitude, but saw the obvious snag. 'Won't people think it a bit strange, you and I buying Spike a ring between us?'

'I don't find it strange,' said Marianne. 'Do either of you?'

And they both readily agreed that they did not. Dean, however, took off George Porter's ring and gave it back to Spike.

'For the time being though, will you wear this? I'd like you to wear it for a while before I do. Then I can wear it with twice as much pride, too. And you never know, there's still the possibility you'll go first. You might be run over by a steam-roller outside the house tomorrow.'

'If I was I'm not sure that would do the ring much good!' laughed Spike.

'Well,' said Dean, 'if we're lucky you might land with your hand sticking out from under the steamroller. And then Marianne and I could rush out and feel really pleased that the ring had been saved.'

Marianne concurred that it was a lovely thought. 'We could go straight to the pub to celebrate!' she laughed.

It was not until much later, just before he bade them good night, in fact, that Dean plucked up the courage to ask them a question that had been troubling him since the afternoon. Seeing them there now, looking so pure and innocent, brought it to mind again.

'One thing puzzles me,' he said. 'You made this baby at Christmas, I gather. But as I recall you borrowed a packet of condoms off me that night. A pack of four, in fact. I remember it had one extra free. What exactly happened to them? You surely aren't going to tell me they were too small!'

Marianne and Spike looked down guiltily.

'Well, no...' Spike said, and added with unconvincing bravado: 'though since you mention it they were a bit on the tight side, but er...no.'

'Well,' said Dean, making the most of this rare opportunity to give a pious lecture, 'don't you think you were a bit irresponsible not using them?'

Marianne and Spike looked suitably ashamed. They looked briefly at each other and then at the glasses on the table, each obviously hoping that the other would be able to talk their way out of the trouble they were in, like two adolescents caught smoking behind the bicycle shed.

'Well, the fact is,' said Spike, after realising that it was most probably up to him to respond, 'there weren't enough. I mean, not for the next morning too. Even Marianne's other boyfriends managed at least four times in all, and as she said, they were a pretty weedy bunch compared to me. I had the Porter name to defend.'

Marianne ventured to look up at Dean while Spike gave this explanation, her eyes expressing something akin to pleading.

Dean stared at them for a few moments.

'Well yes, of course, how silly of me! How could anyone think four could be enough?'

He bit his lip as Marianne threw him a grateful glance.

'We've always made sure we've had enough since,' said Spike.

'Well, I'm glad to hear that,' said Dean, holding his voice steady with great effort. 'I only hope it hasn't created too much of a shortage in the area.'

He got up and just managed to say 'goodnight' before leaving them. He was unable, however, to make it to his own room before bursting into raucous laughter, in fact he did not even complete the first flight of stairs.

'Well,' said Spike, 'I don't know what he finds so amusing.'

'I can't imagine,' lied Marianne, not for the first time.

CHAPTER EIGHT

'You're making it up!' said Roger.

They were seated in their usual pub in Wardour Street. For, unbeknown to Spike and Marianne, it had now become routine for Dean and Roger to meet on a Friday or Saturday evening before going their separate ways to more salacious haunts (to which it would have been impractical for them to accompany each other, given their differing tastes).

'Even I couldn't make that up,' Dean assured him.

Roger sat back in his chair and laughed in his usual silent way with his mouth firmly closed (a technique he had perfected at the back of the class in the fourth form). 'Well, it looks as though we're going to have to revise our opinions about them,' he said.

'I suppose they must have been saving it up.'

'And Marianne told me she's worried that Spike works too hard! The hypocrite! She keeps him working harder than anyone. It's a wonder he has any energy left for the shop. Not to mention his Mother Teresa act.'

'Oh, you know about that, then?' said Dean.

'Marianne told me on Monday when she rang up to tell me about the wedding. It was a bit garbled, she was so full of it all. I'd never heard her be so excited before, in fact I can't remember her being excited at all. And the baby, of course.'

'Oh, the baby!' said Dean, affecting a world-weary air. 'Don't talk to me about the baby. I've had it from them all week. You should hear them talking about it! I didn't know two adults could make so many silly faces. And they've gone through fifty names for it already.'

(Roger did not notice that Dean blushed a little as he finished saying this, as well he should. For it was Marianne who had had occasion to affect a nauseous look as she listened to Spike and Dean discussing the expected arrival for the umpteenth time, and she it was who had first made the point about the silly faces. 'You're like two old women', she had told them. 'It's not the first baby to have been conceived, you know.')

'In fact,' Dean went on, 'Spike's already gone out and bought a Hornby train set. He's set it up in the spare bedroom. I helped him put it together last night. He wants me to go with him tomorrow to buy some more bits for it, a little station and so forth. You can build it up as you go along.'

Once again Dean was not being entirely honest, for his enthusiasm about the train set was hardly less keen than Spike's, something Roger was now beginning to suspect.

'You can get little houses to the same scale,' Roger said, and added hastily; 'or so I'm told.'

'Oh, there are all sorts of things you can get. Even little cows to go in the fields the train passes. Marianne suggested we wait until this BSE business is completely out of the way before we get any of those, but Spike reckons it should be okay now.'

Roger laughed. 'Actually, I was thinking of popping over on Sunday to see them,' he said. 'Will we be able to tear Spike away from his train set to come out for a drink in one of those interesting little pubs in your area?'

'Well, we'll have to play with it for a bit before we go out, I suppose. It's the price you'll have to pay.'

Dean noticed from Roger's satisfied look that it was not a price he minded paying.

'I take it he's anticipating a boy, then?' Roger probed.

Dean gave Roger the sort of look he usually gave Marianne or Spike when they had said something particularly reactionary.

'You're not very up on things, are you? You're supposed to give train sets to girls as well as boys. And you can give dolls in pink frocks to boys.'

'Hmm,' mused Roger doubtfully. 'Are you really telling me that if it were a boy Spike would welcome people giving him dolls in pink frocks?'

'Well, no,' Dean smiled, 'I wouldn't try it myself. Between you and me, I quite like the idea of a girl. It'll stop Marianne feeling out-numbered.'

'I wasn't aware she was,' said Roger, enjoying the look this provoked.

'Marianne thought a boy at first,' went on Dean, ignoring Roger's jibe, 'but then she said it didn't matter anyway, since she already has two little boys. I don't know what she can have meant by that.'

'What indeed?' laughed Roger.

Roger looked serious for a moment, for Marianne had told him something else too, something he had been too cowardly to raise before.

'I was sorry to hear about your news,' he said. He had thought he could handle most situations but this, he surmised, could be the exception.

'Oh that!' said Dean, helping Roger immensely with his cheerfulness. 'I intend to make the most of it, I can promise you. It's already got me this Schott jacket!'

Roger smiled, though inwardly thrown by Dean's courage. He had already had occasion to suspect that Dean was the only man among them, now he was certain of it. Not that he could ever tell Dean that, of course. Besides, their little meetings were primarily intended to be the occasion for laughing about Spike and Marianne and it was clear that neither of them would welcome too much deviation from this agenda.

'I suppose you're hoping to be a bridesmaid,' said Roger.

'Well, I wanted to be, but Spike's told me I have to be the best man. He said that will be even funnier. Actually, old Elizabeth has already put in a bid to be a bridesmaid. Said she never was one but had always wanted to be.'

'The mind boggles! Come back Baby Jane, all is forgiven! I hope the dressmaker is warned to add a little pocket for the gin bottle! And who,' Roger asked, trying to sound more uninterested than he really was, 'will be giving Marianne away?'

'Most probably her uncle in France.'

'Ah,' said Roger, trying not to let his disappointment show. Yet Dean spotted the tone, and the fleeting expression of regret, and decided that he would have a word with Marianne again on the subject. Roger had played his part in helping things along, after all.

'She's going off to France in a couple of weeks to see them. I don't think she's certain how they'll react.'

'I think I know,' said Roger. 'I've met the aunt. From the same mould as her mother, if a little more physically robust. Is Spike going with her? Their seeing him might help.'

'No,' said Dean. 'She's got it into her head that Spike and I should go somewhere together before Spike has the handcuffs snapped on. She wanted to pay for us, but Spike wasn't having that, of course. In the end they compromised and he agreed to let her pay half.'

'And have you decided where you're going?'

'Well, she said it was up to Spike, so I decided on New York.'

'Spike will always be a free agent with you two around, won't he?' Roger laughed.

'Well, he'll always be free to do what he wants,' said Dean thoughtfully, 'it's just that Marianne and I usually know what he wants before he does.'

Marianne did not relish her trip to Angers to see her relatives (she never had much). Still, at least now she had pleasant thoughts to help her pass the time.

Before Marianne and Spike had been able to think of their own arrangements there were others that it fell on them to make, for while Ian's valedictories could not be said to have been their responsibility, they were aware that it was not a duty anyone else was likely to take on. They were not left alone in their task, for Steve and several other acquaintances were happy to lend a hand in organising things, and one or two of Ian's relatives emerged from the woodwork once it had been established that they would not be expected to pay for anything. Ian himself had not left any clear instructions as to how he wanted things conducted, though he had apparently told Spike (somewhat perversely, Marianne could not help thinking) that he would like the song 'I Will Survive' played and that he wanted a party of sorts held at his flat after the funeral.

It had taken Marianne, Spike and Dean three days of hard work to make the flat presentable, though Marianne correctly surmised that their efforts would be largely unappreciated, as few could have been aware just what the place had looked like before. Their supplies of food and drink were welcomed, however, especially by Ian's family who did it considerable justice even if they were vague as to who had provided it. It was understandable, after all, that they should have been a little perplexed as to where Spike and Marianne fitted into the picture, though they found more logical the presence of Dean,

Steve, Miss Brodie and the two leather queens who showed up. Ian's stepmother, a large woman with peroxide hair, had assumed that Marianne was some sort of social worker until she was properly introduced at the flat. She remained wary, however, as did Ian's brother (who sported a pony tale and so many tattoos that they had started to invade his face) and sister (whose hair matched her step-mother's and had only marginally fewer tattoos than her brother). They did not look as though they could normally have been consid-ered a timid family, but this collection of poofs and posh accents had thrown them at first. Only after the drink began to flow did they relax a little, and the discovery that Marianne was expecting a baby before any nuptials had taken place made them feel that she was probably not made of such different stuff as themselves after all.

'Now you make sure you get your name down for a council place as soon as you can,' Ian's stepmother advised Marianne (much to Dean's amusement). 'And don't stand for any nonsense. You have to keep on at them.'

It was clear, however, that her main concern was not to give Marianne and Spike helpful advice so much as to see what was worth retrieving in the flat.

'This settee's not too bad,' she mused, 'and the sideboard would probably do for our Dawn, at least until her Wayne comes out of prison... Didn't Ian have a television?'

'It was rented,' said Spike. 'It's gone back, with the video.'

She looked suspiciously at Spike. She had wondered why he had been so helpful to Ian and now surmised the reason.

'Has it, indeed?' she said tartly.

'You didn't have to let it go back,' said her stepson, not so much suspicious as practical. 'We could have taken them back to Laindon and they'd never 'ave known.'

'There's a radio cassette you can have,' said Dean.

'Oh, is there?' she said, allowing Spike to pour her another gin and tonic. 'That's very good of you!'

In the event Ian's family did not stay very late, as they had to get back in time for the last Bingo session. Spike handed them the keys before they left, and they announced ominously that they would be coming back the next day and had noted what was in the flat ('Not that I'm accusing anyone, mind'). They permitted the party to continue without them on condition that the place was cleaned up properly afterwards.

'There!' Dean laughed when they had gone. 'I knew it. Marianne only got herself pregnant so she could get a council flat.'

'I've been rumbled!' said Marianne, with feigned shame.

'And Spike. Got that TV and video stashed away somewhere no doubt. What a pair!'

Although everyone tried to make what was left of the little party a lighthearted affair (if only to comply with Ian's own wishes), Marianne noticed that Spike's affected levity was superficial. It was only when they were alone later, in bed, that he at last gave vent to his feelings. There had been too much to do to have time before. She wept with him. Of course, it was not only Ian they were thinking of.

More congenial had been the dinner party they had arranged to celebrate their engagement, the first time since they had moved into the house that all twelve chairs in the dining room had been occupied. Elizabeth was in fine form (notwithstanding Daphne's spectacularly unsuccessful attempts to prevent her from drinking too much) and sang them a few songs. Although Roger and Dean groaned every time she started off, there was one song, at least, that inexplicably affected Marianne, so much so that she had to go into the kitchen on the pretext of fetching more coffee. 'Please don't take my sunshine away,' Elizabeth sang and, alone in the kitchen, Marianne felt her eyes moistening. It had to be the pregnancy, she reasoned, something to do with the hormones. Surely nobody could take her sunshine away now. Or could they?

Marianne's biggest worry had been Dolly and how she would react to the news, but if Dolly had any misgivings she had kept them well hidden, at least after the expected grumbles about Marianne 'getting Spike into trouble.' The prospect of the baby, it appeared, was enough to enable her to forgive much. If anyone was a little sad that evening it appeared to be Judith, who would soon be losing Marianne as a colleague. She perked up, however, at the prospect of being a regular visitor to them, as she was invited to be. Indeed, it was clear that they all intended to be regular visitors, which gave Marianne yet another new and pleasant sensation. She had never before known what it was like to be part of such a hospitable and appreciated household.

When the train arrived at the Gare du Nord, Marianne thought it would be pleasant to go via the rue du Roule to visit the hotel at which she used to stay so regularly. She was quite surprised that it was still there, though in truth there was no reason why it should not have been: she had only missed one year, after all. And yet it seemed to belong to a different era. She was able to take coffee and a slice of gâteau in the lounge and deliberately sat on the settee on which she and Spike had once sat. It was enjoyable, but it did not give her quite the intensity of pleasure she had anticipated. And she realised that the reason it did not thrill her as she had expected was because it no longer mattered. She left jauntily, her spirits boosted by the knowledge that she was now too happy to need nostalgia.

As she sat on the train to Angers she began to think about the best way of tackling her relatives, in particular Aunt Bernarde, her mother's younger sister. Not having met Spike, their eyebrows would doubtless be raised a little when they were acquainted with some of the bare facts of the case. They had been thrilled when she had given them the news on the phone, but she had deliberately withheld details of the events of the past seven or eight months, telling them that she would be coming to see them and could fill them in then.

She was met at the station by Marcel, her cousin, the younger of Aunt Bernarde's two children, a studious young man who was now an accountant. He had always looked like the school swot and she noted that he had not changed much. He wore the sort of glasses that in England would once have been described as 'National Health,' and she suspected that his conservative clothes and hairstyle were still chosen for him by his mother. As he drove her to their house just outside town, he began cross-examining her almost immediately.

'Well, you gave us quite a shock,' he said (quite a laugh, he obviously meant). 'And having a baby, too. I didn't think the English did things like that.'

'They do, all the time,' she assured him. It was obvious he shared the vague French prejudice that English people hardly had sex at all, except boys at public school.

'I meant middle- and upper-class ones,' he said, the only ones that mattered, of course. 'And is he rich?' he asked, confirming his position on her mother's side of the family.

'I'll tell you all about it when we arrive,' she promised.

'Ah, so there is some sort of mystery,' he said gleefully. 'We thought so.'

She was greeted warmly by Aunt Bernarde and Uncle Victor, though it was obvious that behind their smiles lurked an eagerness to find out more. Marianne resolved that she should tell them all they wanted to know over dinner, after she had time to gather her strength. Her allegedly arduous journey gave her the excuse to retire for a couple of hours after a hasty cup of coffee.

Even at dinner Marianne did not rush into any explanations, although she was aware that her apparent reticence must only be serving to excite their curiosity - and possibly their suspicions. She spent much of the meal asking Marcel and Simone (her other cousin, a registrar in the local hospital, who had returned home from work while Marianne was resting) about their careers, and her hosts spent the rest of it giving their views about the recent spate of strikes in France and about what should be done with the strikers.

'So,' said Uncle Victor, when dessert was almost finished, 'you haven't told us about this man you are marrying.'

Marianne had brought with her the photographs taken at Christmas and now passed them round.

'But he's a boy!' exclaimed Bernarde, when Spike was pointed out as Marianne's intended (the word she actually used was *gamin*).

'A very good-looking *gamin*,' said Simone, with genuine admiration.

'But,' said Bernarde, 'those people, his aunt and uncle...'

Marianne knew what she meant. Bill had been dressed in his best for Christmas, but his grin betrayed several missing teeth and his colour bore witness to the beers he had downed at The Kitchener's before dinner, not to mention the numerous glasses of wine and brandy he had consumed during and just after the meal. Dolly, too, was in her best clothes but her hairstyle and dress would have confirmed all the popular preconceptions about dinner ladies from East London. And they had not even mentioned Dean yet. This omission was quickly remedied.

'And that is his brother?' said Marcel. 'But how is that possible . . ?'

'He was adopted,' Marianne explained. 'Just before Mr and Mrs Porter were killed.'

And this presented Marianne with a dilemma she had not so far considered. Should she tell them about her having met the Porters twice before in Paris? Should she tell them about her trip to Walthamstow with Daphne and everything that had ensued since that glorious impulse? She began to wish that she had thought things out a little more carefully beforehand.

Victor poured her a second glass of wine. She had deliberately made her first last throughout the meal and had noticed how they had looked at her as though they were some official committee set up to root out un-French activities.

'I shouldn't have more than one,' she protested. 'The baby...'

'Oh, how English!' laughed Victor. 'Rules, rules, rules! Well, I know we have them too, but nobody takes them seriously. But this is a celebration. Bernarde and I got through three bottles of champagne the night we found out she was expecting Marcel. It didn't do him any harm.'

Marianne wished that Dean was there to give a suitable riposte to this. She felt a little nonplussed at herself not being able to recall the French for 'wanker'.

And yet their motives were not totally malign, she could see that. And if she did not tell them everything now it would look as though there was something to hide, and she could see no reason to hide anything about Spike, or Dean, or even Bill and Dolly for that matter. And there was definitely nothing to hide about Lottie and George Porter.

'Well, the house seems nice enough,' said Bernarde, looking again at the photograph of them all seated in the lounge in Snaresbrook. 'Does he own it?'

'Well, actually I own the house,' Marianne admitted. 'But he pays me rent for it.'

Bernarde and Victor looked at each other knowingly.

'When you meet Gregoire,' Marianne said, 'then you'll understand.'

She decided that she would concede to their snobbery only as far as giving Spike his proper Christian name, and translating it into French.

'I'm dying to meet Gregoire,' said Simone.

'We are happy for you,' said Victor. 'Please don't misunderstand us.

If you are content, that is enough. But you have to admit this was not the sort of match your mother would have wished.'

'My mother thought I was only good enough to be paired off to a rich man twice my age,' said Marianne. 'That's what women who are failures have to do. If she knew how happy I am I think she would be happy, too.'

'But,' said Bernarde, 'what do your English friends think of this?'

'Well, you've met Roger haven't you?' said Marianne, knowing perfectly well that Bernarde, on her last visit to London, had both met Roger and been impressed by his ancestry.

'Ah, yes,' said Bernarde, brightening. The ugly *milord*! We always saw him as an appropriate man for you to marry.'

'Well, he knows Spike - I mean Gregoire - well, and fully approves of him. In fact he gave him a job.'

Marianne said this like a conjurer pulling a rabbit out of a hat. If the *milord* approved, she reasoned, then Bernarde would surely be influenced.

'And he did not have a job before he met you?' asked Victor pointedly.

'Oh, yes,' said Marianne. 'That's how I met him again. I went with Daphne to look at a house her sister was buying. He and his uncle had been renovating it.'

'You mean he was a labourer?' asked Bernarde, spitting out the word 'labourer' as only she (apart from Marianne's mother) knew how to.

'You say that's where you met him again,' interjected Simone, both because she had been intrigued by Marianne's accidental de nouveau and because she wanted to steer her parents away from their particular line of questioning.

'Yes. I'd met him in Paris with his parents a couple of times a few years ago.'

And so she had an opening which allowed her to tell them something about the Porters. She also ventured to mention her little flirtation with Spike at the hotel in the rue du Roule, but to her surprise this was the very particular of which they seemed to approve. There was something French about it, after all. And from there she was able to cover subsequent events, loyally leaving out the bits that Spike would have found embarrassing. Marianne became so carried away that she did not notice Victor refilling her glass.

'And yet,' said Bernarde, 'his parents left no money to speak of.'

'It was the property slump,' Marianne explained.

'Well,' said Bernarde, 'he seems to have got back his property now.'

Marianne could not help noticing the real meaning behind this remark.

'If you are thinking what I believe you are thinking, I can only say you are wrong. Gregoire is extremely proud. He has never been remotely interested in my money. As it happens, he himself insisted that our finances should be kept separate, and that he should continue to pay the rent after we are married.'

'And did you agree to that?' asked Bernarde.

'Of course not!' said Marianne, as the knowing glances which had only hitherto passed between her aunt and uncle now took in their children.

'Well, you know your aunt has always had a suspicious mind,' said Victor, adopting a more avuncular tone. 'All the same, I would urge a little caution on your part. Don't let him suggest that you make over half the property to him or anything like that. Not until you've been married a good few years, anyway.'

'Gregory would never expect anything like that,' said Marianne, 'let alone be the one to suggest it.'

'Well, perhaps not. In any case,' he brightened, 'if he was a mere fortune-hunter he would be going for richer pickings than you have to offer.'

'I would have thought Marianne is quite wealthy enough,' said Bernarde.

'Have you come into some money, then?' asked Victor curiously, turning to Marianne.

'Well,' said Marianne (surprised that her uncle should ask such a question. She had assumed that he had always known, more or less, her position), 'I grant I had to sell most of my bonds to pay for the house in Snaresbrook, but I am getting rent for it. My biggest asset remains the flat in Lucerne Court, of course.'

'But is that worth much with such a short lease?' asked Victor.

A short lease? What was he talking about? Marianne had not actually looked at the lease, but had assumed that it was for a suitably safe term.

'Your father could never really afford a flat like that,' Victor went on by way of explanation, 'but he knew your mother had her heart set on living like an English duchess. He found he could buy that one because of the shorter lease - thirty-five years then, I believe. He calculated that would see both of them out. He was not too worried about you. I think he assumed you would certainly be married to your aristocrat by then, or at any rate to somebody who could keep you in comfort.'

Marianne did vaguely recall her father once saying something negative about the lease, but she had not realised that he may have been referring to its length. Not much mental arithmetic was required for her to deduce that, if her uncle was right, it meant that there was barely ten years left to run or, to put it more practically, an asset which she had assumed to be worth in the region of 300-400,000 was probably hardly worth 60-70,000. Oh *merde*. In fact, oh shit! She did her best to make it appear that this information had not come as too much of a shock to her, that she had already taken it on board.

'Well, the house in Snaresbrook is still an asset,' she pointed out.

'Not an asset that can be realised very easily if you are living in it,' said Victor.

They let the subject drop for the moment, embarrassed by their hunch that Marianne had not, in fact, been aware of her true financial position. Bernarde took the opportunity to talk about the Martins who lived in the chateau up the road, and more particularly about their son, Jules, whom Marianne had met some years before on a previous visit. She recalled that at one stage she and Jules had been earmarked by her mother and Bernarde as a possible match, albeit a second-division choice on her mother's part, who had still had hopes of an English aristocrat. Surely Bernarde could not be thinking along those lines again, even now? Marianne relaxed for a moment. Jules, she recalled, had married not long after their last meeting.

'He's divorced now,' said Bernarde, and went on to refer to his wealth and the likelihood of his being a Gaullist Deputy before long.

'Oh, for heaven's sake, Maman,' said Simone, mixing irritation with amusement in equal measure, 'Marianne's not likely to drop Gregoire and run after Jules Martin just because you want her to.

For one thing you forgot to mention that his ears stick out even more than ever and his looks certainly haven't improved with the years.'

'Yes, of course,' said Bernarde. 'But remember, Marianne, there is no shame in changing your mind should you wish to do so. You should see what the alternatives are.'

'I've had thirty years to learn about the alternatives,' Marianne pointed out. 'Besides,' she laughed, 'surely Monsieur Martin will not be too happy about me expecting another man's child.'

'Oh, don't worry about that,' Bernarde breezed. 'We haven't told anyone about the baby. There's plenty of time to sort that out, too, if you wanted to change your mind.'

The implication of what Bernarde was saying did not strike home to Marianne immediately. It was the shocked silence from the others which confirmed to her that her ears had not misled her. Bernarde, realising that she had allowed herself to be carried away too far, tried to give a pathetic little laugh.

'And so Gregoire and his brother are in New York,' said Victor, with forced jocularity.

'Yes,' said Marianne, a little weakly.

'I'd love to go there,' said Simone. 'I don't know how you could have resisted going with them.'

That, thought Marianne, is just what I'm thinking.

Marianne retired not long after dinner. This did not appear to be taken amiss for they were aware, both from her previous visits to them and theirs to London, of the sober hours she kept. She had not, in fact, kept those hours for some time, but they did not know that.

She lay on the bed for a while, fully clothed. She was not so much offended (Bernarde's remark had been almost too offensive to give offence, displaying as it did the state of mind of the originator) as stunned by the strangeness of this environment which had once been so normal to her. She felt as though she had been plunged back into some dark period in her life, the period before that day last year when she had boarded the Victoria line and emerged into the light at Walthamstow. It was only three days since she had seen Spike and Dean but it already seemed like an eternity.

She heard a tapping on her door and her heart missed a beat. She could not but recall the last time, at Christmas, when she had heard a similar knock. Although saddened by the reflection that it could not be Spike this time she was fairly pleased to see that it was Simone. It could have been worse.

'Oh, Marianne,' said Simone, entering and closing the door behind her, 'I don't know how Maman could be so rude.'

'She probably got it from my mother,' Marianne pointed out. 'Yours was the younger of the two after all.'

'They were as snobbish as each other. You'd never think they both started out as poor seamstresses would you?'

'I don't know,' laughed Marianne. 'Some might say their origins were fairly obvious.'

'Anyway, I haven't come to talk about those two old vultures,' said Simone, sitting on the side of the bed. 'Tell me the uncensored truth about Gregoire. Is he good in bed?'

'Yes,' said Marianne, 'very. But if he wasn't it would make no difference. He doesn't have to do very much and he's better than any other man I've known. One touch from those fumbly fingers is enough. Always so nervous at first, always so effective later! And even when he's asleep he does more to me than all the others put together. I wake up before him most mornings - I think I must have trained myself to - and when I see his face just a few inches from mine, that gorgeous stubble so close up, and the eyebrows, the mouth the chin. I try to control myself and just gently touch, but sometimes I give up and just have to take his head in my arms. That half wakes him up and he smiles and goes back to sleep almost immediately and I know I can hold him until the alarm goes off. In some ways that first half hour of the day is my favourite. I know all this may wear off eventually, that we'll settle down into something more mundane as married people always do. I did think for a long while that it might just be lust on my part, and I felt ashamed of it. But there was something from the outset which I couldn't define, something that told me that there were good reasons for loving him other than his youth and his looks. I suppose it helped knowing that his parents had given him such a good grounding in warmth and kindness. But all the same, there are children from such families who don't turn out to be particularly kind themselves, who take affection from others for granted and don't necessarily know how to return it. Yet Spike - that's what we call Gregoire - and in fairness I should say Dean, too, have learned to build on what they were taught. I sometimes wonder if he would have turned out as he did if his parents had not been killed when they were. If they had lived he might have become like so many others, especially when he realised how attractive he was. It was as though he had to lose them to be as he is now. It makes me feel guilty when I think like that, because it almost amounts to my feeling glad that things happened as they did.'

'But that's a dilemma many people find themselves in,' said Simone. 'When a couple who yearn for a child adopt an orphan, they must be glad, in a way, that the child's parents died. When someone marries someone who has been widowed, they must be happy that their predecessor no longer exists. All we can say in such circumstances is that we wish it could have come about without the loss of anyone else, but in the real world that happens to be the way it had to come about. But I never thought I'd hear you talking like this, Marianne.'

'No, I can imagine. It's just that I realise now how little I knew before, certainly how little I felt. When I used to see items on the news about people who'd lost someone they loved or whose child had gone missing, I used to feel sorry for them but I never really had any understanding of what it could feel like to suffer such a loss. Now I can begin to understand. I imagine what it would be like to lose Spike, or how he must feel at the thought of losing Dean, and for a few seconds I really understand that sorrow I've only heard about.'

'But you were always kind. He and his brother must have spotted that or you'd never have got past the first hurdle.'

This thought cheered Marianne, and she suddenly felt guilty that she had allowed herself to be the centre of attention since her arrival.

'How about you?' she asked, realising that Simone must have her own aspirations, too. 'Has anyone passed your way who's worth telling me about?'

'Oh, yes,' laughed Simone. 'In fact your saying Spike was a labourer when you met him touched a raw nerve with Maman for a reason nearer to home. I've been going out with a guy I met when he was working on a new wing at our hospital. He was digging a hole when I saw him. Maman was livid, of course. What she doesn't know is that his family are actually quite wealthy. His father owns the building firm and Luc was only working there at the time to gain experience. It's his father's intention that Luc should take over in a couple of years. We haven't told Maman any of that yet. I thought it would be amusing to let her seethe for a while!'

Marianne laughed, and was about to enquire further about the young man but Simone was determined to bring the conversation back to her.

'Marianne,' said Simone, 'why did you come to see us now? We will be seeing you at the wedding in only a few weeks, after all.'

'Oh, I thought I'd better explain. Perhaps it was my mother I was really trying to explain to. As she's not here Bernarde was the next best thing.'

'But where would you most like to be at this very moment?'

'I should think that's obvious.'

And Marianne involuntarily looked sad. Yes, she would have liked to have been with Spike and Dean. She suddenly realised that Spike was thousands of miles away. She had tried not to be offended by Bernarde's absurdities but she could not put them totally out of her mind. She now craved safety, for herself and for the child she was carrying, and knew that safety could only be with Spike. Absurd, really. Spike, who could panic so easily, who appeared to let others mould events for him. And yet it was his clumsy integrity which gave her a strength she never knew she could possess. Talking about it had not been a good idea. The absence of it was too much to bear.

'Then why don't you go there?' asked Simone.

'Well,' laughed Marianne, 'I'm not one for impulsive decisions, as you know, nor for foreign adventures. Besides, there are practical difficulties. By the time I get back to London, book a flight and get myself together they'll be on their way back. They only went for a week and they've already been there three days.'

'Why do you need to go back to England? The climate in New York is not so very different from here and you have a few days' things with you. You could go tomorrow. I know there are flights in the mid-afternoon from Paris because I saw a friend off a few weeks ago. You could book a flight right now if you wanted to. I presume you have a charge-card with you.'

'Well, yes...' said Marianne, wondering how Simone could be so absurd. She might well have changed, but did her cousin really believe she had changed so much that she would do anything so ridiculously impulsive?

Whether as a result of a genuine change of heart or because Victor had given her a talking to, Bernarde was kindness itself the next morning. They all insisted on accompanying Marianne to the airport and seemed to have become a little infected with her own excitement, not to say impressed at her decisiveness. She politely lied, of course, showing a consideration for Bernarde's feelings that her aunt had never shown for hers. She had half promised, she maintained, that she would join Spike and Dean in New York.

Alone (apart from a few hundred other people) in the departure lounge at Charles de Gaulle Airport, Marianne took stock and realised that her trip to Angers could have been a lot worse. Bernarde's reaction had been anticipated, after all. That, indeed was why Marianne had gone to give them the news herself. It was her own motive for going which, in retrospect, disturbed her. It was almost as though she had believed that she had some explaining to do, perhaps to herself as well as to them. Had she, however fleetingly, believed what her aunt believed about Spike's probable motives? And could he be blamed if the financial advantages had been a partial consideration on his part? And he had Dean to think of too. Were such considerations more dishonourable than loving someone for their body as well as for their mind? An element of the material exists in all love, surely.

On the plane she began wondering if she was doing the right thing in going to New York, though she was grateful that this thought only came to her after they were in the air. She ached for Spike, ached for the safety she felt with him, and the need to be with him had stemmed as much from self-preservation as from desire. But what would his reaction be? Would he think that she was checking up on him? And poor Dean. This was to be his week with Spike, perhaps the last they would have alone together. But no, not the last. She could easily remedy that in the near future. She could afford to let them go away without her once she felt safe. Her conscience partially salved, she made a conscious and successful effort to get in a little sleep. She wanted to feel and look her best when she arrived.

She knew quite a lot about New York already. Spike and Dean had bought three guidebooks in the fortnight between the booking of the holiday and their departure, and they had spent several happy evenings poring over the books and discussing their contents. She

251

had also been with them at the travel agent's and knew the hotel in which they would be staying (her going would have been a pretty fruitless exercise otherwise). 'Why don't you come with us?' Spike had said more than once.

The time difference meant that it was still only eight in the evening when she arrived at JFK Airport and, after having used her cash-point card to draw out two hundred dollars (she was amazed that it could be that simple) she was able to share a cab into Manhattan with an elderly French couple with whom she had conversed during the flight. Their family had presented them with the trip as a fortieth wedding anniversary present and, although excited, they were terri-fied by the stories they had heard of the city. Marianne, the homework she had done with Spike and Dean still fresh in her mind, was able to reassure them that it was not really as dangerous a place as they had been led to believe, just as long as one took sensible pre-cautions and avoided certain areas.

She had correctly anticipated that, at that time of year, she would not have too much difficulty getting a room in the hotel on West 35th Street. It was not large by New York standards though she was impressed by the size of the room to which she was shown. After showering and dressing in under half an hour, and feeling amazed at how awake she felt, she returned to the reception area to ask which room Gregory and Dean Porter were in.

'Number 618,' said the cheerful, fresh-faced young man at the reception, 'but they went out a while ago .'

'Oh!' said Marianne, although she should have expected it, after all.

'I know where they'll be,' he laughed, and added: 'You're not Marianne, are you?'

'Why, yes,' said Marianne, with understandable surprise.

'Name's Al,' said Al, shaking her hand. 'You could say I'm a friend of theirs. I checked them in on Thursday. It was my night off last night and I ran into them in a bar in the Village. They told me all about you. Dean said he wouldn't be surprised if you showed up.'

Trust Dean to think that, thought Marianne.

'Well, the cheek of it!' she laughed. 'I suppose he told you I was so besotted with Spike that I'd drop everything and go to New York to be with him.'

Al coughed a little nervously in an attempt to disguise the smile he had been unable to prevent appearing on his face.

'No disrespect ma'am, but where do you think you are now?'

And it was not until then that Marianne realised properly that she was in New York, that she really had been that impulsive, that it was not one of those dreams she sometimes had in which she was bolder than she really was. What ever had come over her? Whatever it was, she was glad it had.

'So where do I find them?' she asked.

Al hesitated, as though reluctant to tell her.

'Oh, don't worry,' she laughed. 'I know Dean's probably dragged Spike to a gay bar. Somewhere in Greenwich Village, I suppose.'

This hurdle out of the way Al relaxed a little. 'Well,' he said, 'it's called Cousin Oscar's. In Christopher Street.'

'Where else?' smiled Marianne, recalling the information provided in Dean's gay guide. 'But are you sure they'll be there? If they get bored they might want to cruise on somewhere else. Dean will, I mean.'

'Well...' Al hesitated again. 'They'll definitely be there. They'll have to be. The fact is Spike's working behind the bar there.'

Al was surprised at the ease with which Marianne took this information. She almost gave the impression that it was just what she would have expected.

'Look,' said Al, 'if you can hang on till eleven I'll take you there. I finish then.'

'Fine,' said Marianne, brightening. It was only half an hour, after all.

Al brought her a cup of coffee while she waited, which was not long as Al's replacement arrived ten minutes early. Al wanted to take a taxi, but Marianne insisted on the Subway. She knew that there was a line running from the corner of their block to Christopher Street. That was partly why Dean had chosen that hotel.

'Are you sure you want to go this way?' Al asked nervously as they descended the steps on the corner of West 35th. Odd, Marianne thought, that the foreign prejudices dismissed by the guidebooks seemed to be shared by New Yorkers!

'I have travelled on the London Underground and the Paris Metro, you know,' she reassured him.

'It's er... not quite the same,' he said.

Marianne soon saw what he meant, but it did not have the effect on her that he had anticipated. True, London had its beggars, and Paris had armies of them, but Marianne had never before come across so many totally mad-looking people in the course of a ten-minute journey. Moreover, the beggars and nutcases in London and Paris were for the most part puny affairs, whereas these looked as though they were in training for the world heavyweight title. Nice to see that poverty did not prevent them from dining well. Marianne felt an excitement she had not felt since she had first ridden a horse, that peculiar mixture of exhilaration and fear. What sleepy villages London and Paris were compared to this! Nevertheless, she was aware of the nervous Al sitting next to her, and for his sake took his advice and reluctantly avoided eye contact with the three Mike Tyson look-alikes (except that these looked as though they had been in more fights) sitting opposite them and concentrated on the equally large woman with wild eyes who was shouting loudly about Jesus.

'I don't know what you were worried about,' she said, when they emerged at Christopher Street. 'I thought that was most interesting.'

'You could be raped if you're not more careful,' said Al, feeling she should be warned.

'Could I?' said Marianne. 'Still, I'm pregnant anyway so there's nothing to be too concerned about on that score.'

She was joking, Al surmised, but he was surprised nevertheless. He knew the English were supposed to be eccentric but he had not realised they could be that eccentric. Although, he reflected, he had met Spike and Dean.

They entered the bar. It was fairly large and quite crowded. Some sort of show was in progress, for there was a stand-up comedian performing on a slightly raised stage, making rather vulgar comments about people who fart in bed.

'Neither of them seem to be here,' said Marianne, after looking round.

'I think they may be,' said Al, 'and if they're not they will be.'

Marianne insisted on buying Al a drink. While waiting to be served she sensed that Al was gesticulating behind her back to the barman.

'This is Spike's girlfriend,' said Al.

The barman looked at her, as though not understanding straight away.

'Oh, high there!' he said, after thinking for a moment.

'She's come to New York to surprise him,' said Al.

'Well, he's getting ready...' began the barman, and then stopped and looked towards the stage. For the comedian had stopped telling jokes and appeared to be making an announcement.

'Well, those of you who were here last night for our talent show will know that we have a special treat for you now. By popular demand, we welcome back again tonight, from Londonengland, the Wanstead Warriors!'

'That's where we come from!' said Marianne excitedly to Al.

The sound system was cranked into motion and after a few screeches began belting out a tune which seemed to consist of little more than a series of heavy beats. Two young men emerged in military looking dress: camouflage trousers, khaki shirts with white tee shirts beneath and leather Confederate-style caps, and began doing a type of marching tap dance to the thumping sound. From where she was standing Marianne could not see very well, but she observed that they looked rather cute, even if the routine they were doing looked a little silly. Silly or not, the audience, or at any rate the more raucous male part of it, seemed to find it immensely diverting, and the performers were greeted with a series of cheers and wolf whistles. As her eyes focused on the two lads she observed that they looked very much like Spike and Dean. Very, very much like them. The smile on her face froze for a few moments as the reason why they looked so much like them became apparent.

'Jesus!' she gasped, and not because of any conversion brought about by the mad woman on the Subway.

The shock over, she began to enjoy herself. She had no doubt whose idea this was, for Dean was obviously relishing the limelight a great deal more than Spike, who did not appear to be entirely sure what he was doing and took his lead from Dean as to where the routine went next.

'Well,' she laughed to Al. 'I must say, if this won them a talent competition last night I hate to think what the other acts were like! Some warriors! One looks so nervous we can only be thankful he has camouflage trousers on, and the other must have the limpest wrists in Manhattan!'

'They haven't really started yet,' said Al, looking uneasy again.

And as he spoke Dean began undoing his shirt, and Spike followed. Slowly, deliberately, they undid the buttons. The audience became noisier with approval and, when the shirts were finally thrown off, roared in appreciation. Only when the shirts were followed by the tee-shirts did Marianne realise where it was all leading to. She told herself to be calm, but found it increasingly difficult to be so. They squatted, still wriggling in tune with the music, and removed their boots. And then they moved to the buttons of their trousers.

That was enough for Marianne. Instinctively she charged towards the stage, and was seen for the first time by the two performers, who halted their routine in disbelief. Dean, a quicker thinker than Spike, fled from the stage while Spike, still transfixed, was unable to avoid a huge and loud slap which she aimed accurately at his face. He followed his brother into the changing room behind, pursued by Marianne. The audience, perhaps believing that this was part of the routine, exploded with laughter and applause.

'Actually, when I think about it,' said Marianne, 'it's good to see that he was able to be such an exhibitionist for once.'

'Yes,' said Dean. 'I thought it would do him good. That's why I suggested it.'

Marianne narrowed her eyes in a humorous look of disbelief, and Dean smiled in acknowledgment of her doubts.

'Well,' he admitted, 'the 100 dollar prize money did have something to do with it. But we don't take our pants off, you know.'

'So Spike told me at least 20 times last night. Still, I suppose I did over react,' she conceded.

'Well, I suppose it must have been a bit of a shock for you - though not quite as big a shock as it was for us. But you did break your promise. You said you'd let Spike have some freedom, but you wouldn't even let him strip off in a gay bar.'

It was the following evening. They were finishing their dessert after having consumed a leisurely meal in a roof restaurant in Battery Park City overlooking a marina and, in the distance, the Statue of Liberty. Leisurely, that is, for Marianne and Dean. Spike had had to rush off after the main course to attend to his bar duties a mile away at Cousin Oscar's, but they had plenty of time to digest their meal in civilised comfort before joining him there.

'It's funny,' she mused, 'when I went to Walthamstow last year I found him working behind a bar, and he's doing the same thing when I arrive here. But why? This time I mean. If he was mean by nature I could understand it, but why this determination to earn some more money, even when he's supposed to be on holiday? He's not badly off.'

'Well,' said Dean, 'he had to do something with his evenings, and it's something he enjoys. It was an accident, really. Larry was complaining about being left on his own because the other barman hadn't shown up, and I said that Spike had been a barman in England. So the Larry said: "Well get your arse round this side of the bar!" Mind you, I shouldn't have thought Larry would have said that if he hadn't sussed that Spike was likely to pull the punters in.'

Under normal circumstances (but what circumstances were ever normal when Spike and Dean were involved?) a future wife might have been expected to be a little concerned about her prospective husband being ogled by a mainly gay clientele but, after things had settled down the previous evening following the abrupt end of the cabaret, the locals (and, more to the point, the manager) saw the funny side and made quite a fuss of Marianne. Even after the novelty of her presence had worn off, she and Dean had spent an enjoyable couple of hours seated at the bar watching Spike's impressive professionalism as he handled the punters, some of whom would clearly have liked more than a drink from him. His job was made none the easier by the silly comments Dean and even Marianne made from time to time, but he had taken it all in good part.

'And the money is good,' said Dean. 'Not the pay so much, but tipping barmen here is almost compulsory, and I think Spike does better than most as far as that goes.'

'I've no doubt,' laughed Marianne. 'At least in that place.'

'And, to be honest, he actually does want to earn as much money as he can. What with the wedding and everything.'

'I thought we'd sorted that out,' said Marianne wearily. 'The tradition is that the bride's father pays. I know mine's dead, but I've got all his money.'

'Oh, he's not thinking of the wedding itself, but afterwards.'

'We have more than enough to live on. I've agreed that I won't put more into the general finances than he does, but he's earning enough to meet my contribution without any difficulty.'

'But you own the house,' said Dean.

'Oh, God! Is that still a problem for him?'

'Well, he has gone on about it a bit,' admitted Dean.

'Well I don't see that there's anything we can do about that. It's there, paid for, and that's that. If he wants to be so archaic he can look on it as my dowry.'

Dean frowned. 'Look, Marianne, we both know you're better off than we are, but you're not that rich, are you? Not filthy rich. Buying that house much have left a bit of a dent.'

This surprised Marianne. She had almost deliberately given them the impression that she was wealthier than she really was, mainly in an attempt to stop them feeling guilty about the affordable rent she had agreed with them when they had originally moved in. But the truth was she had had to cut deeply into her resources to pay for it, with the result that the income from her investments had been dramatically reduced, and that had been before her discovery that the lease on the flat in Lucerne Court might have less time to run than she had thought. And the income from the museum, small but helpful, would also soon be a thing of the past, for she had no intention of working for some time after the baby was born.

'Well,' she admitted, 'I did have to sell a few bonds...But I'm okay. Don't you worry about that.'

Dean did not pursue the point, but remained unusually serious all the same.

'Marianne,' he said, 'there's something else I was going to bring up with you. You know Steve and Miss Brodie? Well, they've suggested we rent a flat together. Do you think Spike would be terribly upset if I moved out? I think the time has probably come...'

She looked at him intently. This was the last thing she had expected.

'Do you want to go?' she asked.

'Well, in some ways, of course not. But it's an odd way for you to start your married life, with me there. I can see that, I'm not stupid. And besides,' he added, with totally unconvincing cheerfulness, 'I'm quite looking forward to being independent.'

'If Spike was here,' she said gently, 'I think he'd say you were telling porkies again.'

'Well, a bit,' he admitted, 'but it may be for the best.'

'No, Dean, it wouldn't. I remember what it meant to me a few months ago when Spike said "you belong with us". I had no right to expect that, not then. But you do have a right to expect at least that much from me. You belong with us, Dean. In fact, now I think about it, I can't imagine how we'd survive without you there. I think you must have underestimated the feelings I have for you. Yes, Spike has been and will be the focus of my life, I can't deny that. But without you there may not have been a Spike for me to find again. You loved him and kept him for me, and when the time came you handed him over despite what that meant for you. He's my first love, but you're my hero. There will always be something of you in him, and I can never forget that. And without you there he won't be complete.'

'Spike's complete as he is, without either of us,' said Dean, trying to be flippant in an attempt to disguise his real feelings. 'Our job now is never to let him find that out. And don't say he isn't a hero. He may never make an entrance on a white charger, but who could live with a hero like that anyway? His heroism is worth more than that. He just goes on and on being generous and sticking by those he loves, doing what he thinks is right, and nothing anyone ever does can stop him. And that's why I think you're so suited. I've noticed they use the word "cheap" in New York more often than we do. The other barman used it in its most obvious way to describe the flashy punter who left just a couple of dimes as a tip, but that guy we heard arguing with his boyfriend also used it in a different way, to describe the way he treated people. I don't know what the opposite of cheap is in that context' - he laughed - 'I suppose it ought to be "expensive," but that could be even more insulting. All I know is that you and Spike are the complete opposite of cheap. I've seen other couples, straight and gay, who pretend to the world they're madly in love, and they may think they are, but you can somehow tell its not likely to last long because of the way they're for ever claiming their rights and laying down ground rules, sometimes trying to disguise their self-centredness with pseudo-ideological claptrap. I know I pretend to make fun of you two sometimes because you come across as a bit old-fashioned, but I really wouldn't want you any other way. You are a lady and a gentleman in the best sense possible. You both know by instinct what's right, both in the way you treat each other and how you act to others. I've only ever known one lady and gentleman of that sort, and they're both dead now. You know who I mean.'

'Yes, I know who you mean. It's going to be a difficult act to follow, isn't it?'

'If you and Spike can't do it, nobody can.'

They had intended to take a taxi to Greenwich Village, but Marianne felt that a walk would be beneficial. They needed time to restore their poise, to look cheerful again for Spike's sake.

'Let's go via Washington Square,' she suggested. 'It's not far out of our way.'

'Henry James, I suppose,' smiled Dean.

'How did you know?' she asked, surprised again at his perception.

'That's one of the first places I wanted to go to in New York,' he said. 'I went there last night before meeting up with Spike in the bar. The house poor old Catherine Sloper is supposed to have lived in has been pulled down, though part of the terrace still survives, so you can see what it looked like.'

'Why "poor old" Catherine?' asked Marianne. 'She gave the dastardly Morris his come-uppance in the end.'

'Yes, but she must have lived a very bitter and twisted life afterwards. Actually, it's the film rather than the novel that a lot of gays love. Her going up the stairs with the lamp in her hand while he beats on the front door. Every queen identifies with that, and I suppose a lot of women do, too. We like to see ourselves as Catherine, triumphing over all the bastards we've ever met, forgetting we've been the bastards ourselves, sometimes. Though the film doesn't show what she must have felt like the next morning.'

'That's true,' agreed Marianne. 'Films that end on that kind of triumphant note can probably never be realistic for that reason.'

'And haven't you felt a bit like Catherine?' asked Dean. 'For all you knew, Spike could be another Morris Townsend, only wanting you so that he can live a life of idleness.'

They both thought of Spike, slogging his guts out (a habit he would most probably keep up to the end of his life) while they strolled about thinking literary thoughts. They looked at each other simultaneously and burst out laughing.

'Spike has too much pride for that,' said Marianne. 'I sometimes wish he had less. So different from my mother. She let herself waste so much of her life. I feel a bit sorry for her now; all she could do in her last few years was play at being an invalid, although there was nothing really wrong with her. Well, her heart was a bit iffy, but if she'd got up and done something she might have lived longer. I think my aunt would probably say that it was my fault. If I'd looked harder for the wealthy match she had in mind for me she might now be living happily in a dower house as the *grande dame* of the neighbourhood.'

'Ah,' said Dean, 'so it's true, then. Your aunt didn't take to the idea of your marrying Spike.'

'Oh dear!' she said. 'I didn't mean to give that away. Has he said anything, then?'

'Only that you can't have enjoyed yourself much with your relatives to have cut your trip short. He knows he can't be what they'd expected for you.'

'No,' she said, 'he's far beyond what they could imagine.'

Washington Square in the evening was not a congenial place to stand chatting. The kindest thing one could say about many of its after dark devotees was that they were 'interesting.' Unfortunately, one or two of the faces there, they noted, appeared to be showing an interest in them.

'It's okay,' said Dean. 'I think they're only drug pushers.'

Nevertheless, they thought it best to make their way to Cousin Oscar's. On their way they passed a colourful-looking cafe and Marianne suggested they go in.

'Not in a hurry to see Spike, then?' asked Dean.

'I think we'd only embarrass him if we turned up too early,' she said. 'He has his work to get on with.'

This was a good enough reason for stopping off, but it was not the only one. For Marianne was conscious that too much had revolved around her and Spike over the last few weeks, and that she had seen Dean largely as a means of helping her win Spike. Her goal all but achieved she could relax and think more of Dean as a person in his own right. She now perceived just how much she enjoyed his company and that, after Spike, he was probably the best friend she had had or would ever have.

Dean smiled as their coffees were brought to them and Marianne noticed just how pleasing a smile he had, too. Yes, perhaps she had spent a little too much time looking at Spike. Now she could look with Spike, and what was there to discover, she realised, opened up a whole new world of enchantment.

'Live long enough for our children to remember you,' she urged, saying the words before she even knew that the thought had formed.

'Oh, I intend to', said Dean and added, observing her slightly sorrowful look: 'You never know, I might live much longer than you think. Big advances have been made recently, after all. Poor Spike can only think of Ian, but I think the outlook for me is a bit better than that. I hope Spike won't cotton on too soon, though. I want to make the most of it. It's quite nice having him look so worried every time I sneeze. Besides, even if I did die fairly young, that would still be better than outliving Spike.'

'That thought frightens me, too. I mean that I might one day have to live without him. I know I'm a bit older than he is, but women still tend to live longer than men.'

'I think you're jumping the gun a bit,' laughed Dean. 'Besides, you'll have children. And I think, of the three of us, you're probably best equipped to be left alone. Daphne and Elizabeth seem merry enough widows. You could go back to Lucerne Court or somewhere like it and bore everyone rigid talking about your dear late husband and his peculiar brother.'

'Oh, I'll never go back to Lucerne Court,' said Marianne firmly.

'Why do you say that?' asked Dean with some concern. 'That's where you spent most of the first part of your life. Surely you ought to be as attached to it as Spike is to his parents' house? He's said that. He wonders if he's not being unfair to you, expecting you to live in the place that means so much to him.'

'Oh, it doesn't just mean a lot to him,' Marianne said. 'Long before I'd seriously fallen in love with Spike, I think I fell in love with the Porters as a family, although I only knew his parents fleetingly. They were so different from mine. Mine never really learned how to be happy, or to give happiness.'

'But I'm sure they didn't intend any harm,' said Dean. 'Who's ever had perfect parents anyway? And why should we expect them to be more perfect than we are?'

Marianne smiled, although she took the observation more seriously than her face suggested. Dean was right. In general, selfish, callous people are the ones who are quickest to accuse their parents of selfishness and callousness. She only hoped that this thought had not also occurred to Spike.

'But I'd have thought Lottie and George Porter must have come pretty close to that ideal,' she said, knowing the high regard in which Dean held them.

'They came close, but they weren't perfect,' he said thoughtfully. Sensing her surprise he elaborated. 'They were kind and good people, and there can't have been many kids they fostered before me who didn't think they'd landed on their feet when they found themselves in that house. But they didn't totally do right by Spike. They were right to tell him how lucky he was, and that he had to consider other children who weren't so fortunate, but I sometimes wonder if they didn't go too far in that. He always had it drummed into him, especially by George, that he was basically a spoilt brat, and yet he shared his home and his space with a whole string of difficult little weirdos like me, and I can't ever recall him complaining. And then in the last few months before they were killed I saw the beginnings of rebellion in Spike, and if they'd lived he'd probably have had quite a few arguments with his dad, the way older teenagers do. I saw it coming and I was a bit frightened of it, though I know it sounds ridiculous that I of all people should have been worried by the prospect of a scrap or two. It wouldn't have mattered if Lottie and George hadn't died when they did. Spike could have gone through his little period of rebellion and they'd all have emerged from it as happy as they'd ever been. But although George was always half joking when he pretended to put Spike down, he should have found time to praise him just a little for the good he'd done, then perhaps it wouldn't have been so bad for Spike when they'd gone.'

'Perhaps he intended to,' said Marianne.

'Yes, perhaps he did. It's a small criticism, very small considering the basic decency Spike has inherited from both of them. I'm making it now for the first and last time, and I wouldn't have said this to anyone but you.'

'Have you ever thought of trying to trace your own family?' she asked, primarily because she found it difficult to dwell on Spike's suffering, but it was also an opportune moment to put a question that had crossed her mind more than once.

'Yes, I have thought of it,' said Dean. 'It's strange, isn't it? I'm the one who's always been seen as the orphan when it's you and Spike who really have no parents now. Both of mine could still be around somewhere. But perhaps that's why I don't want to pursue the matter. What good could it do? If they don't want to know me I'd only make myself miserable, and if they do want to have me as a son what could that do to Spike? I've only had one family since I went to live with the Porters, and I want no other. Nothing can ever top what they gave me and what I have now.'

Marianne was cheered by the realisation that this compliment was partly directed at her, and felt suitably honoured.

'Come on!' said Dean, his coffee finished and an in impish glint in his eyes. 'Let's stop being all sentimental and do what we're best at. Let's go and embarrass Spike!'

Shortly after their return to London Marianne checked the lease on the flat in Lucerne Court and discovered that Victor's supposition about its remaining term was all too correct.

She began to wish that she had not gone on her literary quest to Washington Square, for while she was confident that Spike was no Maurice Townsend, she still found it difficult to believe that he could be completely untainted by practical considerations, especially as everyone else with whom she had been in contact recently appeared to be. Could he really be blamed if he did see her affluence as part of the package he was agreeing to? And was she deluding him if she were to keep from him that she was not as comfortably off as he had assumed? It had not helped that, two days after their return, he had for the first time raised the subject of money, asking her bluntly if she was in any difficulties (Dean and his big mouth! she thought). She was vague, telling him that she was perfectly all right and that he had nothing to worry about. She wondered afterwards if she really needed to have been quite so evasive. She knew exactly how much he had, after all, and how much he earned.

After making enquiries with the freeholders of Lucerne Court, she decided to turn to Roger for advice, meeting him for lunch one weekday when Spike was safely at work.

'Well,' Roger mused, 'in the short term you could still get a tidy little income by letting the flat, but what then? Besides, letting can have its worries. You might as well cut your losses and sell it for what you can. Added to what you already have you still won't be too badly off.'

'That's the point,' she said. 'I haven't much left apart from that. I blew most of the rest on the house in Snaresbrook.'

This elicited the look she had expected. 'Well,' he said cautiously, 'you could see what they want to extend the lease. If you could add on at least thirty or forty years you could get a good price for the place.'

'I have asked them. They want a hundred and fifty thousand for thirty years' extra. That's more than twice what I'm now in a position to raise.'

'Not exactly a charity, are they?'

'They think they are. If I weren't an existing lessee it would be eight thousand per additional year instead of the five thousand they want from me. So it would make sense for me to have the lease extended before I sell.'

'Well,' he said, 'I could...'

'I'm grateful, but don't even think about it. I wouldn't take it anyway, but if Spike were to find out...Well, let's just say it could cause problems. You are an ex-lover of mine, if that's the right word. He'd most probably smack you in the mouth, which would be a nice thought if it didn't mean he'd be out of a job.'

Roger hesitated before coming out with his final suggestion. He had enrolled Spike on a course on antique furniture and he was curious to see how long it would take him to work out the value of the furniture and paintings in the dining room.

'Are you aware,' he said, 'that some the stuff in the house could be...'

'...Could be worth at least as much as the shortfall,' she completed for him. 'Yes, I know that. I suspected it when I first looked round and I got a friend who works at Sotheby's to look at it before I signed the contract. It was the Porters' secret little nest egg, I suppose. I will tell Spike sooner or later, of course. I didn't before just in case our relationship came to nothing. I'm not that stupid. But you must know I can't get rid of it just now. I think he'd notice.'

For the first time Roger looked at Marianne with something approaching respect.

A week or two later Marianne noticed that Spike began behaving a little oddly. Several times he closeted himself in the study and seemed decidedly embarrassed when, on one of those occasions, Marianne took him in a cup of tea. He swept away an official looking letter and tried to shield something he was writing from her line of vision. Another time Dean emerged from the study with him, thoughtful looks on both their faces. She told herself not to be too alarmed by such goings on but at the very least she could not help being intrigued.

After dinner one Friday evening, a fortnight before the wedding, Dean left them seated at the table, in more of a hurry than usual to be gone. Before going he gave Spike a significant sort of glance which, she noticed, Spike returned.

'I suppose he's going for a drink with Roger before his night on the town,' said Spike, as though looking for something to say.

'And no doubt the two of them will be having a good laugh at us!' she said.

'Oh, don't put all the blame for that on to Dean and Roger. Everyone laughs at us. I gather the latest nickname for us is Albert and Victoria.'

'Yes, I know,' Marianne laughed. 'I wonder if they'd look at us in quite that way if they knew I'd made passionate love with the man who came to fix the washing machine on Monday, with a young soldier who'd knocked to ask directions on Tuesday and yesterday with a policeman who'd come to arrest Dean for being the master-mind behind a gay conspiracy to blow up houses with naff curtains.'

'And which did you like the best?' asked Spike.

'Oh, the soldier, definitely the soldier, even if the uniform wasn't completely authentic.'

'Actually, I think Dean suspects something. I forgot to put his army boots back in his room. Anyway, who do you propose to make love to this evening?'

'Well, it's Friday this evening,' she pointed out, 'and you're going for a drink with your mates. I thought it would be nice to be taken by surprise by a rather rough Cockney type who'd been out boozing.'

'Hmm, that could be arranged,' said Spike thoughtfully. 'I think you'll have to pretend to be a Cockney yourself, though. And not too much of a lady.'

'Ooh, yes, that sounds good. Plenty of verbal. Lots of "you filthy pig!" and "you bitch!"...But no, Spike. I've just thought of a better one, one I've been waiting for since last summer in fact. Do you still have the white jeans and the teeshirt that was your barman's outfit at The Kitchener's?'

'Well, yes. But I've put on a little bit of weight since then. The jeans may be a bit tight.'

'All the better!' she smiled. 'I can be a daft woman from the West End who arrives in a pub in Walthamstow and ends up being swept off her feet, literally, I hope, by the barman.'

Spike chuckled in approval. 'But first,' he said, becoming suddenly serious, 'there's something rather important I have to talk to you about.'

He went into the study for a few minutes and re-emerged looking a little apprehensive.

'Marianne,' he said, brandishing the important-looking papers he had tried to hide from her before. He had obviously taken one last look at them, for he had his glasses on. She found him amusing in his glasses, and she and Dean had often laughed that he looked like Clarke Kent in them, especially now with his suit still on.

'Spike!' she retorted, in a comic echo of his serious tone.

'I'm...er...going to ask you something that may annoy you.'

'Don't tell me! You want to know if your mistress can come and live with us after we're married.'

'Oh, no,' he said, unable in his now tense state to continue with the jocularity, 'nothing like that. It's just that...I'm not entirely happy that I should be living in your house. It's not right. I know it's probably a bit chauvinistic of me, but I think we should own it half and half.'

Marianne felt the blood draining from her face. Much as she wished she could not, she remembered her uncle's words of caution, and her own rejoinder that he had nothing to fear. Had she been naive after all?

'What...what do you mean, Spike?' With difficulty she dragged out the question, with even more difficulty the following one. 'Are you saying you want ownership of half of this house to be made over to you?'

'Well, yes,' he said, his deep voice becoming a few octaves higher as he sensed her unease.

So Spike the innocent, the incorruptible, had caught up with the world at last. She had always known there had to be a fly in the ointment and here it was. And yet did that make him worse than any other man? And were there not quite a few women who would expect at least as much from their prospective spouse? What hurt was the thought that she had not known him quite as well as she had believed. She pondered for a moment.

'If I were to say no, Spike, would that put paid to everything?'

He did not understand her at first, but when her look confirmed her words he screwed the papers he was holding into a ball and threw then angrily into the corner of the room, an uncharacteristically untidy gesture for Spike.

'I'm sorry,' he said, 'I shouldn't have mentioned it. I thought you might be upset. I would be if I owned this house and someone wanted to split it with me. I told Roger I shouldn't ask, and Dean, although they said it was a good idea. Roger even said he would have a word with his solicitors about drawing up the agreement.'

So Roger was behind this! She should have known. Was this his revenge? Perhaps he had let Spike know that she was not as well off as they had all thought and suggested that Spike should take what he could while there was still something left. To think that she had asked Roger to give her away at the wedding in preference to her uncle, Uncle Victor who now, it seemed, had been right all along.

'Look,' said Spike, panicking as usual. 'I'll see if I can cancel the surveyor. He's due to come on Monday morning.'

'The surveyor?' said Marianne. This was becoming more and more bizarre. 'You mean you have to have the place surveyed to make sure it's up to scratch? Well, I suppose one has to check a gift horse's mouth, whatever the proverb says.'

'Well, it's not me who wants one, it's the building society. They insist on it.'

'The building society? What on earth has this got to do with a building society?' But even as she asked the question Marianne knew the answer. Oh dear!

'Well, you don't think I could pay you for my half without a mortgage, do you?'

Marianne said nothing, her feeling of remorse too extreme for her to do so.

'You didn't think...?' said Spike, and her silence confirmed just what she had thought. Spike responded with one of his rare displays of anger, a glorious, justified anger which, in her relief, she almost enjoyed.

'Why have you never trusted me?' he burst out. 'First you thought Dean and I must be a couple of thieves, then you assumed I must be having an affair with someone, now you think I want half of this house for nothing. And all the time you never stopped to ask a few questions before jumping to your conclusions.'

Go on, Spike, she inwardly urged, go on! You have every right. And yet he had asked a question which had to be answered.

'The reason I didn't trust you, however much I wanted to, had nothing to do with you. It had to do with me. You've brought me so much happiness I keep on thinking there must be a catch some-where. I keep feeling I'm not supposed to be so happy.'

He looked down at his coffee cup and sighed. 'But perhaps there is a catch,' he said. 'There could be quite a bit of sadness to come, we both know that.'

'You mean Dean?' she asked.

'Yes,' he nodded, looking intently at the table rather than at her. 'But in a way it's not just Dean. I wonder if I've been entirely honest with you. I know that when people are in love they're supposed to think of each other all the time, to behave as though they're the only ones who exist. It's true you're somewhere in my mind most of the time, and I couldn't live without our times alone together. But often I think of my mum and dad too, and Dean, and sometimes of one or two of the other kids they fostered before Dean came along. And Ian. I even think of Dolly and Bill, and they're only a couple of miles away. And sometimes I wonder if I'm really being fair to you, not thinking of you all the time as I'm supposed to.'

For a moment she had felt the earlier fear returning, but as he spoke it dissipated and she somehow knew then that she would never feel it again.

'Well, I know that if we lived according to some of the love songs we hear we'd be behaving as though we're the only two people in the world,' she said, 'but that wouldn't really be much of a world, would it? I know you'll never forget those you love, and that's the very thing that makes me love you so much. How could it make me feel more secure if you could lightly forget everyone else? If you were the sort of person who could do that the odds are you could forget me as quickly. I'll always love them too, because they made you what you are, and they made an excellent job of it. I know what grief is most likely coming, but I suspect it won't come for a long time yet, after we've all enjoyed a lot of happiness. And if it does come all I ask is that we'll be able to share it, just as we did the happiness. And when the grief is over I know you'll never fully forget your loss, any more than you can forget what you've lost already.'

She got up and switched on the light.

'Come on, you,' she said tenderly, 'it's time you got ready to go on your lads' night out.'

He stood up and she noticed that he flinched a little as he caught sight of the screwed-up papers on the floor. He looked sheepish as she picked them up. As she unravelled them she saw that it was nothing more sinister than a building society's rules and regulations with a draft mortgage agreement attached.

'So you want to go halves on the house, then?'

'Not if it offends you so much,' he flustered.

'But it doesn't offend me,' she reassured him. 'Why don't you tell me what you have in mind?'

'Well, Roger told me that you'd spent most of your disposable cash on this place, and that the lease on your flat wasn't worth as much as you thought...'

'He had no right to tell you that,' she said, not now with much indignation.

'The thing is,' Spike went on, 'he suggested I see about a mortgage to buy half of the house. They'll advance me 80,000, and I have 15,000 of my own. Dean also wants to chuck in his 5,000. I know that sounds daft, but he wants a stake in the place, too, and I think it's right we should let him have one. So that brings us up to a hundred grand. That's half what you paid, isn't it? Furniture included.'

'Yes,' lied Marianne, 'exactly half.' For she recalled that, when answering their original questions about it, she had knocked a third off the price she had in fact paid. The untruth had not been to deceive Spike and Dean so much as Roger and one or two others who, she had feared, might try to question her wisdom and, more painfully, have guessed just how determined she had been to have that house at any price.

'You don't mind, then?'

'Not if that's what you really want, Spike. But I still don't understand why you wish to throw your money away. And poor Dean. That's all his savings.'

'I wouldn't be throwing it away,' said Spike. 'And Dean wants to feel he really belongs here. And let's face it, we'll both see he's okay, savings or not.'

Marianne smiled. She had no doubt that Spike's motives were purely straightforward, but she suspected Dean knew them both well enough to have worked out that his own little stake would be repaid with interest in other ways in the coming years. Spike smiled too, the same thought obviously having crossed his mind.

'So what do you have to do now?' she asked, unsure of the practicalities but prepared to go along with them since it meant so much to Spike.

'Well, if it's okay with you, the building society's surveyor will come. If he's satisfied the place isn't falling down, you'll get a hundred thousand quid.'

Marianne had not so far considered this aspect of the matter, that it actually meant hard cash in her handbag. For all practical purposes Spike was giving her a small fortune, a very small fortune to be sure but one which, to him, would represent years of hard work.

'But Spike!' she said, with pretended horror, 'people might say I'm only marrying you for your money.'

'Do you think so?' he said, his brow furrowing. 'Don't worry, if anyone tries I'll explain that it was my idea.'

She did her best not to laugh, unsure if he was joking. 'It would be a great relief if you could do that,' and then she pointed out, as she felt she had to: 'It's a big commitment for someone of your age to make, you know - and I don't just mean about the house. There's still time to back out.'

'I am nearly 21!' he said indignantly.

'As old as that?' she laughed.

'And you're not that much older than me. You look just as you did when you were 20.'

'But you never knew me when I was 20.'

271

'No, but I've seen the daguerreotype. But seriously, I think both of us have a better chance of making things work than a lot of people. I know what a good marriage is because I spent the first sixteen years of my life looking at one. And you, too, Marianne, although you talk about your parents as being a bit cold and stuck-up, they provided you with a good home and stayed with each other to the end. I think you should be more appreciative of that sometimes.'

Apart from his earlier impetuous outburst, this was the nearest he had ever come to rebuking her, a gentle and fair rebuke which thrilled her. He was coming on, she noted with pride. He somewhat spoilt the effect by instantly looking embarrassed, and seemed on the verge of apologising.

'Go on,' she said, getting in first before he could do anything so silly, 'your friends are waiting for you.'

'Why don't you come?' he asked.

'No, Spike. Friday night's the night you're supposed to be a Jack-the-lad with your other laddish mates, remember? I'll be very annoyed if you don't stick to the deal.'

'Don't be daft,' he said, kissing her. 'It's not really like that. Come on, let's celebrate my becoming a home owner.'

'I'll come along later, then,' she promised, 'but you go now.'

For Marianne genuinely wanted to be alone for a while. She wanted to contemplate the life with Spike that lay ahead of her and the reverie was too delectable to share with anyone, not even Spike.

He went upstairs to change. While he was gone, she savoured his joke about the daguerreotype, and pondered how she would get her revenge later that evening. He returned, wearing his jeans and bomber jacket, and he had taken off his glasses. Superman again!

'I know this must all seem a bit pathetic to you,' he said, perhaps misinterpreting her smile. 'Me, scraping together everything I can to pay for half a house. And your mother wanted you to marry into the aristocracy.'

So many others had reminded her of that, some with reproach, some with amusement. All she had been able to do in response was to mutter something about their not knowing Spike. And yet all the time there had been an answer she could have given them, an answer so obvious that she wondered why it had taken her so long to find it.

'I am marrying into the aristocracy,' she said, and it was not laughter she was trying to suppress now.

Despite her efforts he could not help noticing the quiver in her voice. As he passed the lake on his way to the pub, he remembered reading somewhere about the effects stress could have on pregnancy, and he wondered if he had not been responsible for causing Marianne some unnecessary stress that evening. Apart from the business of the house he also recalled telling her that he didn't always think only of her. Had it come out right? Did she really understand as well as she said she did? And he had virtually accused her of being an ungrateful daughter, not to mention his joke about her age. He sighed to himself, regretting his insensitivity.

'Well, Gregory,' he could imagine his father saying derisively, 'you really know how to charm a woman, don't you?'

'Oh, shut up!' said Spike, who did not like being told what he already knew.

'Oh, I don't think he did too badly,' said his mother.

Spike proceeded on his way, but as he turned the corner he scowled as he heard his father saying, obviously so that he would hear: 'How Dean has managed to resist putting a firecracker under him and Droopy Drawers I'll never know!' Then he brightened as he remembered that his father only made fun of those he loved (well, usually). The remark also suggested that his parents did not know everything about his and Marianne's antics, which he found something of a relief. They probably even thought that he knew nothing about the furniture in the dining room. He felt a bit guilty about that, even though he knew his parents must have intended it for him. He would tell Marianne, of course. But he sensed that it would be easier all round if he were to make the discovery after the deal had been struck.

Meanwhile Marianne took the photograph album from the bookcase, the album Lottie herself had put together. So often it recent years it had been scanned with sorrow; now, at last, it could be perused with undiluted joy. There was Spike, the Spike she had first seen in the rue du Roule, and the young Dean, a cheeky grin on his face. She looked at Lottie and George themselves, looking back at her with, she sensed at last, approval, and she remembered her earlier words to Spike. They were indeed the ones who had made him what he was. And as she looked at them she realised that she missed her own parents, too. She had loved them really, it was just that it had never before occurred to her that she had. And they had loved her and wanted the best for her, misplaced though their view of the best may have been.

She went to her bedroom and took out some photographs of her mother and father which she kept there. These she brought down to the lounge and placed in the album with the Porters. 'Perhaps you will get on after all,' she said cheerfully.

'Yes,' she could almost hear her mother saying, 'he is a pleasing boy. But I really don't think you should let him go out wearing jeans like that. He looks so much better in a suit. You both have standards to maintain, you know, and I don't...'

'*Oui, maman,*' Marianne sighed, closing the album.

As she changed, she smiled to herself, wondering what jokes Spike was picking up at that moment, carefully noting them, no doubt, so that he could recount them to her when she arrived. Most of them would be dreadful but she always loved the way Spike told them - and sometimes got them wrong, to the good-humoured vexation of his friends who would endeavour to put him right where necessary.

She left the house and crossed the road so that she could walk by the lake, as Spike invariably did. And as she surveyed it, shimmering under a full moon ('There's going to be a full moon tonight,' Dean had said before leaving, 'I'll have to lock my door with you two in the house.') she realised that she had been dreadfully remiss. She stopped and looked into the water, that same water into which Dean, during that terrible period for Spike, had deposited Lottie and George Porters' ashes. She knew that Spike took comfort from his imaginary conversations with them, and thought that it was high time she said something of her own.

'Thank you,' she said. 'I almost forgot to say thank you. I promise I'll look after him - I'll look after them both. And we'll try to be as good parents as you were. But for now, thank you.'

She assumed that it must have been her imagination, that it was simply a fanciful echo of those kind words Lottie Porter had once said to her, but as she walked on she could have sworn she heard, 'Thank *you*, Marianne,' behind her.